W9-CEK-262

White Apples

Books by Jonathan Carroll

The Land of Laughs
The Voice of Our Shadow
Bones of the Moon
Sleeping in Flame
A Child Across the Sky
Black Cocktail
Outside the Dog Museum
After Silence
From the Teeth of Angels
The Panic Hand
Kissing the Beehive
The Marriage of Sticks
The Wooden Sea
White Apples

White Apples

Jonathan Carroll

A Tom Doherty Associates Book
New York

This is a work of fiction. All the characters and events portrayed in this novel
are either fictitious or are used fictitiously.

WHITE APPLES

Edited by Ellen Datlow

"Absence" by Pablo Neruda, translated by Donald D. Walsh, from
The Captain's Verses, copyright © 1972 by Pablo Neruda and Donald D. Walsh.
Reprinted by permission of New Directions Publishing Corp.

A Tor Book
Published by Tom Doherty Associates, LLC
175 Fifth Avenue
New York, NY 10010

www.tor.com

Tor® is a registered trademark of Tom Doherty Associates, LLC.

Library of Congress Cataloging-in-Publication Data

Carroll, Jonathan, 1949–
    White apples / Jonathan Carroll.
        p.   cm.
    "A Tom Doherty Associates Book."
    ISBN 0-765-30388-4 (hc)
    ISBN 0-765-30401-5 (pbk)
    1. Death—Fiction.   2. Fatherhood—Fiction.   3. Reincarnation—Fiction.
4. Pregnant women—Fiction.   I. Title.

PS3553.A7646W48   2003
813'.54—dc21   2003042648

First Edition: October 2002
First Trade Paperback Edition: July 2003

0   9   8   7   6   5   4   3   2   1

To   Andrea L. Padinha—
      once a student,
      then a friend,
      forever my hero

      and

      Neil Gaiman

And a thousand thanks to

    Niclas Bahn,
    Boris Kiprov,
    and
    Chris Rolfe

for keeping me up and running
while *White Apples* was being written.

Love, sleep and death go to the same sweet tune;
Hold my hair fast, and kiss me through it soon.

—A. C. Swinburne, "In the Orchard"

White Apples

Chocolate-Covered God

Patience never wants Wonder to enter the house: because Wonder is a wretched guest. It uses all of you but is not careful with what is most fragile or irreplaceable. If it breaks you, it shrugs and moves on. Without asking, Wonder often brings along dubious friends: doubt, jealousy, greed. Together they take over; rearrange the furniture in every one of your rooms for their own comfort. They speak odd languages but make no attempt to translate for you. They cook strange meals in your heart that leave odd tastes and smells. When they finally go are you happy or miserable? Patience is always left holding the broom.

She liked candles in the bedroom. As far as Ettrich was concerned, candles were for churches, power outages, and the tops of birthday cakes. But he never said that to her, not even as a joke. She was very sensitive—she took whatever he said seriously. Soon after they met he realized he could hurt her easily, too easily. One nasty word or sarcastic phrase was enough to knock her flat. She confessed she had only recently gone beyond the point of feeling she had to please the whole world.

She said things like that. "I did drugs even though I hate them. But I wanted my boyfriend to love me so I took drugs with him. I was a terrible coward." She admitted to mistakes. Early on, she was willing to tell him some of her most revealing secrets. It was thrilling and disconcerting at the same time. He loved her a little.

One day while walking through town he passed the store. When it came to women, Vincent Ettrich's eyes were the most voracious part of his body. Even when he wasn't fully aware of it, his eyes saw everything that had to do with women: what they wore, how they smoked, the size of their feet, the way they pushed their hair, the shape of their purses, the color of their fingernails. Sometimes it took a second for him to realize something had already registered in his mind—a detail, a sound, a *wisp*. Then he would look again. Invariably his unconscious sensors had been correct—the sheen of sunlight off a green silk blouse pulled taut over a great pair of breasts. Or a hand on a table, a rough stubby hand, surprisingly connected to a chic woman. Or unusual almond-shaped eyes reading a French sport newspaper. Or just the radiance of a plain woman's smile that transformed her face completely.

The day they met, Ettrich walked by her small store. He'd passed it many times before on his way to work but never looked in the window. Or if he had he didn't remember what he saw. Part of the daily scenery, his life's backdrop. Today he looked and there she was, staring at him.

What did he notice first? Later he tried remembering that moment but came up blank. The full-length glass door to the shop was closed. She stared through it straight at him. Small. Maybe that's what struck him first. She was small and had the thin carnal face of a naughty angel. The kind of minor cherub lost in the corner of a fresco in an Italian country church. One with a holy expression, but something else is in that look, something wanton. It says the model for this heavenly spirit was probably the artist's mistress.

She wore a short blue summer dress that fell to just above the knees. Her looks didn't overwhelm him as some women's did, but he slowed and then did something strange. Ettrich stopped and waved at her. A small wave, his hand rose to about chest height. At the end of the gesture he thought why am I doing this? Am I nuts?

The air around him suddenly filled with the smell of hot pizza. He turned slightly and saw a guy walking nearby carrying a large white and red pizza box. When Ettrich turned back, the woman behind the glass door was waving back at him. For an instant, a second and a half, he wondered why is she doing *that*? Why is she waving at me? It was a nice wave, very feminine. Her right hand was pressed close to her chest, going back and forth like a fast windshield wiper. He liked the gesture and the way she smiled behind it—warm, not tentative at all. He decided to go in.

"Hi." He felt no hesitation. His heart was happy and calm. He was in his element. Vincent Ettrich had approached so many women over the years that he had his voice down to a science. This time it came out bright and friendly, good to see you! There was nothing dark in his voice, dark or macho or sexy in any way. If things went well in the next few minutes, he could use that stuff later.

"Hi." A small one in return from her, like a small child that looks at you hopefully and wants to come over but is wary. Her hand had turned in and rested on her left breast as if she were checking her pulse. "That was so nice. I liked that you did that."

His mind blanked. "Did what?"

"Waved to me. I don't know you but you waved. It was a little gift from a stranger."

"I couldn't resist."

She frowned and looked away. She didn't like that. Didn't want to hear yet another man say she was good-looking and he wanted to make contact. She just wanted that unexpected wave from a stranger and then return to her life.

"I saw you before you saw me," she said but still wouldn't make eye contact.

"I often walk past here but never looked in." He lifted his eyes and saw what was around him. It made him smile and then chuckle. They were surrounded by women's lingerie. Boxes and boxes of it—white, peach, black, mauve . . . Bras and panties, thongs and eggplant-colored slips, sheer nightgowns were on display everywhere. Everything a woman loves to put on and everything a man wants to take off her. Ettrich loved lingerie stores. He had been in so many and bought so much of it for different women.

"A 34-B?"

"Excuse me?"

She pointed to his chest and wiggled her finger. "I was guessing you were a 34-B in a bra?" She smiled at him and it was a great one, full of humor and mischief.

He caught her line drive and threw it right back at her. "Do many women come in here who are actually happy with their breasts? Just about every one I've known thinks theirs are either too big or too small. Breasts are a touchy subject with women." He waited a beat to see if she would catch his double entendre. The sly look that slid across her face and the way her eyes widened momentarily said she got it. Heartened, he went on. "It must be tough working here."

"Why?"

"Because every day you've got to please customers who generally aren't happy with their equipment."

Her smile returned slowly. She had small slightly crooked teeth. "Equipment?"

Ettrich didn't hesitate now. "Sure, and your job is to outfit that equipment with the latest battle gear."

She moved her arm in an arc meant to take in the whole store. "Is that what all this is, battle gear?" She kept smiling. She was enjoying him now. He had one foot in the door.

Ettrich took a copper-colored satin bra off the counter and held it up as if it were a piece of evidence in a court trial. "Put this color on top of beautiful black skin and you've created a binary weapon." He put it down and picked up a periwinkle-blue thong that weighed as much as a whisper. "And *this* is a ground-to-air missile. Deadly at any range."

"If you wear it for your boyfriend he's a goner?"

He nodded. "Right. And there's absolutely no equivalent for men. Do you realize that? There is nothing a man can wear that has the same effect on women that these things have on us. It's not fair."

Her eyes appraised him. Was this man being fresh or funny? Did she want the conversation to continue? He felt he could almost see the question mark above her head. One of those great early moments had arrived. They'd had their hello, the first talk and banter. Now the "should we go on?" pause was here. The next play was hers. He was eager to see what she would do.

"What's your name?"

"Vincent. Vincent Ettrich."

She put out her hand to shake but then for some unknown reason pulled it back. It threw him off until she said, "My name is Coco. Coco Hallis."

"No! Your name is really Coco Hallis? That's amazing."

"Why?"

"Because it's an unusual name but I know someone else with the same one."

Now she didn't believe him although it was the truth. He could feel his connection with her weakening so he went for the dramatic gesture. Taking his cell phone out of his pocket, he dialed a number. The young woman crossed her arms and leaned back on her heels—a gesture that said nothing else but "Show me."

Bringing the phone to his ear, he waited a moment and then quickly handed it to her. "Listen!"

Taking it hesitantly, she listened. In time to hear a female on the other end say in a firm professional voice, "Hi, this is Coco. I'm out of the country for the next two months. You can reach me in Stockholm at—"

Coco Two handed the phone back to Ettrich while the recorded message was still playing. "That's *unbelievable*. What are the chances of that happening? What does she do?"

Ettrich slid the phone back into his pocket. "Oil exploration. She travels around the world looking for undiscovered oil deposits. Comes back from crazy places like Baku and Kyrgyzstan with great stories about—"

"And what do you do, Vincent?"

Part two had arrived. Because he was quick-witted and adept at guessing what the next big thing would/could/should be, he was an early success. But a career in advertising did not impress women unless they were in the biz themselves. No, women wanted to be swept off their feet by both a man AND his profession. The majority wanted to imagine themselves on the arms of titans, geniuses, or adventurers: at the very least artists, whom they'd inspire to even greater heights of imagination.

"And what do you do, Vincent?" How many times had he been asked that question in all the years he had pursued women? What did he *do*? He tried to move people to buy ketchup, sanitary napkins, and mediocre automobiles. He splashed color and greed and beautiful people in viewers' faces to persuade them to buy whatever he'd been hired to promote. That was the true description of what he did; however, he had learned to distort and finesse his answer. "Creative consultant" was a favorite phrase of his, whatever the hell that meant. But he had long ago learned women's eyes lit up when they heard one was "creative" so he threw it in whenever he could.

"I'm a professional hot air balloonist," he said to Coco Two.

Spontaneously she barked out a great big laugh and waved both hands around, dismissing him as if even the idea was ridiculous. "You are *not*!"

It was exactly the response he wanted. He'd read her correctly. "You don't believe me?" He smiled innocently.

"No, I do not. Do you always dress in a suit and tie when you're going ballooning?"

"You never know who you're going to meet up there." His voice was calm and self-assured. She'd just called him a liar but he hadn't raised an eyebrow.

"No, really Vincent, what *do* you do?"

"I'm a crane operator."

"A *crane?*"

"Yes, you know those birds with the long legs—"

She hooted her laugh this time but it was as loud as the last one. It said she loved his joking around. "Come on, tell me!"

"I'm a French fryer. You know, dip them in oil, beret first—"

With some women the gimmick worked wonderfully. Distract them, make them laugh, but don't tell until you see their laughter fading and a wee bit of annoyance creeping in. That way when you did tell them, they were happy for the truth and almost grateful.

He watched the merriness fade in her eyes although her mouth was still lit with a big smile. The moment had come where if he didn't fess up she'd either be irked or think he was a weirdo.

"I'm in advertising."

"Are you good at it?" she asked without hesitation.

"Excuse me?" He'd never been asked that question before. Certainly not by someone he'd met only ten minutes before. Was he put off or intrigued by her chutzpah?

Picking up the blue thong he'd held moments before, she thrust it at him. "Sell me this. Tell me how you'd get me to buy it."

This was good, a sudden fun idea. Coco Two was turning out to be terrific. Playing along, he took the skimpy thing and stared at it. Ettrich *was* very good at his job and within seconds he had an idea.

"I wouldn't try to sell it sexy because that's what would be expected. You know the scene—a typically beautiful girl on a beach facing the water with her back to us, naked except for this. Nearby a cool-looking guy is staring at her. Forget it. Too mundane, too *done,* we've seen it a hundred times before. Are we doing a magazine campaign or TV?"

Coco crossed her arms and shrugged. She was pretending to be the client he was trying to impress. "Either. So no naked girls?"

"No naked girls. Use sex to sell dull things, things you don't think about—shaving cream, kitchen stoves. If you want to sell something that's already sexy, you should go in another direction."

"Like?"

In his pocket was a postcard he'd received that morning from his ex-wife Kitty. Although she loathed him, Kitty always sent good postcards. It was one of her ways of communicating with him without having to talk directly. This one was a photo of a tan Chinese Shar-Pei dog, that bizarre breed with so many wrinkles on its face and body that it looks like a large piece of melting caramel. The dog in the picture wore an ornate Mexican sombrero and looked heartbroken. Ettrich laid the postcard down on the counter. He took two empty three-by-five-inch file cards and a thick black marking pen out of his other pocket. With the pen he drew a large "X" across the dog's face on the postcard.

Coco looked at the picture, then at Vincent. He laid the picture down next to the thong on the counter. He wrote "MAN'S BEST FRIEND" in large block letters on both file cards. He put one above the X'd-out dog picture, the other above the blue panties.

"Something like that. Go in that direction."

Vincent didn't look up once to see her reaction. Holding his chin in his hand he kept staring at his advertisement, still considering it. He was in her shop but more than that he was in his own world. His work mattered to him, even when he was being lighthearted about it.

———

Some weeks later he took her to the restaurant Acumar. Everything about the place was obnoxious but Ettrich knew that because he was a frequent customer. It was the favorite restaurant of the executives in his company. Even the waiters there wore beautiful double-breasted suits, white shirts, and ties. They handled both food and customers as if either might stain their expensive sleeves.

If you are a success in life, there are places you must go and pay to be humiliated. It is an unwritten law that human beings must be tormented throughout their lives in one way or another. If you are fortunate enough to have risen to a social level where no one does it to you for free, then you must pay for the service. Trendy restaurants, exclusive boutiques, any Mercedes-Benz dealer, or your very own personal trainer saying how fat and out of shape you are being a few examples.

"Why is this place called Acumar?"

Ettrich was about to eat a thimble-sized wedge of bread topped with what looked like a sardine head resting on top of a dandelion. "I think it's the name of the owner."

Coco kept looking over her shoulder and turning in her seat to check out the elegant restaurant and the other diners. Ettrich could have told her she wasn't supposed to do that in a restaurant like this because it made you look like a rube, but he didn't. Anyway it was kind of nice watching her do it. He was used to women who played things so cool that nothing short of the Second Coming made them raise an eyebrow.

She picked up her sardine/dandelion hors d'oeuvre, looked at it and wrinkled her nose. "I don't like fish. Is it okay if I don't eat this?"

"Of course." He put his back down as a show of solidarity.

"Acumar. It's funny—If you have a name like Bill and call your restaurant Bill's, it sounds like a dump. Call it Acumar, it sounds mysterious and exotic." She looked at the long silver menu open under her hands. "Everything looks good here, Vincent. What do you think I should have? Oh no, look at that!" She frowned at the menu and her eyes narrowed.

"What? What's the matter?"

"Look at the name of that one dessert—'Chocolate-covered God.' That's not nice. It's not funny and it's not nice."

Ettrich had to fight down a smile. Was she really that prudish and uptight about things? "Does that offend you?"

She was about to answer when a waiter passed in an obvious hurry. She put up a hand like a traffic cop to stop him. Something in the gesture or the look on her face stopped him instantly.

"I'm not your waiter but I'll get him for you."

"I don't want my waiter. I want *you* to answer a question."

"I'm really in kind of a hurry—"

"I don't care."

Both the waiter and Ettrich reacted the same way—they came to attention and watched her very closely.

"What is Chocolate-covered God?"

"Excuse me?"

"This dessert on the menu. See? 'Chocolate-covered God.' What is that?" She pointed at the menu and tapped the item with her finger.

Puzzled, the waiter leaned forward a little for a better look. He clapped a hand over his mouth. "Oh, that's a misprint! It's supposed to be chocolate-covered *gob*, not God! I've got to go tell Acumar immediately. Chocolate-covered God. Is that a scream or what?"

After he'd rushed off, Ettrich and Coco looked at each other. Neither said anything. When too many silent seconds had passed he chirped, "Looks like you saved Acumar's day."

She shook her head. "I doubt they'll take back all the menus and change them. I was only making a point. You were surprised by my reaction, huh?"

He knew she would be irritated if he lied so he didn't. "I'm not very religious. I gotta admit I thought it was funny too when I first saw it." He couldn't read her expression. Her normally active face was empty. She raised her eyes and looked at something behind him.

"Vincent?"

Glad for the distraction, Ettrich looked up and saw Bruno Mann standing above him. Mann worked for the same company. The men had frequently traveled together on business and were almost friends. Bruno looked deeply shaken.

"Hey, the Mann! How goes it?"

"I'm—Vincent, it's really you!"

"Well, yeah. Are you all right?" He hadn't seen Mann for a few weeks but the surprise on the other's face and in his voice made it sound like Ettrich had just returned from space exploration.

Still staring, Bruno touched his own cheek with two fingers and shook his head incredulously. His eyes were full of fearful wonder. He looked at Coco. She looked right back and didn't break eye contact.

"Bruno, this is Coco Hallis."

The two shook hands but nothing special passed between them—no friendly smile or nod, no how-do-you-do vibe. Neither seemed interested in the other. Ettrich's cell phone rang. Taking it out of his pocket, he looked at the screen to see who was calling. Kitty. His ex-wife never phoned unless it was very important, usually something to do with their children. He excused himself and walked the short distance out to the street to talk. He stood with his back to the restaurant, a finger in his free ear to block out the roar of city sounds around him.

"Hello?"

"Vincent? It's me, Kitty."

"Hi, you. What's up? Is everything all right?" He always tried to be friendly with her, friendly and upbeat. He still loved her in many ways, but she hated him cold black and deep and always would after what he had done to her and their marriage.

"The strangest thing just happened, Vincent. I don't know why she called *me*. I didn't even know the man very well. He was your friend but she called me instead."

Despite wanting to go back to the restaurant and Coco, Ettrich smiled. Kitty talked too much. Most of the time it was charming and he had learned over their married years how to tune in and out of her chatter without her ever seeing any sign of it on his face. Now while she rattled on, he turned and looked through the window back into the restaurant.

To his genuine surprise he saw that Bruno had sat down next to Coco and the two were talking. Coco was throwing her hands around, now and then pointing a finger at Bruno Mann. To all appearances it looked like she was scolding him. Bruno seemed contrite. He kept looking guiltily down at the table and then back up at Coco.

"—died. He just died. Isn't it amazing? The man was our age!"

Ettrich heard that red-light word and snapped to attention. "What? Who died? Kitty, I didn't hear what you just said. We've got a bad connection. *Who* died?"

"Bruno Mann. He had a heart attack. His wife just called me. She wanted you to know but why did she call me? She knows we're divorced—"

Ettrich was so stunned that he literally could not focus on anything. He blinked again and again as if he'd gotten something painful in both eyes. And he forgot he still held a telephone against his ear.

"Vincent?"

"I—Kitty—I'm . . . let me call you back. I can't handle this." He put his other hand to his forehead and closed his eyes. He could feel his heart racing in his chest. It was running away with him.

"Are you all right? I didn't know you were that close to Bruno." Kitty's voice was low, hesitant with concern.

"I'll call you back." He thumbed the disconnect button before she could say more. He continued to look at the small phone in his hand as if it could somehow help him. Maybe he could call someone and ask what do I do now? What the hell was Ettrich *supposed* to do? Go back into the restaurant and talk to the dead man? How could the man be dead and at the same time be sitting talking to Coco? Should Ettrich run away? He didn't want to do either. He didn't even want to look again to see what was happening at his table, but he did.

Bruno Mann was gone. Coco sat alone holding her long glass of red wine near her mouth while she looked around the room. Eventually they made eye contact. Smiling, she gestured for him to come back in. The dead man was gone. But where? Ettrich could go and ask her what they had talked about. He would have to be careful though because Bruno might still be nearby and who knows what would happen if he returned. Ettrich was many things but not a coward. Holding the silver phone in his hand as if it were a talisman against evil spirits, he made himself pull the door open and walk back into Acumar.

A lit candle was in the center of every table. They were a striking, unusual blue-gray that matched the color of the tablecloths. Coco had commented on it when they sat down, saying she would love to have a dress in that color. Walking across the room toward her now, Ettrich found himself looking at the candle on their table. The flame stood straight up in the air, unmoving.

"Vincent?"

For a second, half a second, a small but terrifyingly large moment, he was sure Bruno Mann had said his name. But then it came again and it was a woman's voice, Coco's voice. Because everything in his brain had run for cover, it took time for Ettrich to mentally regroup and think clearly once more.

In the meantime she said his name again, now more insistently. There was no question mark at the end of it.

All this time he had been looking at the candle flame. Suddenly he realized he was not looking at the blue candle in the restaurant but a yellow one. A yellow candle on the night table beside the bed. The bed Ettrich was lying on. On his side, he could feel his arm beneath him pressing against his body. He was lying in a bed looking at the unmoving flame of a yellow candle. All this came together and formed solid in Ettrich's mind. He sat straight up and barely choked out an "Uh!"

Behind him Coco asked, "What? What is it? You okay?"

They were in her bed. Seeing his bare knee, Ettrich realized he was naked. Shock. Recognition. Relief—all these emotions flew through and around him like a flock of banking, soaring birds. He was not in Acumar restaurant but in bed with Coco Hallis, staring at her yellow candle. Coco and her candles. No Bruno Mann. Ettrich must have fallen asleep and dreamed the whole damned thing!

She put a hand against his back and slid it slowly down his spine. "What's up? What's going on with you?" Her voice was sweet and sensitive.

"Jesus, I just had the most *amazing* dream. It was so fucking vivid, right down to the smallest detail. Even the color of the candles!" He shook his head and roughly rubbed his face to get the blood back into it.

Her hand slid slowly down and off his back. She yawned loudly. It annoyed him. He was still shivering from a tornado of a nightmare and she was yawning. But that wasn't fair. He'd had the dream, not her. He tried to will his irritation away. He wanted to turn around and look at her, put a hand on her and feel that soft skin. *That* would bring him back to earth. Coco was a sensational lover. The only woman he had ever been with who laughed like an ecstatic child whenever she came. The first time it happened she hesitantly asked if that bothered him. No, he liked it very much. Why was she asking? She said some men hated it because they thought she was laughing at them, no matter how much she denied it.

He wanted to touch her now and have sex. As he was turning to her she said something he didn't hear. She was lying on her stomach. The curves of her back and high round ass were on full display. She was easy with her body; said she liked it when he looked at her naked. Head turned away from him; her arms were stretched above her like a swimmer floating on the water. Ettrich put his hand on her ass. She didn't move. He slid it slowly up over her back, enjoying the rise and dips of her curves. Her skin was warm. He liked that very much—Coco's skin was always warm.

His hand went up higher to her shoulder blade and then over to the thin neck. She wore her hair short. He pushed it as his hand slid up the back of her head. He stopped. There was something dark on the back of her neck. Narrowing his eyes, he tried to make out what it was in the flickering light of her candlelit bedroom. He still couldn't see it. He didn't remember her having anything back there like a mole or a birthmark of any sort. Holding her hair up, he leaned over and looked more closely.

It was a tattoo. Looking black in the room's dim light, it was definitely a tattoo. Simple block letters that spelled "BRUNO MANN." The dead man's name was written into the back of Coco Hallis's neck.

Ettrich leapt up like he'd been scalded. He *had* been scalded. "What is this? What is that?" Backpedaling, he stopped halfway across the room. He jabbed an accusing finger at his pretty young lover who still hadn't moved. Coco remained in the same lifeless position. On her stomach, face turned away, arms over her head.

"Coco, look at me for Christ's sake! What is that? What is that tattoo?"

She said nothing and still did not move. For a moment Ettrich thought she was dead. He had seen her impossible tattoo and somehow his seeing it killed her. But that was insane. He wanted to go over and touch her. He also wanted to get dressed as fast as he could and get the hell out of there. "Coco!"

Finally she lifted her head and turned it slowly in his direction. She opened her eyes and looked at him. "What?"

"What is that tattoo? Why do you—"

She mumbled something he couldn't understand. It sounded like she was talking in her sleep.

"What? What did you say?" He took two steps closer to her. He had to. He had to know what she was saying.

She spoke louder. She sounded annoyed. "I *said* it was your dream. You know who Bruno is." Putting a finger to the back of her neck, she rubbed it up and down over the name there. Just that gesture made Ettrich do a whole-body twitch.

"But why—but how did it get on your neck? It wasn't there before. I know you never had it before today."

Coco pushed herself into a sitting position and looked at him. "That is correct. It's brand-new. Chocolate-covered God, Vincent. Remember that part of your dream? The part where you said you were not very religious?"

He froze. The woman knew his dream!

She reached over to the night table and picked up her pack of Marlboro Lights cigarettes. Pulling one out, she lit it from the yellow candle. The light in the room flickered as the small flame went from the table to her hand and back to the table again. She took a long drag and, letting her head drop back, blew the smoke in a thin gray line toward the ceiling. "Sit down, Vincent. Come smoke with me. You like to smoke." She looked at him and smiled.

Obediently Ettrich went over and sat on the corner at the foot of the bed. What else could he do? He wanted to say everything but could think of nothing to say.

"Come closer. I want to touch you." She motioned him over with her cigarette hand.

He shook his head, closed his eyes. "No, here is fine."

Slowly she lay back down and looked at the ceiling. Taking a drag off the cigarette, she tried to blow a smoke ring but it didn't form well. "How long have we known each other?"

She was so calm. Ettrich's world had just imploded but she was asking how long they'd been *dating,* for Christ's sake.

"A month and a half, two months. I don't know. Tell me about the tattoo, Coco. Please."

"I will but first you must listen to me carefully, Vincent, because what I'm going to say now is very important. All right?" Her large eyes moved slowly to his. Her expression demanded his attention. He nodded.

"Good. Do you remember your life before we met?"

The question was so peculiar and out of place that he wasn't sure he'd heard her correctly. "Do I remember my *life*? Of course I remember it." Anger like a blowtorch flared in his chest. What was this bullshit? "Why wouldn't I remember my life?"

"Then do you remember the hospital? Do you remember all the time you spent in the hospital when you became sick?"

"What?" Ettrich had the constitution of a dray horse. He was never sick. Once a year he caught a mild winter cold that usually lasted three days and gave him the sniffles. Sometimes he took an aspirin for a mild headache. Nothing else—even his teeth were healthy. The only reason he ever went to a dentist was to have them cleaned.

"What hospital? I was never in the hospital!"

"You don't remember Tillman Reeves or Big Dog Michelle?"

"Big Dog who? What are you talking about?" As soon as he asked that question, a picture slowly filled Ettrich's mind like thick liquid pouring into a glass. It was exactly that sensation—his brain slowly filled with the image of . . . a black man's disease-ravaged face looking straight at him and laughing. The man's teeth were yellow and large. His cheeks and eyes were very sunken but he was laughing.

Standing behind him was a BIG black woman wearing a white nurse's uniform. On her breast was a red nametag: Michelle Maslow, RN. She was smiling too but sternly, as if against her better judgment. Like a high school principal who's caught bad boys up to no good. Her size and the blazing whiteness of her dress were in severe contrast to the shrunken man in bed in front of her. Where she emanated health and strength, he looked more dead than alive.

Hands on her massive hips Nurse Maslow announced, "Now I *know* you made up that nasty nickname for me, Professor. Mr. Vincent Ettrich is a gentleman. He's not an ungrateful *hamster* like a certain Professor Tillman *Reeves*." Her voice was stentorian and magnificent. She could have ruled the universe with that voice.

His jolly albeit gravely ill eyes never leaving Ettrich, the man in bed barked. "Woof. Woof. Big Dog's in *da house*."

The nurse made an exasperated face and went tsk tsk tsk. "You keep it up like that and see what happens. A squeaky little hamstuh is all you are. Not like your very nice roommate here. Just because you're sick, Professor, doesn't mean you can be rude to your nurse."

Reeves's smile grew wider. He said to her over his narrow shoulder, "Just because I call you Big Dog Michelle does not mean I respect you any less, Nurse Maslow. *Au contraire*. One of the great experiences of my life has been meeting Cerberus before I die. I only wish I'd known you were a she and not a he all these years. In his *Theogony*, Hesiod said Cerberus had fifty heads, but having had the pleasure of your inimitable company all these weeks, I know that your one head is sufficient, madame."

She crossed her arms. "Fifty heads, huh? Well, you know what? I looked up that Cerberus you're always talking about. That's right. And if you're saying I'm the dog that guards the gates of hell, then you better watch out because I got a whole lot of bitin' teeth!"

"Woof."

She leaned forward as if about to reply. Her face broke into a big smile. Watching her, Ettrich realized she wasn't fat at all, just strapping. Her bare arms were packed with muscle. He was sure she could probably pick either of them up with no trouble.

And then the tent collapsed. That's what it felt like when Vincent Ettrich began to die. His whole being felt like a tent, a big circus tent, and someone jerked away the poles that held it up. His life collapsed like that tent while Michelle Maslow and Tillman Reeves laughed. It was more amazing than frightening because it happened so fast. He could not breathe. All at once everything stopped working—his mouth, his throat, his lungs. From one second to the next all of him just shut down. No gasp or cluck or choke even; a hand fluttering up for help. Because he was finished. Life left him a moment before he realized he was dying. Watching two nice people laugh, Vincent Ettrich died.

Of course things went black. Of course there came a total void. But it was palpable, tactile. It felt like he was standing in a small closet with the lights off. It *felt*. That's right: Now dead, Ettrich could feel. And as that astonishing realization sunk in, light came on again in a blinding blitz, like a flashbulb going off straight in his eyes.

"Congratulations, Vincent. It's about time you started seeing these things. Here's a souvenir for you. Hopefully the first of many."

The light still blinded him when he felt something being put into his hand. Hand. He had a hand. He could touch. He could *feel*. Slowly he looked down and felt/saw what had been placed there: a small square. A piece of paper, a photograph. Vision returning, he was gradually able to decipher the image there. When he did, his head reared back like he'd inhaled ammonia. Because it was a photograph of what he'd seen the moment he died: Tillman Reeves and Big Dog Michelle facing him and laughing.

Ettrich looked up from the photograph and realized he was again in Coco's bedroom, still sitting naked on the corner of her bed.

"Finally! I was beginning to lose hope." She sighed bluntly and got up from the bed. Without looking at him she padded across the floor and left the room. A few moments later he heard her pissing into the toilet next door. The sound of the flush and then a short burst of water in the sink. She came back into the bedroom and stopped. She looked at him, clearly amused.

"I died?" He almost couldn't say the word, the hard "d" at the beginning, the hard "d" at the end.

"Yes, Vincent, you died."

"I'm dead?"

"No, you *were* dead. Now you're alive again. Look around. Just like before. Your life continues."

He was shaking his head. He didn't realize it for a while. "Why? Why did I come back to life? Why can't I remember dying?" His voice was so small. It felt like it came from somewhere very far away but it came from him. Even his voice was betraying him now. At once, everything he had ever known made no sense at all.

Standing a few feet away, Coco took her hands off her bare hips and turned them upward as if to say "I don't know."

"Then who are *you*? At least tell me that."

She danced her head from left to right and back again—a silly little gesture. "I'm Coco the underpants girl."

"Please don't joke around. Who are you?"

"I'm your lover. Your treasure. Your treasure map. X marks my spot. You saw." She touched the back of her neck where Bruno Mann's name was written. "I'm here to keep you honest. Your guardian angel." She sang the title line of the song "Someone to Watch Over Me." "I'm all of the above and none of them. I'm here to help you find your way through all this, Vincent." And in a slight, silvery voice she added, "The moment you saw me for the first time in my store that day was the moment you were reborn. That's why I asked if you remembered your life before we met."

It was unbearable, too unimaginable and ghastly to absorb. Ettrich felt like puking. He put his face in his hands and tried to drag his sanity back into the corral. "I died? I died but came back to life, this *same* life?" He said it more to himself. He needed to say it out loud to hear how it sounded. Jerking his head up, he cried out to this woman and to God, "Then why don't I *remember*? Why don't I remember dying? Or being dead? How's it possible not to remember that?"

Coco squatted down like a baseball catcher ready for the next pitch. "You were in the hospital for a month with liver cancer. In the end they moved you into a room with Tillman Reeves who was also about to die. He called himself Tillman the Terminal. Big Dog watched over both of you."

Ettrich shouted, "But I don't remember that! Nothing! How can it be? How is it possible?" He thought he was going mad. "And I do remember things from before I saw you. I remember what I did that day. I remember putting on my clothes that morning . . ."

She shook her head. "No, you're making it up out of the life you used to know. The old days, Vincent. All those thousands of Tuesdays and Fridays and holidays and rainy days when your heart was still beating. You were sure you had all the time in the world. But you're scared now so you're just putting your hand into that sack and pulling out old memories."

The part that stuck was her saying, "when your heart was still beating." Ettrich had been about to say prove it—show me what you're saying is true. He was going to cross his arms, throw out his chin, and say "Prove it." But she stopped him with that phrase "when your heart *was* still beating." Past tense.

His left arm was leaning on his knee. He slowly turned it over. He put two fingers of his right hand on the inside of his left wrist and felt for a pulse. He did it while she spoke, hoping she wouldn't notice.

There was no pulse. He pushed harder with his fingers, searching. Nothing. He had no pulse. He put his fingers to his throat and felt for it there. Nothing. "When your heart was still beating." Vincent Ettrich's heart had stopped beating.

He began to shake. He shook like someone in the last throes of a terminal disease. His teeth chattered and he could not stop them. His sanity was drowning, barely clinging to a small piece of the wreck that until an hour before had been Vincent Ettrich—successful businessman, philanderer deluxe, satisfactory father, casual vegetarian, etc.

Face in his hands, eyes tightly closed, elbows on his knees, Ettrich began to rock back and forth. Without being aware of it he was making a sound—a kind of high humming or groaning. An almost inhuman sound that began in the pit of his stomach and rose sinuously up to his mouth and out into the world. It was fear and grief and desperation transformed into noise. Even Coco seemed disturbed by the eeriness of the tone, the pitch.

"Vincent."

He ignored her and kept keening. Face hidden, he rocked his body back and forth like a mad Jew at prayer.

"Stop wasting time. Pay attention to me."

He didn't stop. Fuck her! Wasting time? His entire being had just been given a cosmic enema but she was telling him to pay attention.

He heard gasps, catcalls, laughter, street sounds. So loud and close that he had to see what was going on. He opened his eyes just as a yellow cab passed nearby, splattering him with viscous puddle water. He leapt up. He had been sitting on a curb two feet from a snarl of rushing city traffic. He was still naked. The nightmare we all have at one time now surrounded Ettrich: the one where we alone are naked in the middle of some downtown city street. Everyone else around us is properly dressed and staring.

People were certainly staring at Ettrich. Staring, pointing, hooting. A few feet away, Coco Hallis stared at him too with furious eyes but she was naked too. Despite everything that had just happened, everything he had just learned, Ettrich still self-consciously covered his package with his hands. That made the crowd laugh and jabber even more.

A handsome thug in a brown leather jacket walked over to Coco and after looking her up and down appreciatively said, "Hey, baby, I'm buying whatever it is you're selling."

Ignoring him, Coco asked, "Are you ready to pay attention now?"

"Hey baby, don't be rude. I'm talking to you."

Coco turned slowly to the guy and said just loud enough for him to hear, "And now I'll talk to you, Bernie. You made two women pregnant but you won't take any responsibility for the children. You've never even seen them. You didn't go to your mother's funeral, and the woman you're sleeping with these days, Emily Galvin, is doing it a lot with another guy when you're on the road. Would you like to hear more?"

Bernie's eyes widened in trapped-like-a-rat alarm. He backpedaled away from Coco fast.

"Can we go now, Vincent? I'm getting cold out here." She gestured around them, taking in the whole city and the growing crowd that seemed to have gathered for the specific purpose of staring.

"Yes! Get us out of here."

Before he'd finished speaking, they were back in her bedroom. It was warm and dark and still funky smelling from their good sex not so long before.

"What am I supposed to do, Coco? What do you want me to do?"

She watched him but said nothing. Her silence was intimidating (especially in light of what she had just done), but not threatening. Ettrich knew for certain that she was waiting for him to figure out what to do next. Clueless, he felt for his pulse again and couldn't bear the fact there was nothing beneath his skin to certify that he was alive.

He remembered what it was like having a pulse. How it would thump hard in his throat when he was nervous at a business meeting or putting the first serious moves on a woman. If he lay on his left side in bed he could hear its dull double drumbeat, a sound that always made him vaguely uneasy.

We know the heart is there, we know the blood is there. But hearing the lub-dub of our pulse reminds us that we are only chugging machines and there is little godlike or immortal about our makeup.

Feeling his silent wrist now, he looked at it a long time as if trying to remember something. He took a deep, deep breath and let it out slowly, saying, "Man! Man oh man oh man . . ." As he said it he could hear a doorbell ringing way in the back of his mind's house. Some part of him went to answer it. Standing there larger than life was the word "Man" and behind it the name Mann: Bruno Mann.

It took a moment for it to sink in. Ettrich looked at Coco and said the name. She remained impassive but was clearly waiting for him to continue.

"If Bruno is dead but I saw him, then he's in the same situation as me. And you were talking to him in the restaurant. You said I came back to life the moment I saw you." One of the candle flames on her dresser sputtered. Ettrich glanced up and licked his bottom lip while his mind caught its breath and moved to the next thought. "So it's probably true with *everyone* this happens to—you meet them the moment they come back." Now he was talking out loud to himself. Coco was there but she was not as important as his own understanding. "I've got to find Bruno and talk to him about it." He tapped one index finger against the other and kept doing it. Things were becoming clearer; a plan was emerging. "Obviously you're not going to tell me more. So I've got to find him and compare notes. That's a plan. That makes sense, right?"

He looked up from his tapping fingers but Coco was no longer there. He remembered her saying she was cold. He assumed she'd gone to put on something warm. He sat there making a mental list of things to do next. He didn't feel good but he felt better. Ettrich was a pragmatist. He had more questions for Coco but was pretty sure she wouldn't answer them. He would just have to figure these things out on his own.

But there was one thing he had to know before he could proceed and only she could answer it for him. He couldn't go on with his planning until she gave him some kind of answer. Suddenly impatient, he stood and went to find her.

For a Guardian Angel or Grim Reaper or spirit or whatever she was, Coco chose to live in a pretty meager apartment. One bedroom, a living room that doubled as a dining room, kitchen, bathroom, basta. It took Ettrich all of two minutes to walk through her place and discover she was gone. It didn't even surprise him. He could only shrug. What did it mean? Was she gone for good or had she just disappeared for now?

A white couch sat under a window in her living room. In front of it was a round glass table. Ettrich saw two things lying on it he knew hadn't been there before. Coco didn't like things on the table. She had told him that. He walked over and saw they were photographs. One was the picture he had already seen of Big Dog Michelle and Tillman Reeves laughing. The other was a close-up of Coco's neck with the Bruno Mann tattoo on it.

Holding one in each hand, he looked back and forth between them. A tattooed neck and two black people laughing. The images meant little but he knew they were his new beginning. As he walked back to the bedroom to get dressed, it came to him that if he couldn't find Bruno then he would next go looking for Michelle Maslow.

Lost at C

When he got back to his apartment, Vincent Ettrich looked at his possessions and surroundings with the kind of cocked head a dog makes when it hears the sound of a harmonica. As he sat down at his desk, his eyes fell on a thought he had written on a Post-it note and stuck on a lamp: "Some women are meant to be worshipped, others are meant to be fucked. Men's greatest problem is they keep mistaking one for the other."

Some people are defined by their job, or the damage they do, the children they have, the legacies they build, the way they see the world, or the way they trick the world into seeing them as other than they are. Vincent Ettrich would not have minded if someone said he was defined by the number of women he had known and sometimes loved in his life. Now that he was dead, or *had* been dead and was back alive for whatever reason, he looked at that quote and thought nothing is different. I still feel the same about women. I still feel the same about life. If I *was* sick and died but don't remember any of it, then what good does it do me? What have I learned? What I want today is the same thing I wanted yesterday— an interesting job, a few bucks in my pocket, and some women in my life I like to hang around with. So what did it matter that he had no heartbeat anymore and this impossible knowledge about himself if he could do nothing with either?

He remembered an article he'd read about reincarnation. An expert on the subject was asked, if reincarnation really exists, then why can't we remember anything about our past lives? The expert's answer made Ettrich laugh because it was so appropriate. "I can't even remember what I had for lunch two days ago. How am I supposed to recollect what it was like to live in ancient Egypt?"

Remembering this, Ettrich smiled a little and let his eyes wander around his desk. He saw an old letter from Isabelle in Austria and was reaching for it when he noticed the light on his answering machine blinking. Someone had called while he was out. He leaned to his left and pressed the button.

"Vincent, this is Bruno Mann. We have to talk. You know why. My number is 133–7898. Call as soon as you get this."

Ettrich sat forward so fast that his neck snapped back and it hurt. What stunned him almost more than the fact the person he needed to talk to most had called, the telephone number Bruno gave was the same as his: 133–7898.

For some odd reason, he had developed the habit of tapping in telephone numbers with his thumb. People commented on it, women invariably thought it was cute. This time his hand was shaking so much that on the first try he clumsily punched in the wrong number.

"Shit shit shit." For the first time in years he slowly used his index finger to press in his own telephone number. To his dismay the line was busy. "Who the hell is a dead man talking to?" And then he thought of himself and made a face. He redialed four times in the next two minutes but the line remained busy. He knew that if he kept doing it with no luck he'd go nuts. Looking around for something to do, he snatched up Isabelle's letter and read it.

"There is always something terribly urgent I need to tell you about, Vincent. Something always important. A nuance, a gesture, a sound, a belief, a memory, a vision, an anonymous black steel grave marker in the town cemetery, a flock of birds flying overhead outside Hansy's *Gasthaus* window, the man and his retarded son we watched eating lunch that day, the smell of a kiss, the sounds of sex, the sweat in your palms, the tears on my cheek, the coffee smell in the air at AIDA, that white-gray of a winter evening's breath. There is always something terribly urgent I must tell you about. Because you are essential, because you are mine, because you understand, because you have brought my life back to life again. Because of so many other things. Thank God for you.

"I have this one wish. Take whatever time you need, and if it takes you years that doesn't matter. Here it is: write me a letter with your own hand, in your beautiful handwriting, telling me all you want to tell me, all I am for you, all I am, all you are for me, all we are, so that if one day I will not be able to take baths anymore, I can read that letter and it will be beloved water."

The great, the sublime Isabelle. Isabelle Neukor. Three quarters perfection, one quarter broken glass. But he would have walked barefoot back and forth across that glass, he would have *eaten* it if it meant he could have her. They met when Ettrich was in Vienna because his company was hired to do promotion for the Viennale film festival and he spoke fluent German. She was the only woman he had ever known who he honestly believed he could be content with, but she never let that happen. He had tried for years and sometimes she said yes, I'm ready, give me your life and I will give you mine. But then something always scared her off—sometimes a minute later, sometimes at the last minute. At that point she would disappear—always to another country and sometimes into the arms of another man. She would write Ettrich how happy she was there and how she would always love him as a friend, but . . .

Invariably though a letter like this one would arrive and always always always his heart leapt up like a child waking to Christmas morning. In his beautiful handwriting he once copied down a quote he found and gave it to her. "Those who cross the sea change the sky above them, but not their sails."

Now a wicked chill ran through him when he thought of something Coco had said—he was reborn the instant he saw her for the first time. Did that mean Isabelle was not real? Was his memory of her and all the things in his life simply a macabre illusion?

He had no time to think about it because the telephone rang. He snatched it up and hello'd? as fast as his mouth could move.

"Vincent? It's Bruno."

"Thank God."

There was a pause on the other end until Bruno said, "Are you sure He exists? Right now I don't know what I'm thinking about God."

"Amen to that, brother."

"You did die, didn't you, Vincent? I *did* go to your funeral. You were sick and then you died, right? All of my memory is totally confused and distorted. When I saw you in the restaurant today I almost wet my pants. I went to your funeral! I went to St. Julian's hospital when you were there and brought you flowers!"

Ettrich picked up a pen and wrote "St. Julian's" on the bottom of Isabelle's letter.

"Yeah, it's true, Bruno, but I don't remember any of it either. Or any of what happened to me. I had to be told. And when I didn't believe it she showed me. She had to prove it to me."

"Exactly! Exactly! That's what happened to me too. So where can we meet? Can we do it now? I'm going out of my mind. Nothing's changed, Vincent. I died and I'm back but nothing's changed! I don't remember anything except what he told me and then showed me in the restaurant."

Ettrich frowned. In his mind he saw Coco talking to Bruno in Acumar. "*He?* Who's he?"

"Brandt. The man you were sitting with in the restaurant— Edward Brandt."

"I was with a woman, Bruno. I introduced you two. Her name is Coco Hallis."

Bruno cackled a crazy laugh that stopped as fast as it began. "It was a man, Vincent. I met a man at your table, no woman. You introduced me to Edward Brandt."

On each end of the connection, both men wore almost exactly the same bewildered, haunted expression. They thought the same words too—Oh my God.

Before he left the apartment to meet Bruno, Ettrich made one more call. He didn't want to make it but knew he had to. He called Kitty and she wasn't happy. She immediately asked what he wanted in a peeved voice and said it was very late, please be quick. In as nice a voice as he could muster, he asked if she had heard anything more from Bruno Mann's wife. In an even more irritated voice she asked why Nancy Mann would call her?

"Well, you know, because of what happened to Bruno."

"What happened to him?"

Without being aware of it, his voice took on an edge. "Kitty, you called me this afternoon. You said—"

"I said nothing. I've been out all day, Vincent. I was busy. Why would I call *you*?" She hung up.

To her and the rest of the world Bruno Mann had never died.

On his way to meeting Bruno, Vincent Ettrich performed his first miracle. He lived on the south side of town, Bruno way in the western suburbs. They agreed to meet at an upscale bar named Hof's that specialized in rare kinds of whiskey. Ettrich liked the place because Isabelle Neukor had introduced him to it. One of her many remarkable surprises. At work one day he received an e-mail from her. Isabelle loved any kind of mail and often wrote him three or four times a day when things were going well between them. Sometimes a letter in the post to his office, others waited in his computer like kisses made of words. This time she sent him only the name and address of an unfamiliar bar and told him to be there at one that afternoon for a surprise. He smiled, thinking she'd arranged over the telephone from Vienna for him to be served a nice lunch, her treat. When he arrived, Isabelle was sitting at a table talking to Margaret Hof, the owner of the bar. It astonished but didn't surprise him.

Once when they were in bed, Isabelle asked him to describe her in one word. She was always doing things like that—asking him to condense his world into one word or phrase or picture that showed her how he saw things. He thought a while and then said, "An Italian opera."

She shook her head. "That's three words."

"There's no one word that can contain all of you, Isabelle."

"Try."

He thought some more and abruptly the right word came to him. "Sea."

" 'C'? Like the letter?"

"No, like the ocean." There was a glass of water on the night table. He lifted it. "Most women I've known are like this glass of water. You're the sea."

This memory crossed his mind as he waited on the street for a taxi. To his surprise tears came to his eyes. But tears often came to his eyes when he thought of Isabelle. She was an Italian opera *and* the sea. He could never believe the depth of his emotion for her and often it frightened him.

A taxi pulled up. Ettrich got in and gave instructions to the driver as they moved away from the curb. He began to think about what he wanted to say to Bruno, what he wanted to ask. But once again the whole thing became so crushing and impossible that for the moment he pushed it aside as best he could and just stared out into the night.

He thought about the angry tone of Kitty's voice when they spoke earlier. For the thousandth time since they separated, he felt terrible regret for what he had done to that good and loving woman. The irony being that for the first time in his adult life he had done it solely out of love and no other reason.

For years, for most of his married life, Vincent Ettrich had been a complete dog when it came to pursuing women. Not that he treated them badly. On the contrary, he was the king of the female heart and that was the trouble. He adored women. He adored everything about them and they immediately sensed it the moment they met him. So many said they fell hard for him because in many important ways he possessed both a woman's heart and her way of perceiving things. That is a deadly combination in a man who cannot get enough of them. His best friend, a long-ago lover named Leah Maddox, called Ettrich her best girlfriend and was entirely serious. He was the rare kind of man who could sit and listen happily for hours to a woman talk about whatever mattered to her. It was not a trick, not a ploy to con her into thinking she interested him. His curiosity was genuine, his concern palpable. The fact he usually wanted to fuck every one he listened to was something else. Most men he knew saw women as a challenge, he saw them as marvels.

"Excuse me?"

Ettrich blinked his musing away and looked in the rearview mirror. The cabdriver, a thin balding man with large eyes and a small nose, was looking at him.

"Listen, I'm real sorry to ask this, but I got the worst heartburn. I was wondering if you'd mind if I stopped at a drugstore and got something for it? I'll just be a few minutes and I'll give you the rest of the ride for free."

"Sure, go ahead. Take your time."

"Hey, that's great. Thanks very much. I know a place in the next block. I'll be as fast as I can."

"No problem." Ettrich knew he'd arrive at the bar long before Bruno and there really was no hurry. They were no more than five minutes away from the place. Besides, he knew what bad heartburn was all about because it was one of the lousy side effects of work in advertising. Everyone in his office carried a bottle of Tagamet in their briefcase. Heartburn. Now that he no longer had a beating heart did that mean he would no longer have heartburn?

"Here we are," the taxi driver said and pulled slowly to the curb in front of a brightly lit all-night drugstore. He turned off the engine and looked again at Ettrich in the mirror. "Anything I can get you in there? Dental floss, film, ice-cream cone?" Ettrich smiled and shook his head. The driver nodded and turned to open his door. He stopped with his left hand in the air. It looked like he was about to say Wait a minute! His hand fell and, with a harsh gasp, he pitched forward onto the steering wheel.

Ettrich slid forward. "Hey!" He reached up and touched the driver's shoulder. The muscles were loose; there was no tension at all in his body. And then it happened: Up through Ettrich came the feeling of slowly sliding his hand into warm water. Something liquid and warm was moving languidly up his arm toward his shoulder.

And with no thought, Vincent Ettrich knew that it was the other man's life entering him. This "liquid" flowing up his arm and out of the other was *numen,* the divine substance, the sacred spirit that lives in a certain place in the body and sustains us all. A moment before, he did not know the word or what it meant. As soon as he felt it enter his arm he knew everything. The man was dying and his numen was entering another who had already died. Instinctively Ettrich also knew that it would give him back his heartbeat and other things, living things he had lost when he died. Indispensable things.

But he could not accept it, could not take the flame that lit another's life.

Lifting his hand off the cabdriver's shoulder, he felt a strong jolt go through his body, as if a powerful electrical connection had suddenly been broken. In the next instant he put both of his hands on top of the man's head and willed the numen out of his body and back into the other.

At first it felt like trying to push through water—slow and useless. But the more he concentrated on the substance itself, the more it took a concrete shape and hesitantly allowed itself to be moved in the other direction. Halfway up his elbow to his shoulder, Ettrich willed it back down with all of his might. The longer it was in him the more he hated pushing it away because feeling this stuff inside his body was an ecstasy beyond imagining.

And then it was out. The last slip of it left his fingertips quickly and completely. He was exhausted and fell back against the seat. The cabdriver moaned. It was a completely sexual sound, as if the man were having an orgasm. It filled the inside of the car. His head twitched and he moaned again, this time in pain.

Ettrich fumbled for the door handle and pulled it up. The door swung open and he got out. Bright light from the drugstore made him squint. Inside the store he saw people moving around, oblivious to what was happening on the street. He took a few shaky steps and it was difficult but he kept moving. He turned once and looked back at the car. The drugstore lights burned across the taxi's windshield and he could not see inside. The driver would be all right though. Ettrich was sure of that.

When he got to Hof's he felt nervous and almost afraid. Not because of what had just happened. He was glad of that because he knew he had done the right thing despite the fact he had sacrificed something of great value. No, Ettrich was afraid of what Bruno Mann would say. He worried that in comparing notes the men would find no common ground. Their experiences would be wholly different. And then what? How would he proceed from there?

The bar was full of couples. Normally Ettrich would have liked that. He liked to sit alone watching men and women go through the moves, do the dance that either brought them together or to the point where they realized there was no point in going on. He could read people brilliantly which was one of the reasons for his success in both business and romance. His mother had said if you can read a face then you can read a soul and he believed that. Waving to Margaret Hof working behind the bar, he sat down at a small table that faced the front door. Margaret brought him a glass of the single malt whiskey he liked. Hands on hips, she asked how he was doing. He smiled at her and said fine, I'm okay.

"I've heard from Isabelle, you know. A couple of days ago she sent me a letter." Margaret was from Austria and had known Isabelle for years. They had met in Vienna when Margaret was working at the Silberwirt restaurant there. She spoke English with the quirky fluency of someone who had been in the country a long time but didn't give a damn if she got the language right. She knew all about their on again/off again relationship and had sometimes acted as referee in their battles. She liked Vincent very much but was mercilessly honest with him. She always called it as she saw it and more often than not her judgments went against him. When Ettrich left Kitty for Isabelle, he lived for weeks in a studio apartment that belonged to Margaret.

He frowned and looked at his glass of whiskey. "Do I want to hear what she said?" Isabelle had not contacted him in two months. Twenty times a day he wondered how she was.

"You can ask her yourself. She is coming here the day after tomorrow."

"What? Why? Why is she coming now?"

"You must ask her yourself, Vincent. She wants you to pick her up at the airport. I was going to call and tell you. Friday night, eight o'clock. Flight 622 Austrian Airlines." She patted his shoulder and started away.

"Margaret?"

"Yes, Vincent?"

"Is there something you're not telling me?"

She hesitated, nodded. Reaching into the pocket of her beautiful silk slacks, she pulled out a piece of folded paper and handed it to him. "She sent this to me last week. Said I should give it to you when I thought the time was right."

He took it from her, eager to see what was there. "Why didn't you give it to me before?"

"Because no matter what happens next, your life is about to change."

He wanted to know what she meant, but more than anything he had to read Isabelle's note. They looked at each other a moment more and then Margaret left. Unfolding the paper he saw it was a poem. He hadn't heard from her in so long.

You, on one foot

Something I cannot forget
nor do I want to
is you, standing on one foot.
Almost naked, your underpants
a white blur in your hand.
Looking at me, you slide them off
your lifted leg.
All skin you are then, except
for that vivid touch of crumpled white
in your fist.
I loved you even more

if you tottered a little,
off balance before you stood again
and came to bed, smiling.
I saw you on one foot like that
in many places.
But I remember best at Miriam's
because that is where it happened
the first time.
In that cluttered bedroom of hers—
laundry hanging around, stuffed animals
and the bed that was never friendly.
How happy we were there!
You lifted your leg,
slid that white down and off
and I thought—
If a moment like this exists
then there must be a God.

I am pregnant, Vincent. Pregnant with your child. Our child. I haven't decided what I am going to do about it yet. I will be in touch.

His mind raced around like a fly caught between two hands. She was coming. She was pregnant. How could it be? Why hadn't she told him? And when that first blast of questions had come and gone, the real one came. How is this possible if I was dead? He reached for the glass of whiskey and drank it all without tasting it. While his head was raised he happened to glance toward the bar and saw Margaret watching him. He could not read the expression on her face. There was no time for that now.

Taking out his pocket notebook, he carefully wrote down Isabelle's flight number and when it was due. Without thinking he picked up the glass again and drank what was not there. He wanted another but wouldn't ask for it because that meant Margaret would bring it and he would have to say something to her. Not now. Not yet. The atomic bomb had just been dropped on his mind and the mushroom cloud was still rising and expanding outward. He stared at what he had written on the page and wiggled the pen up and down in his fingers.

"Vincent? Fuck, man, sorry I'm late."

Bruno pulled out a chair and sat down across the table from Ettrich. The man looked like he had run out of a burning house. His hair, always so carefully combed back flat and gelled to a seallike gleam, stood up all over his head. A meticulous dresser, who prided himself on the number of Kiton suits he owned, Bruno wore a rumpled sweatshirt with a rhinoceros on the chest and a pair of tattered carpenter's pants. Reaching down, he began to tie the laces on a pair of dirty tennis shoes. He pulled too hard and one of the laces broke off in his hand.

"Fucking bastard. Fuck!" Holding up the frizzy piece, he stared at it with absolute hatred.

"Take it easy, Bruno. What do you want to drink?"

"Nothing. I've been drinking all day and it only gave me a fucking headache. Maybe when you're dead you can't get drunk. What do you think, Vincent? You think all the rules are different for us now?" His voice was both laconic and worried. He wanted to sound like a tough guy but it didn't work.

"Have you taken your pulse? Do you have a heartbeat?"

"No." Bruno looked suspiciously around, as if spies might be watching their every move. He shook his head. "What else? Is there anything else different about you since you discovered the truth?"

The guy was so distraught that Ettrich didn't think it was the right moment to describe what had happened earlier with the cab-driver. Later. He would drop that one on Bruno when he was a little more stable. Ettrich said no, feeling the slightest bit guilty for lying.

"Me neither. But what do we do, Vincent? What does this *mean*?"

"First tell me something—do you remember dying? Do you remember being dead? Anything at all?"

"No. Nothing. Absolutely nothing. That's what's so goddamned creepy about this—how can you die and be dead but not remember it? I don't remember one thing."

Ettrich sighed and rubbed his mouth. "The same with me. I was hoping you'd remember something and we could start from there but obviously that's out now. Look, I'll just tell you how it happened to me and we can compare notes."

"Yeah good, that's good. Tell me."

Slowly and with as much detail as he could remember, Ettrich told Mann about meeting Coco, their affair, and the events of that evening. Bruno said nothing, only nodding sometimes and making hand gestures for more detail, or "wait a minute" while he digested the facts. When he heard about his name tattooed on Coco's neck, he closed his eyes and sucked in his lips. Then he laughed but said nothing. Instead, he picked up the empty whiskey glass and spun it around and around in his hand.

When Ettrich had finished his story, the only things he left out were what had happened in the taxi and the news about Isabelle.

"But why did Coco go on all those weeks letting you think things were normal? What was the point?"

"She said I had to figure it out for myself. She was just waiting for a sign from me. When I saw you after you died, that was it. But I don't know what to believe, Bruno, because then she disappeared. How did it happen to you?" He sat in the chair with his legs spread wide, shoulders slumped, elbows on knees. He looked both tired and defeated, as if he had just gotten bad news or spent an especially difficult day at work.

Bruno rubbed his eyes with the heels of his small hands. He was a handsome man. He had a certain gravitas that gave him a substantial and trustworthy air. You wanted him on your side of an argument.

"I'm gay, Vincent. It took me a whole lifetime to realize that and then admit to it. When I did, it felt like a stone had been lifted off my soul. Don't get me wrong—I have a wonderful wife and we've had a good life together. But it was a lie and part of me always knew it.

"Know what I like about you, Vincent? How much you love women. Not so much the way you behave toward them because from what I've seen, sometimes you're a stinker. But you were always so sure they were the best thing on this planet. Sure. You were always sure of who you were and what you wanted.

"Not me. Looking back on it now, I was your classic closet gay. I won't go into detail because who cares, but all the time it was there and I pushed it away like it was the plague. But eventually you have to deal with it. Especially today, when it's not the worst crime in the world to want to be together with another man.

"Then I met Edward Brandt."

"The guy you said I introduced you to at Acumar?"

"Right. For your benefit we pretended to be meeting for the first time. But we've known each other for months. He owns La Strada, the men's store. Do you know it?"

"No." A thought came to Ettrich like someone stamping a foot hard on the floor. "He owns a *store*? Where is it? Where is the place?"

Bruno was annoyed at the interruption. "On North Wells."

Ettrich slowly put both hands flat on the table. "678 North Wells, right?"

"How do you know?"

"Because that's the address of Coco's place. Both of our friends run different stores at the same address. Interesting, huh?" The men stared at each other until Ettrich grew a slight smile. "And both sell what we love in their stores: I'm crazy for women so Coco sells lingerie. You're into fashion and Edward Brandt sells men's clothes. It would be interesting to go there right now and see what kind of store is there. Maybe neither. How did you meet?"

"I went into La Strada."

"The same way I met Coco. *Was vor ein Zufall.*"

"What?"

"That's German. What a coincidence."

They spoke for another hour without getting anywhere. They discussed exhaustively the question of their shared experience and, more importantly, what they should do now. They came to no comfortable conclusions. In the middle of the conversation, Bruno asked whether Vincent had experienced any odd powers since his "discovery."

Ettrich didn't hesitate. "Besides no heartbeat? Unh-unh. You?"

"No, but I keep hoping there's some kind of upside to this, you know? Like maybe tomorrow we'll discover we can fly. I'm tired, Vincent. I've got to go home and get some sleep or else I'm going to collapse." He chuckled. "Resurrection takes a lot out of you."

After putting Bruno in a cab and watching it move away, Ettrich unexpectedly became very wound up and nervous again. He knew that if he returned to his apartment now he would only pace around or turn the television on and off as if it were a light switch. In fact the *last* place he wanted to be right now was at "home." A small bachelor apartment in the good part of town, it had a river view and nothing in the refrigerator but an unopened bottle of Chopin vodka and too many microwave pizzas. He decided to walk the seven blocks from the bar to Coco's shop to see if anything was different there.

It had rained while he met with Bruno. The streets shone from it now. Cars passed in a sexy hiss. The night air smelled of wet stone and metal. Two women went by laughing and he was given the gift of their good perfumes. Colored lights from various store windows fell across his feet, turning his shoes different colors as he walked by. As he passed a bar, the door suddenly opened and three burly guys in baseball caps came out accompanied by the sound of Queen's "Another One Bites the Dust." The tune's bass line stayed in Ettrich's mind as he walked on.

Kitty liked rain, Isabelle snow, Coco liked hot sunny days. Walking along, head down and the Queen song going somewhere in his background, Ettrich started making a mental list of the similarities and differences between the three women. Kitty tried so hard to be a vegetarian. Coco seemed to eat only junk food. Isabelle loved meat—the heavier the better. She often called herself a farmer and said she fit right into van Gogh's painting *The Potato Eaters*. What a laugh. With her Swedish-blond hair and big bee-stung blue eyes she looked more like a beauty in a cosmetics commercial than a brown van Gogh peasant.

One thing that struck him as he walked along was that with the exception of Margaret Hof, Ettrich never spoke of Isabelle to anyone. He kept his thoughts about her to himself. Even when there had been trouble between them and he'd desperately wanted to talk with someone about it, he'd remained silent. What did that signify?

He turned a last corner and was on North Wells Street. Coco's store was at the end of the block. He walked toward it with curiosity rather than trepidation. The day had been so insane that one more piece of madness would have fit right in. But to his surprise the store was still there. No La Strada, nothing but that familiar shop with its glass door and window full of lingerie. Hands in pockets, Ettrich stood in front of it for a good five minutes, thinking things over. He was lost in his thoughts when the car pulled up behind him.

"Hey sport, what are you doing over there?"

He turned around and was faced with a policeman staring at him from inside a patrol car.

He smiled. "Thinking about buying some lingerie."

The cop wasn't amused. "It's one in the morning. You planning on waiting around till that store opens?"

Ettrich saw that a second cop, the driver, was looking straight ahead and smoking a cigarette. "No, Officer, I was just taking a walk and stopped to look."

"Well then, why don't you keep on walking."

Ettrich was about to respond when he saw something. Something that was going to happen to the driver in a few days. It was a family thing. It wasn't a terrible thing, but it was ugly. The man had caused it to happen but was unaware of what the consequences would be. Ettrich saw the man's next few weeks and they were full of sorrow. He saw the policeman's future as easily as he saw the man's face wrapped in its gray veil of cigarette smoke.

He walked away.

My Heart Is a Clock

Two nights later Ettrich parked his car in a half-empty lot just as a
747 came in overhead, taking up the whole sky and then the whole
world for a few thrilling loud moments. He loved picking people
up at the airport. Loved the feel of airports—the comings and go-
ings, the tremendous emotions that filled the air like ozone—part-
ings forever, welcome homes after years away, the tactile immediacy
of right this moment when so many important things ended or
began.

He took a few steps, hesitated, and looked back at his car. He'd
washed and vacuumed it like a demon an hour before. Normally
this new auto looked like hell. It went weeks, sometimes months,
without being washed. Inside lived a dizzying mess of papers, candy
wrappers, magazines, books, numerous coins, and other now-fuzzy
ephemera that had rolled beneath the seats. On the back floor lay
a music cassette with the tape unspooled. Next to it was his daughter's headless Barbie doll (the head had fallen into one of the cracks
and was stuck to a breath mint). The variety of junk went on and
on in a sometimes surprising, always disgusting array. The only time
Ettrich cleaned the car was when he knew someone important was
going to ride in it, or he had it tuned and the repair shop threw in

a free wash. Kitty's car was immaculate. Isabelle drove an ancient Land Rover that was also messy inside but nothing like this. No automobile was like this. While riding in it one day, Isabelle said his car must have done terrible things in its last life to be damned to living this one with him.

What would Isabelle say when she saw his gleaming car now? Would she be impressed or skeptical that he had transformed it for this occasion? He thought of the postcard that he had sent her after she ran away the last time. On it he had written: "In leaving, you took away a part of my life that didn't belong to you. It was mine, Isabelle, not yours, and not ours in common. Which makes you a thief." What had she thought of that? He never knew because whenever Isabelle fled, she stopped communicating with him altogether. Even more than her running away, he resented the heartlessness of her silence. It bled all the substance out of the relationship they had created together and the closeness they had attained. Her abrupt silence was nothing but cowardice and a betrayal of a deep, important trust. They had agreed time and again that the best thing going for them, and what both relished most, was their ability to talk frankly and intimately about everything that mattered. Isabelle's silence rudely finished that. Although she was only half of their dialogue, she had taken both sides with her into that wordless black hole.

He checked his coat pocket to see if he had the camera with him. Another Isabelle quirk—she had an obsession with picking people up at airports or train stations when they came to visit her. She said it was an important custom in her family. She felt it was something you must do whether you liked it or not, to show your visitor you cared and make them feel welcome from the first minute. Ettrich thought it was sort of loopy but he also liked how committed she was to the tradition. So he went along with it and was always there to meet her wherever in the world they chose to rendezvous.

Isabelle invariably brought a camera with her to photograph

whatever person she had come to meet as they came through the gate. She loved looking at these arrival pictures and had literally hundreds of them.

Ettrich had his camera—the beautiful digital Leica she had given him for his birthday two years before. When he had opened the present, she asked him to take pictures every day of his life and send them to her via e-mail. Nothing special or arty, just whatever interested him enough to want to show her. From the first it surprised him how much he liked doing this. Liked e-mailing her his photographs of a puppy jumping over a puddle, or three bums eating popcorn from big yellow tubs, and of the little girl who could not have been more than five years old sticking out her tongue and giving him the finger at the same time. He sent Isabelle so many pictures. Sometimes she would comment on them, usually not. Sometimes he was disappointed when she said nothing because he really wanted to hear what she thought.

The worst was when she left and he stopped sending her his pictures. He kept taking them and many were stored on computer discs. But they were for Isabelle and now she wouldn't see them. So there was a strange deadness to these photographs when he looked at them. Stillborns. It made him resent and miss her even more.

Walking into the terminal he asked himself if he felt nervous. He had to take a wicked piss which always meant *some* part of him was nervous. But which part was it? Some of him was nervous, some delighted, a large chunk still simmered with anger . . . Ettrich was a tossed salad of emotions. And he was *dead*. He was dead, dead, dead. Or *had* been before he was back in his life. But no one seemed to notice a difference, including himself, until Coco had enlightened him with her slide and snapshot show. Would Isabelle see any difference? Did his return to life have anything to do with her?

How would he appear to Isabelle Neukor? Would she see a sullen man, a happy one, hopeful, or only a fool? Worst of all, would she be the one to see a dead man? What did she *want* to see? The thought "Why is she coming here now?" galloped across his mind. Followed closely by "She's pregnant with *your* child, stupid. That's why." But it really didn't make sense. Because as far as he could figure, the last time they had slept together was almost three months before. Isabelle had a very regular period so she must have known for over sixty days that she was pregnant. Why hadn't she contacted him then? Why had she waited so long? And why tell him about it in such a roundabout way via Margaret Hof? Why hadn't she just called him and said this has happened and we must talk about it?

Because she was Isabelle. Her line, often repeated, only she usually phrased it "That's just me." Over time it had become both the most endearing and infuriating sentence he'd ever heard a woman say. She used it to explain her intelligence, perception, and consummate generosity. But she also used it to explain her neuroses, disappearances, and selfish silences. At the beginning of their relationship he had begged her to say more about what this phrase meant. "That's just me." *What* was just her? But Isabelle shut down hard and cold when he persisted in asking. Ettrich quickly realized it was a place in her he was not meant to go.

On the afternoon of the day she was to arrive, after pissing six thousand nervous times and otherwise trying to keep himself busy until it was time to go to the airport, he took down a photograph of her from the mantelpiece. Turning it over, he read again what she had written on the back:

> Like a hand on your face
> that puts my blood next to yours
> I want you so much.

You tick in my chest.

All the seconds.

My heart is a clock.

He never fully understood what those mysterious lines meant but nevertheless they touched him deeply. He read them often.

The photograph had been taken in their room in Krakow, Poland. It was the oldest hotel in that singular town of high looming shadows and medieval spires. Above the front entrance of their hotel was written, "May this house stand until an ant drinks the oceans and a tortoise circles the world."

Ettrich had been in London on business and wasn't planning on seeing Isabelle that trip. But she called a day before he was to return to America and said in her deep resonant voice, "I've discovered a town. You must come. *Please*. It will haunt you for the rest of your life. It's Venice without the water. There's an amazing restaurant called Peasant's Food where you sit at hand-carved wooden tables and drink hot peppery borscht. It will be our city. We don't have a city together yet, Vincent. Please, please come."

It was the beginning of the end of his marriage. He could look back and say right there—that moment. He changed plans immediately and bought a ticket to Krakow. He had never been to Poland before. But that's what his life with Isabelle had become: He dropped everything and flew nine hundred miles to an unknown city deep in Central Europe on her excited say-so.

In this photograph, the two of them are standing in front of the full-length bathroom mirror. Ettrich holds the camera out from his body to take the picture. His other arm is wrapped around Isabelle. Both her thin hands are on his. Eyes closed, her head is turned up toward him. She is smiling beatifically—as if she were in the middle of orgasm. You can see her perfectly, but the camera flash obscures him. Ettrich is only a dark suit and the white of his lower jaw. But he loved that aspect of the picture—it was as if her radiance was the only thing allowed to show through the flash. He didn't know exactly why, but as he was leaving the house to go to the airport, he slipped the photo into the breast pocket of his sport jacket.

Because it was Friday night, the start of the weekend, Ettrich had expected the airport to be mobbed. It was notably empty. What's more, the few travelers there seemed in no hurry. People ambled about, no one ran, no one shouted orders or desperate last-minute instructions. Those who were flying moved toward their departure gates with the leisurely pace of window shoppers. It was nice to see for a change but also vaguely disconcerting.

As usual, Ettrich had arrived much too early. This man liked punctuality, liked to check in early for a flight, a hotel, for anything. He liked to be at a restaurant first, liked to be waiting for whomever he had a date with. This habit pleased certain people but exasperated others because if they arrived late they could see in his eyes that he was clearly not happy. Nevertheless Ettrich thought it was a proper and courteous sign of respect: a small gesture that said he cared. Isabelle was just like him in that regard—it was a game between them to see who would be the first to arrive. On their first formal date in Vienna, she had already been waiting inside the Café Diglas ten minutes when he arrived ten minutes early. He was already in love with her by then. It had never happened so fast to him. She wore a black cashmere sweater. She wore several thin gold necklaces. Her white hands on the gray marble table were still.

At the airport he stood under one of the big digital boards that listed scheduled arrivals and departures. Djibouti. Buenos Aires. Dublin. Isabelle would arrive within the hour carrying their child in her belly. Dublin. He'd gone there with Kitty on their honeymoon. They stayed at the Shelbourne Hotel and had tea there every afternoon at four. He thought he would never again be so happy in his life. Staring at the board, its flickering yellow numbers and exotic names, he wondered for the hundredth time what was happening to him and why? Dublin. Kitty. Isabelle. Death. Pregnancy . . .

With all this whizzing in his head, it took a moment to realize he was staring at her flight number—622—and the fact the plane had landed half an hour early.

Suddenly Ettrich was the only person running in the airport. He knew the building and its distances by heart but had no idea where she would be by now—clearing customs, baggage claim, or already out in the hall looking for him, dismayed to find he wasn't there.

All he could think to say while he sprinted toward her gate was "Perfect. Perfect. Perfect." The only time in the last five years he had been late for anything and it had to be *this*. Perfect.

Zooming along, he heard a man call out his name but Ettrich didn't even glance over to see who it was. The never-ending corridor seemed as long as the one leading to the wizard in the film *The Wizard of Oz*. Perfect. Then someone else called his name, another man's voice. Was everyone he knew at the airport tonight?

Distracted, he actually jogged by Isabelle who was passing in the other direction on the moving walkway. She didn't see him because her head was down and turned away. One of the wheels on her brand-new suitcase wobbled badly and she was checking to see why. The only thing that stopped him was the jacket she wore.

Isabelle always dressed with great flair. She was vain. She liked clothes that showed off her graceful body and long legs. She wore tight slacks and thin jackets. Boots. Boots always, but the leather on them was thin, chic, and never practical. In the winter she was forever cold, often shivering so hard her teeth chattered. As a joke Ettrich ordered a fat goose-down jacket from the Lands' End catalog for her. It was navy blue and yellow. A road repair worker could have worn it in the middle of the freeway and never worried about being hit by traffic because the thing was so conspicuous. To his great surprise, Isabelle loved the jacket. When she wasn't wearing it, she allowed her dog Soup to sleep on it.

She was five feet past before he was able to get the surprise out of his mouth and say, "Hey you!" Their greeting always, the "you" stretched long and lovingly.

Isabelle's head came up fast and there was *the smile*. He once asked if she had a million teeth because her smile was that big and radiant. She put her pinkie on a front tooth and began counting them. He pulled her finger to his lips and kissed it.

Now she brought her hands together and held them under her chin. "I thought you weren't going to come, Vincent."

Instantly on guard, he had no rejoinder for that, witty or otherwise. Instead, he remained silent and only continued walking backward quickly to keep pace with her on her moving sidewalk. It was just as well that he said nothing because he saw that in spite of her smile, Isabelle was crying. Her beautiful blue eyes brimmed with tears that now spilled over and slid down her cheeks, making them gleam. "You weren't there and you weren't there and you weren't there, so I thought—" Overwhelmed, she threw her hand in the air to complete the sentence. She continued to smile but there was more sadness in her expression than he had ever seen. Ettrich almost fell to his knees with pain and pent-up longing for this woman. He had missed her so much. She was the only one who had ever mattered. For months he had thought she's gone now, gone for good. He had honestly believed that. But now here she was near him again, saying she hadn't thought he would come. How could she believe that? How could Isabelle ever think he would not come when she called, wherever she was?

What happened next was without precedent. A big bearded man carrying a stained canvas duffel bag over his shoulder hurried down the moving walkway in the same direction as Isabelle. Once there, he banged into her so hard that she yelped in shock and staggered badly. Not even flashing her a glance, the man said "stupid cunt" and kept going.

Leaping over the barrier between the corridor and the moving walkway, Ettrich ran after him. When he was close enough, he timed it carefully and stuck out his leg, tripping the other perfectly. The man flew forward, landing on his head and elbow with a thick *clunk*. Ettrich wasn't finished. As soon as the guy hit the floor, Ettrich bent over and punched him in the face. Only once. Ettrich was cool—he was completely in control of both the moment and his actions. He was only doing what was necessary. *Nobody* touched Isabelle like that. Especially now, with the baby.

"Vincent!"

Still bent over, he turned slowly and looked back at his love.

At the same time, the big man came out of his daze and erupted. "What the fuck—"

Ettrich jabbed three stiff fingers into the guy's red cheek. "Don't move. Don't think. Don't do a thing." The tone of his voice would have frightened anyone. It said I'll kill you. The man's eyes widened and he froze.

Ettrich stood up and gestured for Isabelle to come. When she caught up, he lifted her suitcase over the fallen man whose eyes were now glued to the ground. She stepped over him and the two moved quickly away.

The man on the floor rode all the way to the end of the line sitting in that position without once looking up to see if they were gone.

"Is it really your car? The home of the headless Barbie doll?" Holding the sandwich in one hand, Isabelle looked slowly around the spotless interior of his car. Then she turned to him and eyes happy for the first time, took a big bite and moaned. "Umm, it's delicious, Vincent. Thank you."

It was one of their rituals—whenever she came through the gate in the U.S., he handed her a pastrami sandwich slathered with coleslaw and Russian dressing fresh from any nearby delicatessen.

Isabelle never ate on a plane because she said she was wary of food that came in rectangles. When Ettrich arrived in Vienna, she had an *Extrawurst Semmel* waiting, the best bologna sandwich he had ever tasted.

They had been sitting in his car for fifteen minutes and he had yet to put the key in the ignition. It was bliss having her there. His world had suddenly become whole again. For the moment life was perfect. The car was redolent with the striking aroma of her cologne—Creed's Royal Water—the same kind Ettrich used. On their first date after smelling it on him, Isabelle literally demanded to know the name so she could buy and wear it "for the rest of my life." He loved the cologne but never wore it when they were together because he wanted to associate it with her.

Still admiring his oh-so clean car, she began to eat the bulging sandwich and drink from a bottle of cream soda, another favorite. While she ate she didn't say much but that was fine. She appeared just as content to sit there as Ettrich so he didn't worry about it.

After finishing, she carefully folded the piece of shiny wax paper the sandwich had been wrapped in. "I could eat another one of those right now."

He smiled until he saw she meant it. He didn't know whether he was impressed or dismayed because that sandwich had been as big as a dachshund. "Really? You want another?"

She nodded. "I need to eat something more, Vincent. These days I have the appetite of a sumo wrestler. I could eat the moon for dinner." She patted her tummy. Because she was wearing the down jacket he hadn't been able to see much of her body. Was she bigger now? Did the baby show yet? While she ate, he sneaked peeks at her stomach but couldn't see a difference.

"How do you feel otherwise? I mean, does your back hurt or have you had morning sickness or—"

"The usual suspects?" Unexpectedly, she took his hand and held it in both of hers. "Yes, a little, the big differences are my appetite, and for some reason I'm cold all the time. Thank God for this jacket which I basically live in now. But my side effects are nothing compared to those of other women. The first three months are supposed to be the worst and I've been very lucky. I just keep lots of candy bars in my pockets and walk around wearing this blue igloo you gave me. No big deal.

"Look, do you want to talk about this now or can we wait a little while? I'm still kind of dopey from the flight and I really do want to get something more to eat. Preferably sweet, if you don't mind."

"A hot fudge sundae?"

She squeezed his hand. "Maybe two."

Ettrich reached for the ignition key and, sighing contentedly, turned it. Isabelle was *here*. She was sitting two feet away from him and now they were going to eat ice cream. How could life be any better?

"I heard that."

He looked at her. "Heard what?"

"Your sigh. Was it a happy one or a sad one?"

Before he had a chance to answer, she asked another question which changed the color of the rest of his life.

"Vincent, what's it like to be dead?"

They were followed. If Ettrich had been paying any attention, he would have seen a perfectly restored 1969 Austin-Healey 3000 Mark III convertible in the rearview mirror when he drove out of the parking lot and onto the highway. It remained three car lengths behind them the whole trip to the restaurant. What's more, the vintage machine was fitted with a muffler that made it sound as loud as a racing car. Plainly this Healey was never intended for surveillance assignments, but the woman driving didn't care. Now that

Vincent Ettrich was aware of his situation to a certain degree, Coco Hallis was going to do things her way.

He did not know that she owned the car. Plus she had parked far enough away from him in the airport lot so that he probably wouldn't notice. Even if he had it wouldn't have been a problem. *Let* him see her—sooner or later he would have to know she was to remain very much a presence in his life for some time.

While waiting for them to come out of the airline terminal, she amused herself by thinking of ways she might introduce herself to Vincent's glorious girlfriend. "Hello I'm Coco, the woman he's been sleeping with while you were avoiding him." Then she could add in her most fawning voice, "Vincent's told me *so* much about you." Which was a lie because Ettrich almost never mentioned Isabelle to Coco. In general he was happy to talk about anything and anyone, but *that* woman was strictly off limits. Coco had repeatedly tried to worm details about Isabelle out of him but to no avail.

She lit a cigarette and realized halfway through smoking it that she was more than a little jealous of Isabelle Neukor. Wasn't that funny? She wanted to laugh but couldn't because there is little laughter in a jealous heart.

And then suddenly there they were. Coco sat up straight in her seat and flicked the cigarette out the window. It cartwheeled across the night and hit the ground in a bounce of orange sparks. She recognized their body language before she knew it was them. Lovers ahoy!

Ettrich was pulling a large suitcase that wobbled on its wheels. A thin blonde walking two steps behind him had her arms wrapped tightly across her chest as if she were very cold on this balmy fall night. The two of them kept bumping into each other like they couldn't get enough contact. And Isabelle kept reaching out to touch Ettrich—his arm, his hand, the back of his head.

Coco put on her large horn-rimmed glasses for a better look at Ms. Isabelle Neukor. Was she beautiful? Vincent sure thought so, but it was hard to tell in that humid chemical light. She was tallish and had very animated features. When they weren't locked under her armpits, her hands danced around like an orchestra conductor's whenever she spoke. A great open smile came often to Isabelle's face that would have delighted anyone. Blond hair fell to her shoulders but Coco couldn't tell if it was real blond because the light over the parking lot distorted everything.

Yes, okay, Isabelle *was* beautiful but not annoyingly so. Hers wasn't the kind of face which, on entering a room, drew men's looks like a vacuum cleaner and left every other woman feeling diminished.

Sorrow. That was it—there was a great deal of sorrow in Isabelle's face that both diminished her beauty yet gave her a distinctive compelling look. It was the face of someone who had seen both great and terrible things and was carved by the hands of both.

The two lovebirds got into the car. But then they just sat there for some unknown reason. Coco saw Ettrich hand Isabelle a small white package that turned out to be a sandwich. Which she proceeded to eat—and eat and eat for minutes on end while he sat next to her doing nothing. They didn't even appear to talk much while she ate. *This* was Vincent's razzle-dazzle, soul-frazzling romance? Lovers meet again after three gut-wrenching months apart. He's back from the dead, she's pregnant with his child, and the first thing he does is give her a *sandwich*?

Coco didn't begin to understand how any of this worked, but that wasn't the point. She wasn't there to study human behavior. She was there to protect Vincent Ettrich against all of the bad things that were likely to happen to him from this day on. That was what she had been sent to do. What she hadn't planned on was falling for the man, however long or short that fall was. Watching his car from her corner of the airport parking lot, Coco knew she had at least a big crush on Ettrich and that was bad news. Human emotion could cause problems. Frowning, she rolled her eyes in disgust at herself. In doing so, she looked up at one of the lights above the parking lot. What she saw there no mortal could have seen.

The parking lot was shaped like a large square. There were streetlights at each of the four corners and three down the middle of the lot. Coco's eyes jumped back and forth between them. The same thing was happening to all seven—some of the light streaming from each was slowing and coalescing into different recognizable forms. But human beings would never have apprehended it because human perception was crude and simplistic. It was like bringing a dog to the opera: the animal might notice and even bark excitedly at the hubbub, but the Mozart would only have been noise to its ears.

Although she was well aware of what this particular light show augured, it was impossible for Coco not to watch raptly because the scene was unquestionably beautiful. Light streamed down from the lamps. Slowing, some of it began to curve and drift, stop or break apart, at times floating back upward. Like hot lead or candle wax poured into water, the light froze or curled or spread, often joining with other threads to form indescribable, repeatedly lovely forms.

If asked what was happening, Coco would have calmly said it's gaining consciousness. Emanating from the giant lamps as a solid, once out in the world parts of the light divided then met others and rejoined into different shapes, all of them alive. Coco could have named each of these living forms but there was no need. She had seen the process happen before and her reaction to it was the same—fascination and fear. Anyway there was nothing she could do about it *but* watch. These events were created by beings eons beyond her understanding and capabilities. She could only watch the occur-rences unfold and then, if necessary, act on them within the limits of her power.

The light forms swirled lower. Touching ground, they began rolling like fog across the pavement. Some of them were searching and quickly found what they sought—Vincent Ettrich's car. Coco knew this would happen the moment she saw them forming in the air. She knew they were here to find Ettrich and his Isabelle.

Oblivious to what was happening, the couple continued sitting in his car—Isabelle eating her sandwich, Vincent staring straight ahead with his hands on top of the steering wheel. Light slid up the door on the passenger's side. On reaching the window it split in two and moved in opposite directions. This learning light watched both passengers now. Languorously circling the car, it looked in from different angles and vantage points, learning about them. Things they didn't even know about themselves, things only the light could understand. Throughout this inspection both people remained oblivious. Isabelle folded the sandwich paper and said something to Vincent. He smiled but it suddenly stopped, faded and disappeared. The light, moving across the top of his shiny car, paused as if listening to what they were saying. Then it began moving again. It wasn't fully cognizant yet so the couple had some time. Soon though. When the light had its full strength and intelligence it would be unstoppable.

Coco lit another cigarette and wished she could call for help. Being this close to the light was extremely dangerous for her too. But her job was to protect Ettrich as best she could, so she had to stay. For a moment she raged at how horribly unjust all of this was. Against it she was powerless to protect Vincent. And he certainly had no way of defending himself against what was coming.

The cigarette tasted awful. Why did people like these repulsive things? She had started smoking only for Ettrich's sake and then found herself doing it more out of habit than for any other reason. She quickly rolled down the window and tossed it out. But she was so nervous just sitting there helplessly watching that she had to do something with her hands. Pulling the cigarette lighter out of its socket on the dashboard, she bit into it. Now *that* tasted a lot better than cigarettes. Coco sat there more or less contentedly eating the still-warm object while watching the beautiful menacing light move over Vincent's car. The sound of plastic and metal being crunched and chewed was surprisingly loud in the small cockpit of the Austin-Healey.

After having swallowed the last curl of metal, she was still hungry. Looking at the dashboard and then lower, her eyes stopped on the gearshift knob. It was fat and round, made of a beautiful burled walnut. Normally she didn't like the taste of wood but beggars can't be choosers. Like Isabelle Neukor across the parking lot, Coco wanted more to eat. Her hand dropped onto the knob and with a twist of immense strength began to unscrew it. All the while her eyes never left Ettrich's car.

Anjo

"What should I get?" Isabelle's beloved voice rose from behind the large black and yellow menu she had been studying. They faced each other in a booth by one of the windows. This booth was so large six people could have sat in it comfortably. But the diner was half-empty so they didn't feel guilty being there. It was that time of night when people don't think about eating. Most of the customers were either drinking coffee or eating dessert.

Ettrich had driven here from the airport because he remembered Isabelle liked the place very much. It was the kind of basic but good restaurant that advertised breakfast twenty-four hours a day, and served meat loaf with real mashed potatoes to guys wearing baseball caps indoors or women in pantsuits and running shoes. The friendly waitresses were all middle-aged and had 1950s' names like Elsie and Doris. When they asked "You ready for more coffee, hon?" Isabelle grinned and nodded like a child. As a European, she loved the genuine friendliness of most Americans. She was a great fan of America. Many times he had heard her defend it to skeptical condescending Europeans who saw his country as a great place to shop but who would want to *live* there?

"A banana split." She closed the menu with a *whop* and gave him a big smile. "With extra *Schlagobers*."

He nodded and looked for a waitress. "Do you feel more comfortable speaking German or English? I never asked you that before."

"Both. Either. It doesn't matter. It's just that you can say certain things better in one language or the other. *Ich liebe dich* is an ugly-sounding way of saying 'I love you.' English is softer and fits the emotion better." She looked around the room, taking it all in. He had never known a person so attentive to the world around them.

"Isabelle, how did you know about what happened to me?"

Her eyes slowly moved to Ettrich's face. When they stopped he saw that they were calm. "You waited so long to ask, Vincent."

"I was afraid to. I *am* afraid to."

She nodded that she understood and sighed. "Do you remember the last time we made love in Vienna? That night?"

"Yes, of course."

A waitress appeared. "Hi, folks. What can I bring you?"

Ettrich was so distracted that he could only stare at this stranger standing above him and wonder who the hell she was. It clicked in his brain a moment later and he tried unsuccessfully to think of something to order.

Isabelle said, "I'd like a piece of peach pie with a scup of vanilla ice cream."

"You mean a scoop?" The waitress nodded encouragingly.

"Yes, yes, a *scoop*."

"You've got a cute accent. Where are you from, if you don't mind my asking?"

"Austria. Vienna, Austria."

"No kidding? You came all the way from Vienna to eat a piece of our pie? And you, sir, what would you like?"

"I'll have a Coke."

"Gotcha. I'll be right back." She winked at Ettrich and took off.

Isabelle lifted her chin and looked down her nose at him. "I saw her wink at you." She smiled.

"I thought you were going to have a banana split?"

She shrugged. "Never trust a pregnant woman." She dipped her index finger in one of the glasses of water the waitress had brought. Taking it out, she ran it across the top of Ettrich's hand.

"Talk to me, Isabelle."

"Before I do, tell me about the last time we made love. It's important. Tell me everything you remember."

Ettrich sat back and steepled his fingertips over his stomach. "I said let's eat dinner at your favorite restaurant. So we went to the Stella Marina—"

"What street is it on?" Both her face and voice were a challenge.

"Windmuhlgasse. Sixth District. Is this a test? Come on, Isabelle, you know how good my memory is."

"We'll see. Go on."

For the moment Ettrich was on safe ground because his memory really was extraordinary. People commented on it. It was a good friend, having helped him countless times in both business and romance. He remembered whole reams of statistics, obscure facts and details, poetry, a woman's middle name five years later.

"It was a beautiful night. We couldn't decide on whether to eat in the restaurant or at an outside table. You even started laughing because we couldn't make up our minds. Finally I just said *inside* so we could talk without all the street noise. Should I tell you what we ate?"

Isabelle shook her head and pushed a glass back and forth between her hands. The water inside swayed to the edges but none slopped over.

"After dinner we walked on Mariahilferstrasse and bought ice cream. It was melting down all over your hand and I kept telling you how to lick it so that wouldn't happen." The memories made Ettrich smile. What a nice night that had been! Putting his hands flat on the table, he looked at them. For the first time he noticed a liver spot on the back of his left. "I always assumed I'd grow old. I never imagined myself dying before I had white hair growing out of my ears and lots of liver spots on my hands. But I was wrong, huh? I left the party a lot earlier than planned." His eyes were full of sadness and dismay.

"I don't remember any of it, Isabelle, *nothing*. Not getting sick or going to the hospital . . . I don't remember *dying*. How is that possible? Not remembering *death* I can understand—you die and go someplace completely different. When you come back to life you can't remember that place because it's unimaginable. But how could you forget dying? That scares me most. I don't remember anything about it—not one thing."

"Here you go, folks—peach pie à la mode and a Coke."

Neither of them looked at the waitress, so caught up were they in the intensity of their moment. The woman was about to say more until she sensed what was going on between these two, and then she hurried away.

Gently Isabelle urged Ettrich to continue describing their last night together in Vienna.

He made an exasperated face. "Why? Is this going anywhere? Does it mean anything?"

"Yes, Vincent, trust me. It means everything."

"All right. We ate the ice cream walking back to your apartment. We stopped in the courtyard of your building for a few minutes to look at the trees. I always like to watch the way the streetlight comes down through the leaves in that eerie yellow-green . . . I said how it reminded me of what the city must have looked like a hundred years ago."

Isabelle's eyes never left his face while she spooned up pie and ice cream. A white creamy drop fell onto her chin. Without thinking, Ettrich reached over and wiped it off with his thumb. Then he licked his finger. Neither of them paid attention to his gesture.

"When you opened the door to your apartment, Soup went crazy. She jumped up in the air and started spinning around like a whirling dervish. You wanted to take a shower, so I went into the living room and played with her."

Isabelle dreamily looked down at her plate and was surprised to see all of the pie and ice cream was gone. She had been so involved in his account that she didn't remember the flavor of anything except that it had been sweet and heavy. To remind herself of the tastes, she rolled her tongue around the inside of her mouth.

"On your bookshelf was one of those rawhide bones she loves to chew. So I took it down and started playing tug-of-war with her with it——" Ready to go on, Ettrich was puzzled to see Isabelle raise a finger to stop him. Like running back into the house when you forget your keys, he ran back into his memory to see if he had forgotten anything important while recounting their last night together. No, he had everything. Why was she stopping him? Her eyes took on an expression he couldn't decipher. She had been moving her mouth around in a peculiar way, but then she stopped abruptly and *that* look crossed her face. What did it mean? Ettrich always kept a close eye on Isabelle because her facial expressions often said what she was thinking long before she actually said anything.

She opened her mouth and lifted a hand at the same time. For a moment he thought she was going to pull a hair off her tongue or a bad bit of the dessert she had just eaten. Instead she reached into her mouth and took out something silver, something round and large—a bell.

"Jesus!" The object was so unexpected and odd to see that it was like a slap in Ettrich's face.

Isabelle stared at it with delight and appreciation. Her face said she was not surprised to have found a silver bell in her mouth. As she jiggled it in her hand, the thin tinny sound of the metal clittered in the air. Isabelle looked at Vincent, her eyes shy and sly at the same time. "He's here."

Ettrich leaned forward and asked carefully, "*Who's* here?"

She put the bell down on the table and tap-tap-tapped it toward him with the back of her index finger. "Your son is here; our son. This is his way of saying hello." She pushed the bell again.

Vincent Ettrich loved Isabelle Neukor more than any woman he had ever known. She was without question *the* one for him. If ever there was a person he would have died for it was she. But looking at that silly bell in front of him and then at her, he was convinced she had gone mad. For the first time in their relationship he felt repelled by her.

He remembered something: when he was a boy his mother owned a canary. She kept it in their kitchen in a blue cage. Hanging inside the cage was a bell that looked exactly like the one in front of him. Even when he was in a far corner of their house, young Vincent could still sometimes hear that bell when the bird poked it. He put his hand over this one now, as if by covering the object he could make Isabelle's lunacy disappear.

"That's how I knew you died and came back, Vincent. He told me. He talks to me." She put her hand on top of his. Ettrich had to fight the impulse to pull away.

"You're saying our unborn child *talks* to you?"

Her smile could have lit and warmed a city. "Yes, Vincent"— she nudged her chin in the direction of the bell—"and now he's talking to you too. That's his hello."

Nothing. He could not think of one thing to say or do in reaction to what she had just said.

She kept smiling. "You don't believe me."

He shook his head.

"Would you like me to prove it?"

He nodded.

"The name of your mother's bird, the one you were just think-ing about, was Columbus. It died on a hot summer day when you were six. You and your mom buried it in the backyard in a matchbox. Two days later you dug it up again when she was out shopping. You wanted to see if it had gone to heaven yet." She picked up the bell and held it out to him. "Ask anything you want, Vincent. He wants you to be convinced this is true."

"What's on Coco Hallis's neck?"

There was no way Isabelle could know who Coco was. Unless she'd hired a private detective to follow him around for the last three months, but that was not Isabelle's style. Closing her eyes, she tipped her head slightly to one side and then opened them again. "A tattoo, a name: Bruno Mann."

"How're you folks doin' over here? Anything more I can get you?" The waitress's voice cut through that moment between them like a knife.

Ettrich's expression didn't change. He looked up at her and smiled. "Do you want to see a really great trick?"

Taken off guard by his question, the waitress didn't know how to react. Was this guy pulling her leg? She managed to say, "A trick? Sure. But is it a *wonderful* trick or just a good one?" Now she gave a real smile, letting him know that she was a good sport.

Ettrich said, "You judge for yourself, ma'am. Do you have children?"

She arched an eyebrow. "Yeah sure, I got some kids. Why?"

"Watch this." He turned to the pretty woman sitting across the table from him and asked, "What are the names of her kids?"

Isabelle looked at the waitress, paused, and then said, "Ron and Debby. Ron after Ronald Reagan and—" She paused again, thinking. "Debby after your sister Deborah."

The smile fell off the waitress's face. She had never seen this woman before. How could she know those names? Before she could ask that, the woman spoke again.

"Your husband, Dean? Those tests he took the other day? He's okay. It's not cancer."

"How do you know that? How do you know about those tests?"

Isabelle said nothing. What could she say? She looked at Vincent to help.

"*Huh*? How do you know those things about my family?" The distraught woman took a step forward.

"Because she's psychic. Is there anything else you would like to know?"

The waitress was aghast. She had read about psychics and seen them on TV, but never had actual contact with one. This stranger knew about Dean and the frightening dark spot on his lung. But she'd also said he would be all right! Was it true? She was so confused and distracted by possibilities that the only thing she could think to do was write their check, slam it down on the table, and walk away. When she got to the counter she needed to tell someone what had happened. Instead, she only stood there and glared at the handsome couple. Who were they? It didn't matter— She only wanted them to leave right now.

"Do you believe me, Vincent?"

"Yes, Fizz, I believe you. What's going on? What is all this?"

Hearing him use his nickname for her for the first time since she'd arrived, Isabelle's heart opened its till-then clenched fists. It was like a secret password between them—Fizz. No matter what, they could talk now.

"His name is Anjo—"

"The child?"

"Yes."

Unable to hold back, Ettrich jutted his head toward her stomach. "That unborn child told you his name is Anjo?"

"Yes, Vincent, that's right." She knew she must be patient now, knew everything hinged on Ettrich's believing her completely.

His voice was exasperated. "All right, all right. Then who is Anjo? I mean, besides our child?"

She wanted to give a blunt snap answer, but gathered herself instead, thinking of the best way to begin, the right words to say, the phrasing that would be most effective. She had to do this perfectly—it was crucial.

"A week after we slept together and you left for America, I knew I was pregnant. There was no question in my mind. I felt it throughout my whole being. I wanted to call and tell you—"

"Why didn't you? You disappeared again after London. It was so damned unfair." The terrible feelings from those months alone were in his head and heart again—the anger, grief, and resentment. They felt as new as now. He hated them, and like flicking on a light switch, just thinking about that merciless time brought them right back to life.

Isabelle's anger flared. She was barely able to catch it before it leapt out of her throat and fastened onto him. To contain herself she looked out the window. A car's headlights touched her face. "You never knew what you wanted from me, Vincent. Did you want a life partner or only a part-time girlfriend you could meet in Europe and jump around with for a few days before going back to your real life?"

"That's bullshit! I left my wife and family, Isabelle. I gave up a *life* to be with you!" He willed her to look at him but she would not. She continued staring out the window at the street. Why wouldn't she make eye contact? If she had, she would have seen it all in his eyes, the rock-solid truth of every word he had said.

When she spoke again her voice was quiet, quieter than he would have expected. "That last night we were together in London, you said you did it for me. It was the worst thing you could have said, Vincent."

"Why? I left everything to be with you. What's wrong with that?"

"Nothing. But you said you left your family because I wanted you to. You made it sound like you weren't part of the decision— you only did it for me. Not for you, or *us,* only for me."

"Oh Isabelle, don't get grammatical now. You knew exactly

what I meant when I said that. Cut me a little fucking slack!"

"No! Because you didn't only say it, you meant it. Your words and actions were the same. I was watching you. I've never watched someone so closely in my entire life!" Her voice had risen; the sentences came faster. "I understood your guilt, Vincent; the sacrifices you were making. I was on my knees to you in gratitude. But I never got the feeling that you left your family because in your heart of hearts you truly believed life with me would be the best thing. That you had finally found your home and were coming to me with an open heart and an eager soul."

It was the word "eager" that KO'd him. Isabelle's English was ninety-five percent perfect, but sometimes it transcended that— sometimes she pulled words out of her hat that defined things better than someone might whose English was their native tongue. What the hell was an eager soul? He knew exactly what it was and what she meant by the phrase. In response the only thing he could manage was to repeat in a mumble, "I gave up a life for you."

She surprised Ettrich by finally looking at him and reaching for his hand. "Let's get away from that now. Can we move beyond it and talk about other things?"

Looking at their hands he said, "No, I need to talk more about this, Fizz. You tore the fucking heart out of my chest by just disappearing, especially that time. *Pfft.* You vanished completely from my life after I'd done the only thing I could to prove my love for you meant more than anything."

She wasn't having it. "You did it because you thought you were going to lose me if you didn't."

Eyes narrowing, he spoke between clenched teeth. "Wrong. Don't diminish what I did, Isabelle. You don't walk away from two children and a marriage of sixteen years because you're afraid of losing your mistress."

"Men do it all the time, Vincent. Don't be naïve."

How could he be this angry with her so suddenly? He wanted

to pound the table, squeeze his eyes shut, and bite the day. When she spoke again it didn't register because the thunder from his anger was still filling his head. "What?"

"A few weeks after that I met a man."

As fast as it came, the anger left Ettrich when she mentioned another man.

"Go on."

"We went to dinner a couple of times. He was interesting—he said things that stuck in my mind. It was clear that he wanted something to happen between us. The last time we went out he said that and was very insistent about it. Know what I said to him? 'I'm sorry, Berndt, but you're not required reading for me.' "

"Did he understand that?"

"Yes and got very angry. He wanted to hit me."

"What?"

"Yes, but nothing happened. Anjo stopped it. He protects me."

"Say that again?"

"Anjo always protects me."

"Tell me about this."

"I could, but you should see it for yourself." Apropos of nothing, she pointed to the bell sitting between them in the middle of the table.

"What do you mean?"

"You can see for yourself what happened. I think that would be better, Vincent. Pick up the bell."

He picked it up. And the next thing he knew, he was sitting alone at a small table in a different restaurant. It took him twelve blinks to accept that new geography and acclimate himself to where he was. As soon as he did he was angry again. Because suddenly he was in the restaurant Stella Marina in Vienna. One table away, Isabelle was deep in conversation with another man who was holding one of her hands and staring into her eyes with too goddamned much longing. Ettrich smelled fresh baked bread and frying olive oil. All around him German was being spoken, on the stereo Pavarotti was singing "Nessun dorma," silverware clinked on plates as diners tucked into that delicious Italian food.

Ettrich watched Loverboy ply his moves on Isabelle, working through the spectrum of facial expressions and oh-so appropriate body language—earnest, sexy, ha-ha playful, pensive. In response, Isabelle let him hold her hand but it meant nothing because Ettrich knew exactly what the bemused smile she was wearing said—No. What was the guy's name, Berndt? From the look of things he was about to become *Burned*.

Stella Marina is a small restaurant, one oddly shaped room, intimate and warm. Looking away from the Odd Couple, Ettrich checked out the other people in the place. Only on a second eye-sweep did he see the dog. It was so imposing that it startled him, forcing him to do a double take. He didn't recognize the breed but it was a magnificent creature. Over five feet tall when it stood on its hind legs, the 155-pound Fila Brasileiro lay unmoving next to its owner's foot. Its anvil-sized head rested on a paw while its sad eyes watched everything with an unusual intensity. Ettrich had never seen a dog that took up so much psychic space. It was like a beast out of Greek mythology or a Persian folk tale.

Who would own such a dog? An old couple who were both eating pasta with great gusto. The dog sat by the small frail-looking man. How would the old geezer control that monster if it decided to take off after something?

Ettrich looked at Isabelle. She was staring straight at him but without a glimmer of recognition in her eyes. Didn't she recognize him? Was it possible in this setting he was invisible to her? What were the rules here? Who was she seeing when she looked at him so indifferently? He was not disturbed by her blank stare, only curious. Since the night he saw the tattoo on Coco's neck, Vincent Ettrich had been forced to accept whatever this new and untrustworthy universe threw at him. Beamed to an Italian restaurant in

Vienna where the love of his life now looked at him like he was a dinner roll? Accept it. Period. He could do nothing else other than watch and wait to see what came next.

"Isabelle?" Berndt pronounced the name "Ease-a-bail."

Her eyes slid over to her dinner partner, but Ettrich was pleased to see they didn't warm up any when they got there. *"Ja?"*

Berndt spoke a deep, beautifully enunciated *Hoch Deutsch*. He had the voice of a sexy radio disc jockey. Smiling, he looked down, as if what he was about to say was too tough for eye contact. "Ever since we met we've been talking, but so far I haven't had the courage to tell you what's really in my heart. I want to try now."

"Don't." She quickly pulled her hand out of his.

That word and her gesture blindsided him. "Why? Why not?"

"Because that's not why I'm here, Berndt. I thought that was understood. I'm not looking for anything like that."

"Like *what?*"

"Like what's in your heart. I don't want to know that." Beginning with her mouth, the skin on her face tightened. Ettrich had seen it happen many times before. It meant she was shutting down, closing off. Isabelle was looking at Berndt now, telling him with her eyes and blank, taut face that he was walking across a minefield.

Berndt's anger showed by the way that he slowly spread the fingers of both hands to their full length over the table. One index finger touched the other and began tapping the fingernail, as if it were sending Morse code. Innocuous as the gestures appeared, it was clear this man was gathering himself to do something.

"There was no reason before to tell you this, but obviously there is now: I'm very much in love with someone. I'm pregnant." Isabelle said it firmly, only stating the fact.

"Pregnant?" The index finger tapped the other faster and faster. Berndt kept shifting his eyes from his busy finger to her face and back again. Then he began to nod his head. From afar it looked like

he was only agreeing with something his dinner companion had said. But he didn't stop nodding, nor did the finger stop tapping. "Why didn't you tell me this before?"

"I just said why, Berndt—there was no reason to. Whenever we met it was nice and interesting. For me that was all."

"That was all?" he repeated, head and fingers moving, big emphasis on the last word.

"Yes." She did not stop looking at him.

"That's interesting. I had a very wrong impression."

"I'm sorry if I misled you."

"I'm sorry too. Really sorry." Berndt chuckled but it sounded more like something was stuck in his throat.

If this guy *did* start something could Ettrich stop him? Did he have any power here? Isabelle had stared straight at him before but not seen him. Did that mean he was (1) invisible and (2) useless?

"I'm really angry now. I'm really very angry at you." Berndt looked at his hands and slowly closed one into a fist.

Alarmed, Ettrich got up from his seat. At the same time, megadog rose like an extra table coming up from the floor. Staring at Berndt, it began to growl at him in a voice of gravel and blood that would have scared the shit out of the dead.

No one in the room even looked their way. It was amazing because the dog was snarling very loudly now, its head up and tipped to one side, mouth drooling white foam and strings.

This monster was about to attack Berndt but nobody was paying any attention, much less trying to stop it. Even the dog's owners ate their meals in happy oblivion, the old woman slurping up green spaghetti, her husband taking a long drink of wine. People in the room laughed and ate and shook their heads at good stories. Only Berndt, Isabelle, and Ettrich seemed to notice that one of them was about to be devoured.

"Anjo, stop." Isabelle spoke quietly to the dog. It continued to growl and slobber but did not move any closer to Berndt. Its gums were the purple of raw liver. Its teeth were long and white. They could do anything; they could bite off an arm.

Meanwhile, the diners dined. Ettrich finally understood that somehow these others could not see what was happening here. Only the three of them and the dog were involved in it.

Why had Isabelle called the dog Anjo if that was the name of their child?

"Were you going to hit me, Berndt? If the dog weren't here, would you have *punched* me? Or slapped me? Is that your style when you don't like hearing something? Don't shake your head no—I saw what you did with your hand." Slumping back in the chair, she threw her napkin on the table. The dog stared and growled at the petrified man.

Berndt didn't know where to look. He simply could not process all that had happened in the last five minutes: Isabelle said she was not interested in him. And she was pregnant. Then his anger erupted like a volcano. Then this demon dog appeared, ready to bite him. And to top it all off, no one else in the room was even looking! So he did the only thing he could—he cried, "Help!"

"Shut up, Berndt. No one can hear you. They don't even know we're here anymore." To both men's great surprise, Isabelle took her glass and tossed the water in it on the old woman at the next table. It splashed across her face and elegant red silk dress. The woman continued eating as if nothing had happened, although water dripped from her face and her dress was ruined.

Berndt was barely able to whisper, "I don't understand this."

"There's nothing to understand. You were going to hit me because I said no. But Anjo won't let you do that." She looked at the dog. The way it looked back at her said there was no question that this animal understood exactly what she was talking about.

"But what about them—" Berndt gestured around the room. "Why can't they see this?"

She looked at the dog and smiled.

Berndt licked his lips and swallowed hard. What would happen now? "Can I go, Isabelle? Can I just leave here now? I'm sorry. I promise never to bother you again. Please let me go." He twitched when the dog let loose a high unhappy yip. Even if she let him go, would the dog?

"Remember Olga, Berndt? That sweet woman who loved you so much? Remember the way you used to treat her when you were angry?"

"You know Olga?" He was dumfounded. How was it possible?

She looked at the dog again. "I do now. You're a terrible man. Now I know some of the things you've done and you are an awful person."

"But how? How do you know about Olga?"

"Anjo. Anjo told me. You're a piece of shit, Berndt. Leave. Go. Get out of my sight."

After her date had raced out of the restaurant, the dog came over and put its head in Isabelle's lap. She stroked it absentmindedly. It let loose a long contented sigh, like a man putting his cold feet into a warm bath.

Ettrich approached her slowly. "Isabelle?"

Ignoring him, she continued petting the brute and staring into the off. Even the dog didn't open its eyes.

Ettrich sat down in Berndt's chair. "Fizz, can you hear me?"

"What a stupid thing to do! Look at what I did to myself." At the next table the old woman started dabbing at her face and blouse with her napkin, as if the water there were her fault. When she was finished she noticed where her dog was. "Anjo! Come back here. Stop being a pest."

Isabelle waved the order away and said she liked having the dog visit.

The old man piped in, "He doesn't realize how big he is. He imagines himself a cat."

The dog opened its eyes for a moment but, seeing the world was in order, closed them again. For now it could rest.

"You call him Anjo. Where does that name come from?"

The old man made as if to speak but stopped, stumped. He looked wide-eyed at his wife who looked back. Then both of them broke out in similar bewildered smiles. He shrugged and gestured for her to talk.

"We don't know. He was always Anjo. Isn't that funny? As I remember, that's what his name was when we bought him as a puppy and we just accepted it. No?" She looked at her husband who nodded. "Are you sure he's not bothering you? We can pull him back over here if he is. He's big but when my husband scolds him, he becomes timid as a mouse."

"No, he's perfect. We're very happy here together."

To protest that, Anjo squeaked again because she had stopped petting him.

The couple went back to eating their meal.

"Isabelle, do you hear me?"

She did not. She picked up a fork and speared some food; she raised her elbow high so as to avoid bumping the big brown head on her lap. Ettrich watched her eat. The way she cut food into the smallest pieces, the slow-motion trip from plate to her mouth. Without question Isabelle was the slowest eater he had ever known. It was a running joke between them. She used to say she could go to a restaurant half an hour before him, order, and start eating. Chances were he would still finish before her.

But those hours spent over meals together were some of the greatest times of his life. All the things they'd discussed, the jokes, the great and small anecdotes that described and highlighted their lives to each other. Once in the OXO Tower restaurant in London she stood up in the middle of their meal, came around the table, kissed him on the lips, and said in a lewd voice, "I *love* this. I love this more than anything." And he knew what she meant. He knew one hundred percent what she meant by it. Two feet away the view out the window was of all London, glittering. This woman was a city in herself—teeming, confusing, exhilarating, sometimes one big traffic jam.

Ettrich closed his eyes when he felt tears coming. Isabelle could do that to him so quickly and easily. Sometimes he only had to look across a table at her and he would feel them begin. Was that what real love meant—tears? Such promiscuous things—they came when you were happy *and* sad, but for Vincent Ettrich only when it had to do with this woman.

How long did he close his eyes, four seconds? Long enough to touch his thumb against one eye, his index finger against the other to push the tears back. In that momentary dark he heard a familiar sound—the thin tinkle of a small bell. Opening his eyes, he saw he was back in the diner with Isabelle, far away from Vienna, Berndt, and Anjo the dog. She was holding up that bell and grinning.

"Did you order spaghetti al pesto?"

"What?"

Her smile was a mischievous child's. "At Stella Marina. That's your favorite meal there. Did you order it?"

"You know where I was just now?"

"Sure. You watched Berndt and me in Stella Marina."

His head dropped back, he locked his fingers behind his neck and looked at the ceiling while he spoke. "Are you going to explain all this to me, Fizz?"

She didn't answer. He continued looking up and she continued not answering. The silence between them wasn't uncomfortable because it was intermission. They both knew the next act was coming.

"Anjo told me you were sick that same night. It was one of the first times he ever talked to me. He said you had cancer and were going to die. But that you didn't know it yet."

"You knew I was sick before I did?" He lowered his head slowly and looked at her. His eyes were flat. All that she had said was history but in his heart it felt like right now.

"Yes, I knew, Vincent. Everything Anjo told me came true."

"A dog told you my future."

She shook her head. "Anjo isn't a dog. He's whatever he wants to be, whatever is convenient for him. He goes in and out of things—animals, people. He has that power."

"Who is he?"

She shook her head again. "He's our son. More than that I don't know. He won't tell me."

Ettrich looked out the window and then back at her. "Did he make me sick?"

"Oh no, Vincent! Anjo brought you back from the dead."

A Frog Ballet

Fifteen minutes after Berndt fled the restaurant, Isabelle walked out
of Stella Marina smelling her hand. Before leaving, she had taken
the small flacon of Royal Water she always carried in her purse and
tipped some of it onto the back of her wrist. After what had just
happened, she needed to smell Vincent's beautiful cologne. What
she really needed was to smell Vincent but that was impossible. The
Royal Water would have to suffice. She needed him there after what
had just happened. But even his smell did something good for her;
that small trace of him brought her a piece of peace. It never
failed—some drops on the back of her hand, close the eyes, deep
breath—Vincent.

Where was he now? What was he doing? She wondered that
ten times a day. She thought about him twenty. More. Did he hate
her for running away again? He had every right to hate her, especially now. He had left his family and moved into Margaret Hof's
apartment. Only until he could put his life in order and then he
planned to move to Vienna to be with her. He already had a tentative job lined up with a German public relations firm that had
offices here. It would be a huge salary cut from what he was re-
ceiving in the United States but he didn't care.

Vincent was not like other men—he had never made promises to her but then reneged on them when it came time to act. He told her only once that he could not live without her and would leave his family when he felt he had sufficient strength and resolve. She never doubted that he would do it because Ettrich always kept his word to her. But he acted much sooner than Isabelle had envisioned. It came as a shock when he called her and said, "It's over. I'm alone." His voice was breathless when he told her; it sounded as if he had been running for miles.

She already knew she was pregnant then but didn't tell him. She wanted to see his face when he heard the news. They arranged to meet in London that weekend. Isabelle asked if one of those nights they could have dinner at the OXO Tower because of the incredible view it offered of the city and the Thames. She wanted to tell him there. The beauty of the place, the convergence of their lives, and the secret she was about to tell Vincent so overwhelmed her halfway through the meal that she got up, walked around the table, and kissed him. "I love this," she said an inch from his de-lighted face. "I love this more than anything."

Half an hour later their relationship was finished as far as she was concerned. Until that meal, the subject of Ettrich's leaving his family had been left to cool on a side table, as if it were a dish just taken out of the oven and too hot to eat. They spoke of other things; they spoke of what had happened in their lives since they'd last been together. All the time though they kept looking over at that dish wondering if it was cool enough yet to try a first bite. Almost casually he brought it up by saying how weird it was to live alone again in a very small apartment after all those years of space and a noisy family. That began the discussion. Way too soon they were both sitting stiffly in their chairs staring at each other as if they did not like what they saw.

To her dismay, Vincent said he had left his family for her. To his dismay, she glared at him as if he had slapped her face. It was one of those conversations that became an argument that became a bleeding disaster. None of it ever should have happened. These people simply missed each other's points, and because they had brought separate but very charged hearts to the table that night, everything said from that point on was distorted then exaggerated then misunderstood and finally used as ammunition to shoot point blank at each other. It was the worst discussion they ever had. They got up from the table, no, they *staggered* up from the table like dazed survivors of a tornado that had killed their families, flattened their house, and left them with nothing but the breath in their lungs.

What's worse, they foolishly returned together to the hotel room in Chelsea that Vincent had rented for the occasion. They thought they could fix things up in bed. It didn't work and both of them ended up looking at the ceiling, not wanting to touch the other.

Exhausted by jet lag and all the recent upheavals in his life, Ettrich did not awaken when Isabelle rose very early the next morning, packed her few things, and left. She did not linger at the door hoping for his voice, or look back over her shoulder to see if he was watching. She only wanted out of there. Downstairs in the lobby she wrote him a quick note, intending to write more later when her head was clear and no longer muddied by emotion. She gave this short note to the clerk at the front desk. He looked at her dubiously, as if she were a prostitute finishing up her shift. Any other time this misunderstanding would have delighted Isabelle and made her laugh. Instead she began to cry as she turned away and walked toward the ornate front door.

What Vincent said last night still burned on her heart like slow acid. He had left his life *for her*. Not for himself, and not because he finally realized being together meant more than anything did. His great "gift" to her. She smiled bitterly thinking that the word *Gift* in German meant "poison."

Hailing a maroon cab, she told the driver to take her to Heathrow. She had no idea when the next flight back to Vienna was. She would find out when she got to the airport. The important thing now was to get moving, get away from him and this hotel and city, which a night ago, eight hours ago, had held all the promise in the world. God damn him! Damn him and his "I did it for you."

She knew running away wasn't the answer. Knew it was an immature and cowardly thing to do, but Isabelle Neukor was a coward. Much as she would have liked to change, she did not have sufficient inner strength.

She was thirty-one. She had lived a privileged life that had given her character but no backbone or real inner strength when she needed it. She knew this but often pretended otherwise, fooling many people over the years. But those who knew her well knew that Isabelle was a paper lion. They were amused when she roared because it was only tricky sound effects she had devised, much like the Wizard of Oz hidden behind his curtain, furiously working those myriad levers and buttons.

Having money in the family was like cigarettes—the trouble with both was that they were always there for you. It didn't matter if you were happy or sad: They were always at your fingertips, ready and eager to make your life better even if only for a few minutes. Too often in Isabelle's life when the going got tough, she went to the bank. She was thirty-one and had run from too many things. She had severe panic attacks and often took pills to quell them. Once when he was overwrought, Ettrich took half of one of those pills. It was the strongest thing he'd ever ingested and he came close to keeling over. He could not believe Isabelle took a whole one almost every day.

But none of this mattered to Vincent Ettrich. He loved her without reservation. In college he'd had an Italian girlfriend who would say "I love-a you like-a crazy." The sentence always pleased him but he didn't believe the woman for a moment. Until he met and fell for Isabelle Neukor, that is. Then he knew one hundred percent what it meant to love someone like-a crazy.

Within four days of their first meeting, Isabelle had told him almost all of her secrets. She was astonished at herself and thrilled. She told him about the sedatives she took and the neuroses they were meant to diffuse. She told him her fears and her hidden hopes for the future. She wanted to have a child some day. She had never admitted that she wanted to have a child, much to her mother's despair. Although she had certainly had her share of lovers, Isabelle had never met a man she wanted to have children with. Next she told Vincent her deeply ambivalent feelings about her interesting, difficult family. She continued telling this stranger things she had never told anyone, not even the good-hearted boyfriend she had lived with in New York for three years. And when she discovered how good it felt to talk to him, she told Vincent Ettrich more.

Half an hour into their first formal date she already wanted to touch his hands to see if he had cold or warm ones. Instead she asked what he thought was the most important thing in life. She hoped he would say something wonderful or at least stunningly different—not "love" or "freedom" or "individuality." Please, not those lame lumps. She wanted Vincent Ettrich to be creative and imaginative; she wanted to be in awe. If to "love like-a crazy" was Ettrich's goal, then Isabelle's was for just once in her life to be in awe of a man. He sensed that a great deal hinged on his answer to her question. After looking at his hands a long time he eventually said, "To be understood."

How could the man who said *that* have so misunderstood what she needed/wanted to hear at the critical moment last night? Why couldn't he have said, "I left that all behind because you are my life now." Or "Only you, Fizz—you and nothing else." Those would have been fine. Although they sounded a little purple she still could have lived with those sentiments. But *"I did it for you"*? The sound of the guillotine blade slamming down across their relationship filled her ears the moment he said the sentence. That was the correct word for it—sentence. Vincent sentenced their relationship with one sentence.

She looked out the window of the taxi at London, the traffic in Hammersmith, the morning after. What would she do now with her life?

Her cell phone rang. She crossed her hands over her purse to try and smother the shrill sound. She was sure it was Vincent calling and she didn't want to be tempted to answer it. What would he say, come back? What's wrong? Come back and let's work this out. Don't be stupid. You're letting us go to hell because of one sentence. Don't be childish, Isabelle. Don't be a coward. For once in your life stay and fight for what you believe. The phone rang and rang. It seemed to grow louder by the second. She pressed her hands harder onto the purse, as if that might somehow help. What else could she do to make him go away? Shut up. Shut up. Go away. Be quiet. Leave me alone—I'm not coming back, Vincent. She happened to glance in the rearview mirror. The cab driver was looking at her, obviously wondering why she didn't answer her phone. Shit!

She opened the purse and groped around in it for her phone. She'd turn the damned thing off and shut it up altogether. Ring Ring. It was at the bottom of the bag. She pressed the off button and held it down.

The green screen went blank but somehow the ringing continued. She frowned. How could that happen? How could the phone be off but still keep ringing? Ring Ring. She undid the battery and disconnected it from the back of the machine. When she had the battery in one hand and the telephone in the other it continued to ring.

The driver said loudly, "Pardon me, missus, but would you mind answering that? The sound's driving me corky."

She stabbed the on/off button again, then stabbed it six more times. The phone continued ringing, but suddenly the sound changed. It became the famous signature phrase of Strauss's "Blue

Danube" waltz. Daa-daa-daa-daa-daa/dee-dee/dee-dee. The screen lit up again, orange this time. It had never before been orange. A small black logo of a dancing couple moved around the screen in time to the music. Then they disappeared and the sound stopped. The words "CALL ANJO" replaced the dancers on the screen.

Staring at this, Isabelle slowly shook her head, denying the whole thing. She said as much out loud. "Who's Anjo?"

"Thank you."

Befuddled, she narrowed her eyes and looked in the rearview mirror. *"What?"*

The taxi driver tipped up his chin. "Thanks for answering your phone."

Isabelle stared at him, trying to get her mind's lens to focus properly on all this. At that moment she had no idea what the man was talking about. Her haunted telephone was in one hand, the phone battery in the other. The driver was talking gibberish and she was supposed to call Anjo, whoever that was.

Isabelle stopped to take a long drink of water. She watched Ettrich over the edge of the glass, her eyes wide and happy now. She had been speaking a long time. He hadn't interrupted once. He had watched her face, the changing expressions there, the beautiful small mouth and wet dart of her tongue forming the words. Listening and watching, he was remembering her again even though she sat directly across the table telling him this mad story about phone messages from their unborn child.

"So the first time Anjo made contact was when he paged you that morning in London?"

She put the glass down on the table with a small clink. "Page?"

"Uh, SMS. He sent you a message on your cell phone?"

"Right."

They looked at each other and what passed silently back and forth between their eyes was "This is nuts." And "I know, but it's the truth."

"Your phone really started playing the 'Blue Danube'?"

"Yes, and *has* been ever since that morning. I can't change it. I tried." She laughed. "I hate the 'Blue Danube' waltz. Do you know how many times I've heard that thing in my life, living in Vienna?" Isabelle looked over Vincent's shoulder and saw the waitress standing in a corner scowling at them. She knew why: Because the woman was afraid of them, afraid of what Isabelle had said earlier about her family.

It was probably the same sort of fear she had felt when Anjo first appeared and began harassing her. Or was it teasing? She could never decide which it was—clever or cruel—because sometimes when he came it was this, the next time that. Always unexpected and unpredictable, he entered and exited her life either like a surprise bouquet or a violent shove from behind.

"When did he first actually talk to you?"

"At a café in Vienna. Would you like to see?"

"No!" Instinctively Ettrich threw up both hands to ward off her invitation to "travel" to her past again. "Just tell me about it, Fizz."

"It doesn't matter. What is important is when Anjo told me about you and what was going to happen to you."

"Tell me about that." Ettrich caught himself starting to hyperventilate. He rolled his eyes in disapproval. Another one of the conspicuous changes in growing older—his body had become more emotional than ever. It had its own way of reacting passionately to things now. Fierce feelings arose over situations or events that would have drawn barely a shrug from him in the past. Listening to the radio last month, he'd heard The Blue Nile singing "Midnight Without You," their brilliant jazzy ballad about the end of a relationship. Thank God Ettrich had been alone because seconds into the song he began to cry.

These days when he got nervous, he would start breathing strangely or clench his fists until they hurt. Or else he immediately felt the need to take a wicked piss. In certain vivid ways his body was regressing back to childhood where things are simple action/reaction: You're sad, you cry. You're scared, you piss your pants. Maybe growing older meant becoming a prisoner to your body's whims.

"—walking down Windmuhlgasse—"

"Wait, Fizz, stop. I didn't hear the first part. Please go back and say it again."

"When I left Stella Marina, I realized that if I went home I'd just sit in my apartment and be jittery after what had just happened. It was only nine o'clock but I didn't feel like going downtown. Then I remembered the Café Ritter is open late. It was only a five-minute walk so I decided to go there.

"You know the Ritter: it's a big place with a real 1950s feel to it—very smoky and full of shadows even in the middle of the day. It was almost empty. When I first walked in I noticed a baby stroller next to one of the tables. I thought that was strange because it was pretty late in the evening to have a baby out. I sat at a window table toward the back and ordered a glass of wine.

"Cora called me on my pocket phone. I guess I got lost talking to her and staring out the window. Anyway, something touched my knee. I looked down and saw a child leaning against it; a little boy was looking up at me. He was dark—looked either Turkish or Yugoslavian—with thick curly black hair and big brown eyes." She bit her lower lip and giggled. "He was also ugly. I know you're not supposed to say that about children, but this one looked like the kind only a mother could love."

Ettrich envisioned a gnome, a troll living under a fairy-tale bridge. "How so? Weird-ugly or just ugly?"

"Nothing-special ugly. Flat nose, big droopy mouth. Ugly. You'd look at him and think, Well, maybe when he gets older he'll get better looking. But you know he won't. That's why it always touches me when I see women fussing over ugly babies. God bless them, you know?"

Ettrich couldn't resist a jab at her. "Snob. Elitist."

Isabelle nodded and grinned. "I'm just calling a spade a spade."

He kissed the air between them and gestured for her to continue.

"The first thing I thought was that the baby stroller must be for him. I looked toward the table for his parents, but I sat at an angle where I couldn't see them. So little Mr. Ugly and I kept staring at each other. He was very small; you've got to keep that picture in your head. He was barely big enough to waddle when he walked. If you gave him one of your fingers he would hold it with his whole hand.

"After we'd watched each other a while I smiled but he didn't smile back. Instead he said quietly but very distinctly, 'Pick me up and put me on your lap.' He spoke in a baby's voice, Vincent, but it was no baby speaking."

"Jesus Christ." Ettrich sat back and rubbed his hands fast up and down his arms as if trying to brush the cooties off.

"Yes, I know how you feel. But you've got to remember Anjo is naughty or sometimes just playful. After a while you get used to his tricks."

"No, Fizz, I'm sorry. In the same night, he came to you as a hundred-pound guard dog and then as a talking baby half an hour later? There's no *way* I would ever get used to that."

"If you had to you would and I did. I picked him up and put him on my lap. He told me to play with him like a normal baby so the people around us wouldn't think it strange I was talking to him."

Ettrich kept rubbing his arms. "Fucked up."

"What is?"

His voice rose into falsetto. "This whole thing. It's completely fucking insane. We're sitting here talking about these things in measured tones but it's all cra-zy!"

Isabelle waited silently for his verbal storm to pass. Vincent huffed and puffed and prepared to rant more but didn't.

"Should I continue?" She raised an eyebrow and the edge on her voice.

"Certainly! Please describe how baby ugly told you I was going to die."

"Wait a minute—"

"He said 'Wait a minute'? I don't understand."

"No, shut up, Vincent. Something's wrong."

He didn't need to hear it twice. Ettrich's whole being came to instant attention. He scanned the restaurant like a Secret Service agent protecting the president in a crowd. He was so intent on finding an enemy that he didn't see Isabelle gather her things and start to stand.

"We have to leave."

"Why?"

"It's Anjo. He says we've got to get out of here right now."

Ettrich threw a twenty-dollar bill on the table and got up. Isabelle was already out of her side of the booth and heading for the door. She put a hand behind her for his. He took it and they hurried out. At the last moment he caught a glimpse of their waitress. Her face was triumphant—they were leaving.

In the parking lot Isabelle started walking in the opposite direction of his car. He pulled on her hand, trying to stop her. "Where are you going? The car's over here." He pointed.

"We can't take your car. Come on." Now she pulled on his hand.

"Why not? All your bags are in there."

"Forget them. Just come, Vincent!" She looked over her shoulder at him and then past him at the restaurant. Her eyes were so clear and scared that without thinking, Ettrich looked back there too. Nothing was different.

They were in that urban no-man's-land between a large city and its airport where cars speed back and forth but rarely stop, especially at night. A fly-by zone, a bus stop where you never stop, somewhere between here and there that's part of your city but a part you know only through the window of a car. The only businesses in these neighborhoods seem to be open but always empty— fast food joints, defeated-looking karate schools, and discount furniture stores with thick metal safety gates blocking their narrow doors. Occasionally you do see a person walking here but they look drunk, lost, or dangerous.

Isabelle kept tight hold on Ettrich's hand while she moved straight ahead without once turning her head. It appeared she knew where she was going, but after a long time she just *kept* going and they never got there. For a mile he didn't say a word about it, content to walk with her and look at this strange area he had only ever whizzed through on his way to the airport.

Sometimes a brightly lit bus rumbled by, its noise and noxious exhaust fumes filling all the air. After a while Ettrich realized the only sounds around them were the *wush* of cars and trucks passing, and their own footsteps clicking on the sidewalk when no vehicles were around. It was a city silence, the kind you hear at three o'clock in the morning when you're walking downtown after a party and can't find a cab.

"Isabelle, where are we going?"

"I don't know. I'm waiting."

"For what?"

"For Anjo to tell me where to go."

He pursed his lips. "Okay. But can you at least tell me why we had to leave that place so suddenly and walk?"

A silver Jeep Cherokee passed with drum and bass music thundering out of it. A very white elbow stuck out of the passenger's side window.

Isabelle said something the music drowned out.

"What? I didn't hear you."

"We left because you were in danger, Vincent. Anjo felt it coming and told me. The same thing with your car. It wasn't safe." She continued her brisk pace to nowhere.

"Stop." Ettrich grabbed her arm. She tried to keep moving but he would not let her, not for anything.

"Vincent, we must—"

"No. Right now, right here tell me why I'm in danger. How's it possible—I'm already dead. Or was. What more can they do, kill me again? You're the one who's alive and *pregnant*."

She looked left and right as if she were about to cross the street and was checking for oncoming cars. When she turned to him her eyes were all love and dread. "It's so complicated, Vincent. I need so much time to explain it all to you."

He wasn't having it. "Then give me a short version right now. I need something, Fizz. Give me something."

"You shouldn't be here. You died, you're dead. But Anjo brought you back to life because he needs you. You must help him before he's born. He needs both of us to be alive until he's born."

"Why?"

"He won't tell me."

A huge blue truck blew past them followed closely by a black one whomp-whomp.

Ettrich had fifty important questions but knew he had only moments now to ask a few. "Why don't I remember any of it? Getting sick, being in the hospital, *dying*—I don't remember it. Nothing."

"That was how Anjo was able to bring you back—by wiping out all of your memories of that time."

"But it's not just me, Isabelle. Everyone treats me like before:

Kitty, the people at work, Margaret Hof. They don't *know* I died. How can that be?"

"Anjo. He reshaped everything."

Ettrich wasn't having it. "If he's so powerful, if he can do things like that, why does he need me here now? Or you?"

She smiled for the first time in an hour. "He needs me because I'm his mother. Why does he need you, besides the fact you're his father? Maybe because he knows how much I need you. Let's walk to that bus stop. We're going to catch the next one." They moved toward a small metal and glass lean-to fifty feet away. "There's something else you need to know, Vincent: You're very powerful now that you know the truth. You can do amazing things. If you haven't experienced them yet you will." Gently touching his face with three fingers, she said, "You're a mighty guy now."

Ettrich remembered the other night when he sent the dying taxi driver's *numen* back into him, saving his life. Something else came to mind. "There are two other people who know I died—Coco Hallis and Bruno Mann. Do you know them?"

"You mentioned her name before. No, I don't know them."

"This all started for me when I saw Bruno's name tattooed on the back of her neck."

"On her *neck*? Boy, that's love. I don't think I'd do that, not even for you. How long have the two of them been together?"

"They're not together. They didn't even know each other until I introduced them a few days ago."

"And then she had his name tattooed on her neck?" Isabelle sounded both surprised and impressed.

He was about to explain when a green city bus pulled up and stopped in front of them. The doors hissed open. They entered and climbed the two steps up. The driver gave them a quick glance to check if they were a threat. Seeing that they were okay, he pressed the button to close the doors. There were two other people sitting far in the back. The bus began moving again. Isabelle grabbed Ettrich's arm to steady herself. With his free hand he reached into his pocket for some coins to pay their fares.

She stopped him. "No, no, let me."

He remembered that she liked buying tickets, dropping coins in slots, counting out exact change, doing sums with a calculator. Reaching into her purse, she took out the handsome brown leather wallet from the Connolly store in London that he had given her on their last fateful visit there. Even now seeing it again made him wince slightly at the memory of that calamitous trip.

As they walked down the narrow aisle Ettrich asked, "Where did you go in London that morning you left me?"

"What?" The bus grumbled up to speed, hitting successive potholes and bouncing on what felt like no shock absorbers at all. Isabelle stopped and swung down into an empty window seat and gestured for him to join her.

He sat in the empty seat next to hers. "Where did you go that morning after you left me in London?"

Her voice changed, becoming more strident and staccato. "I took a taxi to the airport. Where I sat for three hours, waiting for a flight to Vienna. And cried. And hated you."

He knew not to say another word on the subject now. The pitch of her voice always rose markedly whenever Isabelle was angry or unsure about something. She also spoke much faster, as if the speed of her words would either convince you of what she was saying, or else keep you from protesting. However, if you still disagreed, she would speak even faster and often end up saying malicious uncalled-for things that caused needless hurt.

Seconds later none of this mattered. Because without warning, Vincent Ettrich was struck by pain so excruciating that it should have killed him. It was so intense that he could not close his eyes, breathe, or blink. Worse, his mind remained crystal clear. It immediately remembered that this had been the pain at the moment of his own death. It was what had finished him off weeks before. It was the first time since his return to life that he consciously remembered anything about that event.

But Ettrich had already died once, so the pain this time did not end in the relief of oblivion. This pain did not end at all. Beyond measure, it consumed his bones, brain, and his blood. It was Omnipotent. It was God.

"Fight it. You're stronger."

Somewhere inside the agony of those endless moments, Ettrich heard and, more importantly, *understood* those words. As soon as he did, the pain ceased. It stopped as quickly as it had started, leaving him empty, hollowed out. At once he felt light as air, little more than a small cloud passing high over the earth.

"Vincent?"

Someone was saying his name.

"Vincent!"

Without realizing, he had turned his head and only now registered that he was looking at someone. A woman: Isabelle Neukor. He did not react. He closed his eyes slowly, like a lizard sunning on a hot rock.

"Vincent, what's the matter? Are you all right?" She was touching his hand.

Awareness, then focus, and finally the world slowly came back to Ettrich. First he heard Isabelle, saw her, eventually recognized who she was and was glad. Before long came the smells—the thick insult of car exhaust, a fresh rye bread inside a plastic market bag, oranges. But it didn't stop there. He was now able to smell the three tarnished copper pennies in the bus driver's right front pocket. Haddock being fried at a fish-and-chips restaurant the bus was passing, six-hour-old peppermint lip balm on the mouth of the woman sitting a few seats behind them, more. Ettrich smelled it all. It was as if a filter holding back life's odors had been taken away so that everything now flooded down over him.

The bus slowed abruptly to avoid hitting a car that veered in front of it. Feeling her hand on his and smelling the small patch of her skin, warm beneath the large Breitling wristwatch she wore, Ettrich quietly told Isabelle what had just happened to him. The pain, the mysterious voice, the emptiness after the pain, the smells that filled the emptiness . . .

While he recounted these singular things, their bus rolled on, moving its few passengers across the city. Nothing could have been more mundane—a mostly empty public bus at night. Four passengers, two of them staring out the window with the blank round eyes of stuffed animals. It could have been an Edward Hopper painting. Except that one of the riders, the fortyish man talking to the lovely woman, had died recently and been resurrected by the unborn child the woman was carrying.

"The voice you heard must have been Anjo's. The *fact* you heard it and understood saved you. Because that pain *was* your death, Vincent. It came to take you back. I made us leave the restaurant because Death was coming for you. It was already in your car and that's why we couldn't use it. I thought we could escape but I was wrong. What's great is that you were able to fight it off this time."

"Anjo told you all that?"

She nodded.

"What else did he say?"

"That Death is stupid but very determined. It finished you once with that pain so it tried to do it again with the same thing. But you're stronger now because of what Anjo's done, so it failed. When he spoke to you in the pain he was only reminding you that you're not the same person who died from it the last time. Death wants you back, Vincent, because you belong to it. You shouldn't be here. It will try very hard to get you. The advantage you have is . . ." She glanced away. When she looked at him again, her eyes were glistening. "I was going to lie but I can't. Your chances of beating it are very small. Anjo told me that before he brought you back. Death is stupid but never gives up. It may be very soon."

"Yeah, well, what about people like me though? The ones who come back? Do the same rules apply?"

She shook her head. "I don't know, Vincent. I don't know how it works."

They rode in silence after that, Ettrich slowly regaining his wits and strength after the siege. Isabelle leaned her head on his shoulder and closed her eyes. She wanted nothing more than to go to bed with this man and make love with him until she blacked out.

One hour and three bus rides later they stood in front of his building. Isabelle didn't like the look of the place but would never tell him that. It was too new and soulless, exactly the kind of faux postmodern apartment complex with a good address you'd expect an affluent man to move into after leaving a marriage and while waiting to catch a flight to his new life.

They rose to the fifth floor in a sleek metal-and-glass elevator that smelled vaguely of coriander. Ettrich would not let go of her hand. The corridor on the fifth floor was the kind of beige and salmon color combo you see in upscale restaurants and New Age furniture stores. It made her cringe. Yuppies lived in buildings like this, suspender wearers, Mercedes owners, Microsoft millionaires. People who were considering buying a vacation house in either Costa Rica or on some minor Greek island. Why had Vincent chosen to live here?

The view. When he opened the door to his studio apartment, Isabelle walked straight to the large picture window and pressed her hands against the cold glass. It wasn't a great view but it was a very good one. The television tower across the city was a glowing silvergray finger pointing straight up into the night sky. She spent a long time there looking at everything, feeling safer now in this small flat with Vincent above the city. He came over and handed her a glass of Chivas Regal with a bit of water added—her favorite drink. He knew exactly how she liked it. Vincent knew exactly how she liked many things.

On the windowsill was something that made her smile as she sipped the drink. It was an object of real importance to both of them. Ettrich kept it in plain sight at all times. His apartment was empty, sterile, and depressing. He knew that. The only reason why he'd rented it was because he was exhausted from his separation and needed anyplace to call home for the time being. He only breathed here, ate take-out food, slept fitfully, and spent way too much time thinking of all the other places he would rather be. That object on the windowsill, silly as it appeared, was his talisman. It comforted him and gave him hope for the future. It had been the first gift Isabelle ever gave him.

About ten inches high, it was a green rubber frog dressed in a white ballet dancer's tutu. Arms arched over its head, it stood on one big flat green foot in a classic ballet pose looking both ridiculous and engaging at the same time.

Isabelle bought it for about a dollar at the Viennese flea market when she was twenty-four. It had traveled with her whenever she moved around the world and was one of the first things she un-packed and strategically placed when settling in. She judged people by the way they reacted to it. If someone thought it a silly girlie thing, she wrote them off without a second thought. If they were considerate or delighted or quizzical in their reaction, then she let them come a little closer to her heart. She never explained why she owned the figure until she'd heard what they thought of it.

The first time Vincent Ettrich saw the frog he picked it right up, turned it this way and that, and said quietly to himself, "Ain't it the truth." Intrigued, Isabelle asked what he meant. He made it dance in his hand a while before answering. "This guy is *us*. All us silly frogs dressed up in our tutus trying to dance *Swan Lake*. It's so sweet and sad. The Frog Ballet, with a cast of thousands. No, millions and billions!"

Several days after they slept together for the first time, Isabelle surprised herself by giving him the frog. She was embarrassed by the intensity of emotion she felt handing it to him. Her voice was almost trembling when she said, "I would like you to have this."

He took it and brought it close to his chest but said nothing.

"Giving that to you means a lot more to me than giving you my body. Do you understand?"

Ettrich understood. She saw it in his face. It scared the hell out of her. She hadn't felt this open, vulnerable, and happy with anyone in years, much less a lover. It had happened so quickly.

These memories piled up fast in her mind as she stood with the whiskey in hand, staring at her frog perched on his windowsill.

She pointed at it with her glass. "Did you ever give it a name?"

"No! That would be sacrilege. He's *Jederfrosch*."

She chuckled at his bad joke in German. "But you keep him around?"

"Always. He's my sidekick. And in this apartment he's the entire decor."

Her head moved from left to right, slowly panning the room. "I noticed that. But you love beautiful things. Why do you keep this place so empty? So . . . barren."

He made a face. "I did have a photograph up on that wall but it depressed me because it was beautiful so I took it down. Fizz, this ain't my home. Home is in Vienna with you. Or at least it was supposed to be before I died." That amused him and he smiled.

"Why are you smiling?"

"Because I said that without thinking. Like it's the most natural thing in the world, no big deal—*before I died*."

She put her glass on the windowsill next to the frog and moved up close to Ettrich. "I don't know what's going to happen, but I'm here now. We're together again."

He put his hands on her waist. "Thank God for that."

She reached up and began to undo the top button of his shirt. He hesitated, then put his hands over hers, warm over cold, stopping her.

"Do you think Anjo will mind if we make love?" He meant it; his voice was worried.

She gave him a luscious smile. She loved him for being concerned. "That's very sweet of you but I'm not that fragile yet. I'm only three months pregnant. It'll be fine; we have plenty of time. Plus, if he feels cramped for space he can move back further in his room." She undid buttons number two and three on his shirt, watching her fingers do the necessary twist and slide. "Your apartment needs furnishing."

"But I just told you—"

She gently butted his chin with her forehead. "I mean now, tonight. It needs to be filled with life. I hate thinking of you sitting here alone night after night. It gives me the creeps."

"It's not *that* bad." He watched her fingers work on the last button.

"It's horrible." She pulled off the shirt and, putting her hands on his shoulders, made him turn around, away from her. He knew what she was about to do. It made him so happy.

When Ettrich was a child, his mother would come into his room most nights as he was preparing for bed. After he'd washed his face and brushed his teeth, she would have him pull up his pajama top and lie facedown on the bed. Sitting next to him, she would run her long red fingernails slowly slowly slowly, lightly lightly lightly up and down and all around his back for a long time. She called them her fingersnails. Some nights they would talk a little while she did it, but most of the time it was done silently and both of them preferred it that way. Minutes of quiet together, both of them thinking their own thoughts but joined by those beautiful small fingers skating smoothly, dreamily, here and there across his back. It never failed to calm, comfort, and finally hypnotize this jumpy little boy's skin into submission. Invariably he fell asleep while she was doing it. As a grown-up and parent, what touched him most about the memory was how carefully she must have pulled his pajama top down and somehow gotten him under the covers without waking him.

Ettrich told Isabelle about the fingersnails one morning while he was cooking breakfast in her apartment. He was wearing boxer shorts and a T-shirt. She loved hearing stories about his childhood and invariably sat rapt whenever he remembered a good one to tell. But this time while he spoke she snuck up behind him and, without warning, pulled his T-shirt up and put it like a hood over his head. He stood there frozen, one arm up holding the spatula in midair with the shirt completely covering his head and face.

Isabelle did not have long fingernails like his mother. Hers were short but what she lacked in nail length she made up for in a marvelous, shivery touch. Starting at the base of his neck, she slowly moved all ten fingers down his back. Their sliding, tickling lightness gave him goose bumps all over his body, despite the fact he was hooded, blinded, and holding an eggy spatula in the air, looking like some kind of insane Statue of Liberty.

"Don't you want to hear the rest of my fingersnail story?" he asked from beneath his full-head blindfold.

"Nope. Because I'm about to update it." Her fingers were trickling down his spine like rain just beginning on a window. A moment later so was her tongue.

Ettrich twitched like he'd gotten an electric shock. "Oops! The following program is not recommended for viewers under eighteen. Can I at least put the spatula down?"

"No. If you move I'll stop." Her tongue slid lower. She pinched his ass lightly, then again harder. His breath caught in his throat and then left in a careful hiss. He didn't know what she would do next. He loved that. The bites hurt and were wonderful together. She pulled his shorts down with one hand while stroking his bare stomach with the other. Standing there covered by his shirt and his underpants puddled on the floor, Ettrich looked ridiculous. If Isabelle had looked up at him she would have laughed for five minutes. But she was too busy to do that. Starting at his ankle, she slid her thumb so lightly and slowly up the inside of his right leg. "I bet your mother never did *this* to you."

He dropped the spatula on the counter; its loud clatter meant nothing. Both arms hung helplessly at his sides, bystanders.

Many months later in a city very far from Vienna, Isabelle's fingers were again moving across Ettrich's back. While she did it, both of them stared out the window. A number of planes passed low overhead, making their final approach to the airport. Ettrich remembered how many nights alone he had watched these planes and thought wouldn't it be the greatest thing in life if she were on one of them? Totally unexpectedly she arrives, just like that, and knocks on the door. I'm here, Vincent. I had to come. We have to talk. I love you. But she never did that. And even with her here now, her fingers on his back, the memory was so painful and lonely that Ettrich had to blink hard a few times to push it away.

After a long and peaceful silence, she began to speak in a low voice:

My love,
we have found each other
thirsty and we have
drunk up all the water and the blood,
we found each other
hungry
and we bit each other
as fire bites,
leaving wounds in us.

But wait for me,
keep for me your sweetness.
I will give you too
a rose.

She put her forehead against his bare back and her palms flat on his shoulder blades. "I read that poem for the first time a week after I ran away from you in London. It destroyed me because it's exactly about you and me. And Anjo is our rose. So I made myself memorize it, like a punishment."

Ettrich did not turn around. He couldn't say what he needed to say now if he were facing her. "I hated you, Fizz. Some part of my heart still does. For giving up so easily like that. I can't imagine what I would've done if I'd known then about Anjo. You just took off again. Never even gave me a chance. You never gave us a chance. Just *took off*. You heard one stupid insensitive sentence you didn't like and zoom—out the fucking door.

"It would have been so easy to resolve. We were *there*. We had it—everything was in place. God damn it!"

She nodded into his back, both of them swaying forward with her push.

"And then you found out I was dying but didn't tell me?" His voice was incredulous.

"You don't remember any of that, Vincent. He took away all of those memories." As if for emphasis, she pushed her head harder against his back.

He tensed. "That doesn't matter. I know about it now. I know you weren't there for me."

"I couldn't be. I told you—Anjo wouldn't let me."

"Why?"

She remained silent. He knew she would. It made him very angry and he wasn't going to let it pass this time. *"Why?"* He started to turn but she quickly grabbed his shoulders and stopped him. He sucked in his lower lip. Outrage was in the back of his throat and out to the tips of his fingers.

More uneasy time passed until Isabelle said abruptly, out of nowhere, as if she had snatched the sentence out of the air as it flew by, "Because *I* had to go get you, not Anjo."

"What? What do you mean?"

"I had to go there and get you."

Ettrich shook his head—he didn't understand.

"After you died, Vincent, I had to go into Death and bring you back."

Rez Sahara and the Twenty-Five Mice

The next morning Vincent Ettrich woke up next to a woman he had never seen before.

He came to consciousness slowly, feeling drugged, feeling like his head on the pillow weighed three hundred pounds. Had he slept at all? It felt like he had been awake for days and only fallen asleep five minutes ago. Even opening his eyes and keeping them open required major effort. Had he dreamed? He vaguely remembered something but it was evaporating from his mind like morning mist under a hot sun.

The ceiling helped. Ceilings could be good compasses. They could tell you where you were. Ettrich had spent so much time in recent months lying on this bed, staring at the ceiling, that he knew its every detail. Prison inmates and the brokenhearted often have Ph.D.'s in the study of ceilings.

Almost directly above him was a small brown mark he had come to think of as the potato because he could find no other description for its shape. A result of water damage from the apartment above, the building owners had asked when he moved in if he wanted them to repair it. The thought of painters tramping around his new place and the stink of fresh paint lingering for days convinced him to say no, the stain didn't bother him. Since then he had even grown fond of it during his staring bouts. It was brown Potato Island in the middle of a boring blue ceiling sea.

So now that he had registered Potato Island above him, Ettrich knew that he was in his own bed. And it must be morning because the room was filled with light, the only time that happened in a day. With those facts in mind, he slowly rolled his head to the right and saw a very good-looking blond woman asleep next to him. He froze. After a good number of beats a wicked grin came to his face. Ettrich really had no idea who this cutie was but that was okay. Like a ventriloquist, his lips did not move when he said very distinctly albeit quietly, "Hot dog!"

Unable to think of anything else to do at the moment, he rolled his head upright again, looked at Potato Island and wondered who is she? What did I *do* last night, for God's sake? Where was I? How did we meet? How did I get her here? He knew he could probably slip out of bed without waking her, but what for? Right here was the place to be at the moment. There was no doubt about that.

He turned again to study her face. She really was lovely— absolutely his type. His eyes moved across her face and down her neck to where the lemon-colored bed sheet covered the rest of her. By the glorious look of things, Miss Mystery didn't have any clothes on. To check that assumption, he slid his leg oh so slowly over toward her and as subtly as a leg can explore another body underneath a sheet he put it to work. Legwork. And indeed he was right—she was naked all over.

There had been many firsts in Vincent Ettrich's life when it came to women. God knows there had been a lot of them. A lot of romances in a lot of places under a lot of sometimes wonderful, sometimes peculiar circumstances. But this really was a major event: The first time he could not remember *anything* about a woman lying in bed next to him the morning after, much less what they'd done together the night before.

What was her name? How had they met? How long had they known each other? What was she like in bed? His list of questions was a mile long. She was *in* his bed, but what had brought them here? It was impossible not to remember a thing about her but, hey, there had to be an explanation for that. And he did not mind one single bit the mystery at the moment.

Leaning forward a few inches, he tried to catch a whiff of her. Ettrich was nuts for the way women smelled. In the morning, in the evening, during sex or sweaty or bathed or perfumed or not—he loved all their smells. Right now he wanted to smell *her* and then he wanted to smell her breath. He crept up a little closer and then still more until he was within good sniffing distance.

She opened her eyes and registered him. She blinked a few times and said, "Hey there." She had a killer sleepy-sexy voice. Beautiful teeth too—they all showed when she threw him a great warm smile.

He wanted to touch her but didn't. Not yet. He had to get some info on her first. "Hiya."

She rolled onto her back. Sliding her arms above her head, she stretched and groaned luxuriously. The sheet slipped down her body until her breasts were fully exposed. "What time is it?"

He stared. He told himself to stop but he couldn't help it. "I dunno. Wait." He reached over to the night table for his watch. "Nine."

"That's not bad. I thought we'd sleep till afternoon. After last night." She looked at him and her eyes said sex-sex-sex. She spoke English beautifully but with an accent he could not place.

With no thought or effort he slid on a counterfeit look that said, "I know—wasn't it great?" Over the years Vincent Ettrich had perfected more fake looks than on all the pages of a movie magazine. The worst part was he was so good at it. These expressions were so ingrained in his character that sometimes he literally could not tell which were false and which were real. What is my face saying

now? Is that the truth? Sometimes it disturbed him but overall Ettrich was pretty comfortable with himself and was generally willing
to trade a little self-awareness for some pussy.

He might have spent some time thinking about this, as he lay
there warm and cozy next to this naked enigma. But then she said
something that changed everything.

"Don't forget today's your mother's birthday."

Silence as heavy as a hippo sat down on his chest and squeezed
all the air out of him. Eventually he managed to say, "How do you
know that?"

"Well, last year you forgot about it and she was angry at you.
Don't you remember?"

Last year? He did not know this woman. Maybe last night he
had known her in the biblical sense, but last year? No way.

"What's my mom's name?"

Mystery Woman smiled but kept her eyes closed. Her face was
relaxed, the skin beautiful. She had a small flesh-colored mole way
back on her jaw near the right ear. "Is this a pop quiz? Your mom's
name is Brigitta. Wife of Peter, mother of Vincent and Judith."

Panic flew up in Ettrich like a flock of startled pigeons. They
went in all directions. "How do you know that?"

Eyes still closed; she stuck out her tongue at him. "How do I
know? Uh, because you told me?"

He moved to touch her shoulder, stopped, then did it. "Tell
me your name."

"Ha-ha—very funny."

"Really. Please, tell me."

"Vincent don't. It's too early to be playful. Wait until we have
some coffee."

"Where did I go to college?"

She made a face. "Rhodes College. Memphis, Tayne-uh-say.
First job with the Ortpond Agency in San Francisco." She opened

her eyes finally, ready to tell him to stop this nonsense now because it was annoying. But when she saw the expression on his face she hesitated. "What's the matter?"

"How do you know those things? How could you?"

"Stop it! This isn't funny." She shoved him.

He shook his head. "Who *are* you?"

"Vincent, stop it!"

His face showed only confusion.

She realized he *was not* fooling around. "Jesus!" She slid away from him to the far edge of the bed. Unconsciously she pulled the sheet up around her because in that second he became a stranger seeing her naked and he scared her. "What's the matter with you? Isabelle, I'm *Isabelle*."

He only shook his head slowly. Her name meant nothing to him.

"Oh, my God." She started to rise but he lunged and caught her arm. Without thinking she shouted.

He let go immediately. "No, please don't go. I won't hurt you. I won't do anything. Just please tell me."

She pulled the sheet tighter around her but remained sitting. "Tell you what? What is going on? You honestly don't know me?"

"No." The word came out small, afraid. He did not have a clue.

"Do you remember other things?" She twisted the top of the sheet so that it would stay tight around her chest.

Grateful that she wasn't fleeing, he rubbed his face hard with both hands. "Other things? Well, of course. Sure."

"Tell me."

He tossed a hand in the air, as if what he was about to say was common knowledge. "I'm Vincent Ettrich, work in an ad agency, forty-one, divorced, have two kids."

Isabelle jumped on that. "Why did you divorce?"

"Why?" He made a rueful face. "Because I wasn't the world's best husband. My wife was a good soul. She put up with a lot, but finally it was too much for her and she threw me out."

"But why? Tell me exactly why."

He looked her square on and said, "Other women."

"Not one in particular?"

"Too *many* in particular. I should convert to Islam. Then I could have several wives and I'd probably be a lot better off."

It began to dawn on her what had happened to Vincent. But she wanted to be sure before she said anything. So she asked more questions about his life and who he was.

Ettrich answered them all but grew increasingly more disturbed as he realized just how much this lovely stranger knew about him.

When she could think of nothing else to ask, Isabelle's shoulders sagged in defeat. Now she knew she was right. Like precision brain surgery, everything about her and their relationship had been cleanly removed from Vincent's memory. The rest of his life was there and in place; just she had been excised.

Except—The possibility made her sit up straight and the sheet came undone.

"Do you remember being sick?"

"Sick? What do you mean?"

She made to speak but stopped. Then she tilted her head and appeared to be listening to something. Her face slowly relaxed. Touching her stomach above the sheet, she slid her hand back and forth across it. "All right. I'll try."

Anjo had spoken to her.

Ettrich was confused. "What? Try what?"

She ignored him. Her face was peaceful. "I'd like to show you a few things today. Can we spend some time together?"

He didn't know what to say. He was worried this woman was bad news north, south, east, *and* west. Pretty as she was, he would have preferred that she had gotten dressed and left. But Ettrich was a gentleman. That was one of the reasons why he had been so successful with women over the years. He was courtly, considerate, and never, ever let a woman feel like he had used her.

"Come on, Vincent— It's Saturday—you're free. Let's go have breakfast. We'll eat scrambled eggs and bacon and drink lots of coffee." It was so strange talking to him like this. Restrained yet flirty, trying to win him over while not being too obvious about it. As if the man sitting on the other side of the bed were not the love of her life and father of her child, but rather a handsome stranger she was coyly trying to woo.

"Will you excuse me a minute?" he asked, pointing to the bathroom as his reason. Without thinking he got out of bed naked and was seven steps under way before realizing it wasn't too politic to parade around naked now in front of this puzzling woman. What else could he do but raise his hands in the classic "Whoops!" pose, shrug, and keep going. Behind him she laughed. Was it at his cool, his ass, or the situation?

She was laughing because the gesture was so *Vincent*. She felt a huge rush of love and vowed to find a way through this.

He closed the bathroom door and went over to the sink. After looking at himself a long time in the mirror he asked, "Now what, bro?" Then took a towel off the shelf and wrapped it around his waist.

What was he going to do with her? Have breakfast, take a little walk, and then a sweet but firm *arrivederci*. Where did she live? Hopefully somewhere in the city, a cab ride away.

The bathroom door swung open behind him and she came in wearing one of his T-shirts. She was holding two pieces of chocolate cake in her hands. Taking a bite out of one, she offered him the other.

"What's that?"

"*Sachertorte*. Your favorite breakfast."

Ettrich liked *Sachertorte* and had eaten it often. But he could not remember ever having had it for breakfast. He took the piece she offered and the two of them stood there eating Viennese chocolate cake. He didn't know about her, but it felt kind of nice doing it. Halfway through her piece, Isabelle gestured for him to look in the mirror. He did. Both of them had cake crumbs on their faces.

"Where's your camera? You should take a picture of us like this."

He wiped his mouth with the back of his left hand. "What camera?"

She started to say *The one I gave you,* but stopped. "Don't you have a digital camera?"

"No."

"Oh. Well, then . . . uh—" As she backpedaled verbally, a thought came that widened her eyes. Maybe it would help. "Since we're on the subject of eating, here's the question of the day. But you have to think about it before you answer. Don't just say anything. Okay? Describe the three most memorable meals you ever had. Breakfast, lunch, and dinner."

It was Vincent's question. Actually there were five of them. What he had deemed with goofy fanfare *the five questions.* Watching him now eat the last bite of *Sachertorte,* she looked for a glimmer of recognition in his eyes but nothing showed. He was only thinking about her question.

One night in bed in Krakow they couldn't sleep because it had been such an enchanted day that neither of them wanted it to end. So as had happened often, they lay together after sex talking for hours, their bodies entwined. Somewhere in the middle of that conversation, Vincent came up with his five questions. They discussed them for days afterward, digging deep in their memories, talking about forgotten parts of their lives, savoring, abruptly changing their choices, and describing things in the greatest detail. Isabelle thanked him again and again for thinking up those questions because they were so much fun to play with.

Now standing in the bathroom of his small apartment, he swallowed some cake and brushed his hands off on the towel around his waist. "They can't be three dinners?"

"No. Breakfast, lunch, and dinner." She already knew his answers. Or what once were his answers. How could he forget Café Redolfi in Krakow that sunny Sunday morning? They had a table by the window facing the great square and were drinking cup after cup of the good cappuccino served there. Both of them were jittery from too much caffeine, too little sleep, too much sex the night before that had left them wired and raw, exhausted and exhilarated. They couldn't stop looking at each other. They wanted to go back to the hotel right now but didn't because this place, these hours, this moment in their lives was perfect too. How was it possible to be this happy?

Vincent announced his first. "All right—my favorite breakfast ever? Remember that hot August in Vienna when we stayed up all night and then the next morning drove out along the Danube to Tulln?"

Of course she remembered but waited for him to tell the story. About how all the stores were closed because it was Sunday in Catholic Austria. The only thing open that early was a gas station where they were able to buy milk. Luckily she had half a *Sachertorte* in the trunk of her car, a typically odd gift from her mother.

Sitting on fat boulders next to the river, they ate a breakfast of slightly stale cake and milk. A coal barge from Romania passed by and tooted its horn at them. Ten minutes later a stately white Russian cruise ship glided by on its way back to the Black Sea. Then two old men in kayaks passed—all of them swept by on the fast-flowing current. When he had finished eating, Ettrich picked up a small stick nearby and slowly peeled the bark off it while they sat listening to the rush of the river. When he had it bare, he slid the stick into his pocket. She looked at him and raised an eyebrow. He said only, "Souvenir."

Standing now in the bathroom of his small bachelor's apartment, this new Vincent looked stumped. "I can't answer that question. By the way, where did you get the cake? It was very good."

Where did she get it? At the Sacher Hotel in Vienna and she carried it all the way in her knapsack in its elegant little wooden box. At U.S. customs they'd almost confiscated it. She fought hard to keep it because it was going to be her peace offering to Vincent. Isabelle had the whole thing planned and had been imagining the scene since she left Austria. She would give him the *Sachertorte* and make a joke about it, but both of them would know the gift was both important and deeply felt.

How it saddened her ten minutes ago to open the box and, with no ceremony at all, slip the protective plastic wrap off and quickly cut two slices from the cake.

Something crossed Vincent's face and, sidling by her, he left the bathroom. She looked in the mirror, said, "*Now* what?" and followed him. When she caught up, he was standing by the front door with hands on his hips, looking at her large knapsack.

He pointed an accusing finger at it. "Yours?"

"Yup."

"And that's where the cake came from—you brought it with you? We came back here last night with you carrying that big bag, went to bed, and here we are eating your cake this morning? But I don't remember any of it? Not a thing?"

Before she had a chance to say anything, his phone rang. Both of them were relieved because she didn't know what to answer and he didn't want to hear one more thing from her.

He went over to the phone and picked it up. "Hello?"

"Vincent, this is Coco. Sorry to bother you—"

"Who? Excuse me, who did you say you were?"

"Coco. It's *Coco,* Vincent."

The name meant nothing to him. The woman's voice was unfamiliar. "I'm sorry, but do we know each other?"

"Look, Vincent, I know she's there and doesn't know anything about me, but just give me a minute, willya?"

"You know *who's* here?" He looked at Isabelle.

"Your Isabelle. I know you picked her up last night—"

His temper flared. "Is that right? Well, how do you know that? Who the hell are you?"

"Don't be a jerk. Just listen to me for two minutes—"

He hung up but kept his hand on the receiver. He glared at Isabelle as if she were the enemy. "Why do other people know you're here? Hmm? And why do they know who you are but I don't?"

"Who was that?" she asked as gently as she could.

"Coco. Whoever *that* is. But she knew you were here—even called you by name. Said 'I know you picked up Isabelle last night.' How did she know that if I didn't? And who the fuck is Coco anyway?"

The phone rang again. He snatched it up. "Hello? What?" As he listened his face softened. "Hi, Kitty. Sure, I can do that. It's no problem. In half an hour? Is that okay? Yes." He listened some more and then put the phone down. He cold-eyed Isabelle. "I have to take one of my kids to the doctor. I'm going to get dressed." He turned around and left Isabelle standing there.

She had no idea of what to do next, so she went over to the window and looked out. She was still there a few minutes later when he left without saying another word. With her back to him, she didn't see Ettrich stop a moment at the door, hand on the knob, look at her, frown, and leave.

What could he say—please take off? Or wait till I'm back and then we'll sort this out? How about—could you at least tell me how we know each other before I go? Forget it—if she was here when he got back he would take care of it later.

The next shock waited in the parking garage beneath his building: His car had been stolen. He had an assigned spot. It was empty.

On seeing it and realizing what it meant, his stomach dropped. He was supposed to be at Kitty's house in twenty minutes. Ettrich couldn't believe it—why would anyone want to steal his car? It was new, but it was also a monumentally dirty, nothing-special Ford Taurus. A sexy silver BMW stood in the parking place right next to his empty spot. Why hadn't they taken that one?

He'd never had a car stolen before. It made him feel wounded and vulnerable, like life was no longer his friend. And then there was that woman in his apartment—Isabelle. What the hell was *she* all about? He had no memory of what had gone on between them, yet she knew way too much about him. More bewildered than he had been in a long time, he took the elevator to street level and hailed a cab.

While Ettrich rode toward the posh suburb where he'd once lived with his family, Isabelle cut herself another piece of cake and pulled a chair over to the window. Eating, she looked out at the city. She took too big a bite and a chunk of chocolate icing fell in her lap. Picking it up, she inadvertently looked at the windowsill. Her dancing frog figure was gone. They had taken it too, along with everything else that had to do with her connection to Ettrich.

"God damn it!" There had to be *some* trace of her here. Besides her body at his window and her knapsack by the door, there had to be some sign in Vincent Ettrich's home that she existed in his life. They couldn't have erased her completely—it wasn't possible. And if it was, she was going to put herself right back into it.

So she began searching.

When Isabelle Neukor was young she was an incorrigible thief. But because her then white-blond hair and cobalt-blue eyes made her look like a sprite, Tinkerbelle, or a tiny angel, she fooled people for years. What she wanted she took. Money, candy, toys—whatever caught her fancy went into her pockets. The act never made her feel guilty or nervous either, usually the Achilles' heels of a young robber. When Isabelle pinched something from a store, her heart beat no faster than it had when she was walking down the street five minutes before. She didn't steal because she was wicked or deprived or because it gave her a naughty thrill. She simply took whatever it was she wanted and that was okay with her soul.

To be a good thief one must also be a consummate snoop. Have the imagination to ferret out *all* the hiding places people are likely to use to conceal the good stuff like money, cherished objects, and dirty magazines.

From the age of eight on, Isabelle had the knack and never lost it. She would have been a good watchmaker because successful snooping is like taking apart a complicated watch. You do it layer by layer, careful to place each part in an assigned spot so that nothing is ever mislaid or left out when you reassemble the mechanism.

Even as a child when she opened her mother's lingerie drawer (diaphragm, Dexedrine pills, lots of cash if Mom had recently been to the bank), Isabelle would first study the objects in there a long time, memorizing their order. Then she would go through the drawer (or the closet, the purse, the desk, school bag, her father's wallet . . .) lifting and shifting things around, looking for goodies. But she always made sure everything was returned to its original place when she was done. It was not paranoia on her part—simply good sense. The only time she was ever caught was by a schoolmate who punched Isabelle in the face for stealing her pink ballpoint pen.

Tying the sash of her robe tighter, Isabelle walked into Ettrich's bedroom ready to do battle with those who would erase her and their relationship from Vincent's memory. A bedroom is always the emotional center of any house. The physical passion lives there. So does the greatest peace and sadness. Nor are we ever more alone than when we are in bed with only our secrets and inner voices to say good night or good riddance to a day. If Isabelle ever needed to examine a person's life, which was rare because she didn't care about most people, she began in their bedroom. Although she no longer stole things, sometimes it was essential to get to the bottom of a matter and using her old talent was the best way.

His bedroom was large but just as sparsely furnished as the other rooms. There was the double bed, a thick oak dresser, Eames lounge chair, a black and pink Chinese carpet on the floor. Looking at these objects, she got no "read" on the person who lived here, other than the fact they were willing to spend a couple of thousand dollars for a chair. Next to it on the floor was a book. She walked over and read the title. She smiled and clapped her hands. *The Charterhouse of Parma* by Stendhal.

Vincent had a number of sweet quirks, one of them being a lingering desire to be a good A student. Years ago he had assigned himself the task of reading five classic novels a year. Often when they were together he carried some weighty tome that he was attempting to slog his way through like an explorer hacking his way through thick jungle vines with a machete. But this novel was his nemesis. In the time she had known him, Ettrich had tried to read it three times with no success. He usually reached around page 100 before giving up. Once he even threw a copy out a train window as they were arriving in Salzburg station. He looked at her and said, "I *will* read it. Just not today."

And here it was again. She never understood why he didn't just give up on Stendhal and read something else, but that kind of curious tenacity was Vincent too. Seeing the book now encouraged her though because she knew the history of that novel in her lover's life. She knew *his* history and the important part she played in it. Now she had to find concrete proof of it in this apartment.

Across town, Ettrich and the cab driver were thinking. As a lark he'd asked the man if he could name the three most memorable meals he'd ever had. While they passed through five green traffic lights in a row, the driver described in lively detail his all-time favorite breakfast and lunch. Ettrich didn't know what was more impressive—getting through five lights or the man's memory.

"How'd you know so fast? I couldn't come up with any of them."

The man lit a cigarette without asking the passenger if he minded. "Realize, those meals come with a maybe. Maybe in an hour I'll remember better ones, but I don't think so. That dinner is a pisser to choose though. I've had lots and lots of great dinners." They rode along in an amicable silence, thinking about the meals they had eaten.

Isabelle was sitting on the bed looking at a photograph when the front door opened. She was so deep in thought that she didn't hear it. The picture she held was of Vincent, his ex-wife Kitty, and their two children. They were on a beach in swimsuits; all of them tan as toast, smiling, bunched close together. The way they were placed was what interested her most. Isabelle had seen this picture plenty of times. Vincent often carried it in his billfold and she liked him for that. He always had a picture of his children with him. He loved them and they loved him. He was a very good father.

She had found the snapshot in his dresser and because it was so familiar she had to pick it up and look at it again. But seeing it this time she noticed something new—in the picture, Kitty sat between the children. Vincent was squatting down behind them. His hands were on the kids' shoulders but he made no physical contact with Kitty. Did that mean something? She'd read a number of articles about how psychologists were now studying old photographs and analyzing things in them like body language and figure placement to get an idea of what was really going on in the picture at the time it was taken. It was an interesting concept and in many ways made real sense. With that in mind, she wondered if Vincent's squatting behind his family and not touching his wife "meant" anything. Or was Isabelle just seeing animals in the clouds passing overhead?

"Oh hello."

Startled, she looked up and saw a short pretty woman standing in the bedroom doorway.

"Hello. How did you get in?"

"Key." Pretty woman nodded, as if that were sufficient. But of course they both knew that one word was its own atomic bomb in this situation. Why did this stranger have her own key to Ettrich's apartment?

"Vincent's not here?"

Isabelle's heart suddenly weighed a hundred pounds. She knew who this woman was without knowing who this woman was. Another one of Vincent's tootsies. And she was an adorable-looking tootsie as well, which didn't make it any more fun to think about. She was lovely, she had a key to his apartment, and the tenor of her voice had the confidence of a woman who felt she had every right to be there. The facts all pointed to a tootsie. God damn it!

"His wife called and asked him to take one of their children to the doctor."

Tootsie did something unexpected: she came over to the bed and sat down next to Isabelle. "I'm Coco. Coco Hallis." She put out her hand. "And you're Isabelle."

Isabelle's heart now weighed two hundred pounds. "Yes."

They sat there silently. Coco reached over after a bit and took the Ettrich family photo. She looked at it but the expression on her face didn't change.

All of a sudden Isabelle twisted around, looked at something behind her and shot to her feet like she'd been bitten on the ass. The realization had just come that both women had fucked Vincent in this bed.

"What's the matter?"

"Nothing." She headed for the door. "Would you like some coffee?"

"No. Please stop, don't go. What's the matter?"

Isabelle didn't know this woman. What was she supposed to say to her?

Coco put the photo down in her lap. "You want to know how I know you?"

Isabelle crossed her arms tightly, preparing for the worst. "I guess." After a short pause she blurted out, "No, no I don't! I don't want to know anything about you."

"Yes you do. Because it will make you feel better. Come, sit down." Coco patted the bed next to her.

Isabelle wouldn't budge. She held up a stiff hand that said no— I'm fine where I am.

Coco stopped patting. "Was he weird with you this morning? Was there anything different in the way he acted?"

"He didn't know who I was! He had no idea. He woke up and looked at me like I was a total stranger. He wasn't joking. It was horrible." She described in detail her morning with Vincent. Verbalizing the experience made it even more intolerable.

Coco paused and sucked in her lower lip, as if unable to decide whether or not to say the next thing. "What did Anjo say about it?"

Isabelle twitched. *"What?"*

Coco pointed toward Isabelle's stomach. "What did Anjo say to do?"

"How do you know about—"

"That's why I'm here, Isabelle. To protect you. Ask him. Ask Anjo who I am."

The two women stared at each other with a kind of wary curiosity. Coco wanted to see how the other would react now. As usual Isabelle's first instinct was to run, but where? She knew this had gone too far and that there was nowhere to go. The next room?

Back to Vienna? To the ends of the earth? With every bit of strength she had, she was able to hold it together enough to say, "I'm going into the other room. Please let me be there alone."

"All right. I'll stay here but please ask him now because we really do not have much time."

"Time for what?"

Coco's voice remained calm. "To save the three of you. You saw what happened last night. It only gets worse now."

Trembling, Isabelle walked into the living room and sat down on the couch. A few hours ago, she and Vincent sat here kissing and touching again for the first time in three months. She looked toward where he had sat and noticed the pillows were still pushed down from his body. She touched them, remembering him there, trying to feel his presence. "I'm scared." She said it to herself, to Anjo, to God. But she forced herself to close her eyes and slowly felt the café take shape around her. This is how it invariably happened and by now she was used to it.

The sounds always came first. Street sounds—cars, horns honking, brakes screeching, fat trucks rumbling slowly by. The street in front of the café was busy and even when you were deep inside the building you could hear the ruckus out there. Next, she would feel the seat beneath her—sometimes it was hard, sometimes soft. She had no say about where she would be sitting in the room. Sometimes it was a hard wooden chair with no arms, other times in a booth with worn Naugahyde or soft velvet beneath her. When these things came she knew she was there so she could open her eyes. The Café Ritter in Vienna, where she met Anjo for the first time after her disastrous dinner with Berndt.

She never knew how Anjo would appear to her next. Several times it had been as the ugly little boy she saw that first time. Once he appeared as a tall plain-looking woman who wore too many clashing colors and never stopped speaking bad English in a heavy German accent. Once it was even the waiter who called himself

Herr Karl. Once in a while whoever it was would already be sitting there. Other times Isabelle would have to wait until they chose to appear. On the table in front of her would be a glass of freshly squeezed orange juice, her favorite drink there. There would always be other people in the café but not many. Just enough to make it feel normal and not like a movie set. Thirsty from the night's sleep, she took a long drink of juice. Glass raised to her mouth, she looked at the ceiling as she swallowed. When she lowered it again, Abraham Lincoln was standing next to the table holding a top hat in both hands. "Hi, Mom." He smiled sadly and sat down.

Coco was going through Ettrich's closet when she heard Isabelle's weird burst of laughter. Why was she laughing? Coco wondered if she should go into the living room and see if anything was wrong. But maybe that laugh was a good sign. Maybe something Anjo said to Isabelle had loosened her up.

She took down another of his sport jackets and went through all the pockets. If Isabelle was right, now they had to find some kind of convincing concrete proof to show Vincent that they *were* part of his life. It was essential. Wiping his memory clean of both women had been a clever trick. Yet Coco could fix that with the right tools. She only needed to find them here, among his possessions.

Ettrich was odd about his clothes. He bought only Girbaud—jackets, shirts, jeans . . . the works. But Vincent was odd about many things. He didn't like to use a knife when he ate, if he could help it. But he never left the house without a pocketknife—which he never used. He talked to himself a lot when he drove, as if there were two of him behind the wheel who needed to chat about what to do next. His car was constantly filthy both inside and out although he was Mr. Clean, often showering morning and night. He collected beautiful knapsacks and briefcases but almost never carried them. So the pockets of his chic clothes were forever lumpy and deformed with cell phone, Palm Pilot, miniature sketchbook, paperback novel, and a ubiquitous pocketknife that he never used.

These quirks and others made him both weird and interesting. Coco would not like to have known that fifteen minutes before, Isabelle had had essentially the same thoughts about Vincent while she'd been doing exactly the same thing—poking around in his belongings. While going through the pockets of each of his jackets and trousers, Coco thought about Isabelle until she realized she wasn't concentrating on the job at hand. She wanted to talk to this woman to discover what she was like. The only things she knew were based on Vincent's infrequent comments, and those were invariably biased in her favor.

Unfortunately at that moment she touched a piece of paper in one of his pockets and pulled it out to look. Written on it in Vincent's gorgeous script was the name Lucy Wallace and a telephone number beneath it.

"Asshole!" Coco crumpled the paper tightly in her hand and started to drop it on the floor. Then she thought better of it and put this paper ball into her pocket. Who knows? Maybe Lucy Wallace would turn out to be worth knowing about. But Coco didn't believe that, not for a second. She assumed Miss Lucy was just another one of Vincent's pipkeys. Ettrich and his women. Another thing that so intrigued her about Isabelle—how had she managed to wrestle that man's wandering heart to the ground and get it to willingly submit to her? What was the Neukor magic? All Coco had seen so far was a good-looking woman sitting in a car eating a sandwich, hurrying out of a diner wearing a backpack, and the one this morning who only looked washed out and distraught. Not that she shouldn't be if what she said was true. If Vincent's memory of the two women really had been wiped, then they had a difficult job ahead of them. She went back to rifling through his clothes.

When Isabelle returned to the bedroom ten minutes later, the first thing she saw was Coco's ass sticking out of Vincent's closet. She cleared her throat to catch the other's attention but it didn't work. She tried again but no luck. "Hello?"

From inside the closet came a muffled voice. "I know you're there. Wait a minute because I've got something to show you. Can you find a flashlight? It'll make things easier."

Glad for something to do, Isabelle went hunting. She knew Vincent loved gadgets, but in these monklike quarters she wondered if he would own a pack of matches, much less a flashlight. What was he going to shine it on anyway—his empty living room? She remembered once when they were in her car in Vienna, he picked up a flashlight on the dashboard. Turning it on, he put it against one of his nostrils. He said, "Check this out." She looked and gasped. The inside of his left nostril glowed an eerie dark orange. The light was only on one side of his nose, which made the picture even stranger. But she was used to this kind of nonsense. Vincent did things like it all the time. He wasn't childish as much as a card, a joker, a man who still derived great pleasure from clever pranks and interesting pratfalls.

In his small kitchen she opened several cabinets and was touched to see only two of everything—plates, forks, cups, surrounded by so much empty space. How easily objects can strike us down with sadness. One glance at them can tell us everything about a person's life. She winced at the thought of him alone in a store buying these few things after having left his family and home. Two spoons. Two table mats. All because of Isabelle. Who ran away the minute he had freed himself to start a new life with her.

One drawer near the sink was even worse. It contained many little single-serving plastic bottles of soy sauce and at least twenty pairs of chopsticks, still in their paper wrap. She knew the meaning of this immediately. Both of them liked Oriental food. But Vincent always used a fork to eat it because he was so clumsy with chopsticks. In contrast, she was terrific with them and he admired her dexterity. What the contents of this drawer said was far too much Chinese take-out food and save the chopsticks because one day she'll come back and use them. What other reason could there be for him saving the useless things? Without thinking, she put a hand in among them and stirred the sticks around, touching all those sad single meals, the rustle of stiff paper loud in that quiet room. She started to shove the drawer closed when she realized she'd seen something else in there. Sliding the drawer back open she looked carefully. Below the chopsticks was a sheet of paper half-covered with Vincent's handwriting. She pulled it out and began to read what was on it. Three or four lines through, she realized what was there and put a hand over her mouth.

Vincent was a terrific artist. He had studied painting in college and kept at it over the years, although few people outside his family were allowed to see the results. Isabelle took it as a great compliment the first time he shyly showed her slides of his work. Several months before her birthday in their first year together, he asked what she wanted for a present. She asked if he would make a painting for her. He was genuinely taken aback by the request and said he'd have to think about it. She knew that was because if he did the painting, he'd want it to be wonderful and was afraid he might fail. So she wrote him a letter:

> I asked for a painting because I wanted to see another
> piece of your soul but in a different light. I wanted you
> to paint something you thought would go well "on" me
> so I could see how you perceived that. It could be any-
> thing—a horse or a vase of flowers sitting on a window
> ledge under the stars. Maybe they're there talking to
> those stars about the beauty of distance and the music

of color. People can't share in that conversation because flowers and stars are infinite things and we aren't yet. But they will give us their beauty and perfume. Because flowers and stars smell of the same thing—they smell of hope.

His birthday painting hung on her living room wall but she had forgotten this letter. She wrote him so many. She never thought about what he did with them. Seeing her letter copied in his handwriting, she imagined him sitting alone at this kitchen table copying it out, rain on the window, a mug of tea in front of him. She knew exactly why he had done it—at that moment, it was his only way of being close to her. The thought cracked her in half. She put it on the counter where she could see it while she started searching again for that flashlight.

When she walked back into the bedroom she had the letter in hand but nothing else. "I couldn't find a flashlight."

Coco was in the bathroom washing her hands. "I've got some matches. That closet is too small for two of us. Get down on your knees and go in. I'll be out in a minute."

What crossed Isabelle's mind was Coco might lock her in the closet and leave her there. She knew it was a ridiculous thought but she couldn't shake it. How nice for Vincent: he would come home and find this strange woman he'd spent the night with screaming to be let out of his closet. Then blaming another unknown woman for trapping her in there.

Coco came into the bedroom wiping her hands on a towel. "Go in and take a close look at the left wall down by his shoes. You can't miss it." She reached into her pocket and with two fingers slid out a silver pack of matches with the word "Acumar" spelled across it in thick red letters. "Give those back to me when you're done, please. They're my lucky matches. Have you ever eaten there? It's very nice."

Isabelle looked at the matches again and said no. Coco had to hold back a smirk. She wanted to stick her tongue out and go nyah nyah—Vincent takes *me* to expensive restaurants. Instead she saw something in Isabelle's eyes that made her even happier: distrust. "You don't want to go in that closet, do you?"

Isabelle shrugged fast, like a ten-year-old.

"You think I'm going to do something to you, huh?"

"Look, I don't know one thing about you except you're—" Isabelle bit off the end of her sentence like a cigar.

Dropping the towel on the floor, Coco put her hands on her hips and narrowed her eyes. "Except I'm *what*?"

"Forget it."

Coco took a step forward. "No, I don't want to forget it. You were going to say the only thing you knew about me was I'm one of Vincent's pipkeys, right?"

"*Pipkey?*"

"Girlfriends. Sweetie pies. Fucks."

Isabelle said nothing, which said everything.

"Well, if I'm just another Ettrich orifice, how do I know about Anjo?"

There was nothing Isabelle could say to that because she'd been asking herself the same question. Anjo had told her that Coco was not human but was there to help all of them. Fine, but he had also told her that Coco had been one of Vincent's lovers.

"Come here. I want to show you something." Coco turned around and went back into the bathroom. "You can see it here too—you don't have to go into the closet."

"See what?"

"Just come in here and look, willya? Don't be annoying."

Isabelle entered the bathroom as if it were a minefield. "All right, I'm here. What is it?"

Without any warning, Coco reached over and grabbed her by the nose. "This is not third grade. I am not here to *convince* you to drink your milk. When I say come here I don't give a shit whether you want to come or not. Just do it."

What Coco didn't know was Isabelle Neukor's nose was off limits to the universe. No one was allowed to touch it—not her family, lovers, or infants in their touchy curiosity. Even she did not know why this was so, but there you are—people are strange. Vincent discovered this eccentricity early in their relationship and was merciless with her about it. Sexually they were crazy for each other; giving and taking anything that came to mind. But often after some mad, chandelier-dangling session when they were both sated and happily exhausted, he would whisper, "If you really love me, you'll let me touch your nose now."

To which she invariably replied, "Forget it."

Coco's gesture was so unexpected and outrageous that Isabelle's mind went blank. Holding on, Coco moved closer, so close Isabelle could smell her breath when she spoke. It was pleasantly minty. But it was also cold. Not until much later did Isabelle remember this detail and it troubled her.

"Anjo's in danger. You're in danger and you can't hide from this one, *Iz.*"

Isabelle snapped an uppercut straight into Coco's stomach. It was a great punch, full of rage and power, straight out of nowhere, a bell ringer deluxe. And the only effect it had on Coco was to make her grin and squeeze Isabelle's nose harder.

"Very good, Iz, but that doesn't work on me. Can I please show you something now?"

Isabelle considered nodding but that would have made the hurt worse. She managed to say "Yet" because her nostrils were pinched closed.

Coco let go of her and put up both hands as if surrendering to the police. "Nose hard feelings, okay?"

Touching her nose to make sure it was still in one piece, Isabelle said, "What am I supposed to see in here?"

"Open his medicine cabinet and look closely."

Isabelle spent a good long time doing exactly that. But she saw nothing. Eventually she closed the cabinet door and, looking at Coco in the mirror's reflection, shook her head.

"You didn't see anything?"

"No."

"Then come with me." Unfazed, Coco led the way back into the bedroom.

When they were almost to the closet, Isabelle stopped and looked at the floor as if trying to remember something. "Wait a minute. Wait a minute." She did an about-face, went back to the bathroom and opened the medicine cabinet door again. She reached in and took down a small transparent vial of prescription pills. Unscrewing the top she shook several of them into her hand. They were white and large. A word or two was written in black ink on what appeared to be every one of them. Isabelle saw this before when she examined the cabinet. Black squiggles on the white pills. It had just taken time for the understanding to register in her mind and bring her back for another look.

The first pill that she focused on had the word "Soup" written on it. Which was the name of her dog. The next said "Kracow." One had her mother's name on it. Another "Café" on one side, "Diglas" on the other. The place where they had met for their first date. Every object in Vincent's medicine cabinet had words written on it, every word pertaining to their relationship. A can of shaving cream. A bottle of Royal Water cologne. His orange toothbrush. Every single object had writing on it.

"He knew this was going to happen. He knew they were going to try and take you away from him. That's why he wrote on all those things." Coco was reflected in the mirror again, looking at Isabelle from the doorway.

"But how? How could he have known it was going to happen?"

"I don't know, but some part of him did. And that part was very clever—he tricked them beautifully. There's your proof: He wrote single words about you that meant nothing to anyone but himself. I knew about some of them only because he told me. Like how much you two liked Kracow, and the name of your dog. Come with me. I'll show you something else."

This time Isabelle didn't hesitate to follow. When Coco offered the pack of matches and told her to go in the closet she went right in.

On her knees, she lit a match and asked what she should be looking for.

"The left wall, down by his shoes. You can't miss it."

Swiveling as best she could on bare knees in the small space, Isabelle brought the flame toward the wall. Two seconds, three, and then she saw it just as the match burned down and out. Lighting another, she leaned eagerly forward.

Words, figures, and numbers covered a square space of about fifteen by fifteen feet above Vincent's carefully arranged shoes on the floor. Jammed together, this busy array of sketches, words, and personal hieroglyphics looked like the work of a possessed artist, an accomplished doodler, or a scientist working out some obscure formula. On a wall in a closet with no light to see but whatever was brought to it. The display was fascinating and disturbing even to Isabelle, who was the only other person on earth who understood some of what it all meant. As she stared at it, many different things crossed her mind: the cave paintings at Lascaux in France, a photograph she'd once seen of an Argentine prison cell covered from floor to ceiling with the graffiti of decades of prisoners. She thought of Vincent down on his knees in this cramped space, writing their history on the wall, knowing while he did it that soon it would be his only key to finding his way back to them.

When the second match flickered out she did not light another. Instead she slid the back of her hand across the wall, across his figures and drawings. The sketches and memories Vincent had chosen to put up there. She slid her hand across them tenderly, as if they were her lover's face. And she would have continued doing that if Coco hadn't asked,

"Who's Rez Sahara and the Twenty-five Mice?"

Isabelle had seen that one too on the wall. But hearing the ridiculous name actually spoken made her smile in the dark. "One of Vincent's names for a rock group. He likes to make up names for imaginary groups. It's a silly thing he does. But Rez Sahara was my favorite; so he had it made into a T-shirt and gave it to me. He said I could be their first groupie."

"It sounds dumb." Coco was just jealous. He'd never told her he made up names for rock groups.

"It is dumb. That's why I love it."

"It's kind of dark in there. Do you plan on staying?"

Isabelle touched the wall again and felt such love for him. "I don't think I'm ever going to come out."

Pepper and Pencils

As they rode back across the city to the hospital, their cab stopped at a light in front of the railroad station. Ettrich looked at it and thought *my life has jumped its track today and is plowing right the hell through a nearby field. Or something.*

To begin with, he'd woken up next to a gorgeous stranger who spoke and acted as if they'd known each other for years. Breakfast had been chocolate cake (almost) naked in the bathroom. Then he discovered his car had been stolen from the garage. Then that lunacy over at Kitty's house, topped off by this absolutely unnecessary trip to the hospital. Ettrich loathed hospitals.

"Fucking de-*railed*!" he thought to himself and then announced because it felt good to say the words out loud. His eight-year-old son, Jack, turned from the window and calmly appraised him.

"What'd you say, Daddy?"

"Nothing important, Fighter-Man. How are you feeling?"

"Very hot, thank you." Turning back to the window, the boy pressed his nose and lips to the glass. If Kitty had been there she would have had a fit. Sternly she would have ordered him to take his face off there. But Ettrich didn't say that. Partly because he knew how good it felt to press hot skin against cold glass. Partly because anything his ex-wife said today was double anathema.

No matter how many times he did it, it always felt odd ringing the doorbell at his old house. As if he were pulling a silly prank on his old self. How many hundreds of times had he entered using that blue door, calling "Anybody here?" to whoever was around? Picking up the mail on the side table, smelling what was in the air, listening for the sounds of home. The kids shouting, Kitty singing, the TV or a radio on somewhere, the flip-flop of the dog rolling on its back on the braided rug in the sun. Home is the invisibles, the take-it-for-granteds. The tarnished brass hook where you hang your keys, the spot low on the white porch wall smudged a hundred times by bicycle tires. Things you know by heart, things you never pay attention to until *home* turns into the house where your ex-wife lives now with your kids. Then the place becomes a museum of what once was, full of off limits. Every time you enter now there is some kind of admission charge and new visiting hours. Signs might as well be posted everywhere saying don't do this, don't do that. *You* especially, Vincent Ettrich. Only authorized personnel allowed in here.

So he peeked when and wherever he could; checked constantly to see what was different in his old home, what had the Kitty-dragon changed this time?

He pressed the doorbell and stepped way back, giving her much more room than needed when she opened up.

The door flew open an instant later, as if she'd been lying in wait for him on the other side. If they had still been married he would have made a joke about this, but no more. That sort of humor was long dead and buried between them. When they had contact now they were like two boxers halfway through a bout, sizing each other up from neutral corners, waiting for the bell to ring.

Kitty looked great. She'd cut her hair short and wore a new shade of dark, almost plum-colored lipstick. Ettrich's first impulse was to say she looked terrific but sometimes that kind of flattery backfired, especially these days. While he was racing it around his mind whether or not to give the compliment, she said, "It's his ear."

Ettrich was knocked off balance both by how fast the door had opened and her new look. So that all he heard Kitty say was, "It's Zizir." He thought who's Zizir? What kind of name is that? Neither of them knew many Arabs. And what did that have to do with Jack's being sick again?

"Who's Zizir?"

"What? What are you talking about?" Immediately Kitty's voice jumped to that *tone* again. He hated that tone. Everything that had ruined their marriage had been his fault and he fully accepted the blame. However, he still detested the new spiteful tone her voice had developed since the divorce. It said that everything he was, everything he did and thought, was either stupid or despicable.

Lips tightened, he took a long deep breath through his nose. "I asked who's Zizir. That's what you just said, Kitty. You said, 'It's Zizir.' "

She sneered. "No, Vincent, I said, 'It-is-his-*ear*.' Your son has another badly infected ear and he's running a temperature. Dr. Capshew is at the hospital now and said you should bring him over."

"Hello, Daddy." Little Jack walked around his mother's leg and stopped halfway between his parents.

Ettrich's heart smiled. Besides loving him, he really liked this kid a lot. "Hi, Spider Man. Mom says you're not feeling good."

"My ear, Dad. It's that stupid ear thing again." Jack Ettrich was a punching bag for childhood illnesses. Often it seemed like he had just gotten over one thing when another stepped in and took its place. Ear infections, tonsils, mumps, chicken pox, measles, German measles . . . The poor kid took the best shot from all of them and somehow managed to keep a sunny disposition.

The only thing that was a bit strange about the boy, although a quality Ettrich enjoyed very much, was Jack often spoke and acted like a little old man. At eight years old he was quiet, courtly, and thoughtful. "Please" and "thank you" sat in the front row of his vocabulary. Unlike most kids, he took forever to eat a candy bar because he slowly savored each nibble. If you asked him a question he often gave it long and serious thought before responding. He seldom cried but when he did it was Italian opera; it never failed to break your heart and impel you to do anything in your power to make things all right again. Ettrich had once read an article about a very rare disease called Progeria, which caused its victims to age ten years for every one they lived. Kids died of old age at nine. Sometimes he wondered if God had sprinkled a little Progeria over Jack's ingredients before putting him in the oven.

"Where's your car, Daddy?" Jack was up on his toes with a hand shading his eyes as he scanned the street in front of their house.

"Someone stole it this morning."

"Wow, Daddy, they took your car?"

"That's absurd, Vincent. Who would want to steal that garbage truck?"

"I don't know, Kitty. *Someone,* because someone did."

She crossed her arms. "I don't believe it. You probably forgot where you put it last night because you had other *things* on your mind, and now you think it's stolen."

"Kitty—" He wanted to answer that but knew even the slightest sand in his voice would launch her right into attack mode. He swallowed and looked at the boy. "You'd like me to take Jack to the doctor?"

"Yes. Dr. Capshew is at the hospital until twelve."

"But why can't we wait till after twelve and then I can take him to Capshew's office? It's two blocks from here and the hospital is like five miles across town."

"I think Daddy's right, Mom. I don't like the hospital; it smells weird."

Kitty didn't even deign to respond. "I have to take Carmen shopping for a leotard. Her dance class starts Monday and she's been pestering me all week to get it. How do you plan on getting to the hospital without a car?"

Ettrich pointed to the waiting taxi at the same time that name hit home. "Who is Carmen?"

The boy said with a note of disapproval in his high voice, "Stella. She doesn't like her name anymore and she wants to be called Carmen."

Stella was their daughter. It was also the name Ettrich and Kitty had, to their very great delight, discovered on their first date was the one both of them had always wanted to give a daughter.

"Carmen. That's interesting." Ettrich slid his hands into his trouser pockets and rocked back on his heels. "And you go along with that, Kitty?"

"Yes, why not? Carmen's a nice name."

Instead of answering, Ettrich whistled a few bars from the opera *Carmen*. He wasn't a good whistler.

Kitty touched Jack on the shoulder and told him to put his shoes on and get ready to leave. When he was gone she said, "Bring him right back here afterward."

"Okay." Although he normally loved hanging around with his kids, today this was fine with Ettrich. He had to go to the police about his car. He had to go home and figure out what to do with the stranger with the chocolate cake—

"I do not want you taking him to your apartment. Do you understand? I don't want Jack anywhere *near* there." She sounded like she was about to pop.

"Fine, Kitty. I'll bring him right back. Hospital-home-boom."
There was nothing in his voice but okay.

"Don't make fun of me, Vincent. Don't you do that."

He was dismayed. "I wasn't making fun of you. I only said I'll
bring him right home."

"And do you know why I want you to bring him right home?
Because I know she's in town. Someone saw you two last night at
the airport. So are you happy, Vincent? Did I interrupt your morning
frolic with this? Sorry if I did, but the little chore just happens to
be your sick son!"

"What the hell are you talking about? *Who's* in town? What do
you mean, someone saw us last night?"

Kitty shook her head, never to be taken in again by this dishonest man. Oh no, not her, not again. "Still trying that same old
shit, huh, Vincent?" Her voice changed to deep and deeply stupid.
" 'Wud-dya mean, Kit-ty? I wasn't with another wo-man. Honest!
How could you say that about me?' Bullshit, Vincent. Bullshit!"

"Are you crazy? What the hell are you talking about?"

Luckily their son reappeared at the door. He was wearing the
jazzy sneakers Ettrich bought last week in Los Angeles when he was
there on a business trip. Jack lifted one foot while wobbling on the
other. "What do you think, Dad? How do they look?"

"Very cool. They're great on you."

Jack rushed forward and, jumping on Ettrich, threw his arms
around his father's neck.

"Jeez, you're getting so big. Pretty soon you'll do that and
knock me over!"

Jack giggled and hugged tighter. Out of the corner of his eye,
Ettrich saw Kitty working hard not to smile. A stitch of deep regret
for what he had done to her and their relationship ran through his
insides like a vicious cramp. Still holding Jack up, he walked away
from her without looking again.

As hospitals went, this one was a beauty. It had opened three years before and won numerous awards for its ingenious use of space, light, and the open-air feeling it gave people. Everything inside the building was state-of-the-art. The machines all looked like they should have been on a spaceship traveling toward Jupiter. Whenever Ettrich walked through the hospital and saw these gizmos he wondered how could anyone die if they were hooked up to one of them? How could all those winking lights, pumping bellows, multiple LCD readouts . . . lose a patient? They looked so efficient and unwavering in their silent running—how could they fail? He'd asked Dr. Capshew that question once when Stella was there to have her appendix removed.

Capshew, who was a good guy, brightened at the question. Leaning in close, he pointed across the room. "See the machine over there, Mr. Ettrich? That's a sonogram. It bounces sound waves off your insides and shows what they look like to the trained eye. Costs about seventy thousand dollars. But here's a big medical secret—at the end of the day even that's only a tool. A hammer with a Ph.D. Tools can fix things but they cannot work wonders. Doctors would like you to believe we're miracle workers because it's good for our egos. But the truth is we're just like racing car mechanics: Most of our job is fine-tuning very temperamental machinery."

Hand in hand, Ettrich and his son entered the hospital and took one of the many elevators to the sixth floor. Although their car moved quickly and silently up in fast smooth whooshes, it stopped three times before reaching six. Doctors in white with stethoscopes around their necks and clipboards in hand entered and left. They looked so purposeful and sure that what they were doing with their day was one hundred percent correct. Ettrich was envious, wishing he had a job that was so essential rather than one whose general purpose was to bamboozle people into buying whatever it was he'd been hired to promote. He sighed and unconsciously tightened his hand around Jack's. The boy squeezed back, looked up at him and smiled. He looked down and gave two more short squeezes as their elevator car slowed to stop again. The doors opened on three black nurses standing close by, talking. Two of them stepped in. The third remained standing in the doorway, continuing the conversation. Ettrich noticed her last because he was checking out the other two, both quite pretty. The woman said resoundingly, "All I got to say is this conversation will be *continued*." Her voice was so impressive that it registered on him before she did.

"Oh, Michelle, you always have the last word," Pretty Nurse One said, shaking her head.

At that moment Ettrich looked at the woman outside the elevator. She was big. She looked like she could throw a shot put out of the stadium. Her eyes touched his and moved back to her friends. He knew this woman; he remembered her. But from where? As the doors were closing, his eyes slid to her name tag—Maslow. Michelle Maslow.

Without thinking, he said, "Hey!" but the car was already moving again.

"Whatsa matter, Daddy?"

"Nothing, Jack. I just thought of something."

The question scratched at the inside of his brain like a finger with a long nail. He looked at the metal doors and squinted. Who was she? Why was he so sure he knew her? A big black nurse named Maslow. Who was she?

"Excuse me, but could you tell me where that nurse works?" Ettrich asked the women, gesturing toward the closed doors with an open hand.

"Do you know her, Daddy?"

"I think so." He smiled.

Nurse One looked at Jack and winked at him. "Hey there, mister. You comin' to visit us today?" Her eyes shifted to Ettrich. "Nurse Maslow is at nurses' station four on the fourth floor."

The second nurse added, "You can't miss her," and eyed her colleague who smirked and nodded.

"Thank you."

"How do you know her, Dad?"

"Don't know. I just think I do."

Nurse Two couldn't resist asking, "Have you ever been on the intensive care ward here?"

Her tone of voice was such that Ettrich took her question seriously. "Uh, no."

"Well, that's where you'll usually find her."

It didn't end there. When they were walking down a hall to Capshew's office, Ettrich saw a futuristic freestanding water fountain along the way. He knew for certain that he had never used one here. Yet he also knew—his mind played Ping-Pong with itself—that he had tried to drink from one on another floor of this building. Seeing it now, he distinctly remembered at the time he could not figure out how to make it work. The small failure had made him feel stupid and useless. It had brought him to the verge of tears. He had leaned against a wall to support himself because he felt so tired, tired and weak and sick. He'd been so sick. He remembered that. But when the hell was it? His mind raced. He knew for certain he'd lived all this, knew it had definitely been part of his life. All he'd wanted was a drink of water but he couldn't even figure out how to make a fucking water fountain work.

He remembered being appalled by what his body was doing to

him. In the past it had always been his friend. And in turn he had treated it well—enough sleep, exercise, he ate healthy food. He distinctly remembered saying that out loud once—what are you doing to me? Why are you letting this happen? Because his body had broken their sacred agreement—it had stopped fighting for him, stopped protecting him. It was letting him die.

Staring at the water fountain, he walked slower and slower, his mind a thick but fast-flowing mud slide of memories. But were they his memories? If so, how could that be? How did he know these things? Where did they come from in his life?

"What's the number of his room, Daddy?" Jack's small familiar voice brought Ettrich back to now but not all the way.

"It's just down the hall. We're almost there."

"He always puts that weird thing in my ear. I hate that."

Rowley. There was a guy, an orderly, what did they call the hospital workers who brought your food and changed the sheets on the bed? Orderly? Aide? There was a remarkably handsome young man named Rowley who was their orderly during the day. They called him Jimpy. His name was Jim but he was jumpy, always too wound up. He smiled too much; his fingernails were chewed to the quick. He did everything well but too fast, forever in a hurry to move on.

Michelle Maslow called him "Jimpy." That's where the nickname came from. "Jimpy, you make me so nervous. I think you got a family of mice under your skin. As soon as I see you my heart gets jumpy. And it isn't because I've got a romantic interest either, understand? I can feel my pulse go right up into my throat because you're always rushing around so."

In response to this sort of taunt, Rowley would only flash one of those manic smiles and go about his work.

Michelle Maslow. Jimpy Rowley. How did Ettrich know these things?

They reached Dr. Capshew's office and went in. Several people were already in the waiting room who looked like they had been there a while. Ettrich wondered if this would take a long time.

On a table in a corner of the room was a large pile of magazines, some for kids, and some for adults. Ettrich and his boy each chose a few. But before they had a chance to open them, the receptionist called Jack's name. Rising again, father followed son into the doctor's office, embarrassed to be going before all the others.

Worse, Ettrich was dismissed two minutes after he got in there. The doctor decided he wanted to run a few extra tests on Jack because of his recurring ear infections just to make sure it was not something more serious. Which was why he'd asked that the boy be brought to the hospital. Capshew suggested Ettrich go for a cup of coffee and return in forty-five minutes.

So he slunk back through the waiting room as if he had stolen everyone's wallet in there. Still, he could feel their resentment as he passed. If they'd been snakes instead of people, the sound of rattling would have been deafening.

Out in the hall again Ettrich felt equal measures of relief and unease. He had nowhere to go for nearly an hour. He didn't want to go anywhere in this building because he was afraid of having another one of those too-real visions of a place and time he did not want to know more about. For a few seconds he thought of going down to the fourth floor and finding Michelle Maslow. But what would he say to her, what would he ask? I know you. Do you know me? She would look at him like he was nuts and rightly so. After that? Find handsome Rowley and ask the same question? Hey Jimpy, remember me?

Sliding his hands into his pockets Ettrich thought I just want to go home to that shitty little apartment I hate. Home sweet nothing. Then he remembered who was there and realized going home was no good because Ms. Sacher Torte was waiting. He'd find a snack bar. Have that cup of coffee and wait for Jack. Maybe his earth wouldn't move until then. He asked directions from a passing orderly. The snack bar was on the ground floor. That was okay because it would take time to go down and come up again. He needed something to do, to fill the time. Maybe he'd even go outside and take a walk.

He stopped at the elevator, pressed the button, and waited with his hands behind his back. Kitty always called that his old man pose. He did it unconsciously. At the end of their marriage it actually made her angry to see him stand like that. Then again, women were always angry, disappointed, or upset with men for one thing or another. There was no way of escaping it. The more they loved you, the more you ended up disappointing them. Either you brought too much or too little. The wrong color, the wrong time, the wrong gesture. Pay them a compliment and they brushed it off, or said archly, "You're just noticing?" Thinking about this, he watched the red floor numbers change above the metal doors. The car stopped with a tinny ping. The doors slid open and there was Bruno Mann standing alone inside.

"There you are."

"Bruno! What are you doing here?"

The doors started to close. Mann waved a hand across the doors' electric eye and they obediently slid open again. "Looking for you, Vincent."

"But how did you know I was here?"

"I called around and Kitty told me."

"Why didn't you just call my cell phone?"

"I didn't have the number."

"They have all our numbers at work. Why didn't you call and ask them? It's their phone."

Mann looked confused by that piece of information, but only for a moment. The elevator doors started to close. He waved them open. "I'm not thinking so straight right now, Vincent. We've got to talk. Can we go somewhere?" He gestured impatiently for Ettrich to join him in the car. The doors started to close again and then opened. Ettrich saw this only out of the corner of his eye because he was looking down the hall toward Capshew's office.

"I only have forty minutes. I have to be back to pick up my son."

"Great. Fine. Forty minutes will do it. Come on."

Ettrich stepped into the elevator. This time Mann let the doors close. He pressed the button for the lobby.

As the car dropped, Ettrich waited for the other to say something but he remained quiet. Bruno's arms were crossed and he looked at his feet. He appeared to be silently whistling.

"Well?"

Bruno said nothing.

In an instant Ettrich had a concrete target for all of his morning's discomfort. "Bruno, I don't need your silence right now, okay? You asked me to come along. So why don't you tell me what's going on?"

"They're playing with us, Vincent. They've got us like lightning bugs in a jar and they keep shaking it to see how we'll react."

"What are you talking about? Who's *they*?"

Bruno uncrossed his arms. "Do you have a pulse?"

"*What?*" Now Ettrich wanted out of there because he was beginning to believe Bruno Mann had gone insane and he was trapped in an elevator with Mr. Lightning Bug.

"And have you taken a leak since you found out the truth? Have you needed to use the toilet at all?"

"The toilet? Of course I use the toilet. Bruno, are you on drugs?"

Bruno shook his head. "Not me. Not once. And you know what's funny? I didn't even realize it for a long time. There are so many things you do unconsciously that you never think about until you *don't* do them anymore."

Ettrich couldn't resist asking, "You haven't taken a piss? Since when?" He almost smiled.

Bruno saw that and made a face. "I know, it *is* funny. This whole thing is funny in a horrible way."

The elevator stopped and the doors slid open. No one was there. The doors closed again and the car descended.

Ettrich waited for the other man to continue. "And?"

"And what?"

"You didn't come all the way over here to tell me you don't piss anymore, Bruno."

Mann said nothing for a while. Then sensing something, he lifted his head and frowned. He held up a hand. "Quiet. Sssh."

Annoyed at being shut up, Ettrich kept quiet.

"Do you feel it? Something's in here. There's something in here with us." Bruno's voice had an edge but outwardly he seemed calm enough.

"I think it's time to refill your prescription, Bruno. Whatever it is you're taking." Still, Ettrich straightened up and, with eyes a lot wider than before, he looked around that small space.

"When the car stopped last time no one got in. But those doors opened. Did you notice?"

"So what?"

Mann gestured toward the door. "Well, I think something did get in. We just can't see it."

Ettrich felt the sharp unease that comes when you're too close to someone who just might take wing, fly around the room, and then land hard on your head.

It took an eternity to reach the next floor but they did and thank God, the car stopped and the doors opened. Ettrich started to leave but Bruno grabbed his arm and held him back.

Ettrich looked at the hand on his arm. "Let go of me, Bruno."

"Listen—"

"If you don't let me go I'm going to punch you in the head."

Bruno released his arm. "All right. But I'm going with you."

A handsome older black man in a tailored forest-green suit stood there waiting for them to move. But the fight between the two men had taken so long that they were barely able to step out into the corridor before the doors closed and the elevator was gone. Ettrich looked at the man and apologized. He looked back and smiled. It was his teeth that brought everything back. They were very large and the yellow of old piano keys.

All memory is a cat's cradle of strings and intricate connections. Follow one string down and up and around and suddenly you realize it goes back home again. Seeing those yellow teeth made Vincent Ettrich stagger, literally lose his balance enough so that he almost fell. Because they made him remember. At once his mind was full again of everything he had forgotten that morning when he awoke. Isabelle Neukor was the woman in his apartment. Coco Hallis was the woman on the telephone. This hospital was where he had died. Bruno Mann had died but come back too. This man smiling at him was Tillman Reeves, his roommate during his previous last days on earth.

"There you are, dear Vincent. How good it is to see another face from the old days."

The three dead men sat in the hospital snack bar drinking very good cappuccino. They had been talking for twenty minutes but outside of how good the coffee was, they hadn't agreed on much else.

"So, ever since you died you've been in this building the whole time? You can't go out?" Bruno's voice was skeptical.

Tillman Reeves put two fingers to his chin. "No. It's like being in a Sartre play. And speaking of plays, have you ever read Christopher Marlowe's *Dr. Faustus,* Mr. Mann? An essential work, one of my great favorites. At one point in the story, Faustus asks Mephistopheles where Hell is. The clever little swine answers, 'Under heaven.' " His fingers left his chin and made a little circle in the air, as if to include where they were in that definition.

Bruno looked at Ettrich for clarification. But Vincent's expression said nothing so Bruno turned back to the old man. "I don't understand."

Reeves nodded. "For whatever reason, the three of us died and were brought back to life. To our previous lives, no less, albeit in varying states of confusion and lacking essential memories. We have no idea why we're back here, nor what we're supposed to do.

"Remember how afraid you once were to die? How you would have given anything to remain here, simply living as you were? Well that wish came true for us, but does it make you happy? Hell is under Heaven."

They sat unmoving and glumly silent while that sunk in. Then Reeves said, "I don't understand any of this, but a new part of the mystery is why you two can come and go as you please while I am permanently assigned to this unfortunate place."

Bruno sat back and locked his fingers behind his head. "What do you do here all day? I mean, what is there to do in a hospital all the time?"

"Watch operations, talk to the patients-"

Ettrich interrupted. "And how do they treat you, Tillman? How do people like Big Dog respond to your being here again? The ones who knew you died? The ones who were there when you did."

"Big Dog? Who's Big Dog?"

"She was the nurse who cared for us, Michelle Maslow," Ettrich explained.

"They recognize me but not the person I was. I suspect it's the same way your colleagues and friends relate to you. Everything is normal except for certain fundamental things. They greet me and we have our little chats but only that. People have a collective blind spot in their mirrors to who I am and what I was. When they see me day after day they don't ask what I'm doing here or why I'm still hanging around. They say hello, make small talk, and move on. To them I belong here and as far as they're aware that's correct."

From his own experience Ettrich knew this was true. Until Coco had told him the truth, his life and the people he knew remained the same today as they had been six months ago. "A collective blind spot" was a good way to put it.

"But what are we supposed to *do* now?" Bruno's voice sounded like a lost child's.

"I honestly don't know, Mr. Mann. I keep hoping it will come to me in a flash but so far, nothing."

"Do either of you remember what it was like being dead?"

Mann and Reeves looked at each other.

"Nothing."

"No."

"I was sure you'd say that. But isn't that the strangest thing of all? None of us remember—not one thing about it."

"Because they took it away, Vincent. They don't want us to remember. We might be able to use that memory to our advantage."

Ettrich looked at a clock on the wall. "I have to go. I have to pick up my boy. Bruno, are you coming?"

"No, I want to talk to Mr. Reeves some more. Will you be at home later? Can I call?"

"Sure."

Reeves rose from his chair and, to Ettrich's surprise, embraced him. "Promise me you'll come back and spend some time, Vincent. I miss our chats."

"Of course I'll come, Tillman. But do you remember things like that? Do you actually remember the time when we were in here together? I don't."

"You will. The longer you're aware of the fact you've been resurrected, more and more memories of your last days will return. It's similar to recovering from a form of amnesia. They're not very pleasant memories generally, but it's reassuring to have them back again. They belong to you. They're your life."

Bruno chuckled. "Strange, huh? They always say that about reincarnation—if it's real, why can't I remember my past lives? The same thing is true here: We've been reincarnated but can't remember parts of our past life—which just happens to be *this* life."

Riding back up to the sixth floor in the elevator, Ettrich thought about what both men had said. They were right—the three of them had in a bizarre way been reincarnated. But what good was the experience if you had no idea what to do with it? What good was a lesson if you learned nothing from it?

The elevator stopped at the second floor. Again when the doors slid open, no one was there. He was too deep in thought to pay it any mind. The doors closed and the car began to move. It rose for a minute and then stopped. Ettrich blinked. Confused, he looked around, as if the reason for the stop were somewhere in the car.

"Don't tell me this elevator is stuck. Do not tell me that."

The lights went out.

A moment later Ettrich felt the first thing touch his leg.

It was gentle. He almost didn't feel the first contact because it was so tentative. His pants felt it, the cloth down by the ankle. The pants felt it first and then as the touch became more inquisitive, more firm, the cloth was pushed in until it touched his skin. The same thing happened on his other leg but higher up, near the knee. First touch the cloth and then feel the cloth against his skin.

Paralyzed in the darkness, Ettrich asked, "What is this?"

The touch stopped, went away, came back. For a moment his mind cleared enough to remember what Bruno had said earlier—something was in the elevator with them.

"What is this?" He said it low now, a near whisper.

The touch moved all over him now, more assured. Up then down, traveling across his body in an indescribable way, *exploring*. As if they were fingers made of smoke, they wound and floated over his body, tentative and ethereal but unmistakably *there* the whole time.

They went between his legs and felt his cock through his pants. One finger slid slowly up between the cheeks of his ass. They ran down the backs of his legs. He could not move. He would not move for fear of everything. Up his front—the long line from his stomach up his neck, across his face. Into his nostrils a moment and then swirling around to the back of his head. Like a lover, he thought simply. They touch me like a curious new lover.

How long this went on is hard to know. Because there was no way to resist, Ettrich surrendered to the inspection. But yielding made the experience a little easier to bear. When the fingers moved again to his face and caressed it, he abruptly understood what it was. How he understood he did not know, nor would he ever. Perhaps it was something as basic as recognition. You experience it, you know it. Even something as incredible as this. It doesn't matter. What happened was Vincent Ettrich recognized that the fingers touching him now were his own: The fingers of his dead self stroking his live face.

And then that dead Ettrich spoke.

"Most people should never dye their hair blue." Isabelle pointed with her chin toward a fat man at the bar with cobalt-blue hair drinking a can of Diet Coke.

Coco ignored him and watched as Isabelle dissected her lunch. They were in Margaret Hof's bar eating pastrami sandwiches and drinking iced tea.

"Here's a question: Why do fat people always order Diet Coke? Who do they think they're kidding?"

Coco was too immersed in watching Isabelle work on her sandwich to respond. First she had taken off the top slice of bread. Then two of the thick pieces of pastrami. Those she laid on the side of the plate. Next she elegantly folded what remained in half and took a bite.

"Why did you do that?"

Isabelle smiled while she chewed. She held up a finger for Coco to wait while she swallowed. "I always do. Rearrange it the way I want it. Have you ever gotten a perfect sandwich? There's always too much or too little of what's inside. So I fiddle around with it."

Coco's face was noncommittal. "What does Vincent say?"

"He likes it. Do you think it's odd?"

"Yes."

"That's okay. I don't mind being odd. My family has been telling me that my whole life. I just wish I were stronger."

"Bringing Vincent back from . . . from the dead was a very brave act, Isabelle. A weak person couldn't have done it."

Isabelle touched her stomach. "I did it with Anjo's help. Without him it wouldn't have been possible."

"That's not true. He might have helped, but it was your decision. No one could force you to do it. How did it happen?"

Isabelle was surprised. "You don't know?"

"No. It's different for everyone. There's no one method. Anyway, I'm not from there. I keep telling you that."

"Where *are* you from?"

Coco picked up her glass and raised it to her mouth. "You first."

Isabelle continued eating her sandwich as she spoke so what followed came in bits and pieces. "Once in a lifetime, every person experiences their own death in a dream, down to the last detail. But we have twenty-five thousand dreams in a lifetime, so we don't pay much attention. It's just another dream. Or it's a horrible dream and we wake up from it like any bad nightmare—scared shitless. The only thing we want then is to forget the whole thing because it was awful. So you jump out of bed and start the day and the memory eventually fades."

"How did you learn all this, Isabelle?"

"I recognized the dream when I had it. I knew immediately."

"*How?* You recognized your death dream while it was happening?"

"Yes."

Coco whistled a long note and shook her hand as if trying to cool it off. "*That's* impressive. I've never heard of it happening like that and I've heard a lot of stories, believe me."

Isabelle pulled a long piece of meat from her sandwich. "Maybe being odd has its advantages."

"Clearly. Would you tell me the dream?"

"No. Now it's my turn to ask questions."

Coco did something unexpected—she picked up Isabelle's glass of tea and finished it in one long glug-glug. When she was done she wiped her mouth with the back of her hand. "Go ahead."

"Where are you from?"

"Purgatory."

"It really exists?"

"As humans conceive it, no, but it's a good enough vision to suffice. It'll do."

"So there's a heaven and hell?"

Coco shook her head. "No. Life, death, and purgatory. Man invented heaven and hell to torment himself. Have you ever known a sane or truly good person who believes he deserves to go to heaven? I doubt it. Everyone thinks they're damned for their behavior."

"Then how does it work?"

Coco liked that. The simplicity of the question, five words in search of God.

Isabelle's face clenched and she gasped, like she'd suddenly been punched. A huge, agonizing pain hit her. She fell back in her chair and could not breathe. Her mouth fell open, her tongue lagged to the edge of her teeth.

Coco saw this and understood at once. She shoved her glass of tea across the table. "Drink this. Drink it fast."

Staring at her with stunned eyes, Isabelle had barely enough strength to obey. When she swallowed the cold sweet liquid, the pain faded and stopped. Hand shaking, she slid the glass from her mouth against her flushed cheek.

"Don't stop. Drink all of it just to be sure."

The cold glass on her cheek felt so good. The pain had burnt her up, she felt like ash. "What happened?" Isabelle mumbled.

"It was my fault. I drank from your glass but should have made you drink from mine. I'm sorry—it was a thoughtless mistake."

Isabelle showed no sign of understanding, so Coco continued. "Drinking from your glass, swallowing your saliva and making it part of me, enabled me to explain these matters in a way that you can understand. If I spoke normally, in my language, none of this would make sense to you."

"What is your language?"

"I told you, I'm from purgatory. I'm in your world but not part of it."

Isabelle pointed at her. "This isn't you?"

"A very small part." Coco pointed to her thumb. "If I asked if your thumb was you, you'd say it's *part* of me."

"And the other parts?"

"Even if I showed you, Isabelle, you wouldn't be able to comprehend. But you will after your life is over. That's what purgatory is for—to teach you to understand."

"Why did I have all that pain just now?"

"Your soul was overloaded with unfamiliar information and blew a fuse. I could convey the data but you didn't have the capacity to process it. It's like you needed a much bigger hard drive. Drinking from my glass raised you up a level. Now you're okay. We can talk and you'll be safe."

"How does it work?"

Coco counted off the first three fingers of her hand. "From Life to Purgatory to Death. People think when life ends they die. Wrong. The truth is they must go to purgatory first to learn what death is and how they fit into it."

"Purgatory is a school?"

"Of sorts, yes."

"You die and go to *school?*"

"You *leave here* and go to school, yes." Coco asked a passing waiter for two more glasses of tea.

"Where did I go when I got Vincent?"

"Purgatory."

"But I remember it very clearly. It was like here; things were like here."

"That's right— It's designed that way so you feel at ease when you first arrive. But the longer you're there, the more it changes."

"And death? What is it?"

"Death is a mosaic. It is the mosaic."

The waiter brought their drinks. Coco's answer meant nothing to Isabelle and her disappointment showed. "What kind of mosaic? What do you mean?"

"You create a life and then it ends. But what happens to that being, the Isabelle you created? Does she disappear once your eyes close for good? It makes no sense. Why should all the energy, experience, and imagination of a lifetime go to waste? Seventy years of growth and development simply cease when your heart stops?" Coco smiled. "What happens to the smell of pepper and pencils?"

Despite the tension in the air, Isabelle smiled too. "I love those smells. Vincent always kids me because I sniff pencils."

"And use too much pepper on your food."

"How do you know that?"

"He told me."

"Did he tell you a lot about me?"

"No. Only good things. I can't remember his ever saying any-thing bad about you." Coco pushed her glass from left to right and looked at Isabelle. "It really pissed me off."

"Tell me about death."

Coco started to reach into a pocket of her coat. "Have you ever seen any of the world's great mosaics?" Her face twisted this way and that, as if what she was searching for in her pocket couldn't be found.

"Yes, twice—I was in Hagia Sofia and the Church of San Vitale in Ravenna."

"Excellent." Coco pulled out a large handful of wooden Scrabble letters and small multicolored, multishaped ceramic tiles. She flicked her wrist and they danced out across the table in all directions. Some of them jigged to the very edges of the table but none fell off.

"Do you always carry Scrabble letters in your pocket?"

"Only on special occasions. Arrange them any way you want. Letters and colors together. Or just the letters alone, the colors alone—however you want it." Coco pointed toward the scattered tiles.

Isabelle hesitated a moment, looking at them spilled across the tabletop. Then she started sliding the ones she wanted toward her. She took her time choosing. Despite not knowing what this was about, she would still do it her way.

"Any way I like?" She kept looking at the tiles.

"Yes. This is not a game or a trick. Do it however you want. Sort of like the way you rearrange your sandwiches."

Isabelle found the letter "p" twice, an "e," and an "r." She spelled "pepr" and then placed red, yellow, blue, and black tiles in a square around the word like a frame. She continued choosing and arranging, discarding and adding as she went. Only once did she look up to see how Coco was reacting. The other woman was looking at her fingernails.

Margaret Hof came over to see what her friend from Vienna was doing with those strange little pieces on the table. When Isabelle ignored her, Margaret *hmpf'd* and walked away. Coco kept quiet, drinking tea and smoking cigarettes.

When she was finished Isabelle had used many of the pieces. She began to count them but very firmly Coco stopped her. "Don't do that, don't count them. How many there are is not important."

"I just—"

"I'm telling you, don't do it." Coco's voice was cold and sure. Counting the tiles was definitely not a good idea.

Isabelle did not like being told what to do. Still, she stopped and put her hands down. "Okay. Now what?"

Coco did not move. "Take your hands away. Put them in your lap."

Whatever Isabelle expected to happen next did not. Nothing happened. Nothing but the goings-on in the bar around them. Someone sang a few lines of a Monkees song. Someone else laughed. Isabelle kept looking at Coco to see if she was doing anything. Nothing. After more time passed, she began to grow restive and looked at the tiles to see if they might catch her interest. Two wooden letters, "f" and "h," were too far away from the rest, so she slid them in closer to her design. A green star-shaped ceramic tile suddenly looked wrong where she'd placed it so she moved that too. Then another needed adjusting and another. She became absorbed in getting her arrangement just right, although the whole idea of pushing tiles around a table was silly. She wasn't paying attention when Coco began to speak.

"No one can ever leave their design alone once they've started tinkering with it, and everyone does. If you move this tile, now that one needs realigning. Then another. Your whole life you're moving your pieces around and around, always trying to get the big picture just right. Sometimes it looks okay for a while, it looks perfect. But then you get older, or the things in your life change, and suddenly the pieces need to be shuffled again. Again and again, like what you're doing now."

Isabelle had been staring at her design. Looking up, she saw Coco put one of the unused tiles in her mouth and start chewing it. She picked up another and ate that too. After she'd swallowed, Coco continued talking.

"There are two mosaics. The first is the life that *you* create and live. When it's finished, that life is placed into a greater mosaic. The one where everything goes at the end."

"Aliens too?" Isabelle couldn't believe she had actually asked that question, but in her secret heart she really wanted to know the answer.

"Aliens, ants, amoebae, and Ashkenazim. All the a's, all the b's—everything that has ever lived goes there in one form or another after their life is over. Everything becomes part of the mosaic."

"What does it do? I mean, what's its purpose?"

"It is its own purpose."

"That doesn't help me, Coco. That doesn't clarify a whole hell of a lot."

Coco ate another tile. She shrugged as if to say I don't care what helps you because that's just the way it is.

They sat silently staring at each other for some time. Finally Coco asked, "Do you know that Vincent almost always carries a small red plastic spoon in his pocket?"

"Yes, it's his talisman. I was with him when he got it. We bought ice cream in Vienna one summer evening. Then we walked down to the Danube canal and sat there eating it."

Coco slid around in her seat so that she was facing Isabelle square-on. "How well do you remember that night?"

"Very well. Why?"

"Do you remember the flavor of ice cream you chose?"

"Rum raisin. Häagen-Dazs. They'd just opened a stand in the middle of town."

"Why does Vincent carry the spoon?"

Isabelle couldn't keep a note of pride out of her voice. "Because he said it was one of the happiest nights of his life."

Reaching down, Coco took the "h" tile from the middle of Isabelle's design. She held it out to her. "Eat this."

"What?"

"Eat it. Just do what I tell you."

Isabelle took the small wooden square and without pause put it in her mouth. The first thing that happened was her mouth filled with a strong, distinctive taste. Cold and very sweet—ice cream. Rum raisin ice cream. It was so unexpected yet delectable that she closed her eyes to take the whole moment back into herself and make it larger, more hers.

Opening them again it was to the warmth, lush smells, and soft golden light of a summer evening outdoors. She was standing on the *Graben* in Vienna with an ice-cream cone in her hand. Vincent was two feet away eating his rum raisin from a small cup with that red spoon. He pointed it at her. "What do you want to do now?"

She knew what she was going to say because she had already said it a year ago. She listened to herself with detached interest.

"Let's walk through town and down to the canal. We'll sit by the water." She was aware that two very different versions of her self lived in one body at that moment: Isabelle then and now.

For the next half hour, these two Isabelles and Vincent Ettrich strolled through downtown Vienna past the elegant stores, the street musicians, packs of kids in a hurry, and the packs of Japanese tourists in no hurry. All of them together sharing that warm Vienna night.

When the couple reached the canal they sat on a green bench and chatted with the great joyful intimacy only lovers know. They were delighted to be together. They had found each other and both knew this was the big one, no doubt about it. Life would never be any better than this. Vincent was right when he said it was one of the happiest days he'd ever known.

And for Isabelle, living it now *and* for the second time, the experience was incomparably richer. The prickle of the new and the aroma of the old. Nor did the two parts conflict. It was as if her Now self were driving a car down a new and unexplored road. The other Isabelle, who had been here before and enjoyed it tremendously, sat in the passenger's seat. She listened to the driver's enthusiasm about what they were seeing while noticing all the details she had missed her first time here.

Holding hands, the lovers watched the Danube go dark as evening fell around them. She was just about to say something to him when it ended. In an instant she was suddenly back in the dark bar with Coco sitting at the table covered with tiles.

First she was disoriented, and then filled with a terrible, almost visceral longing for Vincent and that moment together. Like waking from a wonderful night dream and wanting more than anything to go back there for a few more minutes. Just long enough to kiss that dream lover, or eat the sumptuous meal that had been cooked for you. Longing, confusion, disappointment. All those dark feelings moved through Isabelle's heart. "What *was* that?"

"The first lesson in purgatory: Reliving your life from the two perspectives simultaneously."

"A whole life? You relive your whole life? How long does that take?"

Coco grinned. "Not long. We have a sort of fast-forward mechanism."

"But what about the bad stuff? Doesn't that hurt you to relive it from both sides?"

"Yes, but it's very necessary too. Before adding your life to the mosaic, you must know it fully. What you just experienced was the first part of learning to understand what your life *was* and what you made with it."

"Coco, is there free will? Am I . . . am I doing what I want, or is someone pulling the strings? You know—" Isabelle pointed to the ceiling. "Him?"

"How much do you want to know? Do you want a taste or do you want the whole meal?"

Isabelle did not hesitate a second. "The whole meal."

"Good. Watch the table."

What happened next took place quickly. Isabelle might have missed it if she hadn't been told where to look.

All of the tiles not in the mosaic began to move. They slid in toward the center of the table where Isabelle had created her design minutes before. But there was nothing ominous or disturbing about this—just some tiles sliding across a table. Both women watched. Isabelle looked up once to see if anyone else in the bar was paying attention but they weren't.

Coco said, "Think of it this way: The design you created here was your life until now. You chose the tiles you wanted and arranged them. Your mosaic. The ones you didn't use are the future elements of your life."

"Is this true? Is that really my life there?"

"No, but pretend it is. This is the simplest way to illustrate it. See how they're all joining now into a larger mosaic?"

"Yes. Except the ones you ate."

Coco plucked another tile off the table and put it in her mouth. "Hey!"

"It's okay. I just ate the last five years of your life, but you'll never miss them."

As a piece, this new larger mosaic rose slowly and hung motionless in the air a moment before upending itself so that it faced Isabelle.

"There is *your* creation—Neukor envisioned and arranged. On the last day of your life, this is what it would look like. People don't know that because most think their lives are a bunch of scattered, random events that don't add up. They couldn't be more wrong."

The mosaic hung in the air as if held there by invisible wires. Both women stared at it while they spoke. No one else in the bar did.

"But what about the bad things, Coco? The terrible things that strike like lightning? The kid who's kidnapped and tortured. Or a good, brave woman in Florida who gets cancer . . . what about them? They didn't *choose* to put those things in their mosaic. Don't tell me they did. No one does."

"Let me finish explaining this, Isabelle, and then I'll get to that."

Isabelle nodded.

"So there is your finished work." Coco waited a bit to allow Isabelle a good long look. Then she took a folding knife out of her pocket and opened it with a loud click. Reaching forward, she stabbed it into the middle of the mosaic. Twisting it back and forth, she pried out one black tile.

Isabelle said nothing, expecting an explanation for the disturbing gesture. While waiting she kept looking at the spot where the tile had been on the mosaic. It was hard not to because strong white light now shone through it from the other side, as if it were a peephole.

When something important is damaged, we cannot take our eyes (or thoughts) away from the break, the crack, or the wound. The first bad scratch on a new car, the first recognized lie told by a new lover, the hole where the black tile belonged. We knew this would happen, sure, but secretly hoped it never would. Sometimes these things can be repaired but even then they will never really be whole or perfect again. Never.

The black tile lay in the middle of Coco's open palm. "Imagine this is your whole mosaic shrunk down to this size." She pointed to the large one hanging in the air. "Your tile completes that. Alone it looks small and unimportant. Until you see what the finished one looks like *without* it. Are you with me?"

Isabelle nodded.

"That big mosaic is not death—it's *God*. The tiles that create Him are all of the completed lives that have ever existed. Every single one of them has its place in Him. And without them all, He is incomplete." Coco handed her the black one. "Put it back in."

Isabelle reached out and stuck the tile into place with her thumb. "So God is a mosaic and we're the tiles. How we choose to live gives our tile its specific shape?"

"Right."

Isabelle naturally waited for Coco to say more but she didn't. "And that's it, the answer to life: God is a mosaic and we're the tiles? The end?"

"Oh no. Now it gets interesting. Watch."

Isabelle looked up just in time to see the mosaic explode. It burst without a sound. All of its many tiles flew out across the room in a wide pattern like a shotgun blast. They moved silently and *slowly*. Not one person in the room paid any attention as black, red, green, yellow Scrabble . . . tiles flew by and over and under and in some cases *through* them on their separate trajectories. Isabelle saw one tile actually pierce a man's forehead and exit out the back. Slowly. The guy continued eating a pretzel and reading the newspaper.

Some went low, others high; some tiles moved only a few inches from where they started. Others flew out to the highest, farthest corners of the barroom. On reaching their various destinations every tile slowed, stopped, and hung in the air as if frozen.

Isabelle stared with the awed, frightened face of a young child watching a fireworks display for the first time. Coco left her alone to absorb what had happened and what she had seen. When sufficient time had passed she said, "Walk around the room and look at the tiles. Look at them carefully. Then I'll tell you more in a minute."

Isabelle looked, she touched, she peered under and over. People in the bar looked at her but paid no more attention after a glance or two. It was as if she were walking through the room to go to the toilet. At first she was hesitant to touch or get too close to any of the tiles but that hesitation passed. Because after that first look around, she realized something new about the tiles: every one was slowly changing form and color. And as it happened, all of them—starting with the most distant—began moving back toward the table again.

She saw a transparent square change into an orange starfish as it drifted back toward Coco's table. A wooden Scrabble letter transformed into a gleaming metallic silver circle. The fingers of an open blue hand closed and that fist became a white apple. Some tiles transformed from a solid hue to a swirling combination of colors. Others went from swirl to solid. The only constant was all of them changed shape and color as they moved.

Captivated, Isabelle walked through the room. Tiles were everywhere and passed through her whenever she got in their way. She lifted a hand and two floated through it like fish through water. Turning around to look behind, she opened her mouth and a brown pinecone-shaped one sailed in. She felt nothing in her throat. Turning again, she saw the tile traveling in the same direction as all the others. It was changing from brown to electric pink and into another shape.

Coco said something and all of the tiles stopped. But their colors and shapes continued to metamorphose as they hung in the air.

"What?"

"Do you know anything about the big bang theory?"

"Sure. How they say the universe began. Fourteen billion years ago." Isabelle could barely tear her eyes away from the frozen blizzard of color and shapes surrounding her. It was magnificent.

"Isabelle, sit down and listen to me. This is what you wanted to know; this is what it's all about. The big bang is no theory—it's the truth. Mankind is only just beginning to understand the concept. But it isn't the universe that began with a bang—*God* did. Periodically God breaks apart like you just saw the mosaic do. In one huuuuge explosion, parts of Him scatter to every corner of the . . . well, *room*. Like what just happened to the mosaic here."

"But why?"

Coco took a tile out of the air and held it out. "Did you notice how all of them are changing color and form while they're out there?"

Isabelle nodded, baffled.

"Then watch." In an instant, the blizzard came together to form a new mosaic right in front of her. But it was entirely different from the one she had created earlier. It was beautiful and elaborate and she started moving in to take a closer look. But as she did, it blew apart again and the countless pieces, the tiles of this new construct, went flying away.

But this time Isabelle didn't watch them. She turned instead to Coco and in a low exasperated voice said, "I do not understand."

"Every person adds their tile, their life, to the mosaic. And the mosaic is God. This happens with everything that has ever lived in the universe. That's what purgatory is for—to teach you about the mosaic and your place in it. When all the tiles have joined, they are thrown out again. Again and again and again, world without end. They travel a certain distance, stop, and return. But *while* they're returning they change into completely different things. So that when they are joined again, the mosaic is of course different—God is different."

"You mean there have been several *different* Gods?" Although she was saying them, Isabelle couldn't believe what these words meant.

"*More* than several."

"How long does this process take?"

Coco shook her head. "You can't put it in a time frame. It's eons, unimaginable, it's forever. But eventually all of the tiles do return. Like your life—thirty years ago you were sent out into this world and now you are returning, a different person. Who knows how long it will take for you to return? But the beauty of it is there will always a place for you in the mosaic, no matter what you have become. Always a specific place in the design where you belong and where you are needed, no matter what form you've taken. You saw what it looked like without that one black tile. You are necessary, and always will be."

"No matter what kind of life I've lived?"

"Exactly. That's exactly right."

"How long does it take for these mosaics to be completed? For a new God to be formed? If I die now you're saying I may have to wait ten trillion years for this one to be finished?"

"Possibly, but once you're part of the mosaic you'll never think about that. Because you will be too busy experiencing the lives and insights of all the others already there. And as more and more tiles are added, you'll share their experience and knowledge too."

Isabelle's arms remained crossed tightly over her chest and the look on her face remained blank, so Coco went on.

"Imagine you must go to a dinner party where you'll know no one. It's in an apartment you've never been before. You don't want to go. But when the door opens you're greeted by the most delicious aromas you've ever smelled. And everyone you meet at the party is brilliant, funny, good-looking, and most of all interesting. Wits and scientists, artists and adventurers, great beauties . . . on and on and on. Within half an hour you realize this is the most remarkable crowd you've ever encountered. Even better, they're all fascinating and are fascinated by you. This guy recently came back from Mauritania, where he was writing an article on white slavery for the *New York Times*. The woman he's with is a photographer and vulcanologist who's been studying the recent eruptions on Mount Etna. You love volcanoes and her stories alone would hold you spellbound all evening. But every person at the party is like her. And as the night goes on, more and more fascinating people come in. Then the meal is served and it's the most incredible food ever! So you don't know whether to eat or talk or listen or lust after all the handsome men in the room. Or even just look at the room itself which is furnished—"

"I get the point." Although her arms stayed crossed, a small smile rose onto Isabelle's face.

"If you went to a party like that, you'd never look at your watch to see when you could leave."

"Especially not when the man on your right is from Mars."

A Rat in Lipstick

The rat reappeared after Ettrich had dropped off his son at Kitty's house and returned to the taxi. It was sitting in the front passenger's seat. But the driver didn't know that because the animal was invisible to everyone but Vincent Ettrich. A sixty-one-pound talking rat. Its name was Alan Wales.

They had met for the first time in the hospital elevator. It was pitch-black in there because the lights went out when the car stopped. So Ettrich didn't know he was talking to a rodent. He thought he was talking to his dead self. Which in fact he was, but what he didn't know was dead selves return in surprising guises— like giant rats that call themselves Alan Wales.

Now the beast had reappeared and asked, "What are you going to do?"

Ettrich looked at the back of the cab driver's head. "Are you sure that guy can't hear us?"

Alan Wales sniffed because Ettrich had already asked that question three times since they met. "*Yes,* I'm sure. Since I'm you, it's as if our conversations are going on in your head and not in public." The rat had turned completely around in its seat so that its back was to the windshield and its paws were perched on the top of the worn Naugahyde seat. It had black eyes the size of cherries and long silvery whiskers that looked like bicycle spokes.

Ettrich gave the driver instructions to the diner where he'd abandoned his car the night before. Then he asked the rat, "Why do you call yourself Alan Wales?"

The rat responded in an irritated voice, "Don't ask stupid questions. You know perfectly well why."

And Ettrich did: "Alan Wales" was the alias he used whenever registering at hotels with women not his wife. Mr. & Mrs. Alan Wales. He made the name up years before. It sounded British and wonderfully phony, as if it belonged to a mediocre 1940s actor with a razor-thin moustache who invariably played either the sap or the cad.

The first time the rat spoke to him in the elevator, the voice in the dark had said, "You're not going to like what you see when the lights come on. So be prepared."

Remembering the ghostly fingers sliding sinuously up his legs moments before, Ettrich tried to sound composed. "I'm going to see myself, right? That's what you said you are—the dead me."

"You *are* going to see yourself. You're going to see yourself as you see yourself these days."

Ettrich was about to say *what?* when the elevator light blinked back on and he saw a huge rat sitting in the opposite corner. It was mud-brown. It was looking at him. It was a motherfucking *rat*.

And then it spoke again in Ettrich's own voice. "If a soul must come back here, it takes the shape of the person's self-image."

Forgetting his shock, Ettrich spat out, "I don't think I'm a rat!"

"That's true—when I arrived earlier you thought you were a piece of shit. Would you prefer that? I can change if you'd like."

Now from the back of the taxicab Ettrich said, "I'm going to go pick up my car. When I was running away from you last night I had to leave it behind. Remember?"

Alan Wales only stared at him. Ettrich didn't know what was more unsettling—a silent rat, or one who spoke in your own voice.

"You keep mistaking me for Death, Vincent, but I'm not. I'm you, dead."

Ettrich waved a dismissive hand to indicate there was no difference. "Why are you here?"

"I told you—I've come to convince you to return with me. You don't belong here anymore."

Neither spoke for a while after that. When the silence held, the rat turned to face front. Ettrich watched the back of its large head and saw its long whiskers twitch. He had no reason to doubt what it had said. In the world where he now existed there were no rules. Or if there were he didn't know them. What was most grotesque about it was everything seemed normal most of the time. Until these mad occurrences snapped open like a switchblade knife and slashed "normal" into pieces.

"Has anyone told you about the mosaic yet?"

Because the animal had its back to him, Ettrich barely heard the question. He slid forward on the seat. "What? Have I heard about *what*?"

Speaking over its shoulder the rat said, "Have you learned about the mosaic yet?"

"Mosaic? No, what's that?"

While their taxi moved through traffic, Alan Wales told Ettrich some of the same things Coco had told Isabelle earlier. But Ettrich was so rattled and confused by the events of the day that he kept interrupting with *"What?"* or "Huh? I don't understand that." Or "What do you mean, we're all tiles?" Furthermore, Coco had her pocketful of colorful tiles and 3-D visual aids to demonstrate the mosaic to Isabelle.

Inside the taxi, Alan Wales had only his words and furry paws to draw pictures and diagrams in the air for his confused student. Try drawing an invisible picture of God with a paw.

To make matters worse, the Pakistani taxi driver began talking. Now Ettrich had to decipher what he was saying and listen to the rat at the same time.

Five minutes later when they stopped at a traffic light, the door on Ettrich's side of the car flew open. Someone grabbed his arm. "Get out. Pay the guy and let's go."

He heard the words before he saw Coco standing there.

The rat said, "Close the door!"

The driver said, "What is going on?"

Ettrich said, "What the hell are you doing here?"

Behind them a horn honked. The light had turned green. Before he had a chance to think, Ettrich was jerked with tremendous strength out of the cab. Coco said, "Pay him and let's go."

While reaching into his pocket for money, Ettrich saw her bend down next to the passenger's window. She looked directly at the rat and then back over her shoulder at him. "Give me the money." She took his ten-dollar bill and, reaching across Alan Wales, handed it to the cab driver. A horn honked again, this time joined by two more. Coco grabbed the rat by the snout and, putting her head very close, spoke to it in a language that never did and never will exist in human history. Then she pushed its head away and said to Ettrich, "Let's go."

He followed her like a little brother, wanting to pull on her jeans jacket and say, "Wait, wait—how did you know I was here?" And "You saw him? How could you see him? He said only I could see him." And "What did you say to him? I didn't understand what you were saying."

But she wasn't waiting around. She walked four cars back to a beautiful green Austin-Healey convertible and gestured for Vincent to get in. The driver of the car behind hers honk honk honked his horn. He stuck his head out the window and whined, "What the hell you doing, lady?"

Coco gave him a warm smile and waved like a movie star recognized. Sliding in behind the wheel of her car, she pointed at the other seat and said to Ettrich, "Please get in now. I'm blocking traffic."

What else could he do? He looked back at his taxi but it had already driven off carrying the Pakistani and the invisible rat. Ettrich got in and Coco tore off the moment his door slammed shut.

"I have to get my car."

She didn't respond.

"I said I have to get my car."

"I know, Vincent. We're going to get it but we have to make one other stop first."

"You saw it just now, didn't you, the rat?"

Coco snorted. "Is that what you saw, a rat?"

"Well, yes. He said his name was Alan Wales."

"A *rat* named Alan Wales. And you believed that, Vincent? You didn't for a minute think that there might just be a little something wrong with that picture?"

Ettrich became defensive, his voice shrill. "It materialized in the elevator, Coco. The car had stopped between floors and suddenly there was a giant rat two feet away that spoke to me in my own voice. He knew things about me no one could know. What was I supposed to think? That someone was playing a trick on me? *Pretty good fucking trick.* He said he was the dead me."

"How could he be the dead *you* if he was a rat?" She looked at him as if he didn't know the answer to two plus two.

A moment passed that weighed a few hundred pounds. Then Ettrich surprised himself by abruptly laughing out loud. He remembered a line from someone famous about how when things got so bad you either laughed or went crazy. "I don't understand anything anymore. Nothing, not one thing. Since the night I saw that tattoo on your neck, everything in my life has gone nuts."

"Well, Mr. Ettrich, we're about to fix that. I'm going to show you everything you need to know." She downshifted and took a left. The car shot forward into the fast lane. "And when you see what it's all about, it's going to scare the shit out of you."

Ettrich closed his eyes. "Thank you. That's what I wanted to hear. Just what I need right now. So where are we going, to hell?"

"No—to the zoo. Isabelle is there waiting for you."

They drove in silence. Which surprised Ettrich because he was sure Coco would want to know more about his meeting with Alan Wales, but she didn't. He wanted to tell her about how the rat had vanished when the elevator reached the floor where Jack's doctor was and didn't reappear again until after the boy had been dropped at his mother's house. He wanted to describe the other things the rat had said, the secrets it had known about him. Ettrich wanted Coco to hear this story and then tell him what it all meant. But she didn't want to hear. She drove her little sports car through the streets and slapped his hand away when he tried to turn on the radio.

He crossed his hands in his lap and looked at the dashboard. In contrast to this perfectly kept car, a big hole gaped where the cigarette lighter should have been. And there was no gearshift knob.

When they stopped at a traffic light, he saw a woman waiting to cross the street. She was small, almost ugly, and dressed in shapeless clothes the color of old fruit. When he saw her, the first thing that crossed Ettrich's mind was "no man will ever try to make that woman laugh." No man would ever show off for her, try to impress her, or try and convince her he was worth dating.

A few blocks further on, he saw a very beautiful woman standing at a bus stop. They made eye contact at about the same time but she looked away and didn't look again at him. Women never looked back. He had realized that years ago. It was one of his small epiphanies. If a man passed a beautiful woman on the street, chances were he would stop, turn around, and look at her again. But women never looked back.

Over the *rummm* of the engine, Coco said "Her name is Alice Hooper."

"Alice Cooper?"

"*Hooper*. That woman you were just looking at; the one in the black coat."

He rubbed his hands together as if they were cold. The car motor was so loud that he almost couldn't hear the sound of his palms sliding against each other. "You know everything, don't you, Coco? You probably know the answer to every question I have."

"Probably."

"Then why don't you enlighten me to what the fuck has been going on in my life these last few days?"

She smiled but ignored his question. "You know what I *don't* understand, Vincent? Human love. Just when it starts making sense to me, something happens and I'm confused again."

"What's not to understand?"

It appeared she was going to say more but then she shook her head. "Forget it. We're here." She turned left and a block down pulled into the parking lot of the city zoo. Ettrich knew the place well because he had been bringing his kids here for years. It was a run-down place that should have been renovated years ago if for no other reason than humane purposes. The cages were too small, the keepers were at best desultory in keeping the place clean, and the only time you ever saw people there was on weekends and holidays. Even little Jack had once asked, "How come the animals all look so sad, Daddy?" Ettrich felt like saying anyone who had to live here would look sad.

Coco paid for their tickets and walked through the large arched front gates. Somewhere one of the animals let out a long, loud bellow that sounded frightening and weary at the same time. Coco walked fast through the place, obviously knowing her destination.

"It feels strange being here without my kids."

"You never go to the zoo by yourself?"

Her question stopped Ettrich for a moment. "No. I'm not a big *National Geographic* kind of guy. Why would I want to come here?"

"Because zoos are holy places, Vincent. I'm surprised you haven't recognized that yet. What with all of the other things you brought back from death."

"Holy? What do you mean?"

"Animals are on earth to protect mankind. When you gather a bunch of them together like this, you create a safe haven. Nothing can touch you here."

"Bullshit! A year ago a lion mauled a kid here when he got too close to its cage."

"Because he taunted the lion. Never taunt your guardians. I could give you ten examples of children falling into animals' cages and being protected by them."

"I don't believe that."

"You don't have to. Watch and see."

Something else came to him. "If they're here to protect us and these are such holy places, why do animals always look so sad at zoos?"

"Because they hate being kept captive. But they've chosen to sacrifice their freedom so that people can be safe."

Eventually they came to a large open yard that fronted the elephant house.

It was covered in what appeared to be red clay. Ettrich had been here often but for the first time realized that the space reminded him of a baseball field.

Because there were no bars to contain them, at first glance it appeared that the elephants could come right over. But as you got closer, you saw that there was a very deep and wide trench surrounding the space. If an animal went beyond a certain point, it would have fallen in and likely been hurt or killed.

Ettrich followed Coco to a chest-high stone wall that marked the boundary. They stood there listening to the odd and exotic zoo sounds around them. The crowing, screeching, growling, bellowing that is so normal and at the same time ominous at a zoo.

"Did your friend Alan Rat tell you about the mosaic?"

"He started to, but I didn't really understand what he was talking about."

"That's no surprise. What did he say?"

Ettrich was about to answer when he heard the unmistakable trumpeting of an elephant. One of the weird delights of a zoo— the sounds that are so familiar from television and films are real here but it's almost impossible to believe. He looked up in time to see a baby elephant come trotting out of the building, its trunk high in the air, its small eyes wide open and . . . happy. The little guy looked like he was having fun. Blowing its horn again, it kept running across the yard. Then Isabelle walked out of the same doorway, laughing. She stopped when she saw them, waved, and kept laughing. Behind her, a giant shadow loomed a moment and then turned into an adult elephant that looked as big as a helicopter. Without turning around, Isabelle reached behind and patted the helicopter on the trunk. It moved its head a twitch and gave her a good shove forward. She laughed again. The baby stood a few feet away from Coco and Ettrich staring at them.

"What is Isabelle doing in there?"

"Visiting Fiona and April. Fiona's the mother."

"But how did she get into the elephant house, or whatever you call it?"

"You'll see. That's where we're going now."

"I don't like elephants, Coco. They trample things."

"These two big girls are very nice. Didn't you see Isabelle laughing? Come on."

They walked a wide circle around the elephant yard. Ettrich kept his eye on his love because he was worried one of the pachyderms would knock her over or step on her or eat her or something else not nice. In contrast, Isabelle took Fiona's trunk in her two hands and brought it to her face. The elephant did not appear to mind.

"Didn't you even once notice the rat was wearing lipstick?"

Ettrich stopped and put his hands on his hips. "You told me you didn't see him as a rat. You saw him as something else."

"I just went back and relived it through your eyes. How could you not notice that it was wearing lipstick? It was mocking you, Vincent. Here's something you must know and don't forget it—animals never lie. They don't lie, they don't put on disguises, and they are always true to what they are. That's why you can trust them."

"Excuse me, Coco, but I do not trust lions. Or elephants or snakes—"

"Because you want them to be the creatures you imagined as a child. Lions should be the strong but sweet beasts in a Disney cartoon. But they aren't, so when they act like lions you're angry at them for not being the fantasy animals you imagined. Russian bears don't put on top hats and ride unicycles. Or sleep in bed next to Goldilocks. *People* force them to do those stupid things in circuses and films and children's books. Sure, some will be more docile or more ferocious than others, but in the end they will always, always be bears. And you never should turn your back on them. You should never even get near them; it's that simple. They're not being dishonest—*you* are in your perception of them."

Ettrich looked worriedly at Isabelle. "If that's true, shouldn't I be afraid for her in there now?"

"Yes, you should. But generally speaking, Fiona and April like people so you don't have to be *too* worried."

They continued walking and Ettrich had to ask, "So if the rat wasn't the dead me, who was it?"

Coco didn't stop. "It's what I just said to you—animals never lie, so when you bump into a big talking rat you can be sure it's lying."

"I'll remember that next time. But then what was it? It must have been something that knew me because it said all these things—"

Coco sucked in her cheeks, deliberating on whether to give a long or a short answer. "It was chaos, Vincent. And I'm going to explain all that in a minute so just hold on. Chaos is not your friend. It knows lots and lots about you but it is definitely not your friend."

While that thought tumbled around and around in his brain, he followed Coco into the elephant house. The first thing that hit him was the odor of the place. It was neither good nor bad but hugely alien; it was an aroma his nose couldn't have imagined in a million years. He couldn't remember if it had smelled like this the last time he'd been in this building a few months before. Jack liked elephants and always wanted to see them when he visited the zoo. The inside of the building was as big as a school gymnasium. Thick, closely spaced floor-to-ceiling metal bars separated visitors from the animals. There were signs posted everywhere to stay back behind the yellow line painted on the floor. Coco walked over to the cage door. She opened it with a long key she had in her pocket.

Ettrich was incredulous. "We're going *in* there?"

"Yes, you have to. Come on." She walked in and didn't look back. He followed but made sure the door was as wide open as it could be in case he had to run out of there for whatever reason. Vincent Ettrich was used to checking for exits. He was good at escaping, both physically and otherwise. He had to be, considering his history of romantic entanglements.

Coco walked to the center of the room. She turned to face him and once again began explaining the concept of the mosaic. It was a strange place for a theology lesson. Her voice echoed off the walls. The smell of the place and the awareness of what lived there kept distracting Ettrich from what she was saying. No one came into the building while she spoke, which in itself was strange because the elephant house was usually packed on weekends. Ettrich didn't comment on this because he was sure something weird was being done to keep them away. Even Isabelle and the two elephants stayed outside while Coco got down on her knees and, bringing out a handful of tiles, dropped them on the cement floor. "Come down here, Vincent. I want you to do something."

At the beginning of her explanation he kept looking around, convinced that any minute something was going to happen. Or someone was going to come in and ask what the hell are you two doing in here? At the very least, the elephants would return and with good reason want to know what these human beings were doing in their home, pushing small colored tiles around on the floor.

But all that changed when the mosaic Ettrich created rose into the air and exploded out in all directions. Then he was mesmerized, as Isabelle had been hours before. Interestingly, he understood immediately almost everything that followed. Even Coco was surprised when right at the beginning of her explanation he nodded and said simply, "I know. I know all of this."

Taken aback, she started to protest. Then she remembered where he had been. Her face relaxed and she murmured, "Of course you do." She finished quickly, answering whatever questions he had and clarifying a few details here and there.

"Yes, okay, all that I understand. But tell me why I was brought back. Why am I here?"

Coco walked out into the middle of the room, into the middle of that frozen confetti of tiles hanging motionless in the air. Turning to Ettrich, she raised both hands palms up, looked left, right, up, and down. Tiles surrounded her. "One of these is you, Vincent, as you know. One is Isabelle, and—" Without looking, she reached above her and plucked a white tile from its place. Bringing it down to chin level, she held it out toward him. "One of them is chaos. Let's say this white one. Chaos has always been a part of God's mosaic and always will be, no matter what form the mosaic takes or how many times it re-forms."

Ettrich looked at the tile in her open palm and thought it resembled a little white apple.

"But like everything else, chaos is different in every new mosaic. This time it has become conscious." The apple disappeared in her hand when she closed her fingers around it. "Before now, chaos was always just an unthinking force, like nature. When a tornado strikes and kills people on the left side of the street but not the right, that has nothing to do with a conscious decision; it's simply because that energy happened to move one way and not the other. Tornadoes don't think; they don't hate or love or reflect. They're weather and weather is a force. And until now, so was chaos. It just *was,* another element.

"But in this mosaic, chaos has gained consciousness. It has become aware." She opened her hand and the apple, although still white, had grown to twice its original size. "As that's happened, it's realized it likes *this* existence, likes being conscious." She closed her hand but opened it quickly. The apple was now as big as a golf ball. She put it back in the air in its original place. It looked wrong there, too big and out of place among all the other, smaller tiles. Coco looked up at it. "Chaos doesn't want things to change. It doesn't want a new mosaic to be formed. For a long time it has been doing everything it can to stop that from happening."

Suddenly all of the tiles, excepting the golf ball, flew back to the place where they had begun as Ettrich's mosaic. For a moment they became an entirely new one, different in every way from the design he had created. That lasted only long enough for him to register how dissimilar this one was from his own. Then more than half of the tiles fell to the floor and clattered across it. What remained hanging in the air of this new mosaic looked pockmarked and fragmentary, like a jigsaw puzzle someone started to assemble but abandoned.

Coco squatted down and began picking up tiles near her. "It's a lot more complex than this, but basically chaos has found a way to stop tiles from adhering to the mosaic when they return." She took one she had picked up off the floor and put it into the mosaic. It stuck for a moment but then fell out.

"How?"

She shook her head. "I don't know, Vincent. I'm just a worker ant. Those matters are for minds a lot bigger than mine." She smiled. "Like your son."

Ettrich's head snapped back. "*Jack?*"

"No, Anjo."

He looked at her uncomprehendingly until it came to him. Then he pointed hesitantly outside, toward Isabelle.

"Correct—*that* son. He and others like him have been sent out to try and stop this—"

"Sent from where, Coco?"

"From the mosaic."

Ettrich rubbed his chin. "I don't remember anything about what that was like."

"Because you were never actually in the mosaic. You were in purgatory, learning about it, when Isabelle came for you."

"Was that Anjo's doing?"

"Partly. But she was the one who decided to go and get you. It was an incredibly courageous act. Isabelle's not aware of it, but when she got there Anjo helped her find you."

"Why didn't he do it himself?"

"That's not possible. It must be done by a living soul who makes the conscious choice."

"Did she know about this, the mosaic and the chaos, when she went there for me?"

"No, Vincent. She went because she loved you and was given the chance to bring you back."

He slid his hands into his pockets and without thinking curled them into fists. "So you tricked her."

"Not at all. She got what she wanted. It just so happens there are other things you must do now that you're here."

"Like what? Why did I have to come back?"

"Because when he is born, Anjo won't know anything about this. Only through the proper education will he come to realize who he is and what he is meant to do. Most importantly you must teach him what you learned in purgatory so that he is able to use it in his life."

"But Coco, *I don't remember* anything about what happened there! My mind is blank; I have no memory of it."

"Then you're going to have to dig deep and find it in yourself. You must."

"But if I can't?"

She pointed to the half-completed mosaic. Another two tiles fell off it.

In frustration, Ettrich picked one of them up and threw it as hard as he could at a wall. It dropped and hit the floor long before reaching its target. "This is insane." That last word came out like a fist pounding a table.

"What's insane?" Isabelle had entered unnoticed via the elephant's door. Thirty seconds later the baby elephant came in too. It walked up to within a few feet of her and stood there, turning and twisting its trunk in the air. The animal appeared to be waiting for her new human friend to do something else fun.

"Coco's been telling me about the mosaic and the chaos."

Isabelle waited for him to continue. Ettrich expected *her* to say something. They looked at each other. The elephant waved its trunk, impatient now for something to happen. Three people and a baby elephant shared a silence none of them was happy with.

"Do you believe it, Fizz? Do you think what she said is true?"

Two more tiles fell off the mosaic. Isabelle looked at them and spoke. "I had a boyfriend once who had been a navy fighter pilot. He was one of those bravehearts who take off and land on aircraft carriers. Once he told me something I never forgot. Every pilot he flew with took one of his dog tags and kept it in his shoe. Do you know why?"

Ettrich was pissed off to hear about yet another Isabelle boyfriend. When had this guy happened? Ettrich didn't care why fly guys put dog tags in their shoe. He wanted to know how long ago this pilot had landed on Isabelle's flight deck.

"Vincent?"

"No, I don't know. Why?"

"Because when one of those planes crash, especially at sea, they rarely find the pilots' bodies—the impact is too great. But oddly enough, the one thing they often do find in the wreckage is feet. They find the pilots' feet. Nobody knows why, but that's why all the pilots put a dog tag in their shoe: If they crash and disappear, there's still a small chance *something* of them will survive and be recognized.

"I don't know what's true anymore, sweetheart. I know the baby's inside me and I know what I did to bring you back here. To me, Anjo is the dog tag in our shoe. No matter what happens to us, if we do this right now, he'll survive and he is as much us as anything else on earth."

"But say it is true, what are we supposed to do, Fizz? Do you have any idea?"

Before Isabelle answered, the first child entered the room. At first none of them noticed the little girl. She was dressed in new blue jeans, new red sneakers, and a spotless white T-shirt. She was shy. Like so many little girls she tried to remain invisible; she came in and, sidestepping to the left, immediately put her back to the wall and stood there like a small statue, trying to take up as little space in the world as she could.

The baby elephant was the first to say something. It looked at the girl and gave a short honk of hello. No one paid attention. Then a boy came in. He was shorter than the girl and had a very wide Hispanic face. He wore the same kind of clothes that she did. Standing together, they appeared to be in their school uniforms. Slowly more children trickled in, all wearing this outfit. They stood quietly on the other side of the bars separating them from the animals and watched. None of them approached the open cage door. The adults saw but ignored them. This was the zoo. Kids came here on school field trips.

The conversation went on between Ettrich and Isabelle. Coco put in a word here and there but for the most part kept quiet and let them talk it out. She watched them closely. They watched each other closely. None of the three watched as April the baby elephant walked slowly over to the children who were now standing close to the bars of the cage, watching everything.

April wanted them to give her something to eat. To a small degree she understood people and the bars on her cage. She understood how they separated her from people. But she also knew that if a person wanted, they could put their hand through the space between the bars and give her something nice to eat. She had to stretch her trunk as far as it would go to get them, but she had learned to do that long ago. To April, usually things offered her this way were tasty so she trusted most hands thrust her way holding something. Stopping two feet from the bars, she watched as many of the children hesitantly lifted their arms and moved their hands toward her. She knew what petting was too but that didn't interest her. She wanted food. Seeing all these clamoring hands, she thought some of them had to have something for her to eat.

Lowering her great head, she moved it slowly from left to right and back again. She liked to swing her head when she was thinking because it felt good. She also liked to pick things up from the ground with her trunk, like hay or grass or sometimes even carrots, and drop them on top of her head. April looked at the children and then looked away. She put one foot toward them and then brought it back. What did they have in those hands? Was it sweet or bitter? Would it be hard or soft in her mouth? She had been fed everything from popcorn to rock candy to the cork out of a Champagne bottle. She took the step toward them again and lowered her head. She had a small patch of vivid red hair on top of her head. Several of the children pointed to it and made fun. Behind her, the big people continued to talk in loud interesting voices. But the elephant was intent now on finding out what the little people had in their hands. She took another step closer.

"For God's sake, Fizz, you must know more than that. You were there—you brought me back from there!" Ettrich's voice was desperate and angry in equal measure.

Isabelle looked toward Coco for help. She saw something on the other side of the room that froze her.

A shriek unlike anything any of them had ever heard tore everything in half. It was high, desperate, and feral. Coco and Ettrich turned toward the sound. It was very difficult to grasp what was going on when they first saw the scene on the other side of the cage.

The elephant's back was to them. The animal faced a bunch of children who stood on the other side of the bars. But it was screaming and then they could see why—a number of these kids had hold of the elephant's trunk and were pulling it toward them. Despite the animal's size and legendary strength, it appeared powerless to stop this.

Ettrich stared and said in a spooked voice, "No fucking way." It looked both impossible and absurd. Like a stubborn donkey being dragged or a young puppy out for a walk, the elephant had lowered its ass to the ground and was trying desperately to pull its head away but to no avail. The kids had the trunk and were drawing it toward them. April continued to scream while she slid across the floor much too fast—as if her great big body weighed little in their small hands.

Coco understood what was happening almost at once, but she could not believe it. In the world where she had come from there were absolutely fixed rules and this was one of them: Animals protected mankind. Zoos were safe havens.

No more. Chaos had learned how to defeat the animals.

"Run, Vincent! Take Isabelle and get out of here." She pointed toward the giant open door leading to the outside exercise yard. From out there came a loud prolonged growl. It sounded like a lion but turned out to be the older elephant, coming to save her child. She ran through the door at a terrific speed and over to April. Coco ran after her. Ettrich grabbed Isabelle's hand and pulled her toward the door. A horrifying high scream came from behind them. It stopped abruptly and was followed by two other sounds: first a sharp, dramatic crunching and then a slopping, a wet splatter.

Isabelle shouted "No!" and tried to snatch her hand away. Ettrich would not let go. She pulled again, this time looking back toward the animals. He did too and regretted it for the rest of his life.

The children had already pulled April's giant head halfway through the bars of the cage, killing her. The skull had burst and there was blood everywhere. The last synapses, messages, and commands from the crushed brain were still traveling down to the distant corners of her great body, making it appear as if she were still living. Some of her did not yet know that it was over. Parts still moved, twitched, reacted, and tried to escape the death that had already come. Her legs crumpled and the body sank to the floor except for the head, still high and wedged between the now-glistening bars.

The mother elephant went up to April's body and pushed it, pushed it, trying to make it stand, to make it come back, to be alive again. She pushed it with her trunk, her foot; she pushed it with her brown head. When none of it did any good she nodded her head up and down and up and down.

Human beings do not understand death. To them it is only loss, something forever taken away, a new space where before there was none. But most animals understand it, which is why they treat death so differently. Because of this awareness, they smell it, push it, they piss on it and walk away. They know one day it will defeat them but while they are alive they own death; it is there for them to use or disdain.

Watching April die, none of the adults noticed the first children entering the cage. They filed in one by one through the open door. None of them were in a hurry. The expressions on their faces were mixed. Some looked happy, others indifferent. Most of them had blood on their white T-shirts and hands. That made them look like they had been doing something naughty like throwing paint at one another or having a food fight while their teacher was out of the room. The blood on their shirts had already dried to brown. Only the blood on their hands and some of their faces was still red.

Only when all of them were inside the cage did they move toward the grown-ups. Coco moaned, knowing it was too late. There was no way to escape them now, no way to escape this moment.

"Vincent, try to remember."

He didn't take his eyes off the kids. "Remember *what*?"

"Remember death. Remember what you learned there."

Before he could reply or even think of something to say, there was another noise outside. It was so singular that all of them froze when they heard it—the children, the adults, and particularly the elephant. At first it sounded like a kind of drumming but then that changed to a flapping, a scattered rushing, as if thousands upon thousands of birds had suddenly burst up and taken flight somewhere very near.

Ettrich was so tense that he gasped when his hand was squeezed. He looked at Isabelle, her eyes as frightened as his.

"Vincent, what is it? What's that noise?"

His eyes jumped from left to right. Then his whole head did the same thing—turned once left and then right. He whispered, "I don't know."

One of the primal sounds of the world was twenty steps away outside. It was the first time any of them had ever heard it. And that was because it was a sound the world rarely heard. The animals were gathering.

A male lion charged through the door followed immediately by a large flock of low-flying pigeons. All of them attacked the children. The lion, not breaking stride, leapt at them. Four of the kids effortlessly caught it in midair and snapped its thick neck in an instant. They dropped its body and the sound of it hitting the concrete floor was like that of a heavy rug being dropped.

The pigeons were next. Astonished as he was by what was happening, Ettrich still had the presence of mind to wonder what can birds do?

Eyes. They could fly straight at the children's faces and, because there were so many of them, pluck out eyes with their sharp beaks. For some time it even seemed this would work, that it would stop them. Screaming through fingers covered now with their own blood, most of the kids bent toward the ground and put their hands up to protect their faces as the birds pecked at them.

Separately a family of four badgers scuttled in the door and went straight for the children's legs. Never friends to man, these brothers and sisters were eager to put their claws and teeth to savage work.

More and more animals came. Strange and unexpected ones too—a zebra, an ostrich, two anteaters with claws longer than the badgers', mandrills that bit and fought with ferocious speed and agility. How could they not win? Each creature that entered the cage knew its strength and its task. None of them hesitated.

Chaos is stubborn but it is not stupid. In time it realized this would not work. Its children, no matter how strong and vicious, were no match for a zoo full of enraged animals. So chaos broke another rule that had existed since the beginning of time on earth.

Before the eyes of Ettrich and the others, the children metamorphosed into the animals that were attacking them. Four badgers became five. But that new fifth had the ferocity and strength of the other four combined. One moment they were having a joyous time tearing a child's short legs to pieces. Then the child became a badger turning on the one closest and biting all the way through its snout. The others instinctively leapt back but it was already on them, using their tricks and moves, snapping, slashing its claws into the belly of one and across the exposed throat of another. It killed them using their shock and disbelief to its great advantage.

All of this happened so fast.

Without doubt animals sometimes turn on one of their own. A deformed baby is born in a litter and instinctively the mother destroys it. If necessary, alpha males fight to the death for control of a herd or a brood. Or sometimes madness prevails and one is driven to kill another.

But not like this, not every single one of them. All of the animals that had come to defend these human beings were now being slaughtered by their own. It was beyond sacrilege.

Ettrich pulled on Isabelle's arm and this time she didn't resist. They hurried out of the cage into the exercise yard, which at the moment was empty and quiet. The obscenity of sounds coming from indoors made the contrast even greater.

"Where is Coco?"

"I don't know—still inside, I guess."

"Shit." He ran a hand across the top of his head. "Stay here."

He pointed to the ground as if where they were standing was safe.

Now it was Isabelle's turn to hold on to his hand when he tried to pull it away. "What are you going to do, Vincent?"

"Try and get her out of there." He didn't add that he had remembered something. In the midst of the bedlam, a realization had come to him. Ettrich was fairly certain it was true this time and could help them now. "Jesus, look at that!"

On the other side of the yard five animals stood next to each other, staring at them: a llama, an oryx, a panther, a Humboldt penguin, and a rare Saruvian green crane. If it could be said that animals have facial expressions then these all wore the same one— sadness.

All of them knew they must now enter the cage and join the battle. They also knew they would die fighting. They had already sacrificed their freedom to come and live in this dreadful, false place. But even that was being taken from them now.

Their lives had been spent in cages although each of them knew how to escape whenever they chose. All of these animals had sat for thousands of interminable days on cement, tree stumps, or ugly bare earth, doing nothing else but eating the same food in the same amount, talking among themselves, and sleeping. Forever bored, they watched and waited through the tedium for something like this to happen. That was what they lived for, that was why they were here. But they had always been told there would be a chance of surviving. Now they knew there was none. It was as simple as that—they would die.

Ettrich felt their courage and their sadness in equal measure. It was unbearable. He freed his hand from Isabelle's and gently touched her cheek. He did not know that Anjo had told her to let him go, that she must.

Still she couldn't help saying, "But what can you do against *that*? What could anyone do?"

He wanted to say something to her but his mind was blank

because he was very frightened. "Just wait here." He started back across the yard toward the door. As he got closer he was able to see more and more of what was happening inside. The horror of it made him want to run away. Steeling himself, Ettrich did what had come clear to him before: He spoke to his dead self.

Not some giant rat wearing lipstick this time, but the other half of Vincent Ettrich. The half of his being that was born the moment *this* self died in the hospital months before. It was one of the only things he knew now beyond doubt: There was a living self and a dead self. Both were essential to taking us through the complete human experience and back to the mosaic.

He spoke out loud to it. "What can I do?"

It answered immediately. "Nothing. *You* can't do anything to help her. But I can." Something spoke to him but Ettrich wasn't sure if he heard or imagined the voice. It spoke again. "There is no chaos in death, so it cannot perceive me. Take out your knife."

Without hesitating Ettrich reached into his pocket and found the "Lile Lock" folding knife he had carried for years. It was short and fat with a beautiful staghorn inlay. He loved touching it when his hands were bored. He'd always thought of it as a kind of talisman despite the fact he rarely used it for anything other than opening letters or cutting an apple in half.

"You are going to enter your knife and then I am going to take over your body. That way, chaos will not be able to see you when you go back in there and you will be safe. I will do whatever I can for Coco. But you and I can never be separated and that takes precedence over everything else. I will have that knife with me the whole time."

"How do you do that? How do you . . . put me into it?"

There was a wild flurry of strange and violent noises from inside the cage. The animals on the far side of the yard started moving toward it. Isabelle shouted for Ettrich to come back, come back.

"I don't do it—only you can. You move your numen from your

body into the knife. You can do it with any object."

"How?"

Isabelle did not understand what Vincent was doing. He wouldn't come back when she called. Now he stood unmoving thirty feet away, holding something in his hand she couldn't see. The five animals brushed past as if she were invisible on their way to the building.

The beautiful green bird was the last because it was so slow on its big flat feet. It waddled comically after the others like some silly movie sidekick. Passing Ettrich, it jerked its long head around to look at him. Flapping its wings, it lifted off the ground and flew away screeching. But from what Isabelle saw, Vincent hadn't done anything to disturb it. He hadn't even moved.

His knees suddenly buckled and whatever he held fell out of his hand. But then he moved so quickly to catch it that Isabelle didn't have a chance to see what the object was. He put it back in his pocket and walked toward the cage.

Once inside the building, the other Ettrich surveyed the carnage in there with detachment. All of the real animals were either dead or dying. The chaos animals were finishing them off with cool assurance. Some distance away Coco lay on her stomach near the lion. What had been done to her was unimaginable.

As the chaos animals worked on, unaware of his presence, Ettrich took the knife out of his pocket and opened it. He started to walk through the place, touching bodies with the tip of the blade. He did not wait to see what happened—he only bent down, touched whatever was left, and quickly moved on. As he had said, none of the chaos animals sensed he was there although he was close by them at all times. While he moved, it grew quieter and quieter in there as the last animals gave whimpers and died. After touching perhaps thirty of the corpses he straightened up, carefully folded the blade closed, and dropped the knife in his pocket. He had not gone anywhere near Coco's body. Twice while moving he looked over and smiled as if he knew something about it that was reassuring.

One by one the chaos animals stopped and began to clean themselves as any animal might after such dirty work.

This new Ettrich watched them a while. He brought his right hand up to eye level and, looking closely, turned it back and forth, noticing every detail. He brought it to his nose, smelled it, and then the rest of the arm up to the elbow. It held the faintest fragrance, something citrusy and nice—soap. He rubbed his palms together and felt the friction-heat grow between them. He had never experienced any of these sensations and they were pleasant.

When he brought his hands apart, he saw the spirit rise from the first animal he had touched. It came out of the massive leg of the dead mother elephant. Looking like a long white string, it broadened until it was full size. Others were rising now too, one after the other. He had been told about these things but had never witnessed them personally. From an ear, a severed wing, the still-shiny eye of a dead badger they emerged and grew to their proper size. The chaos animals were inches away but sensed nothing. They continued to lick their paws and bellies. With closed contented eyes they rubbed their paws across their faces, knowing the job was done.

When the spirits of the dead animals, the *Pemmagast,* had risen, there were some seconds of almost-stillness that this other Ettrich reveled in. He looked from one side of the great cage to the other. It was full of beings that, like him, did not belong on earth and never should have been permitted to come here. He smelled his hand again, the lemon there, a moment, two. Then he said only their name, *"Pemmagast,"* and the slaughter began.

A Few Miles of Night

"She's dead."

"She can't be dead—it's Coco. She's—"

"Fizz, she's dead. She's gone, believe me."

Isabelle put her hands up into her armpits as if she were very cold. "Okay, she's dead. So then what are we supposed to do? What protection do we have now?"

"For now we're all right."

"What do you mean we're all right? That doesn't sound very reassuring. How do you know?"

"We're protected. For now it's all right."

"Stop being so cryptic. Don't talk to me like this, Vincent. I want to know what you know. It's not right to shut me out. I'm in the middle of this, and maybe even more than you." She pointed to her stomach.

"You're right. The Pemmagast are protecting us now: the spirits of the dead animals I told you about. They're what saved us back there. It had never been done before. They were like a surprise attack and chaos had no defense against them. But I don't know how long their power will last. Chaos is smart—it figures things out."

Isabelle's voice trembled. She hated that but she couldn't control it. "So maybe they can't protect us. Maybe they won't be able to do anything when it comes back."

Ettrich hesitated and then sighed. "Maybe. But it's all we've got now until we can find something better. Anjo is the key to everything. Chaos wants him because he's a direct threat to it. But I know something else now that I didn't before—once Anjo is born, chaos can't touch him. He'll be protected and there's no way it will ever be able to harm him."

"How do you know?"

Ettrich lowered his voice and said, "He told me."

Isabelle knew that "he" was the other Ettrich. "It's the truth, Vincent? You're not just saying it to make me feel better?"

"It's the truth. But there's something else just as important, Fizz. Even though he'll be protected in his life, there's no guarantee Anjo will learn how to do what's necessary."

"What do you mean?"

"If we don't raise him correctly, he won't be equipped to do the things they need him to do when he's older."

"Who cares, Vincent? Fuck *them*! Anjo is our child, not theirs. If he grows up just wanting to play basketball and look at girls, then that's fine with me."

"No, it's not that simple."

She slapped the dashboard with both hands. "Oh yes, for me it is that simple."

They were sitting in his car in the parking lot of the restaurant where they'd eaten the night before.

"Isabelle, you should understand this better than anyone. Your unborn child talks to you. They permitted me to return from the dead. And you've seen what's been happening since you arrived here. Every one of those things is impossible, but they've happened to us. Anjo is not just another kid."

Both of them shuddered when Ettrich's cell phone rang. He

took it out of his pocket and looked at the telephone number on the screen to see who was calling. He didn't recognize it. Pressing the connect button, he brought the phone to his ear and said slowly, "Hello?"

"Vincent, it's Bruno Mann."

Ettrich's body slumped against the seat. "Hey, Bruno."

"Where are you?"

"In my car. What's up?"

"Did you bring your son home yet?"

Ettrich straightened up again. No more, he thought. Please, no more right now. Not Jack. Not that. "Yes, I took him home. Why?"

"And it was all right? You had no problems or anything at home?"

"No. Why are you asking?"

Mann ignored the question. "And you had no other problems with anyone else since we were at the hospital? None with other people?"

There was the incident at the zoo but he didn't want to talk about that. The safety of his children took precedence over everything else. "Nothing, Bruno. What's going on? Did something happen to you?"

"Yeah, Vincent, something happened— Suddenly everyone knows now that I died. When I got home my wife freaked out. She screamed when she saw me walk in the door—literally screamed. 'But you're dead, you're dead!' She kept chanting it. What could I say to her—yes darling, you're right?"

"What did you do?"

"I tried to calm her down. But good luck doing that—try calming someone down after they've seen a ghost. And that ghost is you."

"So where are you now?"

"In my house—downstairs, trying to think of something convincing to say to her. But Vincent, you know what this means? If it's true then we're shut out of everything—no job, no friends or family, no bank account—nothing. We can't see anyone we know anymore. We can't even risk *being* seen because it's too damned dangerous. To the world we're dead, which means—"

Ettrich's voice took on a hard edge. "I get the point, Bruno. I've got to think about this. Let me get back to you in a while."

"Don't you think we should meet and talk about it?"

"No, not till I've thought it through. I'll call you later." Ettrich disconnected before Bruno could say anything else. The only thing on his mind was that if it were true, he would never be able to see his children again. His contact with them would be lost forever. The thought was crushing. He squeezed the phone in his hand until the plastic squeaked. When he heard the sound he released it and the phone fell to the floor between his feet.

Isabelle waited for Vincent's face to relax before asking what happened. In a defeated monotone he told her.

She wasn't having it. Reaching down, she picked up the telephone and dialed his home number. Ignoring her, he stared through the windshield at the restaurant and thought about his kids.

"Hello? I'm calling from the alumni office at Rhodes College. I'd like to speak with Vincent Ettrich, please. Oh, I'm sorry. Yes, I do." She tapped Ettrich's shoulder. When he looked she shook her head and smiled. "Yes, I'm ready. Yes, I've got it. Thank you so much." She clicked off and dropped the phone in his lap. "Your wife was very nice and said you don't live there anymore. Then she gave me the telephone number of your apartment. So I guess you're still alive in the eyes of the world."

His face relaxed but his eyes remained skeptical. "What does that mean? Why would Bruno say that if it's not true?"

"It can be one of two things—they only did it to him. Or he's lying to you."

"Why would he lie? That makes no sense."

She waited to let the realization come to him but he said nothing more. "Do you trust him? Do you believe what he tells you?"

"Well, yeah, I guess. I don't know. I work with the guy. I've known him a long time."

"That doesn't mean anything, Vincent, especially now. You should know that."

"But his name was tattooed on the back of Coco's neck! That's how this whole thing started for me. Why would she have his name there?"

"Did Coco ever tell you?" She put her hand on his knee and gave it a gentle squeeze.

He looked at it. His thoughts were whizzing around so fast now that it felt like his brain was a centrifuge. "No, but I assumed . . ." His voice died, and then rose again. "And what about the hospital? What about that whole thing there with him and Tillman Reeves?"

"I don't know, but I would be very careful about who you trust these days."

He sucked in his lower lip and put his hand on top of hers. Eventually he slid it up and over to her stomach where their son was hiding out. "I was just thinking of something someone said to me years ago: The way to get out of a labyrinth is to walk across the top of it."

"That sounds good but what does it really mean?"

"Kitty's grandfather said it and, according to the way he'd lived his life, it was sound advice. He was almost a hundred years old when he died. The biggest scoundrel I ever met. He'd had three wives and treated them all like shit. In the meantime he slept with any woman who said yes to him. He borrowed money from everyone but never paid it back. He declared bankruptcy I don't know how many times but managed to walk away from all the wreckage . . . The guy was a bad character in a Teflon suit. He lived to be ninety-seven years old. But he was charming; I gotta say that for him. On the last day of his life that guy was more charming than Clark Gable."

Isabelle loved the way Ettrich perceived and talked about life. It was one of the things she had missed most in these long months away from him. Even today with all that was going on, she was so happy to hear him talk about nothing special. "You were with him when he died?"

"No, but just before. He loved Kitty so we used to go visit him in the hospital. Listen to this—that last time I saw him, we walked into his room. Naturally he had finagled a single although he had no money for it. We went in and he was wearing a black GET SHORTY baseball cap, a pair of Ray-Ban sunglasses, and a bright red jogging suit. This was seven o'clock at night in January. On a boom box in the corner *Abba's Greatest Hits* was playing. He said he liked them because they had a good beat. A hundred fucking years old. Walk across the top of the labyrinth. That's pretty good advice, you know?"

"But what do you think it means?"

Ettrich smiled, remembering. "He told me where he got the idea. He was once walking through Piccadilly in London. Someone had put a labyrinth in the middle of the sidewalk. It looked like a giant black-and-white plastic tablecloth. It was maybe ten feet by ten feet; really big. Maybe it was some kind of conceptual art. He said the most interesting thing about it was pedestrians were making a wide circle around it. They'd go way out of their way to avoid walking on the thing although it was clear it had been put there for people to use. The only ones walking on the thing were kids having fun trying to figure out the way to the center. A crowd had stopped to watch.

"After a while an old woman came along. You know the kind who is carrying too many plastic bags and mumbling to herself? Now *she* wasn't having any of it—she needed to get from point A to point B and B was on the other side of this labyrinth. So she just walked straight across it. He said the greatest part of it was all the people who'd stopped to watch were clearly angry that she did it—

that she'd ignored the labyrinth. You could see it in their faces. But then they all looked around at each other and began smiling. As if they understood that they were the fools and she was the clever one. Why not walk across it when you're in a hurry to get someplace?

"I've got to figure out how to do that here. So far we've been saying if we can't go left, let's try right. But this ain't your everyday labyrinth. It's not just made up of lefts and rights, but also ups and downs, a mosaic, the Pemmagast and I don't know what else. It's like one of those games of three-dimensional chess where you have to play on many levels at once if you're going to win."

"But how do we do that? How do you get above this so you can look down and figure out the right path to take?"

Ettrich touched her stomach again. "Maybe Anjo can help."

Bruno Mann was annoyed, but that was nothing new. He hated being human and he hated human beings. Hated the heaviness of the body, the slowness of how everything moved and functioned, how it smelled, the *needs* it constantly had. It needed air and food and warmth and cold. The list was never-ending. A body was continually hungry for something, always unsatisfied or uncomfortable, complaining, unhappy with whatever situation it was in.

He had been human so long that some days he almost forgot what it was like to be anything else. It was a disease that moved into your system and infected every part of you until finally you were terminally human and there was no way back. He knew others of his kind who thought that it was okay. He knew some who had come to like it quite a lot and didn't mind being here one bit. Not him. Not Bruno Mann. The longer he was marooned on this desert island called the Human Race the deeper his antipathy toward it grew.

And the latest insult was this: Vincent Ettrich had said he didn't want to meet. Bruno had been around Ettrich a long time and had played him like a fish on a line, reeling him in and then letting him go out just far enough so that Vincent thought he was free. Then Bruno would yank him back. Not that Ettrich ever knew what was going on. When he was dying in the hospital, Bruno had been one of the only people who'd visited him and Ettrich wept at the kindness of the gesture.

But now the resurrected Ettrich didn't want to meet until he'd figured things out. What a laugh. Vincent couldn't even figure out how to keep his dick in his pants.

Perhaps Bruno was upset only because he'd been so pleased with his "They know we're dead!" plan. It was such a smart and appropriate way to begin the endgame with Ettrich. Further isolate and confuse him, cut him off at every pass, close off all his options until it was just him and his flaky girlfriend. Then go in and finish it.

Originally Bruno Mann had been sent to do five other things. It was just coincidence that he came in contact with Ettrich. But as he got to know Vincent and observed his impressive rabbitlike promiscuity, he realized this man and his obsession with women could be useful in a small way.

Certainly chaos encourages broken hearts and promises. Pathetic as it is, love is the great leveler and nothing other than imminent death causes greater confusion in the human soul. Because he was often bored, Bruno took Ettrich on as a kind of pet project and enjoyed watching him blow through women's lives like a hurricane, leaving little standing in the way of pride or self-esteem. The high point came when Vincent actually left his wife and children for another woman, only to see that new woman reject him and disappear from his life altogether. Then as a kind of afterthought, Ettrich contracted a particularly enthusiastic cancer that metastasized immediately, ravaging his body and killing him in months. Bruno had played no part in any of it but he sure got a big kick out of the scenario as it played out.

So it came as a genuine shock the morning he walked into the office months later and saw Ettrich there flirting with a secretary as if nothing had changed in the months since he had died. What the hell was this? What the hell was going on here?

At first no one could tell him anything because they had all been taken completely off guard. How had it happened? Who were the ones responsible for bringing Mr. Hot Pants back? There were meetings and recriminations. No one had seen this coming—they had all been blindsided. No one was willing to take responsibility either. Someone had snuck Ettrich back into life under their radar. As a result, they all looked like incompetent fools. Sound the alarm! Groups were mobilized. Plans never before conceived of were whipped up and put hurriedly into place. They were winging this one and, boy, was it obvious.

Bruno picked up a magazine, looked at the cover, and dropped it back on the coffee table. What was he supposed to do while he waited for Mr. Ettrich to "think it through"? If it had been anyone else, he would have gone over to their house, fucked them up, and forgotten about it. But since doing a Lazarus on them, Vincent had to be handled very carefully now because no one knew what else he was capable of. Add to that what Isabelle Neukor's special, dangerous child was capable of and you had yourself an unwieldy situation.

He picked up the magazine again and let it fall open in his hands. Before he could focus on a page the telephone rang. Thinking it was Ettrich, he said, "Good boy," as if addressing a dog that had brought him a stick. Then he picked up the receiver.

It was not Ettrich. It was not human. It was Bruno Mann's boss. Speaking in the same mysterious language Coco had used earlier to scold the lipsticked rat, it explained what had happened at the zoo. While it yammered on, Bruno looked at his fingernails and ran his tongue around the inside of his mouth. He wondered again why his boss insisted on using a telephone to communicate. Did he think it was quaint or cute? Worse, had he become one of the complacent fools who liked life as a human and was satisfied with this ridiculous method of being heard? Had he really sunk so low?

One thing Bruno knew was not to interrupt. He emptied his mind and let the voice in his ear have its long-winded say. None of the details surprised him, although they were absorbing. Despite loathing humanity, he believed it was a lot smarter than they gave it credit for. Again and again he had seen instances of how quick-witted and capable people were when it came to recognizing and solving problems. He had said this more than once in planning sessions but was invariably dismissed as being unduly pessimistic or just plain wrong.

Now who was wrong? Dumb old Ettrich had outsmarted them and escaped. Worse, they didn't know where either he or his girlfriend was because of the Pemmagast, who had never had the impudence to show their ugly little faces here—until today.

Bruno's eyebrows rose way up when he heard they had done the rescue. The *Pemmagast?* He wished this conversation was on tape so that he could play it back later and listen again to his boss splenetically splutter about how those shitty little miserable ectoplasmic *nothings* had triumphed. It was unthinkable, hilarious, and right in line with what Bruno had been telling his superiors all along. But he was cynical enough to know that his insight would only make them angrier at him now for being so prescient. None of us likes being wrong, especially when we're offered a chance to be right but ignore it.

The description of the debacle at the zoo finally, finally wound down and the boss stopped talking. Bruno chewed on a thumbnail, waiting to hear if another flood of words would be forthcoming but none was.

Nothing was. For the longest while there was only silence or an almost-silence because there was always some kind of noise in the background when chaos was on the phone.

"Is there anything you would like me to do?" To his surprise, the silence held. He didn't know whether to repeat his question or be still.

"You hate it here, don't you, Bruno?"

"Yes sir, I hate it."

More silence and then, "What would you do to get out?"

"*Anything,*" said the Mann who didn't want to be a man.

"What happened today was very bad."

Bruno was paying full attention now. "Yes sir."

"Demoralizing."

He waited. Maybe, just maybe—

"I want you to go see the King of the Park."

It was all he could do not to piss his pants. The command was so unexpected, the idea so overwhelming, that he tried to swallow but found he could not.

"Bruno, did you hear me?"

"Ye-yes sir. But I thought—"

"Do you want to get out of here or not?"

"Yes sir, but—"

"It's either that or another fifty million years of drinking tomato soup here."

Dropping his head back, Bruno squeezed his eyes as tight shut as they would go. He had just stepped into the biggest pile of shit in the universe and there was no way out of it now. "Yes sir, I'll go."

It was a barbershop. Bruno had often heard it described but like everyone else he knew, he had never gone anywhere near the place because of who worked there. Not even out of curiosity and there was no one on earth Bruno was more curious about than the King of the Park.

His first impression of the place was that there was nothing special about it. It had a black-and-white sign, a narrow façade, and an old-fashioned revolving barber pole in front. It was situated on a nondescript, lower-middle-class neighborhood street that faced a small park. The kind of park you see in any city—full of kids racing around on well-worn patches of grass, climbing on monkey bars, and pumping swings while their mothers watched and chatted among themselves. A few would-be tough guys leaned against a graffiti-covered wall, smoking and sneering at whatever caught their attention. Four giant old trees dwarfed the park and made it look even smaller than it was. Bruno could imagine the place overflowing in the summer with people trying to catch some sun or a breeze, drinking cold beer from quart bottles wrapped in brown paper bags, listening to music, trying to make this little dumpy oasis into some kind of ersatz vacation spot five minutes from their apartments.

On one side of the shop was a shoe repair, on the other a dismal-looking pizza parlor. It was eight o'clock at night. The shoe repair was dark. A few dim lights were on in the pizza joint, making it look even more unappealing. The place was understandably empty. In contrast, the barber shop was brightly lit and appeared to be full of customers. Who went to the barber at eight P.M.? Normally Bruno would have been slightly interested to know why a barbershop in a blah part of town was jumping with people at that time of night. But not now. Given the chance, he would have run barefoot across twenty miles of flaming lava rather than do what he knew he had to do next.

Nervously licking his lips, he hitched up his trousers and started across the street. Halfway there he stopped because he was so damned frightened. He could see individual faces in there now. All men, they looked ordinary enough but this was one of the most unordinary places on earth for those in the know. It was home to the

King of the Park. For the fourth time in a few hours, Bruno's bowels rumbled threateningly, telling him they were close to letting loose because he was forcing them to go into that building. Yet another thing he despised about being human—the way the body revolted against you when it didn't like being told to do something.

Summoning his courage, he continued walking, although nine-tenths of him was moaning no-no-no. This was not part of the job description. Long ago when he had first heard about the King of the Park he had reacted like one who hears about yetis or the Komodo dragon—terrible frightening things, but nothing to worry about because I have no intention for the rest of my life of going to either the Himalayas or Indonesia. But now here he was, through no decision of his own, about to face King Yeti himself. Bruno reached the barbershop and with only a slight hesitation opened the door.

Loud music was playing inside. Elvis was singing "Viva Las Vegas!" A few of the men in there looked up, registered his presence, and then went back to what they had been doing—chatting, reading magazines, catching a little catnap while they waited for their turn in the chair. There were three barber chairs, all of them occupied. Seven chairs against the wall for waiting customers, one of them empty. A barber who looked Turkish or Middle Eastern with a shoe-brush moustache and hands the size of pizza paddles gestured with his head for Bruno to sit in the empty chair. The barber working next to him looked over, smiled, and went back to buzz-cutting the head of his customer.

It was just a barbershop and that in itself was hard to digest. Brown and yellow shiny paint, some autographed photos on the wall of forgotten third-rate celebrities who'd once deigned to visit. A smiling black boxer with both fists up, a baseball player with a bat on his shoulder, a singer with a jelly-roll haircut and a 1950s microphone held in one hand. The place smelled strongly of brewing coffee and hair cream.

A few minutes passed and the song ended. The man in the chair next to Bruno's stood up and went over to the door to look out at the dark street. Was that him, the one, the infamous King? He wore neatly pressed khakis, a denim shirt, and work boots. He had shiny black hair and long sideburns. He was not someone you would look at twice on the street.

But maybe that was the point: No one Bruno knew had ever seen the King of the Park. They just spoke of him with dread, fascination, and thirdhand stories you couldn't be sure were true.

The man at the door turned around and looked at the room. He smiled, rocking back and forth on his heels. Then to Bruno's very great surprise, the guy began to tap-dance.

"Uh-oh, here he goes again."

"Wuds dis, tonight's entertainment in the Boom Boom Room?"

"Shut up! I like it when Gary dances."

And dance he did. Gary's work boots had thick rubber heels so instead of tap, they clunked as he moved around on the yellow and green checked linoleum floor.

The men in there all had something to say about the dancer. Most of their comments were funny or complimentary and not one of them was mean. It was clear they were used to the performance and liked it. Tap-dancing Gary. Bruno was more taken aback by this sweet weird event than if a two-headed Cyclops had appeared breathing fire.

"Hey, buddy, you're up."

Realizing the barber was talking to him, Bruno looked at the other customers.

"Don't worry about them. They're just here for the floor show," the barber said and patted the headrest of his chair. "Come on. Let me cut your hair."

Bruno went over and sat down. The barber wrapped a stiff piece of paper around his neck and covered his front with a sheet.

"How do you want it?" He looked at Bruno in the mirror and

snipped his scissors together a few times to show he was ready to begin.

"Uh, I guess trim it all around."

Gary kept dancing but slower now. Looking at his feet, he threw his hands out from his sides and dipped his knees now and then. Some of the men went back to their conversations and magazines. The barber with the moustache put in another CD. More Elvis came on—"Suspicious Minds."

"Fuckin' Elvis. A man cannot come into this shop without getting drowned in Elvis."

"My shop, my music."

Hearing that, Bruno whipped eyes-left so he could better scope out Mr. Moustache. *This* guy was the King of the Park? Watching closely, he looked for some sign or indication that there was more there than just a barber with thick hands. He wore a black short-sleeved polo shirt and khakis. Khakis. The tap dancer wore them too. Did they mean something? Did all of the men in the room wear them? A quick check around told him no. No one else wore a black polo shirt either.

"So where's the donuts? I don't know about the rest of you, but I'm ready for my glazed."

"Yeah, it's about time. Who got them tonight? Dean?"

"They're right here." Dean reached under his seat and pulled out a very large box emblazoned with the logo of Krispy Kreme donuts. He opened it and, with the look of a saint either expiring or achieving religious ecstasy, stared at the contents and inhaled deeply. "Fresh, boys. I saw them take these fresh out of the oven." He chose a shiny glazed donut for himself and passed the box to his right. Ooh's and aah's followed its progress around the room.

Bruno nervously watched this, the whole time thinking, "This is nuts. This whole thing is insane." His eyes ping-ponged between the traveling box and the barber with the moustache. Something had to happen. But nothing happened. The men ate donuts and some got white powdered sugar on their chins and fingers. Even Bruno's barber stopped his haircut, slid the scissors into a breast pocket, and chose a cinnamon twist when the box reached him. Bruno looked sideways and caught the guy's eye.

"And what kind would you like, sir? A plain, a French cruller, and a chocolate-covered are left. Which one for you?"

Bruno's hand rose beneath the sheet when he unconsciously pointed a thumb at his chest. "Me?"

"Sure! That's the tradition here: Every night we have donuts. And whoever's here gets one."

"Gotta have the donuts," someone added.

"That's right," the barber nodded.

Baffled, Bruno said, "Uh, plain. A plain would be great."

The almost-empty box came to him. The barber winked and took a big bite of the cinnamon twist. He gestured with his chin for Bruno to do the same. What else was there to do? He took a small bite and it was delicious. He loved donuts and had them almost every day for breakfast.

"Aren't they good? Nothing beats a Krispy Kreme."

If someone had happened to pass by outside at that moment and looked in, they would have seen a bunch of men contentedly eating donuts—every one of them. It was an odd picture but de-lightful too. They looked like a bunch of grown-up kindergartners at milk-and-cookie break. All of them looked like they were very happy.

When he was almost finished eating, Bruno looked in the mirror and froze. It was the first time he had actually looked at himself since the tap dancer began the evening's entertainment. What he saw was so shocking that he didn't realize the music had stopped and every man in the room was staring at him.

Slowly raising his hands to his face, Bruno touched it with ten-tative, frightened fingers. Because it was a face he had never seen before. But he could feel his fingers touching the skin on the cheeks.

"What is this?" he managed to ask himself, the barber standing nearby, and everyone there. None of them said anything. It was not a horrible face. It was not even very special but it was definitely not his. Yet he could see and feel his own fingers touching it. They felt the unfamiliar cheeks, eyes, and nose. They ran across the lips of the long, flat mouth and then a square chin that did not really fit the structure of the face.

"I'll be finished soon." The barber was at work again cutting his hair. But the hair was gray-blond now, not the dark brown it had been half an hour ago.

"What is this?" Bruno asked again, staring only at the barber now.

"You came here looking for the King of the Park, right?" The barber pointed at the mirror in front of them, toward the new Bruno Mann there. "Well, you found him."

"Me?"

"You. Whoever comes here looking for the King, we help them find him. See those guys?" He gestured toward the other donut eaters. "When I'm done with you here, then they'll do their work on you. Each guy's got a special talent. Mine is heads." He gently touched the scissors to Bruno's temple "And brains."

"*I'm* the King of the Park? How can that be?"

The tap dancer said, "This time you are. Next time there will be somebody else. We make a king when we need one. When he's finished with his job, he leaves."

Bruno Mann understood *that*. "You mean he goes back? He gets to go—"

"That's right. Life here is finished for him. We fix you up, you do your job, and then you go home."

Now it was sinking in and it began to feel good. "So there's never been just one King of the Park?"

"Like one Big Bad Wolf? No, the job is too big for one person.

There's been a bunch of them and that's why he's got such a scary reputation. One King does one job and then out. You're home free, Mr. Plain Donut. That's what you wanted, wasn't it?"

"It sure as hell is. What am I supposed to do?"

"First we'll fix you up. Then we'll tell you everything."

The man who walked out of the barbershop the next morning did not look anything like the blond Bruno saw in the mirror a few hours before. This fellow was short and fat enough so that he pen-guin'd slightly from side to side when he walked. His shoes were shiny black and unwrinkled. He had a big head but not enough ginger-colored hair to cover it. As a remedy, the hair was brushed from the back of the head over the top to the front. He could have passed for a member of the court of Julius Caesar. The hairdo looked ludicrous and generally speaking so did he. Both his blue suit and rigid white shirt had the reflective sheen of cheapness on them, not a natural fiber in either. His tie had a yellow and green paisley design that looked vaguely bacterial.

After leaving the barbershop, Bruno could not resist trying his new powers on the first person he encountered. It was an old man who had little left besides good posture, a meager pension, and happy memories of a successful long marriage that had ended six months before with the death of his beloved wife.

The new King of the Park recognized this. Even before the old man noticed him, Bruno blinked and turned all of this stranger's happy memories one degree to the left or right and made them either sad or bitter. Nothing major, because one or two degrees is usually enough to destroy a moment or a life. The kiss that goes on too long, the one word that wrecks everything, the choice of mean-ness instead of silence . . . With one flick of his new mind, the King of the Park poisoned most of what had mattered in this man's life.

The only sign of its effect on him was that he lost his good posture and bent five inches forward, as if someone had put a heavy package on his shoulders that he must carry into what was left of the rest of his life.

The men in the barbershop had disagreed on just how uninteresting he should appear. Bruno had no say in the matter. They talked around and through him as if he were not there. But that didn't bother him though because just listening to how much they knew and the intelligence of their debate more than confirmed he was in expert hands.

He was transformed five times over the course of the night. They permitted him to leave the barber chair only to piss and throw up once in the sink when, in their eagerness, they altered him too fast and his inner organs revolted.

What was most surprising was that he did not feel any of these changes. From one moment to the next he would be an entirely different man in height, weight—everything. But he did not sense these things taking place, outside of the time they did it too fast and made him puke. The fact he felt nothing was almost more astounding than looking in the mirror and seeing each new version of himself sitting in the chair. It was bizarre times ten. After all, he *was* the clay they were working with.

His barber's name was Franz and eventually Bruno got up the nerve to ask why none of this affected him.

Franz was washing his hands. "Because all the ones we're giving you are dead. We're just trying their bodies on you like costumes. Since they don't feel anything anymore, neither do you."

"Where are you getting them?" Bruno was squeamish about certain things. He did not like the idea of human corpses dug out of graves, brushed off a few times with a whisk broom, and then put on him like some used sports jacket from a thrift shop.

"Don't worry. We catch the ones we want as they die—like the safety net under the trapeze at the circus." The barber dried his hands on a red towel. The others stood behind Bruno conferring. "The guy you are now just drove off a cliff outside Dubrovnik. A German tourist going way too fast in his brand-new Opel. Everything we try on you is fresh, Bruno. There are always people dying."

Did that explanation make him feel better? He didn't know.

The man who brought the donuts said, "Franz, we all agree on one thing—He's got to look like he's walked a few miles of night. Do you know what I mean?" All of them were staring at Bruno now. The speaker put four fingers to his chin. "This guy sells magazine subscriptions over the phone, or some other crap no one wants. He lives alone and cooks all of his meals in a forty-dollar microwave oven. He's not completely invisible yet but you can already see through him."

"Why is it important that I be invisible?"

The tap dancer answered. "There are two categories of invisible people: The old, and the nonentities like Dean just described. Growing old here is a process of gradually turning invisible. Haven't you noticed that yet? The only time old people are ever noticed is when they make trouble, or they're difficult, or they die. Otherwise no one sees them because they're of no importance. They have nothing to contribute except what they learned from life and who wants to sit around hearing about that?

"Losers are the other kind of invisibles. Like old people, they add nothing so they mean nothing. Their whole lives are like scraps of paper blowing down the street—you only notice them when they cross your line of vision. Then you forget them a second later. And why shouldn't you? We call them 'night walkers' and use them all the time because no one notices them. And for good reason—their lives mean nothing. They live and they die and the only difference between the two is a moment later there's one less piece of paper on the planet.

"Ettrich will be suspicious of you now after that stupid false alarm you gave about people knowing you're dead. Bad move,

Bruno. You weren't thinking. You should have had everything in place before you made that phone call. But you were too eager to show off your clever idea. You should have waited and done your homework first. So his girlfriend outsmarts you by calling Ettrich's wife immediately and finds out the truth. You can't afford more mistakes like that. No more mistakes, no more Pemmagast, no more fuckups. We don't have time. We're going to turn you into a night walker and then you can do whatever you want to them because they won't even know you're there most of the time."

The others nodded their agreement or crossed their arms as if to say the discussion was finished.

"No."

"What? Did you say no?"

"That's right. No." Bruno rubbed his nose. Or rather the German motorist's nose. "I won't do it like that. I don't want to."

Dean the donut man looked at the men and asked their question. "And why is that, Bruno?"

"Because I hate Vincent Ettrich. When I get him, I want him to know that it's me doing it, not some German clod he's never seen before."

"Hate? What's there to hate about him? He just seems like a shallow pussy chaser. Why expend all the effort hating him?"

Bruno shook his head. "No, it's more than that for me. Ettrich's ex-wife once said he was like a pigeon on the street just before a car hit him. Forever an inch away from being squashed, he always manages to escape at the last second. He's lucky and I hate luck. Plus he doesn't deserve it. He doesn't deserve to escape, doesn't deserve to be back here . . . How did he end up being the father to that kid? Can someone tell me that? How did this clown end up father of *that* kid?"

"Don't go there, Bruno," Franz said softly.

"What do you mean? Is it against the law to ask a question?"

"Because even unborn, that *kid* is more dangerous than you, or us, any King of the Park, and whoever else you can think of. If he's born and learns what he is capable of, then we are all in deep shit.

"There's no way to know what he's doing or thinking . . . He could be here now and we wouldn't know it. So I really strongly recommend you stop talking about Anjo. The less said the better."

Bruno looked around the room. It was plain by their expressions that none of the men was comfortable with this topic. "All right, but I've got to ask one last thing: If Anjo's so strong, how can we beat him?"

"*We* can't, but his parents can. We're going to convince them to kill him."

Anjo was there, all right. He was in the green comb Franz used to smooth Bruno's ugly new hair. Then he was a piece of chewed chocolate donut sliding slowly down someone's throat. He flitted, he spun, he danced on Bruno's optic nerve a while to see how much spring it had.

He heard everything the men said. He heard they wanted him dead. He wanted his father to hear it too and understand, but Ettrich's mind was forever closed to him. There was so much Anjo wanted to tell his father but he could never get through. Why was that? He had tried so hard. With his mother it had been easy from the start. But with Ettrich nothing worked.

Anjo was outside when the men left the barbershop. He was a black and brown pigeon standing in the middle of the street waiting for a car to come along and squash him. He wanted to know what it felt like to dive upward and escape at the last moment. He wanted to know the experience because that's how Bruno had described his father. Anjo wanted to know everything about Ettrich, even what other people said about him. But it was very early in the morning and the streets were empty. He strutted stiffly around, bobbing his head and making odd little sounds—coos and glubbles. So this is what it's like to be a pigeon.

The men stood outside the building, talking and smoking. Clearing his throat, Franz spit into the street and saw him. For a few delicious seconds the barber watched the bird. Did he recognize him? Did he know the boy had heard everything and was already planning on how to defeat them in the most crushing way?

Pecking and cooing, the bird walked in a small circle, all the time watching the man in the white smock ten feet away. Somewhere down the street the rumble of a truck coming their way grew louder. The bird heard it but continued to look at the barber.

Of course Anjo waited until the last second, until the truck's shadow was across his body and he had only a second to leap into the air or be killed by the wheels. And he did leap, he did escape, but then something happened that threw everything else into the air as well.

At the exact moment the bird fluttered up, the early cell groups in Anjo's brain reached the miraculous moment when mid-brain structure begins to develop. From one second to the next he became completely human and forgot everything. Gone was the green comb, the dog in the restaurant that had protected Isabelle, and Abraham Lincoln. The pigeon flying away was only a pigeon now and Anjo was back inside his mother for good, just another baby waiting to be born.

A Water Sandwich

"For men, sex is gym. For women, it's church."

"Did you really write that, Vincent? You're a pig." But Isabelle was smiling. She sat with her back to the wall, knees drawn up as far they could go to her chest. On the other side of that wall Ettrich was sitting inside his closet with a flashlight, reading things to her he had written on the wall in there. This had been her idea. Maybe he wrote something there that might help now. Neither of them had any better idea of what to do at the moment.

"Only the ridiculous survive."

"Why would you write that on your wall? In the dark, in a closet?"

"Because I thought it best to write everything that came to mind so when I was trying to find my way back, something there might ring a bell."

Isabelle suddenly felt a big *glump* in her stomach. Alarmed, she looked down at it. She'd never felt anything like that before—as if someone had dropped a big stone into a still pool. She asked Anjo if he was all right but got no response. That was strange, but sometimes he didn't talk to her for days. It made her wonder if he was going to be a moody child.

Vincent crawled out of the closet on his hands and knees. "Do you remember my five questions?"

"The ones you asked in Krakow that time?"

"Yes. Do you remember them?"

She raised her head and closed her eyes. "What three meals from your past would you like to eat again? What two objects would you like to possess again? What is the one act in your life you wish you could take back or erase? Umm, I don't remember the other two."

Ettrich crawled over to her and arranged himself against the wall in her same position. "What one person would you like to see again, and what one experience do you wish you could repeat?"

"That's right. I love those questions. They're great to play with. They really make you go back and rethink your life, like doing a big housecleaning. Had you written them in there?"

"No, which is very strange because they're exactly the kinds of questions that would stir up my memory."

She put her hand on his knee. "What are you saying?"

"That I think someone's been in here and erased some of what I wrote. I'm almost sure of it. Like those questions. But more importantly when I remembered them, I remembered something else too."

"What, Vincent?"

His face lit up like he was about to tell a wonderful story. "When you're dead they teach you how to make a water sandwich."

"Huh?"

"Would you like to see?"

"Well, uh, yes. I guess."

"Come on." He stood up and took her hand. "It came back to me the minute I remembered those five questions."

He led her into the kitchen and gestured for her to sit at the small table. When she did, she thought again how sad it must have been for him to sit here alone those months eating his Chinese take-out food.

Ettrich went to the sink and turned on the tap. When the water was running, he cupped his hands beneath the jet and raised them. The flow of water broke perfectly in two and formed swirling transparent pinwheels in the air. Ettrich slowly lowered one of his hands and turned off the tap. The water he had raised remained in the air, turning and turning. Isabelle slapped a hand over her mouth like a child and watched, mesmerized.

Vincent put his hands beneath the two pinwheels and began to prod and form the water as if it were very soft clay. In a short time he had sculpted it into what looked roughly like a large sandwich. But a water sandwich, transparent and glassy.

"My God, Vincent, how did you do that?"

"That's what I was saying: They taught us how to do it. That was one of the first things I made. Isn't it crazy, a water sandwich? But it was the only thing I could think of then."

"Where? When?"

"When I was dead, Fizz. And just now I suddenly remembered how to do it."

"It's wonderful, but what's the point?'

"The point is that I remembered something from the time I was dead."

Isabelle looked interested but unimpressed. "That's what happens when you die—they teach you how to shape water?" The only thing she could think of was one of those arts and crafts classes where the teacher, a middle-aged woman in a smock and beret, taught other middle-aged women how to oil-paint. "But it's *death*, Vincent. There's got to be something more—"

Ettrich heard the skepticism in her voice and responded forcefully. "There is: They teach you that everything you once thought was *only* this is also this and this . . . and this." He lifted his water sandwich toward her. "Now watch." He ran a hand over the top of the sandwich. Blue flame rose up from it. "You can make water burn. You can make it hard as stone or soft as silk. When you're alive you think water is just water. But that's wrong. And it's one of the things that you learn there.

"I remembered something else too."

"About death? What?"

"Here, take this." He moved forward with the sandwich so that he was almost upon her before she began to rise. She was about to say "How do I hold it?" when he threw it in her face. Blinded momentarily by the water, she was more shocked than anything else. Why did he do that?

When she opened her eyes and rubbed the water away, she was no longer in the room with him. Instead she was in another room she recognized instantly. It was a place of great happiness for Isabelle.

She was in a bedroom with many pictures on the walls. Someone was lying in the bed watching television. It was Isabelle's grandmother who had died five years ago. She had lived the last part of her life with Isabelle's family and helped raise the children. All of them adored her. One of the things the kids loved most to do was climb into bed with the old woman every morning and watch television with her. They had their favorite shows and they would cuddle together under her thick down duvet that smelled faintly of her hand cream. For an early hour in the morning, there was no better place on earth than in bed with Grandmother.

"Isabelle, *komm zu mir.*" The old woman smiled and beckoned her over with a thin slow hand—an incredibly familiar gesture. The adult Isabelle hesitated but could not resist the invitation and walked over. She sat down on the edge of the bed and came close to swooning when she heard Austrian folk music playing on the television. Grandmother was watching the early morning national weather report. She had always liked to see what the weather was like around the country.

She did not appear at all surprised to see Isabelle. In her inimitable way she spoke about this and that, nothing important, just the sorts of things she had always talked about which made these moments even more dear.

Isabelle heard something behind her and turned around. Vincent was standing at the door, smiling. She tried to smile back at him but the impact of the moment and the experience left her speechless. She could only raise her hands toward him and then let them float back down to her lap.

Vincent nodded, understanding everything. In Krakow that night she had told him the one person she wished to see again was this woman whom she had loved most of all.

Her grandmother was watching television again, seemingly oblivious to Ettrich's presence in her room.

"This is the other thing I remembered how to do, Fizz. Will you be all right here for a while?"

"Here? Yes, of course, but where are you going?"

"Back to the hospital. To the time before I died. There's got to be something there that can help us." He looked at her grandmother.

Isabelle looked too, and then at him with great love. "I can't believe you were able to do this."

"What's it like to see her again?"

"There's so much I want to tell her, Vincent. Is that all right? I mean—"

"Yes, it's okay. It's like the water sandwich—we think time is only the past, present, and future but it's much more than that. You can tell her whatever you like and it won't make any difference. Whenever you want to come back, just call for me and I'll know. I'll bring you back in a second. Okay?"

"Yes. Will you be all right?"

He was about to say sure, but the truth was he didn't know if he was going to be all right and he didn't want to lie to her. "I hope so. But listen, if something does go wrong, you'll stay here. It's five and a half years ago and you're in Vienna, obviously. The only thing you'll have to do is explain to your *Oma* why you're pregnant. I forget—what's the word in German?"

"*Schwanger.* I'll tell her it's a love child. She'll like that. She was always making fun of my mother for being so conservative."

"All right. If you need me, call me. But you're safe here. I promise you that. They can't touch you or Anjo here."

"I'm not worried about us. Anjo has always protected me."

"Still I'm glad you're here and not there. I'll come and get you when I can." He took one of her hands, kissed it, and walked out of the room.

Grandmother turned from the television and said, *"Komm hier, Schatz. Sag mir alles."*

Isabelle lay down on the bed. After looking one more time at the door she turned to her grandmother and began to talk. The old woman, as was her way, kept watching the TV but her granddaughter knew that she was listening closely to every word.

Ettrich returned to his apartment only long enough to gather the few things he would need. When he had them he left for his own past.

Half an hour later there was a knock on the apartment door. When no one answered and sufficient time had passed, it opened and Bruno Mann entered. Or rather the man he had become. He was carrying a cheap fake-leather briefcase now. He looked like a man who had come to sell you something. Normally Bruno would have had no hesitation marching right in, but to everyone's great surprise, Ettrich had proven dangerous and much cleverer than any of them had imagined. Bruno had been advised to be very careful.

"Hello? Is anyone here?" He knew if someone was they would probably be angry at him for entering uninvited. But he would find the words to fix it. This stout man with the Caesar haircut was one smooth-talking guy.

To his mild surprise no one was there. That was okay though because it gave Bruno the chance to look around Ettrich's apartment unhindered.

He had never been in Vincent's place and was curious to see how the man lived. It frankly startled him to see how sparsely the rooms were furnished. He had imagined Vincent Ettrich would have cluttered his home with furniture the way he cluttered his life with women. But that was not the case.

When he was certain no one was there, Bruno walked through all of the rooms, looking in random drawers and cabinets, picking up a photograph and wondering what the moment was like when the picture was taken. He looked in the bedroom closet and under the bed.

There was one apple in a bowl on the kitchen counter. Pleased to be taking the last one, he bit into it and poked around the kitchen some more. He discovered a drawer full of only chopsticks and white plastic soy sauce packets. On a high shelf above the sink were two unopened bottles of Branston Pickle condiment from England. Bruno had been with Vincent in England. They'd had a fine dinner together at Langan's restaurant in London. Fine until Vincent laid eyes on an intriguing woman across the room. From one moment to the next he lost all interest in being with his colleague. His ego hurt, Bruno reciprocated with a malicious and unnecessary prank that later made Ettrich's painful death a little more sad and bleak.

Bruno Mann preferred those cruel ongoing pranks to any kind of single grand operatic killer blow. He was a whittler, his method incremental; he carved off bit after bit of his prey until there was nothing left. When Vincent Ettrich was dying of cancer, Bruno did several inventive things to remind the man of how much he would soon be missing, as well as how little he would be missed by others. His great dislike of Vincent was made up of one part jealousy, one part boredom, one part maliciousness, many parts detestation of the human race, and the simple overriding fact that Bruno Mann was a total shit. He was sure that's why he'd been chosen to be the new King of the Park.

He looked through Ettrich's CDs and books. He wondered if there was any significance in the fact the man owned four copies of Stendhal's novel *The Charterhouse of Parma*. He opened each one and riffled through the pages looking for incriminating love notes, unpaid bills, or any other dirty goody he might use later to make trouble for Vincent. Any little bit helped. As he looked around he whistled an array of Barry Manilow songs. "Oh Mandy" kept looping back.

He found photos of Vincent's children, one of Isabelle in white cotton underwear holding a pair of cowboy boots, one of his ex-wife in a green silk bathrobe. Holding up both pictures of the women, he looked from one to the other trying to decide which he would choose if it were up to him. He remembered the one time he met Kitty she was pleasant but rather aloof.

The telephone rang. He walked over and, putting his hand above it, deliberated on whether or not to pick it up. He could do a perfect imitation of any human voice so Ettrich's would be no problem. He couldn't decide on what to do and finally the answering machine kicked in.

"Hey Dad, it's your amazing son Jack."

Bruno listened attentively as the boy prattled on. He tried on Jack's voice, repeating his words as they came. It was truly unnerving to see this middle-aged man telling his father how much he loved him in the voice of a little boy. When that grew boring, he thought about how he might use Jack, his sister, their mother, or all three of them to tear Ettrich apart. He found a hard candy in his pocket and, unwrapping it, popped it into his mouth.

"Well, that's about all, Dad. I'll talk to you later." Jack hung up and the dial tone came on. Bruno made the sound of the dial tone deep in his throat. There had to be something in this apartment he wasn't seeing or that he had ignored. There was always a secret something in a person's house; something that shamed and thrilled them equally. Something they would never want anyone to know they possessed. Ettrich's apartment was Spartan but Bruno was sure something important was here and that he could find it.

The phone shut off and the apartment became silent but for the sucking sound Bruno made around his hard candy. That stopped too when he saw what he was looking for.

The wooden cake box Isabelle had brought from Vienna lay on the floor near the window.

"Woo, oo, oo, what have we here?" Bruno prided himself on never biting down on a hard candy. He had the patience to suck on them until they were tiny slivers small enough to swallow. But now he was so pleased to find this box that against all his principles, he couldn't resist a hard victorious chomp down on the butterscotch lozenge. He had what he needed.

Ettrich made a mistake. It was certainly understandable because what he had remembered of death came back at him as such a huge jumbled mess that the force of it almost knocked him over. It was a wonder that he had been able to bring Isabelle to her grandmother on his first try. In fact that might have been the thing that threw him off—it had been so easy that he thought hey, this won't be a problem. I know what I'm doing. But he did not know what he was doing and where he was now proved *that*.

He didn't know where he was other than a hotel room some-where. By the look of the yellowing wallpaper and the old sink and bidet in a corner, it was probably Europe but he couldn't be sure. He had wanted to go back to the hospital where he had died but instead he was in a cheap hotel room maybe somewhere in Europe. But whether he recognized it or not, this room had to be in his life somewhere because that's the way this thing worked: In death you could go back and forth across your life as if it were a railroad track. They encouraged you to do it because studying your life, sometimes frame by frame, brought greater insight into the experience you had just completed. So this room was part of Ettrich's life. But because he didn't recognize it at all, the question was *what* part? He didn't have long to wait.

He hadn't even given the place a good once-over before the door opened and he heard a woman's laughter. To his great surprise, he recognized the laugh because it was unusually deep and sexy and belonged to his mother. But the woman who walked into this room was very different looking from the one who had made him five hundred or so peanut butter sandwiches and folded his underpants neatly in the underpants drawer of his dresser when he was a boy.

This woman had a long lustrous 1940s movie-star hairdo. She was wearing a thin blue and green sleeveless summer dress that showed off her full breasts and long legs to their absolute best advantage. The old Vincent Ettrich would have pursued this woman big time if he had met her at a party. He had seen photos of his mother when she was young, and yes, this was that woman. But it was also so different because this was the real, living Ruth Ettrich and she glowed. That laugh, the rustling clinging dress and every inch of her thin but shapely arms showing . . . she was a knockout.

Then a man came into the room and of course it was Vincent's father, Stan. He was wearing a black polo shirt and old jeans. He was thin and his face was interesting looking almost to the point of being handsome. He also had a full head of hair which fascinated Ettrich because he'd only known his father as a bald man. They were a striking couple. How old were they—late twenties, early thirties? His dad had two suitcases in his hands which he lowered slowly to the floor and let out a sigh of relief. Ettrich remembered for the first time in years how his father always complained that his wife packed too much when they went on a trip.

Ruth went to the window and looked out. She gestured for Stan to join her there. He walked over and, standing behind his wife, put his hands on her shoulders. Such a familiar gesture! How often had Ettrich seen his parents standing like that—his tall father towering behind his mother, her hands on top of his as they rested on her shoulders. With a great hot pain of love and longing, Ettrich suddenly missed them both terribly. Both had died years ago in a horrendous tunnel fire on an *Autobahn* in Switzerland, leaving him bereft because, among other things, he lost two very good friends.

"Oh, look at the view, Stan. It's beautiful down there." She nuzzled his hand and kept looking out the window.

Vincent wanted to take a peek out that window at what was so beautiful. But he was wholly content just to be in a room again with his living parents. Ironically, they were both much younger than he was now.

"What's the name of this town?"

"Recey."

Ettrich's mouth dropped open because hearing that name, he knew exactly where he was, what was about to happen, and most importantly why he was here. This room was the home of one of the nicest stories of his parents' life together. While he was growing up he had asked them to tell it again and again. Sometimes it would be his mother's version and sometimes his dad's. It didn't matter which because none of them ever tired of hearing it.

Three years after they were married, the Ettrichs were hired to teach at an international school in Zurich. Neither had ever been to Europe so the summer before school began they came over early, rented a car, and drove around looking at this new world.

One evening near the French–Swiss border they stopped in a

small nondescript French village. Exhausted by a long day in the car, they asked directions to the only *auberge* in Recey which from the outside didn't look like much. But there was no other option at that hour after twilight so they went in and rented a room.

To their happy surprise it was charming inside the small family-run hotel, especially the view from their window, which looked down on a large meadow where sheep were grazing.

The hotel dining room was straight out of another, enchanted age. Garlands of bone-colored garlic and red onions hung from thick wooden beams and rafters. A six-foot-high fireplace burned pungent pine logs and warmed the uneven stone floor beneath their feet. Ruth slipped off her rubber sandals and kept sliding her feet slowly back and forth across the floor. A friendly giant Irish wolfhound that belonged to the owner of the auberge greeted them and never left their side from the moment they entered the room. There were only two other couples in the restaurant the whole evening. Both ate quickly and left the Ettrichs there alone to feast on rack of lamb and fresh vegetables from the restaurant's garden.

Afterward they drank Calvados in giant brandy snifters because the weather outside had turned cold and just because it was Calvados, Saint-Exupéry's favorite drink. In his bag upstairs, Stan Ettrich had a copy of *Wind, Sand, and Stars,* which he read from to Ruth every night in bed before they went to sleep.

One of the windows in the dining room had been left open so they heard when the thunder came and it began to rain outside. A hard, driving rain that made them feel even luckier to be here. The owner of the auberge, delighted to have Americans staying at his *établissement* for the first time, insisted they try his crème brûlée for dessert. Neither of them had ever tasted the sweet before but after that it became Ruth's favorite.

They made love for a long time that night and nine months later Vincent was born. Both of them were sure he was conceived then and they even had a magical sign of it hours later.

Around three o'clock the next morning Stan awoke and went to the window. The rain had stopped and the light from the moon was an incredibly bright silver-gray. Although it was so late, everything down below was illuminated. He wanted to wake Ruth so she could see this silvery world too but he decided against it. Yet it was so beautiful that he knew he needed a longer look.

Quietly taking the chair from beneath the desk, he placed it next to the closed window. Naked, he sat on it with his elbows propped on the windowsill and watched the empty meadow against the pitch-black night sky. He thought about the grazing sheep they had seen down there earlier. With a start he realized the savory lamb they'd eaten for dinner had likely come from that flock. Even so, it had been a perfect evening and now this. He thought of how he would describe this scene to Ruth tomorrow morning. He loved words and loved telling his wife things, loved to watch her open interested face while she listened, wholly attentive to whatever he had to say.

He was thinking about this, thinking about the words he would use, when the dog and the deer ran onto the meadow together. It was the Irish wolfhound from the restaurant. The deer was somewhat larger than the dog. Later they figured the deer was probably quite young and therefore not afraid to play with a dog nearly its size.

In years to come the Ettrichs asked people who knew about these things if they had ever read or heard of a dog and a deer playing together but everyone said no. Naturally that made what they witnessed even more special. Because that night in the meadow behind their auberge that's exactly what happened: These two large animals loped and darted, feinted and came to sliding stops together, the greatest pals in the world. They would freeze for a moment and then be off again in a burst, racing each other, racing away and then toward each other, playing some kind of mysterious tag and then dashing away full speed as if they were both on fire or being chased by wolves.

Stan went over to the bed and shook Ruth awake. She was a heavy sleeper and didn't appreciate being brought back to the surface in such a rough manner. She was about to tell him that when she saw the look of excited awe on his face and the urgency of his gesture for her to join him. Normally shy about her naked body, she got right up without covering herself and accompanied her nude husband to the window. That was Vincent's favorite imagined picture of his parents—the two of them young and naked standing at that window, watching the mystical dance of the dog and the deer in the moonlit meadow.

Now he stood across the room from them while this was actually unfolding. The sight of their two bare bodies standing at the window made him cry. Then a great idea came and it moved him quickly out of the room. His parents took no notice of him for even a second. He wanted to see them from down below. He wanted to stand in that meadow, look up at their window, and see them framed there. See these two beloved people and the looks on their faces as they watched the animals gambol nearby. On this magical night, he wanted to see them from every angle so that he could remember it all later.

From the many times he had heard the story, he knew the animals stayed in the meadow for almost fifteen minutes and that his parents had watched them the whole time. So there really was no need for him to hurry downstairs but he did anyway. The steep creaky staircase, the wildly dissimilar patterns of wallpaper on the different walls, the great pungent smells that came at him from every direction—old wood, pipe smoke, soup. He kept thinking, I must remember these things; I can't forget them. But a moment contains so many fragile things. It's a wonder we are able to keep any of them alive later.

There was a large brass bell on the front door which made it a task for him to open and close the door without waking that bell. For a short funny time Ettrich felt like a kid sneaking out of the house without his parents knowing. But the reality was he was sneaking out so he could look at his parents from a different angle.

A cobblestone path led to the street. Then he had to walk around to the back of the auberge to reach the meadow. Hurrying along, he tried to watch where he was going while taking in as much of the surroundings as he could. Remember this, he kept thinking. Look at this and this and try not to forget any of it.

He rounded the building and saw a low stone wall between the meadow and the auberge's large garden. The vegetables in the garden were blooming and the eerie thing was that all of them were either black or blue-white under the uncanny light of the moon.

Now Ettrich could actually hear the animals. Their paws pounding the ground, their heavy breathing as they ran close by as part of the large circle they were apparently making. It reminded him of the sounds of a horse race—the feet galloping by, the fast chugging hard breath. He stood for a moment with his hands on his hips, watching them. The dog jumped in the air and slammed its head into the deer's flank. The deer grunted but did not stop or turn. It was winning their race and was not going to be distracted by its opponent's tricks. Racing past, they were so beautiful together that Ettrich forgot everything else and just watched, enthralled.

When they were gone he climbed over the stone wall and out into the meadow. The grass was heavy with rain and dew. His pant legs were quickly soaked and he felt them wet against his bare legs. He inhaled the fecund, deep-natural smell of the soaked world around him.

Fall often begins at night and that is why few notice its entrance. A weather change, or rain like the one that had just fallen was much colder than a summer rain, or it stayed cold on the ground long into the morning. The clouds that brought it are not black with August thunderstorms but the bruised purple that carries snow later on in the year. Although it was still summer, Ettrich could sense fall in the air that night. It made him feel like he was the only person on earth to know.

He walked out into the meadow about thirty feet. Turning around, he looked up at the building and searched for them. There they were. He could see his young parents standing on the other side of their closed window looking down. His father was behind his mother. At this distance her slim beautiful body was now the color of ivory. Both of her hands were pressed to the glass as if she were trying to push open the window and get closer to the racing animals. Ettrich wanted to hold that picture of his parents, that moment. He wanted to kiss them and take them both so deep inside himself that they would be safe there forever.

Still looking at the window, he heard the dog bark out in the field somewhere. Taking several steps back, Ettrich almost tripped over something on the ground. Assuming it was a large stone, he looked down. To his great surprise it was a wooden box. What was that doing out here? Bending over to pick it up, he read the writing on top of the box: "Hotel Sacher, Vienna."

He stopped moving. His mind went blank and the only word he could manage was a slow *"Whaaat?"* Because it was the cake box Isabelle had brought from Vienna. He was sure of that. Here in a French field forty years ago, below the room where he had been recently conceived, was a box he had last seen this morning in his apartment.

He did not touch it. He wanted to but something in his gut said leave it alone—get away from it. They had found him. They were here. Did that mean they had found Isabelle and the baby too?

He straightened up but too quickly. He lost his balance and staggered. Throwing his arms out, he tried to right himself. He had to get out of here now. His first thought was to go to Isabelle and see if she was safe. But what if they didn't know where she was and his going would lead them to her?

Ettrich moved a few steps to the left, stopped, and then moved right. Panicked and confused, he reflexively looked up. For a moment he caught a last glimpse of his parents at their window. This time who they were did not register on him.

Hietzl

Bruno was disappointed that Vincent hadn't opened the cake box. Like a magnificent picnic organized by a master chef, he had carefully prepared the contents of that box for maximum effect. But then that cretin just ran away, leaving Bruno's handiwork untouched and unappreciated. Oh well.

He walked over and picked it up. Holding it close to his head he shook it, thinking fondly about what was inside. Something in there rattled, something hard and metallic. Perhaps he could use it later. Yes. Perhaps he could find a perfect time and circumstance to use the box again where Vincent would have to open it. He slipped it under his arm and started across the meadow. While he was walking he looked up at the Ettrichs' window. Earlier he had seen the animals running around the field. He knew the whole story and found it vaguely interesting but nothing more. If it were up to him, he would have done something vicious to ruin the oh so charming Ettrich family fairy tale forever. Like stab one of the animals as they pranced by, set fire to the auberge, or lightly poison the couple's croissants the next morning. Give them both memorable cases of food poisoning. But Bruno was not able to lay a finger on the past. Chaos cannot touch or alter history because it is fixed. The present and the future are fair game for muddle and mess, but the past is permanent. What was *is,* forever.

No, to achieve his goal Bruno knew he must somehow lure Ettrich and Isabelle back to the present. Then he could get them. Walking across the wet meadow, he was already thinking of ways to do it. Now came the fun part.

Isabelle did not know how she felt about seeing her grandmother again. On the one hand it was a marvelous thing. Grandma was exactly as she remembered her and so many of the little details about her that Isabelle cherished and had held on to so tightly in her memory were there and alive again.

But there was also something in the experience that felt wrong, something that kept Isabelle from embracing it one hundred percent. She wondered what it was, what ineffable force held her back from living fully in this encounter.

"Do you remember Peter Jordan?" The old woman was sitting at the table next to her bed, drinking chamomile tea from a delicate cup made out of Augarten porcelain.

"No, Grandma, who was that?"

"He was a friend of ours from the country. He painted portraits of animals. One circus that came to town had an old camel. It was very sick and they thought it was going to die, so they asked if he would like to have it. He took it and the animal lived another five years. It was the strangest thing to go over to their house and see a camel sitting in the backyard. He never did much . . . might even have been blind in one eye."

"Peter Jordan or the camel?'

"The camel. Peter died a few days after my eighty-third birth-day. He came to the party. Would you like to meet him?"

"What do you mean?" Isabelle knew that at the end of her life, her grandmother had been a little dotty in the head.

"What do you think I mean? Would you like to meet Peter?"

"But you just said he was dead, Grandma."

"So am I, dear. What difference does that make?"

Isabelle sat down slowly on the other chair at the table. "You know that you're dead?"

"Of course. He's a very interesting man. I'm sure you would like him."

"Grandma, I don't want to meet Peter Jordan. I want to talk about what you just said."

"What, that I'm dead? What's there to talk about? You already know that." She poured herself more tea. Her hands shook but that had always been. The pot made a small clinking sound when it touched the rim of the cup. When she was done pouring she lowered the pot carefully to the table. As always, she put her hands around it an instant to steal its heat. She saw Isabelle looking at her thin, age-spotted hands. "When I was a girl I could never have done this. I was so sensitive to heat and cold. I couldn't even eat ice cream because it tortured my teeth. Now look at me. I'm like a lizard taking the sun."

Isabelle, who loved her grandmother almost more than any person on earth, wanted to shake her now. "Grandma, talk to me about this. Don't talk about lizards. You know you're dead but haven't said anything about it to me since I got here?"

The old woman took a long sip of her hot tea before answering. Smoke came up from the cup as she breathed into it. Making a sour face she said, "Isabelle, you knew I was dead when you came here. What are you so surprised about?"

Isabelle felt a gush of guilt go up through her like ice water, as if she had been tricking the other woman by not telling her what she knew. "But how do *you* know?"

"Believe me, when you're dead you know it."

"I mean—"

Her grandmother nodded. "I know what you mean. Everything you see here is a little bit off. Have you noticed that yet? Look at it carefully. That's because this room was created from both of our memories combined. So if you look closely, you'll see that things everywhere in here are not quite right."

Isabelle knew the room intimately. In her last years, the old woman had rarely left it except to go to the toilet. Isabelle had spent so many hours in there that she had unwittingly memorized most of it.

But now, almost as if these familiar surroundings had suddenly become her enemy, she looked fearfully at what she had known so well for such a long time.

Her grandmother reached over and took her hand to reassure her. "There's nothing to be afraid of. Did you see me a minute ago when I was drinking tea? How I squinched up my nose? That's because the tea suddenly became hot chocolate."

Isabelle forgot her fright and added eagerly, "We always used to drink hot chocolate in here. Almost every afternoon when I came home from school; it was our ritual."

"That's right, but now I can tell you a secret, dear: I loathe hot chocolate. It makes my throat feel mossy."

Isabelle laughed hard. For years and years it had been their tradition. She would run into her grandmother's room, full of stories from the day at school. There at the table next to the bed would be Grandma with a pot of fresh *kakao* and vanilla *kipferl*.

She had to laugh again. "The truth comes out after all these years."

"That's right. There are benefits to being dead. One of them is never having to drink *kakao* again. To get back to what I was saying, I imagined tea in my cup. But you imagined cocoa because that's what we always drank. Your memory was stronger than mine so suddenly I had *kakao*."

"If this isn't your room, Grandma, where are we?"

"Where? Well, I'm dead and you're visiting. Your boyfriend asked if you could come here while he tried to make things safe for you."

"This is death?" Reluctantly Isabelle looked around the room.

"It's somewhere between life and death. You came here from one direction and I came from the other." Her grandmother smiled in a way which Isabelle remembered from old times meant she was about to say something she thought witty. "We're at an *Autobahn* rest stop between Salzburg and Vienna. Do you need to go to the toilet while we're here?"

"You sound just like my mother when we would go on a trip. Do you know where Vincent is now?"

"No, dear."

"Can you do anything to help him?"

"No, dear. I'm very new to this. I've only just begun to understand how to look at my own life with any kind of objectivity. I have no special powers."

Isabelle remembered what Coco had said about first going to purgatory and then later to the mosaic after dying. "Can you tell me what it's like?"

"I could but you wouldn't understand. Not because you're stupid, but because life must be over before you can see it clearly. You must have no more stake in it, no more ulterior motives or hopes . . . Telling you what I've learned would be like trying to explain something while you were having an orgasm."

"Grandma!"

"It's true. It's the difference between the calm clearness that comes just after sex, and being in the middle of an orgasm."

Isabelle smiled crookedly. "I thought life was supposed to be a cabaret. Now you're telling me it's an orgasm?"

———————

Ettrich opened his eyes slowly, wary of what he was going to see. And he was right to be worried because what he saw was definitely not what he had hoped to see. Once again he had tried to go back to the hospital in the time before he died.

Instead he was outside somewhere, and it was night again. He saw the flames of a large fire. In between their crackle and snap he heard the lapping of water on a shore.

Lifting his head to get his bearings, he saw that he was on a beach somewhere. A bonfire was burning thirty feet away. In the middle of wondering where the hell he was now, Ettrich heard a Medusa voice and froze. It was Isabelle's phrase and perfectly described the total paralysis that came whenever you heard certain familiar voices. Voices you might not have heard for half a lifetime, but when you heard them again they turned your whole being to stone because of who was speaking.

This Medusa voice was high and nasal, a voice that had only one tone, one range, one inflection—whine. The only thing it was capable of doing (although it did it brilliantly) was to whine. Whether it was happy, sad, in the throes of ecstasy or despair—no matter what, that voice always came out sounding like a whine, a bleat, a bellyache, or a gripe.

"Can't you at least wait till it's really dark so no one sees?"

That was what paralyzed Ettrich. Not only was it the voice, but it had said that sentence. One of the few truly unforgettable sentences from his past that had been notched on his soul with a sledge-hammer and a chisel.

She was lying under him on the sand. Out of the corner of his eye he could see her yellow shorts. He did not need to look down to know that it was Gigi Dardess, the first girl he had ever had sex with. She had a pleasant face, a reasonable body, a filthy reputation, and that voice. Sixteen-year-old Ettrich had invited her to this end-of-the-school-year party because he was desperate to lose his virginity and all indications were that Gigi was the most likely to help him do that.

Like all young men on the planet, he had hoped and dreamed that the golden girls in his school, the Andrea Schnitzlers and the Jennifer Holberts, would one day magically say yes to him. But Vincent Ettrich was invisible to those great beauties and in his secret heart he could understand why. So, like most young men on the planet, in the end he set his sexual sights lower and then still lower until they eventually submerged like a submarine. Looking out the porthole one day, he saw Gigi Dardess swim by at full fathoms five.

She did not seem surprised when he invited her to the party. In fact her acceptance consisted of a sigh, broken eye contact, and a flat "Okay" that made going to the party with him sound more like duty than a pleasure.

Nevertheless, two weeks later here they were and things between them had gotten hot fast. As darkness fell, the couples at the party wandered off to different far parts of the beach.

From the first kiss on, Gigi had unresistingly let him put his hands wherever he wanted on her body. This carte blanche confused Ettrich as much as it excited him because he had not the slightest idea of what he was doing. In the past he had talked endlessly about it with his friends. But none of them knew anything about it either so whatever they came up was only hopeful conjecture. He had also zealously read "The Playboy Advisor" on such matters. But what good did dry words on a page do when you had presumably willing female flesh under your fingertips right this minute? Now that the moment had come, he felt like he was driving a truck full of nitroglycerine down a narrow mountain road in a blizzard.

Desperately trying to figure this puzzle out, he slipped his hand back into her panties for a third try. Maybe this time he would be able to locate her clitoris. A moment later he was reduced to ego-rubble by her whining, "Can't you at least wait till it's really dark so no one sees?"

The only interesting thing about reliving that memorably dreadful, life-shriveling moment was the fact that this time, both the teenage and adult Ettrich existed in it simultaneously.

Young Ettrich was an interesting mess of emotions. On the one hand he was dying to get laid. On the other he wanted to at least try and make Gigi happy. He wanted her to show him how to do this thing right because she had obviously had a lot more experience at it than him. Yet he wanted her to come away from the night thinking Vincent Ettrich was a pretty damned good fuck.

He was not kidding himself about that: If things went right tonight he would fuck for the first time in his sixteen years. Later in life when he was a real *bon vivant,* he would find a spectacular woman and they would make Hollywood love until the day they died. But that was years from now and, as with anything else, you had to learn the basics first. But how could you learn the basics if your partner was no help? Yes, she was letting him have it, but what good is a sandwich if you don't know how to eat it?

When he had waited for what he thought was a sufficiently long time, he started to kiss her again. Just that—no touching or other hanky-panky. Innocent-as-lemonade kissing to try and get things going right between them.

But Gigi kissed like she was licking postage stamps. Even in those days Ettrich was a good kisser but nothing he did tempted her. Whatever sexy tricks and clever lip dances he offered up, she just licked his stamp in return.

When this went on for far too long and the elder Ettrich couldn't stand it anymore, he spoke to his younger self. "Touch her face. Run your hands over it. Touch her ears and neck very gently. Then kiss her wherever you touched her."

He said it out of frustration, not because he thought that he could really get through to the other him. It was like talking to the screen when you go to a horror film. "Don't open that door!" "Don't go in the basement!" But the actors in the film always go in the basement and get devoured. So Ettrich did not for a minute think that his younger self would hear and actually heed him.

He was wrong. A moment later in the middle of yet another dud kiss, the boy opened his eyes and looked at Gigi an inch away as if she had just dawned on him. Slowly his right hand rose to her face and began to touch her cheeks and rounded chin. Something came over both of their expressions as if sparkle really was happening between them.

What followed was the first of many lousy lays Vincent had in his life. But this was the most memorable because it was the first. Gigi's passion moved up a degree or two because of young Ettrich's unexpectedly sweet caresses and the elder Ettrich's coaching. She was never going to be Cleopatra when it came to this stuff but at least some warmth came to both her heart and skin.

Most importantly, the advice from the elder Ettrich, unbeknownst to the younger, saved the experience from being a sexual Waterloo, *Titanic,* or an Edsel—one of those hideous experiences of youth that cripple some part of us forever when they are over. Ettrich would always remember Gigi's callous line about waiting till dark. He would also remember how difficult it was to put on the unlubricated condom he had optimistically carried for so long that the leather of his wallet had molded around it.

Because it was his first time, he remembered many details of that night. But not the fundamental one, which was that his older self's advice made the experience merely mediocre and not disastrous. It ended up being a shrug, a rueful grin, and a good story to tell rather than a permanent knife in his heart.

The past was fixed, that was a given. What happened with Gigi Dardess that night was exactly what had happened twenty-five years earlier:

A little passion + a little response = one less virgin in the world

However, the senior Ettrich now knew that he was capable of

going in and out of his past life as if it were rooms in a house. Although he could not change the dimensions of the rooms or any of the objects in them, he sure as hell could move the furniture around. Slide the bulky dresser away from the window so that more light could come in. Or push the beautiful couch into the center of the room so that it would be used, not only admired.

Then he remembered Coco's tiles and how you chose to arrange them into a personal mosaic. He began seeing connections between all of these things. It gave him hope that if he connected all of these dots the right way, he might succeed.

When the sex was over, he and his younger self lay on their back looking up at the stars. One Ettrich was happy it had happened but was just as happy that it was finished. The older Ettrich was looking for the constellations in the sky above them, trying to connect the trillion stars into coherent forms.

"You always were the optimist."

Time had passed. Ettrich was still looking up at the stars when he heard that familiar voice. His unconscious recognized its owner before he did. That part of him asked the rhetorical question, "Coco?"

"Yes, Vincent." She stood a few feet down the beach, her hands shoved into the pockets of a pair of tight new jeans. She wore a black T-shirt and rubber sandals. Everything on her looked new, just bought. The biggest change was that her hair was long now and fell to her shoulders. She was a small woman but this new hairdo somehow made her look taller and wider. He didn't know if it was very flattering.

"What are you doing here?" He wanted to say more. He wanted to say I saw you dead earlier. I saw what was left of your body after they were through with it. But he held back and waited.

"Come walk with me. Let's leave the lovebirds in peace."

"Can I do that?" He didn't know how he was going to separate from himself and go with Coco.

"You're doing all of this to yourself, Vincent. None of it is real. Come on." Without another word she turned and walked away.

He moved out of himself—just like that, just that easy—and followed her. He looked down at his body to see what was there. Everything was there—one whole adult Vincent Ettrich. He turned and looked at young Ettrich who was still lying on his back, one arm under his head. Gigi turned to him and started talking.

A few minutes later Coco came to a lifeguard tower and climbed the ladder to the top. Ettrich had been walking some steps behind. He caught up but did not follow her up the ladder.

"Nice view. Don't you want to come and join me?"

"I'm fine down here. Tell me what's going on, Coco."

"You're trying to take the easy way out, Vincent."

"What do you mean?" All of his defense mechanisms jumped up and growled at her.

"You can't give yourself advice in the past, Vincent. That's absurd. Didn't you learn anything when you were dead? The past is finished. Gigi didn't get turned on because *you* suggested kissing her neck. *He* thought of it—sexy little sixteen-year-old Vincent Ettrich.

"First you went to France and had your look around there, and now you're here. No one sent you to these places. You chose to go. Now you want to go to the hospital where you died to see if any clues are there that you might be able to use.

"I'll save you the trip—there aren't. You hope you can find answers in the important parts of your past but you can't. No one can because the past is finished and fixed forever. Listen to me—it's all in the present. Everything you need and must do is here now. There is no way of avoiding that anymore.

"Do you know who put that cake box on the ground in France?

Bruno Mann. You're so interested in connecting all the dots, then start there with your pal Bruno. Do you remember how this whole thing began?" Pulling up her new long hair, she pointed with the other hand at the back of her neck. "Do you remember my tattoo here?"

He looked up the ladder at her. In that dim light she was only a variety of grays. But it didn't matter because he was thinking about what she had said and the first time he'd seen the tattoo on her neck.

"Why did you do it that way, Coco? Why start this whole thing like that? It was such a weird way of showing me the truth about all this."

She threw her hands up in the air and looked at the heavens. "Vincent, I didn't do it that way, *you* did! *You* put that tattoo on the back of my neck. I was like a human Post-it note for you, but still it took you forever to read your own message."

"Holy shit." The truth hit him like a flame. She was right. Of course she was right.

"Yes, friend, holy shit. You must start seeing and understanding the notes you've written to yourself. They're all over your life now. Not in the past with Gigi Dardess and not in some obscure corner of the universe. *Here.* Right in the middle of your right now.

"You knew you had died and been resurrected. And you knew what you had to do here. You knew it all from the beginning but you didn't want to face it because it's so dangerous and hard."

In a voice as young and wobbly as an unsure child's he said, "This is scaring me."

Her voice softened. "I know. It's a very scary thing."

"Coco, when we were at the zoo, did I really talk to the other me, the dead one?"

"Yes, of course you did. That's what I've been telling you. It was one of the only times you have consciously used the powers you have to survive. You could have been using them all along. But most of the time since you have been back you've chosen, consciously chosen, to ignore what you know and what you can do so that you don't have to face what you're here for."

A long silence followed and only after some time did Ettrich mumble just loud enough to be heard, "I guess because it's easier to work in an office than it is to fight the gods."

She chuckled. "And pick up women in lingerie stores."

"Yeah, that too." He felt so dumb, so weak, and so utterly incompetent to handle this. Squatting down, he picked up a handful of cool sand. Letting it slide slowly through his fingers, he watched the night ocean rise and fall in front of him, white on black, forever. Far down the beach he heard a woman's high laugh. Was it Gigi? Had his younger self made her laugh that night? He hoped so but he didn't remember. He hoped after it was over that they'd had a good laugh together. He remembered that at some point late that night he had taken her hand and the two of them had run down to the water and jumped in with their clothes on. The water was freezing and the cold went right into his balls but it felt good. He smiled at the memory and picked up another handful of sand.

A short time later the sound of music came from the same direction. The Beatles were singing "Get Back." Ettrich listened for a while and then couldn't help singing along a little. A song so lively and familiar lifted some of the great fear from his head and heart. He sang along some more and then stood up. Turning to the lifeguard tower, he gestured for Coco to join him.

"What's up?"

"Come down here."

She climbed down quickly thinking something was wrong. She was surprised to see when she got there that Vincent was dancing by himself. He was a terrible dancer but it didn't matter.

Grinning, Coco took a step toward him and shyly began to dance too. She was even worse at it than him. But they sort of danced together until the song ended and when it was over they were sorry. Luckily another good one came right on—Major Lance singing "Monkey Time."

Now fully caught up in it, Coco's style was to dance around in small circles while waving her hands excitedly above her head. She looked like a fanatic at a revival meeting. Ettrich was more reserved, dancing with his hands in his pockets—a little Fred Astaire there— and his shoulders bopping up and down to the beat.

"This is good. Who's singing? I like the song."

"Major Lance. It's called 'Monkey Time.' I think it was his only hit."

"It's got a great beat. But why are we dancing, Vincent?"

"Nietzsche said sometimes you reach a point when things get so bad that you can only do one of two things—laugh or go crazy. Tonight the third alternative is to dance."

Both of them had things they wanted to say to each other but now was not the right time for it. Too much had already been said. Too much had happened. Things had to sink in. Dancing was better.

A dog that had escaped from its yard dashed full speed down the beach for no other reason than it felt great. The dog had no plans, nowhere special to go, no females in heat giving the siren call. It was just running. The beach was the perfect place for that because it was flat and straight and soft on the feet. The dog also liked running here at night because there was never anyone around and those who were rarely paid attention to him. They didn't scream or try to catch him. They would only look and go back to their business. Sometimes one of them patted him as he passed by but that was all. It was okay for anything to be on the beach after dark.

The dog ran past two people dancing and a while later a bunch of young people sitting around the last flickers and cracks of a dying bonfire. They were listening to a portable radio. The music from it sounded small and tinny out there in the middle of the ocean's night. The dog had been hearing it for almost a mile as he ran toward it. The music carried. The only sounds at that late hour were the waves, the wind, that small music, and the animal's paws beating across the sand.

Adult Ettrich saw the mutt run by. It seemed to be moving to the music.

Young Ettrich, his back to the sea, did not see the dog. He was looking deep into the bonfire and thinking, "It happened. It really happened this time." But he didn't know what to do with that fact and it would take him a long time to put it into the proper perspective.

After another half-mile the dog stopped, lifted its head, and appeared to be listening to something. Then it changed course and started inland. Because the ocean was receding behind it, the world was quieter here. The houses loomed dark and silent, hunched. Now and then a light someone forgot to turn off shone out. In one window too high for the dog to see, a woman sat wearing an overcoat at a table, crying. A single candle burned in front of her. As the dog passed, she reached out to touch the soft wax dripping down the side of the white candle.

The dog continued running. It ran across town, it ran across America. Then it ran across the Atlantic Ocean and much of Europe until it arrived in Vienna. The next morning just after the sun came up, it stopped beneath the window of a large house in the Eighteenth District. The animal's pink tongue hung out. It was panting but wasn't tired. Energized and alert, it sat on its haunches and looked up at a particular window. Perhaps ten minutes went by before the curtain up there slid aside and eventually someone looked down at it, smiling. They waved but the dog did not react. It sat there waiting.

"Isabelle, come to the window. I want you to see something," the old woman said in a dejected voice to her granddaughter. They had talked for many hours and then fallen asleep next to each other on the bed, holding hands as they had always done in the past.

The old woman slept only a few hours but awoke clear and refreshed, ready for whatever the day had to offer. As soon as she was up she wanted to wake her granddaughter and talk some more. It was such a long time since they'd been together. But even asleep Isabelle looked exhausted. So her grandmother rose and puttered around the room, putting her few things in order, turning on the electric kettle for tea. In the cupboard were two fresh *Topfen Golatsch* from the AIDA *Konditorei*—Isabelle's favorite breakfast. She took them out of the pink and white bag and put them on a plate in the center of the table. Looking at the pastries, she moved them around three times before she was satisfied with the arrangement. Everything had to be perfect for this breakfast together. She knew their time would be short but not how short.

Coming back here from death had made her see things more clearly and appreciate them better, but it did not make her miss life. It was too lopsided, too unfair and unclear about telling you what it wanted and what it was willing to give in return. That was one of the chief lessons the old woman had learned in death—life wanted things from you. If you did not have them, or give them, then life scowled and stopped caring about you. It was temperamental, biased, and in no way fair. If you had somehow been able to ask it point-blank what the meaning of life is, it would not have known—because the meaning of life changed from day to day and from person to person. She wanted to tell Isabelle about that. She wanted to tell this beloved child so many things that she had learned since dying. Some she could; others she was forbidden from doing.

Going to the window, she looked at the new day. The sun was out and reflecting off surfaces everywhere. So many dissimilar things connected by the rays of the morning sun. She looked all around outside—at the trees, the street, at the few passing cars and the gray plumes of smoke streaming from their tailpipes. Lastly she looked down at the yard in front of the house. Her breath caught in her throat when she saw the dog sitting there looking up at her. Knowing exactly what this meant, she let the air out of her lungs in one long bitterly disappointed breath.

This wasn't fair—it really was not. Why hadn't they given her more time? One night was nowhere near enough. One *lifetime* was not enough, but that was a different matter. This was genuinely unfair. They could have told her you will have one night. You will be allowed to talk with your granddaughter about these crucial things and nothing else. Then she could have planned everything better. As it was, Isabelle and she had spent most of the time reminiscing about people, the old days, and various shared memories that were delightful to discuss but of no importance when it came to helping her grandchild confront what was coming now.

The old woman put an insincere smile on her face and waved at the dog. It did not respond other than to continue looking at her. She knew what it wanted and that she must act now because there was no more time. Letting the curtain drop back into place, she moved to the table. She touched one of the *golatschen* with her finger. Joys like sitting at this table and talking together over long intimate breakfasts were over forever. They had told her she could return and see Isabelle. They also named the conditions of the visit and she had readily agreed. The only thing she hadn't been told was how long she would be able to spend with her granddaughter.

Her room was small but she found a way to pace around it. She slid her hands into the pockets of her robe but then impatiently took them out again. She wanted to pull the curtain aside and look out the window again. The insane, impossible hope that the dog was no longer there crossed her mind. But she knew it wasn't gone. It was out in the yard waiting and there was nothing in death or life that she could do now but wake Isabelle and tell her she must leave.

"But why, *Oma*? I just got here yesterday."

"Because your friend is ready and he needs you."

Standing next to her grandmother, Isabelle looked out the window at the dog. "What's its name? Do they call it anything?"

"Hietzl." It sounded like she was saying "heats'll."

The name was so preposterous that in spite of herself, Isabelle gave a short hard laugh. "*Hietzl?* What kind of name is that?"

"I don't know, dear. That's just its name."

Isabelle said it again, trying to get something out of it. "That's a ridiculous name."

"It is. Are you all right?"

The younger woman dropped the curtain and turned to her grandmother. They were standing shoulder to shoulder now. "No, *Oma,* I'm not all right but what does that matter now? If I have to go then obviously that's all I can do."

"Yes, it's out of my hands. You know if it were up to me I would keep you here as long as you liked. I was just so happy to have this chance to see you again. I was sure we would have more time." Her voice was so stricken that Isabelle forgot some of her fear and felt compelled to comfort her oldest friend.

"If they are sending me back so soon, that must mean Vincent has learned something important and is all right now. He must have learned how to fight them."

Her grandmother crossed her arms tightly high on her chest and looked at them. "No, it means you must go back now because there is no more time. He needs you with him because you are his balance and his hope. Within the last day they have suddenly begun doing things, putting things in motion that must be stopped or else it will be irreversible." She thought of how at the beginning of World War Two the Polish army had heroically and quixotically sent their cavalry to try and stop the tanks of the German *Wehrmacht* from invading their country. Granted, Vincent Ettrich would not be alone in his fight against chaos, but he was on horseback while his opponent rode into battle atop the sleekest, most advanced weapons ever conceived. Her heart wept for Isabelle and her Vincent, but there was nothing that could be done about it.

Except—

She went to her small cedar dresser and opened the top drawer. Inside, it was empty except for her treasure—an old silver Faber-Castell ballpoint pen. She took it out carefully, handling the pen as if it were made of the most fragile glass. She walked to the table and just as carefully put it down next to the breakfast things.

"Isabelle, come here. I have something to give you."

Isabelle remained at the window. She was still looking at the dog. "I don't want anything."

"Get over here! I don't *care* if you want to or not."

Isabelle turned around at once, stunned by the tone of her grandmother's voice. She had never talked like that. Certainly not to Isabelle who had known this beloved woman all of her life.

"What is it, *Oma?*"

"Just come here and I'll show you." Her voice was still curt and unfriendly. The child in Isabelle cringed. She never wanted to make Grandmother angry at her. That was unthinkable. She hurried to the table and sat down.

"This pen is the most important thing I ever owned. You are permitted to bring one object with you when you die and I chose this. It was given to me by the only person I ever really loved with my whole heart. But don't ask me to tell you the story because I won't."

Isabelle wanted to say five things and ask six but by force of will she managed to keep her mouth shut, although her eyes were very wide open now.

"I'm going to give it to you. Take very great care of it because it has my death in it."

"Excuse me? I don't understand." Isabelle instinctively reached forward to touch the pen but stopped an inch away and slowly brought her hand back. "What do you mean?"

"My whole experience of dying, where I went, and what happened to me afterward—all of that is inside this pen now. If you are ever in danger and need to hide, turn the top of the pen like this, as if to bring out the point. You will enter my death and you'll be safe there."

"Vincent said that I would be safe here too when he brought me." Isabelle's voice was resigned.

"You are safe for now, but it's slipping. If you enter my death, you can stay there as long as you like because it has already happened. It is a fixed part of the past and cannot be touched."

This time Isabelle reached out and picked up the pen but still handled it very cautiously. She looked at her grandmother and then at the pen again.

"Do you remember when you were a little girl how you used to watch cowboy movies with your father? You'd always get scared by them and go run and hide in the laundry room. Well, think of the pen as another laundry room."

"You're not telling me something, *Oma*. You're leaving something out."

The old woman looked at her calmly and lied. "No. There's nothing else but that."

"Then what happens to you if I do it; if I enter your death?"

"Nothing, Isabelle. Why would anything happen to me?"

Her lie sat on the table next to the silver pen and the golden pastries. It shone jet-black like obsidian. It was cut as beautifully as a diamond. The old woman could see it. The younger woman could not. But because she had traveled to death once to retrieve Vincent, she could feel it, feel its presence and size. She even looked at the spot on the table where it was and frowned.

Seeing this, her grandmother casually reached a hand forward and brushed it across the table as if she were sweeping away crumbs. The glassy black stone, her lie made manifest, flew off the table and rolled under the bed.

The real truth of the matter was this: The instant Isabelle entered her death, the old woman would be fixed for eternity in this room. She would never be permitted to leave. She would not return to purgatory. She would sacrifice the opportunity to enter the mosaic.

Outside the dog barked. "You must go now. He's telling you." She was just as glad. She had almost never lied to Isabelle and knew if asked too many questions now that she might not be able to finesse her way around them.

"It's just a dog barking, *Oma*. How do you know it's him?"

Overcome with love for this girl, this *woman* pregnant with a child, the grandmother reached over and put her arms around Isabelle. "I know because I know. It's time for you to go, darling. But I'm so grateful we had these hours together."

Isabelle squeezed tighter. "What will happen to you when I go?"

"I'll sit here and have some tea. It's a beautiful day; a great day to go downtown."

Isabelle pulled back. "Can you do that? Can you leave the house and go downtown?"

"I was talking about you. That's what you have to do now. You'll see." She let go of Isabelle and stood up. Taking the pen off the table, she put it firmly in her granddaughter's hand and bent her fingers around it. She whispered, "Guard this," because she was referring to Isabelle's safety as well as her own death. Without any hesitation she hoped her granddaughter would use the pen if she needed it.

In that moment of pure unselfish love, she realized that no matter what happened to her now, she would be all right. Whether she remained forever in this room, or returned to the places beyond death she so much preferred, she felt . . . full. She remembered a proverb—"Empty vessels make the most noise." But at this moment her heart and head, miraculously, made no noise at all. She could not recall a time in either her life or death when she had felt so brimming.

Isabelle closed the front door behind her and did not look back. She had no idea whether she would ever see this house again. She had no idea of anything now but that she must follow the dog as her grandmother had ordered.

It sat in the same place on the lawn, watching her impassively. She walked up to it and said, "Hi, Hietzl." She half-expected it to say, "Hi."

But it did not respond. For a time she wondered if her grandmother had been playing a trick on her by saying that was its name. Who called their dog that?

Hietzl was not helpful. He looked at her with large brown eyes but did not even lift a paw to shake.

"Do you understand me, dog? *Sprechen-sie Deutsch?*"

"I know he's always wanted to learn." A middle-aged man came up with his hands in the pockets of a chic long, green, loden coat. Isabelle had never seen the man before.

"Hello, Hietzl." The man snapped his fingers and the dog began jumping around in happy circles, overjoyed to see him. Once in a while it leapt up on him. The man rubbed its head and did not seem at all upset that it was tracking mud and wet grass on his beautiful coat. "And good morning to you, Ms. Neukor." He was standing with the sun directly behind him. Isabelle had to shade her eyes to see his face.

"You know me?"

"I do."

"What's your name?"

"Chivas. You can call me Chivas."

"Like the whiskey?"

"Yes, exactly. You said you didn't like odd names like Hietzl, so let's use the name of your favorite whiskey."

"That's regal of you."

He smiled at her joke and patted the jubilant dog some more.

"And am I supposed to go with you now?"

"If you'd be so kind. My car is right over there." He pointed to a large dark green Audi parked nearby.

"And what about Hietzl?"

"He goes with us. He rides in the back."

"Where are we going, Mr. Chivas?"

"Just call me Chivas, that's fine. Downtown—I'm to drop you off at the Café Diglas."

Isabelle was taken completely off guard. "The Diglas? Why are we going there?"

"Because Mr. Ettrich will be waiting there for you."

"*Vincent?* At the Diglas?" Dismayed, she touched her forehead and narrowed her eyes, as if trying to better focus on all this. The dog sat down on the grass and furiously began scratching its chin with a rear paw. The scratch-scratch-scratch was the loudest sound around them.

Chivas smiled and nodded. "It was his idea. He said it was where you had your first date?"

That much was true, but why was Vincent in Vienna at a café when he said he had so much to do? "All right, let's go."

As if it understood exactly what she said, the dog stood up and trotted toward the street.

Isabelle looked at the car and looked at the car because she knew something was wrong about it. Something—"Wait a minute. Now I *know* what it is: That's a new car. You have a new car. I know the model. My friend Cora Vaughan bought one this year. But we're five years ago."

Chivas shook a finger at her and winked. "Very good, Ms. Neu-kor. Very observant. I've even got a CD in the car from the Blood-hound Gang. Do you like their music?"

"I don't know who you're talking about. Why do you have this year's model car when everything else around us is five years ago?"

"Because Hietzl and I are *from* this year. We came back here to get you." He went to the passenger's door, unlocked and opened it for her.

"Explain." She wasn't going to budge until she heard an answer that satisfied her. And she definitely was not getting into that car with Mr. Whiskey and Hietzl the wonder dog.

"We have to get you back to the present, and this is the most comfortable way of doing that. By the time we reach the café downtown we'll be up to date."

Isabelle did not like that answer. But then she was hailed from behind by her grandmother's voice. Turning around, she saw that the old woman had opened the window to her room and was leaning out on the sill. Both hands were fanned around her mouth to make a megaphone. "It's all right, dear, you can trust him. He's telling you the truth."

Isabelle yelled back, "He says by the time we get to the First District it will be five years from now."

"If that's what he says then it's true. Really, you can trust him."

The dog barked twice, impatient to be going.

"What if I don't go with you?"

Chivas put up both hands in surrender, not wanting to offend. "You don't have to. It's your decision, but it's really a lot faster this way. Would you prefer to take public transportation? Does a tram run near here?"

She was looking at Chivas, sizing up both him and his words, when her grandmother called out to her again.

"Isabelle, go with him. Trust me—it's all right."

"Yeah? Well, I have a better idea—I'll go with you, but I'll drive. You said we just have to go downtown, right?"

The man in loden nodded. "Right. That's fine with me." He handed her the keys to the Audi. Taking them, she waved a last time at her grandmother and got in the car. Chivas walked around to the passenger's side, gestured for the dog to jump into the back, then got in and closed the door. He reached across his chest for the seat belt. Isabelle only watched him because she never wore a seat belt.

He clicked in and said to her, "I would suggest you wear your seat belt. We're going to pass through some ugly weather on the way there and you never know what the roads will be like."

Before answering, Isabelle looked through the windshield at the splendid summer morning spread out like a feast around them. "What are you talking about? What are you telling me, Mr. Chivas?"

"Only that I think it would be a very good idea if you wore your seat belt. Again though, it's your decision."

"A good idea" was an understatement. They had not traveled more than a block when the weather changed completely. Stranger still, there was no gradual transition from one season to the other. One moment it was A and literally the next it was B.

In front of Isabelle's house the trees and flowers had all been in full gaudy bloom. The sun on them was a friendly summer-morning pale yellow. But the moment the car went around that first corner, the sky was an ominous leaden/purple gray. A late November gray that says snow is very near. All of the flowers were long dead. The trees were leafless and a brown so dark that from a distance they looked black. In fact there seemed to be no color around them at all. From one second to the next, the world had gone from Technicolor to a black-and-white movie.

Shocked, Isabelle hit the brakes so hard that the dog slammed the back of her seat with his head.

"Sorry, Hietzl, sorry. What is this?"

Chivas took a blue pack of Airwaves chewing gum out of his pocket and took a piece from it. "I told you before: There's going to be a lot of changes in the weather between here and downtown."

"Why? Changes like this?"

"Worse. Much more extreme. In the last five winters there have been some very heavy snowstorms here."

She dipped her head and regarded him skeptically. "And we're going to pass through all of them in a twenty-minute ride?"

He looked at her as if she had asked the most obvious question in the world. "Well, yes, five years is twenty seasons. Between here and the First District we must go through all twenty of them if we are going to return to our time. That's why I brought a four-wheel-drive car."

Isabelle looked at her hands on the steering wheel and then, for no logical reason, at Chivas's hands. "What kind of driver are you?"

"I placed third in the Acropolis Road Rally and fourth at Monaco when I was alive."

"Okay, you drive then." As the first giant flakes of snow flickered into view and swirled around in the air on the now-whipping wind, Isabelle got out of the Audi and traded places with the one-time rally driver.

On the back seat, Hietzl watched all of this mysterious human moving around with calm indifference.

Five minutes away at Gersthof, they came upon the first major traffic accident. The snow on the ground was four inches thick. A silver moving van had skidded on a patch of ice and gone right into a red and white tram. The whole area around the two giants had come to a standstill. In the street many people wearing their thickest winter clothes braved the snow and bitter wind to see what the damage looked like.

As soon as he took over as driver, Chivas had turned the heater on to full and slipped the transmission into four-wheel drive. Still it was very treacherous going because the temperature outside was below freezing and the roads were all snow and ice.

In her thin cashmere sweater and T-shirt Isabelle was cold despite the heat being turned on full blast. She held her elbows tightly but didn't pay much attention to this cold because what was going on outside the car was fascinating. She spoke loudly so as to be heard above the blower. "How much longer will we be in winter?"

Chivas stared straight ahead and kept tight hold of the wheel. "No idea. I know as much about this as you do. Hopefully not much longer. But it is getting worse. The roads are covered with black ice."

He steered them expertly around the truck/tram wreck and under an elevated train overpass into . . . spring. On one side of the overpass it had been snowing. On this side it was still cloudy but nothing threatening. The sun kept peeping through the clouds. There was no snow anywhere. Parkas had been shed for jeans jackets and pullovers. A few brave souls even wore shorts and sandals. A man carried a bouquet of exotically colored flowers. But another block farther on it began to rain, then pour. A short time later they were driving through a torrential thunderstorm. It became so dark that they had no idea what time of day it was.

Isabelle reached forward and turned off the heat. The blower quieted but the slam and drum of rain on the car replaced it in intensity. Lightning kept coming, coming, coming, followed instan- taneously by great bone-shaking cracks of thunder. The storm was right above them and the runoff of the rain grew higher and higher in the streets until it was a speeding small flood.

"I think—" Their car or something very close was hit by light- ning. BANG! Everything around them lit up like a bomb going off. Isabelle shouted in surprise.

Chivas said he was going to pull over for a few minutes and let the storm pass. Without waiting for her answer, he started to turn slowly in toward the curb. The car behind them smashed into the Audi. The sickening crack and thud of metal hitting metal. Then something large fell off and hit the street.

"Jesus!"

Both of them turned and watched as the driver of a white Suzuki

SUV pulled drunkenly around them and sped away.

"Hey, that guy's doing a hit-and-run!"

Unaffected, Chivas opened his window a crack and spit out his chewing gum. "It was a woman. Didn't you see her long blond hair?"

"So what? She's still doing a hit-and-run."

"We've got more to worry about than that now."

Isabelle stiffened. "Like what?"

"Did you notice the car she was driving?"

Isabelle pointed toward where Ms. Hit-and-Run had sped off. "A Suzuki SUV. Why?"

Chivas stared at her but said nothing. It looked like he was waiting for her to figure out something. The storm kept crashing around them. It was still directly overhead. Maybe it was listening to their conversation and found it so interesting that it didn't want to leave yet. Was she supposed to discover something in Chivas's facial expression, something that would tell her what he was really saying?

To fill the void, she said as an afterthought, "I had a car like that once. The Suzuki, I mean."

He stared at her. Without looking behind her, she was almost sure Hietzl was staring at her too.

"My car was white too. I was a terrible driver then. I had an accident in it and totaled it." She looked at the driver and raised her eyebrows. "You're not being of much help here. Am I supposed to be deciphering something?"

He kept staring at her but then slowly pointed in the direction of the hit-and-run driver. "Help? All right, I'll help you decipher. Think about it, Isabelle. The car that just hit us was a white Suzuki SUV. The driver was a blond woman. We're a long way from the center of town, which means we're still a few years ago. You just said you owned that kind of car a few years ago—"

Isabelle slid all the way over in her seat until her back touched the passenger's door. "That was *me* in that car? That was me who just hit us?"

He nodded.

"How? How can that be?"

"Because you brought her back. You brought her back to stop us now. You don't want us to get downtown to your meeting. Next you'll bring other versions of yourself to keep us from returning to our time. That was just the first attempt."

"*I'm* doing it? Why? Why would I stop myself? I want to be with Vincent; now more than ever. That's all I want."

Chivas's hand came down off the wheel, cutting the air between them like he was throwing a karate chop. "No you don't! You're afraid of what will happen the next time you're with him. And you just proved it by trying to run us off the road. You're afraid of what will happen to the baby and what will happen to you.

"You're a terrible coward, Isabelle, and have been your whole life. Luckily your family and their money have kept you safe from harm. But it hasn't made you stronger. Just the opposite—given the choice, you have almost always run away whether physically or psychically." He reached into his shirt pocket and took out a slip of paper. "You once read this passage and it had such an impact that you wrote it down in your diary. Because you knew it was so true about yourself.

" 'Fear's greatest weapon is its ability to blind us to anything but ourselves. In its presence we forget there are others to consider, things to save besides our own skins, our own feelings.'

"If you join up with Ettrich again now, you know you're going to have to be braver than you've ever been—"

Livid at what he had said, she slammed her hand down on the dashboard. "That's bullshit! I went into *death* to get him! No coward does that."

"*You* did not do it, Isabelle; a small and very remote part of you did—a part you never knew existed before. Like a tiny island in the middle of an ocean that's never been mapped. If you weren't pregnant, you would never have looked for that island. And without doubt you never would have discovered it in your normal travels. You went to get Vincent because of the baby. Don't deceive yourself about that. You did it for Anjo. You found that extraordinary courage within because of the child. No other reason."

She hit the dashboard again. "That's not true! I did it for Vincent. I did it because I love him."

"Wrong. If you loved him, you would *never* have run out on him in London. Don't lie now, Isabelle. You've been lying to yourself your entire life. It's made you deluded and more frightened the older you've gotten. That's why you almost always run away from difficult things. It's part of your nature now. Then you make up a lame excuse to justify your spinelessness. Until Anjo, you had never stood and fought for anything important in your life. That's why you are a coward.

"I'm not telling you something you don't already know in your heart."

She had no chance to digest what he said. While he spoke, Isabelle looked out the window on her side so that she wouldn't have to look at him. When she heard the car start up again and felt it pull out, she was still looking out her window.

"I can see her down the block. She's coming this way."

Isabelle looked quickly through the windshield. In the rain she saw the white car coming toward them from the opposite direction. She tried to keep her voice calm, especially in light of what he had just said about her. "What are you going to do?"

His voice was cool and knowing. "With her? Just scare her. She's not the one I'm worried about." Chivas drove toward the white car as he spoke. Thirty feet away he veered into the oncoming lane and, accelerating, went straight at it. The Suzuki tried to stop. They could hear the skitter of its brakes and skidding tires across the wet distance, through the closed windows of their car. Isabelle had no time to protest or be afraid because what Chivas had done was so unexpected. It all happened within seconds of her seeing the white car moving their way. All she managed was a peep of surprise.

Just before impact, the Suzuki veered to the right and drove off the street straight into a lean-to tram stop. Luckily no one was standing there because the car demolished the flimsy metal structure before coming to an abrupt full stop after hitting a light pole square-on.

Isabelle saw the driver raise her blond head off the steering wheel. She had obviously hit it there on impact with the pole because Isabelle Neukor never wore a seat belt. The older woman stretched her neck as far as it would go to see what had happened to her younger self.

Chivas knew. "She's all right—she only banged her head. Luckily the car is totaled so we don't have to think about *her* anymore. Not that she's the one who worries me."

"Who does worry you?"

She found out minutes later. They had stopped for a red light a block before the Gürtel, the road that circles the inner city and is the demarcation line between the outer districts of Vienna and downtown. Isabelle was torn between wanting to respond to the cruel things he had said and being hyperalert to their surroundings in case they were attacked again.

Chivas seemed content to simply drive and not continue the discussion. It was difficult enough because, as he had predicted, the weather kept constantly changing around them. Sometimes the change was extreme; others it was hardly noticeable. The trees bloomed again. There were window boxes full of summer flowers. A few blocks later the boxes had been taken inside because it was too cold. There was more rain and snow but nothing as extreme as what they had passed through. But both of them knew that meant nothing because it could all change in a blink.

In front of them at the traffic light was a black BMW. Isabelle knew little about cars so she could not tell in what year the car had been produced. She was about to ask Chivas when the first stone hit. It landed with a loud metallic thunk on the roof of the BMW. About the size of a large grapefruit, the stone was so heavy that instead of bouncing off and falling to the ground after hitting, it bowed the roof and stayed where it fell.

Neither of them connected this new shock with what had happened already. Then another stone as big as the first hit the middle of their windshield and rolled down onto the hood. If it had not been shatterproof, both people would have had faces full of flying glass. As it was, they could not see ahead because the windshield was spiderwebbed into a million crystalline cracks.

"Shit, shit, shit." Chivas reached into the pocket on the driver's door and brought up a ball-peen hammer. "Watch your face!" He did not wait for her to cover up. He smashed the windshield with the round end of the hammer head.

Behind upraised arms, she turned her face to the side and felt fear thick as wood in her throat choking her. Squinting and holding her arms up, she cautiously looked toward the now-blind windshield. With his hammer Chivas was knocking a hole through it on his side. She thought of ice fishing. She thought he's hammering through ice.

When the hole was about ten inches wide, he stuck his head forward over the steering wheel. He looked both ways through the hole to see what was going on outside. Another stone hit the very front of their car. Chivas put the Audi in reverse. Immediately they hit a van pulled up close behind them. He swung the steering wheel to the left, then forward-and-backed their car in its place until he could get around the BMW and pull away. Another stone hit the ground nearby. Stones rained down all around them. The sounds were amazing, frightening. But this was good too because it had stopped all of the traffic around them, allowing Chivas to pull out and keep on going.

There were glass shards and dirt on his hands from the hammering. He wiped them across his coat. "Those were cobblestones. Those stones are hundreds of years old and heavy! She must have dug them up from the street. Then climbed all the way to the roof of that building with them to drop on us."

"It was me up there, wasn't it; another scared version of me trying to keep me away from Vincent?"

"Yes, it was you."

"Turn around and go back." Her voice was strong and determined.

Chivas looked at her. "What'd you say?"

"I want you to turn the car around and go back there."

"No, I can't do that." He took a hand off the steering wheel and pointed it forward, as if giving instructions to something straight ahead. "I'm not permitted to go backward. Only forward."

"You're joking?"

"No, Isabelle, I really can't go backward. It's against my instructions."

"Then drop me off here. I'll get to the café as soon as I can by myself." They were two blocks across the Gürtel toward town. He pulled over to the curb again. It had begun to drizzle.

"What are you going to do?"

She looked at the sky and gave a sheepish chuckle. "You said I'm a coward. So now it's time for a change."

He nodded but did not ask what she intended to do. They were both silent a while, swimming around in their own thoughts. Finally he said, "I'll wait for you here."

She had her hand on the door release. "That's nice of you, but I don't know when I'll be back. I don't know if I'll be back. I don't really know anything except that I have to go back there."

"Then take Hietzl with you."

"What can he do?"

"Hietzl? All sorts of things. He's also good company."

"No, I have to do this myself. Without any help or magic or . . . I just have to do it myself."

"I understand, Isabelle. We'll wait for you here."

She nodded and opened the door. Getting out she felt the drizzle on her head and hands. She wanted to say something more to him but could think of nothing so she started to walk away. Then a thought came and she doubled back. When he saw her standing by the passenger's door again, Chivas lowered the window there. She bent down and said to him, "Thank you for bringing me this far. And thanks for telling the truth."

Ten minutes later she stood at the intersection where they had been pelted. Someone had moved the stones off the street and up onto the sidewalk in a row. The black BMW was also parked on the sidewalk. Its driver was talking to two attentive policemen.

The BMW driver was pointing to the roof of a building across the street. Isabelle assumed that was where the stones had come from. She stayed away from the men because she didn't want to get involved in any conversation. Standing on the corner, she looked up at the roof of the building. People walked by her in both directions while cars stopped for the traffic light and then moved on.

The two men finished talking. The BMW with the dented roof pulled back onto the street and drove off. One policeman put his pen and clipboard under his arm and the two cops walked over and entered the building.

As soon as they were gone, a small blond head appeared over the edge of the roof five stories up. Isabelle was not surprised. Nor was she surprised when another stone came flying down from there. It fell far away and rolled.

Putting a hand to either side of her mouth as her grandmother had done earlier, Isabelle shouted up to the figure on the roof, "Come down here. I want to talk to you."

A pair of arms hurled another stone at her. This one hit closer. When it landed, Isabelle walked over to have a look. It was black, striated, and looked quite heavy. But when she put both hands beneath to try and lift it, she discovered to her very great astonishment that the stone weighed almost nothing: as much as a tennis ball, balsa wood, or an empty cardboard box.

She looked up just as another stone hit the street with a loud *plock*. A passing car could not avoid it and ran over the stone. It did not move. The car went bumpity-bump as its tire passed over the unbudging rock. Seeing this, Isabelle thought that one must be different—it must weigh a lot. Without a moment's hesitation she dropped the first and walked quickly into the street to this new one.

Nudging it with her foot, at the first second of physical contact she felt a substantial weight there. But then, almost as if it *realized* who was touching it, the heaviness of this second stone disappeared. It suddenly weighed as little as the other.

She picked it up with one hand and walked back to the sidewalk. She looked up at the roof. There was that blond head again, watching her from on high. What was she supposed to do now? What *could* she do? Thinking about this, she instinctively brought the stone up to her nose and sniffed it.

Right away she smelled more than thirty years of her fear, lies, and deception. Those things do have an odor. It is common, metallic, and not unlike the smell of fresh blood. It is fresh but it is also old, ancient even. Everyone knows the aroma but does not admit it because we have smelled it on ourselves too many times. It is ugly and deeply embarrassing. Good intentions, good love, good hope. We were so sure it would work this time. We were so sure *this* was the right person, or the ideal situation, the thing we had been waiting for our whole lives. But we were wrong. And as our fear, lies, and other deceptions moved in to those new situations, the odor began again.

All of that was in Isabelle's head now because she recognized it was her odor emanating from the stone she held. This wasn't a cobblestone—it was one of the weapons she had used to destroy herself. At the same time she also realized it had become harmless the instant she touched it. She guessed that was because she'd gotten out of the car and deliberately returned to face the woman on the roof, the stone thrower.

The whole thing made her angry. Furious. It made her furious; she made herself furious, the woman on the roof who was the Isabelle in London who had run away from Vincent when she hadn't heard exactly what she wanted to hear . . . All of it made her want to—

The stone was the size of a grapefruit but weighed only as much as a tennis ball. Isabelle could think of nothing else to do to vent her anger but throw it with all her might back at the stupid woman on the roof. And that's what she did. When you are as angry as she was, it is not difficult to throw a tennis ball five stories in the air. It will even go higher if you are as angry as Isabelle Neukor was.

It sailed over the roof of the building not far from that damned little blond head up there. In fact, although the stone went wide, the head ducked fast out of sight, clearly afraid that it would be hit.

One stone wasn't enough. Still enraged, Isabelle went over to the other ones that had been lined up on the sidewalk. One after the other she threw them all back up there. She didn't think about aiming or anything else. She just flung the fuckers as hard as she could. When they were gone she narrowed her eyes and scanned the rooftop looking for that head but it was gone.

An old fat woman carrying two plastic bags full of cheap cabbages from the *Naschmarkt* had stopped to watch. She'd never seen anything like this. When the young woman was finished with her astonishing athletic feat, she asked her how she had done it. The old woman was not interested in why someone would be standing in the middle of the sidewalk in the middle of an afternoon throwing large octagonal stones onto a roof. She just wanted to know how it was done.

The young woman rubbed her nose as if it itched mightily. For a moment the cabbage shopper thought she was preparing to do something else violent. But Isabelle was only trying to frame what she wanted to say. When she had it, she pointed at the shopper and shook her finger at her.

"You can't change the past, but the past is always coming back to change *you*; both your present and your future."

The shopper thought that was sort of interesting. But all she really wanted to hear was how this skinny, ethereal-looking woman had thrown heavy rocks onto a roof.

"The past is fixed, it's permanent." Isabelle was on a roll now, thinking out loud, not about to stop. Her voice got louder, her words faster. Soon the shopper could barely follow what she was saying. "It's dead, but it keeps coming back and stops us from moving forward. It gets in the way of our present . . . and our future." She pointed up to the roof but kept looking at the old woman. "All those things she threw at me were *old*—stuff from my past. But it always stopped me before."

There was a pause while she caught her breath, the words sank in, and cars moved by.

"But how did you lift those big rocks?"

Isabelle looked at the other woman as if she had just spoken in Urdu. "What?"

"Those rocks—how did you throw them up there?"

"I'm sorry—I have to go now." Isabelle started away.

"Was it a trick? Are we on television?" The shopper suddenly brightened up, thinking they were on *Candid Camera*. She looked around expectantly but no cameras emerged from hiding.

Walking backward in the direction of Chivas's car, Isabelle pointed her finger again at the woman. "Don't let your past scare you out of doing anything now." Still backpedaling, she put her hands together at the wrists as if they were bound. She shook them. "It always wants to tie your hands or trip you, but don't let it." She turned and walked quickly away.

The shopper gave a last look around, her last small hope fading that perhaps the cameras would show themselves now, but no luck. Sighing, she got a better grip on her bags and started again toward home and the cabbage soup she would prepare this evening.

Because this interaction was going on between the two women, neither of them looked up at the roof and saw the blond figure throw another stone at them. But as soon as it left her hands, this stone was wafted high in the air like a tissue or an empty candy wrapper. Then it was whipped away in the opposite direction by a strong breeze that was searching for something to play with.

Chivas was feeding a spicy *Debreziner* sausage to Hietzl when Isabelle tapped on his window again with the back of her hand. He pressed a button that unlocked her door. She heard it and walked around to the passenger's side.

"Wow, you're back already? That was fast."

She took the sausage and cardboard plate that it had come on away from him. Hietzl sat patiently in the back seat watching its meal change hands. Isabelle broke off a small jagged piece and fed it to the dog. It chewed slowly and savored the taste. Before offering it another chunk, she looked at what was left of the bumpy red sausage on the paper plate. "Maybe I should have told her instead, 'Never let your past salt your meat for you.' "

Chivas didn't know what she was talking about but he liked the sentiment. "That's true. Your sense of taste was different in the past. As a kid I loved cottage cheese. Now I can't even see the stuff without thinking it looks like white vomit."

She fed the dog the last morsels while Chivas turned on the engine and drove away. At the Ringstrasse he turned left rather than going straight into town.

"Why are you going this way? I thought we were going to the café."

"There's been a change of plans. You're going to the airport."

"Why the airport? Is Vincent out there?"

"No, he's in America. You're flying there to meet him."

"I just *flew* to America."

"I know, but this is the only way to get you there now. When we crossed the Gürtel, we were back in today. I have no magic now except this last piece." He took an airplane ticket and a passport out of his pocket—her passport, the one she had left in Vincent's apartment.

She took them from him, inwardly groaning at the thought of having to get on another airplane for twelve hours. "How did you get my passport?"

"Hietzl did. He just got back. That's why he was so hungry."

She twisted the rearview mirror around so that she could see the dog. It was busy licking its balls. "How did you know I'd come back, Chivas? How did you know—"

"My only experience with you, albeit short, is that you have just become a fighter. You rose to this occasion and went back to face what scared you."

It was so good hearing that. She was sure she was blushing but didn't care. "Thank you. But why isn't Vincent at the café now?"

"Because he was in a serious car accident. He's in a coma and they don't know if he will survive."

My Eef

Ettrich was up on stage, rocking the house. The audience was laughing so much that he had to pause longer than usual between jokes. In the middle of the bit about Satan and padded mailing envelopes, he knew by their reaction that he was home free. You can tell quickly whether an audience is with you or not. It's like putting the first moves on a new woman: If you win their smile right away and it stays, you're off and running. Or if their head is pushed forward a little so they can more carefully hear everything you're saying because they *want* to hear everything you're saying. Their arms aren't crossed because they're not blocking you out . . . signs like these were what you looked for. Yes, it was very similar to when a new woman opened up to you.

This was one of his favorite dreams of all. Whenever he had it he would wake up the next morning happy and full of energy. Awake, he knew damned well he had no talent to be a stand-up comedian. Asleep he was as good as any of them and better than most.

"Have you ever noticed that fat women like patent leather? Why is that?" Now he was moving into the sweet spot, the chocolate center of his routine. The best jokes, the nuttiest insights came now.

284

Even when the first part of his act bombed sometimes, he knew he'd have an audience in his pocket from here on out.

Stepping away from the microphone, he rubbed his palms together. He took a deep breath because the next bit was long and he had to hit the lines boom-boom-boom if it was going to sound perfect. When he took the mike again someone in the audience stood up. Ettrich wanted to yell Sit down! You're going to love this next part, I swear to you. Hold off taking that piss for five minutes. Just listen to this—

A man had stood up, a tall man. Ettrich could not see him very well because the room was dark and the stage lights pointed directly at him. But he could make out a tall man at a table up front, stepping sideways.

A comedian has two ways of dealing with this situation—ignores it, or addresses it. Ettrich felt so good about this audience and the energy in the room that he decided to go after the guy.

"Look at this man leaving in the middle of my act. Now that means either—" Before Ettrich had a chance to finish what he was saying, the fashionably dressed black man stepped close to the stage. With a start, Ettrich recognized him—Tillman Reeves, his roommate in the hospital before he died.

"Hello, Vincent."

"Till! What are you doing here?"

Someone far back in the room shouted out, "Louder! We can't hear you back here."

"Can we talk, Vincent?"

"Here? *Now?*" Ettrich looked at the audience, amazed that Till would make such a ridiculous request in the middle of his act.

"This is only a dream, Vincent. You can do whatever you want in a dream."

"I know, but I'm doing a *show* here, Till—"

"You're also dying, friend, which is more important. Don't you think we should talk about that now?"

"Louder up there! We can't hear you."

Tillman put out his hand, gesturing for Vincent to go ahead of him. Right in the middle of his act! Resigned, Ettrich stepped down and walked to Reeves's table. He felt like a kid being called out of class and made to go to the principal's office. The audience didn't mind. The emcee jumped up on stage and called for a round of applause for Victor Ettrich. They gave him a halfhearted one. Ettrich knew that if he'd been able to finish his routine they would have clapped for him big time.

Since it was a dream, the guy who immediately followed him on stage was Richard Kroslak, Ettrich's archenemy in fifth grade. This Kroslak was an adult but he began telling the same fart and sex jokes that no one liked even in fifth grade. But this audience loved them. They were howling at everything he said. To Ettrich's great chagrin, judging by the intensity of their laughter it sounded as if they liked Richard's routine much more than they had liked his.

"Do you know what happened to you, Vincent?"

Although he was sitting at the table with Tillman, Ettrich couldn't stop looking and listening to that dumbbell Kroslak.

"Vincent?"

He blinked once then turned both his head and attention to his friend. "Yes, Till?"

"Do you remember what happened to you?"

"You mean the accident?"

Reeves's face relaxed. "Yes. Do you remember it?"

Ettrich thought a bit and eventually said, "I was driving through an intersection and another car blindsided me."

"Good! You remember that."

"Why wouldn't I? They were trying to kill me."

Till shook his head. "No, they wanted exactly this to happen. They wanted you either seriously injured or in a coma."

Ettrich showed no emotion. He laced his fingers over a knee. "I don't care that it happened. It's not bad here." When he was alive he had always heard that when people died and looked back at life, they realized how empty and unfulfilling it was. *I fought so hard to stay* there? Now he knew it was true—living was a silly, worthless thing. A pretty waitress came by and, without having been told, brought the men their favorite drinks. Taking the glasses from her, they raised them in a toast to each other and had a first sip— perfect.

Tillman put his down on the table. "Comas are pleasant places. They're the ideal place to go when you're trying to decide whether to live or die."

Ettrich kept drinking from his glass. "Do people always go to a comedy club when they're in a coma?"

"No, they can choose any place they want—the Maldives Islands, a hammock in the backyard where you watch fireflies punctuate the summer evening . . . Some place where you're at peace and can think clearly."

The comedian on stage must have cracked a great joke because wild laughter erupted from the audience. Ettrich looked around. "Then why the hell would I choose to come to a comedy club where Richard Kroslak is bringing down the house?"

"I don't know, Vincent. You'd have to ask yourself that question. Have you decided yet what you're going to do?"

"Now?"

"Yes. Are you going to die again?" Till turned his glass around and around on the table with long fingers.

"I haven't really thought about it." Ettrich realized something and looked at Till. "I'm in the hospital again, aren't I? That's why you're here. The last time we saw each other, you said they wouldn't let you out. So I'm back in the hospital dying again, huh?"

"Hospitals are where most people go when they're in comas,

Vincent." Coco came over to their table and sat down. She wore a clinging silvery silk dress that made her look like a sexy letter opener.

"*Whoa* Coco, you look great!"

She beamed and kissed him on the cheek. "Thank you. It's our last time together, Vincent. I thought it would be nice if I dressed up for you."

A big raucous round of applause rose all around them. Kroslak left the stage in a phony jog, both hands in the air waving to his adoring fans. The houselights came up and the audience started talking.

"You've got nine lives, Coco. I thought the last time we'd seen each other was when they killed you at the zoo."

"It was—in *that* dimension. But we're in a different one now and this definitely is our last time together." Leaning forward she took both of his hands, squeezed them, and let them go.

Then both Coco and Tillman watched Ettrich closely, as if expecting him to say something significant or decisive. But there was nothing to say. He liked this dream and had little desire to leave it. He enjoyed doing his act on stage and knew that if he practiced enough he would become a great comedian. Somewhere far back in his mind were thoughts of Isabelle and Anjo, but they were like foreign cities he'd visited long ago and enjoyed but had no attachment to now.

Frustrated at his silence and the bland look on his face, Coco decided to go for broke. "What about my Eef, Vincent? Have you forgotten that?"

His body went rigid and his eyes flared. He stood up. "Fuck you, Coco. You had no right to do that." To Reeves's great surprise, Ettrich walked away from the table and did not look back.

Coco slapped her forehead and said, "Shit!"

Tillman Reeves said nothing but she was so embarrassed that she wouldn't look at him.

"That was so stupid of me, Till—really really stupid." Without saying more, she got up and followed Ettrich out of the room.

Still not looking at her, Reeves picked up his drink and made to take a sip, then gently replaced the glass on the table.

Coco knew the rules and she had just broken a very big one. Human decisions had to be made voluntarily. There could be no coercion or trickery involved. When that happened, things were often tainted, causing useless or even disastrous results.

But she had been so impatient to get Vincent out of this stupid dream and back into his life where he was so urgently needed that she went where she was never meant to go to find what she wanted.

Until then, the only ones who knew about "my Eef" were Vincent and Isabelle. It was their secret and treasure. Neither had ever told anyone about it. When Coco saw how indifferent he was about returning to life, she went into his mind. Without any hesitation she went looking for just such a jewel to dangle in front of him and say look—*this* is why you must go back. This is reason enough.

Early in their relationship, when both Ettrich and Isabelle knew beyond doubt that this was going to be huge, they were making love one night. In the middle of it, Isabelle began to cry. Initially the reason her tears came was because she was so afraid of the intensity of her feelings for this new man. Then the crying went beyond that into something much greater.

Ettrich didn't know what he should do. While she cried she wouldn't let go of him, wouldn't stop making love. She kept moving, touching him, tears flowing down her face onto his bare skin. More and more tears, sobs, her body moving quicker and wilder. He knew they weren't happy tears but he couldn't tell anything else about them. Was she sad? Overcome? As her crying intensified so did her lovemaking until it became a kind of glorious attack he could barely handle.

In time some part of it swept him up too and pulled him into its center. He stopped thinking and his body took over. Ettrich lost control. He had never, ever lost himself in sex but now it was happening. He was just *gone* and the experience was overwhelming.

Out of nowhere she abruptly came, her voice going high and shrill. For moments it sounded almost as if she were talking in tongues. Then as she climaxed she said "My Eef." Her orgasm went on and on and the "e" in that strange word held. To Ettrich it felt like she came forever, the whole thing becoming more intense as it went on. He didn't think about having an orgasm, so caught up was he in the intensity of the act itself.

When it ended and she slowly floated back down to earth again—her body unclenching, her fingers no longer steel on his arms—they looked into each other's eyes. Everything they had ever wanted in another person was there. For that time, those holy seconds, both of them were complete and the feeling was transcendent. Neither would ever experience anything like that again.

When life had returned to breathing normally once more, Ettrich said in that moment he felt they had given birth to a being that was wholly theirs but separate at the same time. It lived now; it was on the earth and would survive as long as either of them was still here. Isabelle had once read a poem that said much the same thing but did not tell him that because she was so in awe of the experience and thrilled by Vincent's coming up with the idea himself.

Shyly he asked her what "Eef" meant. She gave him a blank look so he explained.

"I don't know where it came from, Vincent." She paused and stroked his face. Her palm was hot and wet. "Maybe that's its name—that thing we made together. It's My Eef. Our Eef."

Either because she was self-conscious, or because those words immediately became sacred to them, Isabelle never said "My Eef" again in her passion. And the only time either of them ever referred to them was when they were talking about that night and its importance. They agreed that it was the only holy experience either of them ever had.

Opening the back door of the club, Coco was met by the bitter odors of fresh asphalt and exhaust fumes—two smells Vincent said he liked very much. The building was near a freeway—she could hear the constant passing and hum of traffic in the background. Stepping out into the parking lot, she looked all around for Ettrich. Because it was his dream, this world lived by his rules. A few feet away the adult Richard Kroslak was being beaten up by two boys wearing high school jackets and Beatles haircuts. Kroslak kept hollering, "I'll never do it again. I swear to God I'll never come back here." But his assailants kept punching.

Leaning on a candy-apple-red Chevelle, two pretty teenage girls smoked and rhapsodized about what a stud Vincent Ettrich was. After listening a while, Coco sidled up and asked if they had seen him recently. They both gestured off to the left and went back to their conversation.

"And that tongue! Do you believe the way he uses that tongue on you?"

Hearing this, Coco had to admit Vincent was an excellent kisser. And an excellent lover. He'd once said that in his experience, the vast majority of women were lousy lovers. But the poignant thing was most of them believed they were terrific in bed. Coco wondered if she was good in bed. She certainly enjoyed it. Unlike Vincent now, there were many things she would miss about this life when she was gone, sex being one of them.

She started quietly whistling "My Favorite Things" from *The Sound of Music* (she also loved musicals) as she walked across the parking lot in the direction the girls had indicated. What could she say now to convince him to go back to his life?

"Nothing."

In the first second, Coco thought she had said the word aloud to herself but she hadn't. A row of cars was parked in front of her. Sitting on the hood of one was Bruno Mann. Against all the advice he had been given at the barbershop, the King of the Park had decided to change himself back to the person Ettrich had always known. He wanted to see the look on Vincent's face when he realized who Bruno Mann really was.

"Hello, Missy."

She stopped where she was and watched him as if he were a tornado coming right at her. "Bruno, you're not supposed to be here. I'm sure Vincent would not include you in his dream."

His arms were behind him on the hood. He leaned back comfortably, totally at ease in the moment. "That's true, but you were not supposed to go fishing in his mind for things like Eefs. So we've both been naughty. I won't tell anyone if you won't. Plus, aren't you impressed that I'm here? It's not easy to enter people's comas if you're not invited."

"Why are you here?" She looked around quickly to see if anyone else was with him.

"Why would I need anyone else to come with me? I got you, babe." Bruno finished speaking by singing the last line. He was reading her mind which wasn't fair but there was nothing she could do about it. He also emanated a force now that she had never felt before in him. It frightened her.

"Tell me why you're here, Bruno."

He grew an easy triumphant smile. "To witness the last act; the results of my handiwork. Did you hear they made me King of the Park? I've got so much power now that I can more or less do whatever I want. Cool, huh?

"But with Vincent I don't have to do much because either way, he's going to self-destruct.

"You heard what he said before—he's happy here. Isn't it incredible after all he's been through and experienced? The man lived and died, and then was resurrected with all *sorts* of extraordinary powers and reasons to live. But none of that matters because he *still* wants to stay here, doing his lousy act in a coma comedy club. Unbelievable. Human beings really are unbelievable. They don't deserve a place in the mosaic. They're so fucking blind."

"He just doesn't understand."

Bruno thought that was very funny. "Oh, sure he does—stop making excuses for him. You've lost, Coco, admit it. Look at the man—he's learned nothing. Look at the way he's thinking now— he doesn't care about living, or his girlfriend, or their kid and what will happen to it if he dies . . .

"Either way Ettrich loses. If he chooses to die now, obviously he won't be able to teach Anjo. Notice that—if he *chooses* to die. But say he *chooses* to return to life. If he does then he's in a deep coma from the accident and needs blood. Did you know that he and his girlfriend have the same rare blood type? The hospital where he's staying is now filled with our people.

"Isabelle will arrive and ask what she can do for him. Our doctors will say Vincent needs a blood transfusion right now to survive. Which he does." Bruno gave a push with his arms and slid gracefully down off the hood of the car.

"Now comes the beauty part—she'll tell them she and Vincent have the same blood type. The doctors will look grave and say only the truth—that it is *very* dangerous for a pregnant woman to give blood. Because they're anemic and losing any could seriously damage their baby.

"But because she loves Vincent so much now, and is sure of it, she will risk it. She will consciously choose to trade Anjo's life for his. Because by giving her rare blood to the man she loves, brave Isabelle *will* harm their special child.

"It'll be okay, but just a little slow. Not Down's syndrome slow, but enough not to understand anything Dad might want to teach it later on.

"So no matter how this unfolds, whatever happens will be their choice. They get to choose their failure. Is that brilliant or not? You've got to give me credit for this one."

"How do you know when she finds out how dangerous it is for the child that she'll give her blood to Vincent?" Coco knew as she said it that she was grasping at straws.

"Because theirs is a real love story, honey, and real love is always chaotic. You lose control; you lose perspective. You lose the ability to protect yourself. The greater the love, the greater the chaos. It's a given and that's the secret.

"There I was, thinking up all kinds of cunning ways to ruin them. Then it dawned on me—all I had to do was stand back and let their love do it for me. I didn't have any more work. Love is a petri dish for chaos. Just put it in there and let it *spawn*." He put one hand on his stomach and extended the other arm out as if he were ballroom dancing with a partner. To the tune of "My Favorite Things" he sang:

"Love is a vi-rus that de-stroys your hard disk,
Love is sure death to all your care-ful lo-gic—"

He danced by himself, he spun slowly. He moved in and out among the parked cars, pausing here and there to dip his invisible partner, to twirl her in the air, hamming it up and having the greatest time. Bruno had all the time in the world now because he was finished with his job. At that moment he was King of this Parking lot too.

Coco watched with loathing because she knew he was right. He didn't have to do anything more. Just let the Vincent/Isabelle connection run its course and no matter what direction it took, Anjo was doomed.

When fireworks started exploding in the night sky directly above them, illuminating their startled upturned faces with bursts and streamers of brilliant color, each thought the other had done it. Bruno thought it was Coco's unexpectedly gracious way of applauding him. Coco thought it was Bruno's way of applauding himself.

It was such a beautiful, bewildering sight that they remained silent a while and just watched. Beaming, Bruno thought it was his due. Coco thought, What a prick, what a prick, what an arrogant prick.

There were flowers and flags up there, rockets and rabbits lit the sky, lit their faces and the cars, the parking lot, and everything around them. A white birch tree that was hiding in the night suddenly glowed. The fading divider lines painted on the parking lot were visible again in the burst and sprinkle of radiant light from above.

It was an amazing display, one of a kind, an event that forced you back to being a child full of wonder. Both of them wanted to talk but couldn't tear their eyes away from all the flash and dazzle. In the middle of the finale—a multicolored waterfall that sprang and bubbled and seemed to take up every inch of up there—Bruno heard someone say close to his ear, "How do you like my show?"

He turned and there was Vincent Ettrich a foot away looking him straight in the eye.

The crackle and pop of the fireworks drowned out Bruno's first try. "They're yours?"

Ettrich put a hand behind his ear to show he couldn't hear. Bruno shouted out, "These are your fireworks?"

Ettrich yelled back, "Yes. It's my dream, so I decided to have some. Make it a festive atmosphere."

Bruno had nothing to say. Vincent didn't seem the least bit surprised to see him there.

"How are you, Vincent?"

Ettrich slapped him on the shoulder too hard. "After you tried to kill me in the car? I'm good, Bruno. I'm glad you made it."

Bruno was taken aback. "You are? You're not angry that I'm here?"

"I'm delighted."

Coco did not hear them talking. She was entranced by the fireworks and waited till the last bright light had died in the sky before looking over. She hadn't expected to see Vincent there. He had his hand on Bruno's shoulder and was leaning in toward him like an intimate friend telling a ripe new dirty joke.

Her voice was full of regret when she spoke. "Vincent, I'm so sorry about what I said in there—"

He shook his head—no more needed to be said on the subject. "So Bruno, aren't you going to ask me about my fireworks? Don't you want to know why I had them?"

"Okay, Vincent: Why did you have the fireworks?" Bruno's voice was campy and melodramatic—he was willing to play straight man to Ettrich.

"To celebrate my return. Thanks to you, I've decided to go back and live some more."

Without thinking, Coco clapped her hands together with joy. But then she remembered what would happen if Ettrich went back.

Bruno's voice was condescending. "That's very nice, Vincent. I'm happy for you."

"You don't sound happy."

Bruno Mann shrugged. There was no reason to pretend anymore. He didn't give a shit about Ettrich. He just wanted to leave. Or maybe as a last gesture when it was all over he would send up some fireworks of his own just to rub it in some more. Fireworks had been a great idea. He wished he had thought of them himself.

"I heard what you said before to Coco." Ettrich turned to her standing nearby. He could feel pity coming off her like heat.

"Yes, well, sometimes you lose, Vincent."

Ettrich squeezed the other man's shoulder. "You never understood the big picture, Bruno. That's why you were lousy at your job. Did you know that everyone in the office called you the doofus in a nice suit?"

Bruno started to say something but Ettrich squeezed harder on his shoulder to shut him up.

"Love *is* chaos, you're right. But it's not only chaos. Yes, you do lose control—*your* control. One person. Singular." Ettrich grinned now because he knew exactly where he was going with this. "Because when there's real love, it's not just you anymore. That's the hardest lesson to learn—it's not just you. Together you've created something new, a third thing . . . My Eef, and in the end that's what saves you—"

"Am I interrupting?" Tillman Reeves came walking across the parking lot toward them. None of them had seen him emerge from the building. His sudden appearance like that might have bothered them if all three weren't so caught up in the events of the moment.

Ettrich was pissed off. He had it clear in his mind now and wanted to say it all while it was still there, both for himself and the others. But Till's voice broke through that clarity.

Then something miraculous happened. When Vincent looked at Tillman Reeves this time, it dawned on him who the man really was. Awestruck, Ettrich opened and closed his mouth several times, unable to do anything else. Eventually he covered it with his hand and was silent.

None of the others said anything. They just stared at him. Bruno was certain it was the first sign of Ettrich's caving in to the inevitable.

"I know who you are!" Ettrich managed to say while looking at Till as if there were nothing else to look at in the world. His thoughts were moving so fast. It was like sitting by the window of a speeding train, trying to catch glimpses of the landscape rushing by outside. He remembered Tillman Reeves lying in the bed next to his before he died. Then meeting him in the hospital the time he'd gone there with Jack. Then a few minutes ago standing by the stage saying to Ettrich, "You're also dying, friend . . ."

"Now I know who you are! You're my Eef."

Till did not react but he didn't deny it either.

Ettrich became more animated. He counted off the proof on his fingers. "You were in the room when I died. You were also in the hospital when I bumped into Bruno. Then you were the first person I recognized in this dream—"

"And right now I'm in that same hospital keeping an eye on you, Vincent."

Despite all of their powers, neither Bruno nor Coco had known who Tillman Reeves really was. Now these enemies looked at each other with alarm and genuine trepidation because even they had been fooled by the way this situation was unfolding.

"But what does it mean, Till? I don't understand."

Bruno had had enough. He did not like how his moment of triumph had been turned into a love lecture by Ettrich which then segued into a chat with this old black guy. "Time's up, Vincent. In the real world you just took a turn for the worse. If you're going to go back, do it now." There was a note of petulance in his voice, as if things had better start going his way soon or else he would start making big trouble.

Tillman Reeves ignored him and spoke only to Ettrich. "Chaos creates nothing—it only destroys. It may be able to think in this mosaic, but it has no ability to make—it can only unmake. That's why it hates people—because they're always *creating* things, whether it's great love or castles made out of Coca-Cola bottles. You and Isabelle created me and I've been watching over you ever since."

Coco couldn't help saying, "There are no guardian angels."

"I'm not an angel. I'm Frankenstein, sort of—but a good one."

Tillman pointed at Vincent. "They took all of their best parts and made me."

Ettrich didn't understand all of this but great tears came to his eyes because his dumb patient heart understood everything.

Bruno stepped away from Ettrich and punched Tillman Reeves in the face. The old man was tall but very thin and frail. He staggered backward and fell down, landing on the base of his spine. Paralyzed with pain, he yelped like a small animal.

Now Bruno Mann stood directly above him, kicking at Tillman's head and face, connecting every time, the sound a horror of repeated *thuck* and *umph*. Almost as bad was neither of them made any other noise—no more yelps from Till, no laughter or words raining down from Bruno as he struck.

Vincent Ettrich was not a fighter and never had been. The few times in his life he'd seen people fighting for real, he'd been either amazed or amused. That amazement was back as his initial reaction to seeing old Tillman attacked. But it passed quickly and without another thought Ettrich leapt forward to stop Bruno. Somewhere in the background he heard a woman's voice, Coco's voice, shouting, "No! Don't touch him." But even if that had registered in Ettrich's mind, it would not have stopped him. He grabbed Bruno Mann's shirt and, pulling him back, wrapped his arms around the King of the Park.

One second, two, five—how long did he have hold of Bruno before being flicked off like a fly? It doesn't matter. In those seconds, Vincent Ettrich held chaos in his arms. No man, no more Mann, no mortal. Chaos.

It went into and through him like an injection of pure heroin that travels at the speed of sadness straight to the heart and brain. He had died once and been brought back to life. Now he died again but return was not so simple. Because Ettrich remained alive this time while the things that made him human died in the hopeless swirl of chaos all around him, world without end. No Lazarus could emerge reborn from this landscape because there was no landscape. Only the process, only the swirl, the unmaking, as Till had so rightly put it. It was an invisible tornado, a tidal wave without water drowning, *unmaking* him forever.

Not even bothering to turn around to check and see where Ettrich was, Bruno continued to beat the old man. Till had somehow managed to curl into a kind of ball, his thin arms barely protecting his head. The blows made terrible sickening sounds as they fell all over his body, wherever Bruno felt like kicking next.

Brought to consciousness by the electric shock of touching chaos, *all* of Vincent Ettrich was in that moment for the first time. Vincent Ettrich who had lived a comfortable empty life and then died an agonizing death, accompanied only by his fears and Tillman Reeves. Ettrich who had been in Death, seen what it was, and learned things there he could show his unborn son. And the Ettrich who had been brought back from Death by Isabelle and her love. All of them awoke and rose together in him. Looking across time and experience, death and resurrection, they saw and recognized each other.

Kick kick kick. Bruno's back was still turned. Why not—what did he have to fear behind him or anywhere in this repellent world? He would deal with Vincent when he was finished dancing on the old man.

Rising off the ground again, Ettrich came at Bruno more slowly this time. For an instant Coco saw his eyes and she immediately screamed. It was so loud and such a peculiar scream that even Bruno stopped and looked up. Lifting his head like that, his neck was exposed. Ettrich saw it, spun Bruno around and bit into and through his windpipe.

He tasted blood and flesh, he tasted chaos. His mouth was full of wet chaos. Every cell of his human self roared, "Spit it out, spit it out." But the other parts of him knew that he must eat all of this and swallow it if he were to prevail. So while Bruno Mann writhed on the ground, his hands to his half-throat trying to hold himself together, Ettrich *chewed*.

Most shocking was it did not all taste bad. Of course it was bitter and black, if you had to give it a color. It was every taste you had ever hated, made you sick, made you retch. Yes of course it was. But something in it was delicious because chaos *is* delicious too. It came as the second taste, the aftertaste that surprised the back of your throat after you'd almost spat out the first in utter revulsion.

Some part of Ettrich, who knows which one, wanted more of this taste and probably would have taken it if Coco hadn't grabbed his arm and made him look at her. She knew. His crazed eyes saw that in her face—she knew what he wanted to do.

"No, Vincent—stop."

Her words touched him slowly. Not all of Ettrich agreed. Some said no. Other parts of him were already dropping away, fading. They had done their job. He tried to stop them, to hold them. He would need them all if he were to continue but right now they did as they wanted.

Coco would not let go of him and that was good. At their feet Bruno Mann was dead, his face full of wonder. Tillman Reeves was slowly moving but he was alive. Chaos moved through Vincent Ettrich's system. Sometimes he shuddered as it touched him everywhere inside.

He looked at Coco. She said something but he didn't hear her. A terrible pain, a pain the size of the moon, tore across the length of his stomach. Chaos moving.

"Vincent?"

He had barely enough strength to stand and look at her.

"You won."

There were so many machines in and near Vincent that Isabelle had barely enough room among them to hold his hand. Thick white translucent tubes ran into his nose and mouth. There were wires clipped to his chest and fingers. Beige machines nearby drew yellow lines across black backgrounds. Things all around her made professional-sounding blips and bleeks. This section of the intensive care ward was more about machines than people, it seemed to Isabelle. The only person reportedly not hooked up to a machine lay near to Vincent. A curtain was pulled around the bed, blocking the view. She hadn't paid much attention. The wonderful ward nurse, Michelle, went about her work silently and with no fuss. She told Isabelle the unseen patient was a man who had been mugged and sustained serious internal injuries.

Kitty Ettrich and their children had visited Vincent earlier. Before they arrived Isabelle went to the waiting room at the end of the hall so that they could be alone with him. About half an hour later Jack entered the waiting room and sidled up to her. No one else was in there.

He put his hands behind his back and announced, "I was in this hospital with my dad just a few days ago."

Isabelle wanted to take his hand, kiss it, and then kiss his small plump cheeks. But she only nodded as if that were very interesting information she needed.

"My dad is a great guy."

If she spoke she would start to cry. So she only lowered her head and nodded so that the boy couldn't see the expression on her sorrowing face. When she looked up again he was gone. Only after a while did she realize the boy did not know who she was—he had just wanted to tell someone what a great guy his father was. And that in itself broke Isabelle's heart.

A long time later she went to the nurses' station to ask Nurse

Michelle if Vincent's family was still there. The nurse said no but
that the doctor would be coming to the room soon and wanted to
speak with her. Michelle was normally chatty so her curtness now
was chilling. What did the doctor have to tell her that he hadn't
already said? Isabelle hurried back to the room to be by Vincent's
side. Proximity to him always made her feel better.

A few minutes later the doctor came in and quickly explained
the situation. Vincent's condition was becoming unstable. He needed
a transfusion as soon as possible or else things would become very
grave. The problem was that he had an extremely rare blood type
which they did not have in the hospital, nor did any of the blood
banks in the city.

Right away Isabelle brightened and told him that was not a
problem because she had the same blood type as Ettrich. At first
the doctor was as relieved as she. Then he looked at her stomach
and remembered that she was pregnant. He said it was extremely
dangerous for a pregnant woman to give blood because there was a
very good chance it would endanger the fetus. She did not react.
He further explained why but was at once rebuffed by Isabelle who
said simply, "I don't care about the risk. Use my blood." It felt to
the doctor like she knew all along something like this would happen
and had already thought it through. "Use my blood." It was a line
he would remember a long time but never figure out whether he
admired her sureness or thought her a fool.

Isabelle Neukor was not a fool. She had returned from her
travels an optimist, even in this cheerless place surrounded by aus-
tere machines that normally did not lend one much hope for a rosy
future. If he were still alive it was very possible Bruno Mann would
not have understood her thinking because never once was she confused by the question of either/or. Either Vincent's life or Anjo's.
She thought both—first we save one and then together we raise the
other. Chaos never once took part in her decision. She fully under-

stood the risk involved in giving blood while in her condition. But it did not matter because she believed with all her being that things would work out.

When the doctor was gone she pulled a Walkman out of her bag and plugged the silver earpieces into her small ears. She turned the machine on. She was listening to a compilation tape of music she'd made in Vienna. Leonard Cohen's song "A Thousand Kisses Deep" came on. She began to hum along quietly. Vincent liked this song too. Taking his motionless hand, she pretended they were listening to it together.

On the other side of the long white curtain separating his bed from Ettrich's, the other patient opened his eyes for the first time since Isabelle had reentered the room. He heard her conversation with the doctor and started smiling halfway way through. In a while, soon, he would speak to her. He would say excuse me, I know it was obnoxious, but I must admit I overheard your conversation just now with the doctor.

I happen to have the same blood type as you and would be most happy to give some to your friend if he doesn't mind an old man's blood. What he wouldn't say of course was that it was *their* blood running through his veins. He closed his eyes again and listened with great pleasure to the beautiful woman humming across the space that was their home now for a little while.

About the Author

Jonathan Carroll is a past winner of the World Fantasy Award and the author of the acclaimed novels *The Wooden Sea, The Land of Laughs, The Marriage of Sticks, Black Cocktail, From the Teeth of Angels, After Silence, Outside the Dog Museum, A Child Across Sky, Bones of the Moon*, and *Voice of Our Shadow*. He lives in Vienna, Austria.

Visit Jonathan Carroll online at www.jonathancarroll.com.

Tor Books

Reading Group Guide

WHITE APPLES
by
Jonathan Carroll

TOR®

www.tor.com

White Apples

Readers familiar with the work of Jonathan Carroll know that the Vienna-based author has his own unique view of the universe and its workings. In *White Apples*, Carroll again allows us inside his brilliantly tilted cosmology, in a novel of hope and wonder that at once dissects the structure of life and death, explains why the past and future are mere details of perspective, and asks the question, "What happens when we die . . . and then come back to life?"

This particular dead man walking is Vincent Ettrich, a womanizing ad man whose own human experience is about to take a series of unexpected twists. The first comes when his new girlfriend gives him some bad news: that he has in fact already died and been released from Death for a reason of nearly unimaginable significance—and that she's been sent as a sort of lingerie-wearing guardian angel to help him discover his true purpose. The second shocker is that his one true love, the impossible and fascinating Isabelle Neukor, is pregnant with Vincent's child, an infant whose birth must be safeguarded if the totality of human existence is to be ensured. And third, Vincent learns that he can only fulfill his mission by confronting and defeating the determined forces of Chaos, whose gnawing malevolence grows stronger with each passing moment.

With wit, intelligence, and a firm sense of both the nobility and absurdity of human existence, *White Apples* takes that singularly human predicament—the nagging awareness of our own mortality, and the knowledge that we're powerless to prevent death from claiming us at any time—and challenges us to find a new way of looking at ourselves, our relationships, and our reality, so that we may learn to embrace life, and each other, with renewed vigor and passion.

⊰QUESTIONS FOR DISCUSSION⊱

1. Among the central themes of *White Apples* are transition and transformation. Such transitions include that of life to death, ignorance to enlightenment, and changes in personal growth and responsibility. How are these transformations manifested in Vincent, Isabelle, and Bruno? Which seems to have the most dramatic impact upon each character? What other kinds of transitions are described in the book?

2. In one early scene, Isabelle says to Vincent, *"Death is stupid but very determined."* Later, Chaos is also ascribed such human traits as jealousy, anger, and hatred. Compare these "personality traits" to those of the main human characters. Which characteristics are shared and which are unique? How do the characters' traits influence their actions and reactions throughout the story?

3. Discuss the idea of the great Mosaic. How does it work as a religious philosophy? Compare it with major religious and philosophical doctrines, and show how it might impact such tenets as Creation Theory, concepts of the Afterlife, Good and Evil, and Free Will vs. Predestination.

4. The scene at the zoo is one of the most powerful and disturbing in the book. In it, the zoo animals, or *Pemmagast* as Carroll designates them, have willingly accepted their captivity to serve

as guardians of humanity. How does this define the place of humans in the universal pecking order?

5. According to Coco Hallis, there isn't a Hell, per se, but Purgatory is very much a reality. She compares Purgatory to a school where we are taught the secrets of life and have the opportunity to review the choices we made during life. How does this compare to other major religious philosophies?

6. Coco says to Vincent, "Here's something you must know and don't forget it—animals never lie. They don't lie, they don't put on disguises, and they are always true to what they are. That's why you can trust them" (page 188). What does this statement say about humans? Further, describe how animals are portrayed throughout the novel and their importance to the story. Does Carroll's presentation of animal characteristics strike you as fair?

7. Many times in love stories, the hero and heroine are so perfectly fitted that they have no choice but to fall in love. In real life, this is hardly the case. Discuss love in relation to Vincent and Isabelle. How did their own imperfection strengthen their love?

8. Discuss how the author uses Chaos as both a concept and a central character in the story. Is there any contradiction to the idea of Chaos, usually defined as the absence of order, being described as a thinking, feeling, and desiring entity? Are Death and Chaos the same thing? Are they related?

9. What roles do children play in the novel? Are the portrayals of Anjo, Jack, and the children at the zoo realistic or symbolic in nature?

10. Sacrifice is a theme repeated throughout the novel. Describe the various types of sacrifices made, their context in the story, and the motivation for each act. Which examples do you think are the most poignant? Are all the acts altruistic? Which impacts the story the most? How would viewing these various sacrifices

from another character's perspective change how they might be perceived?

11. Which characters in *White Apples* do you feel are the most interesting? Which are the most realistic? How do you think you would react to the news of your own death and resurrection?